PLOUGHSHARES

Fall 1998 · Vol. 24, Nos. 2 & 3

GUEST EDITOR
Lorrie Moore

EDITOR
Don Lee

POETRY EDITOR
David Daniel

ASSOCIATE EDITOR
Susan Conley

ASSISTANT FICTION EDITOR
Maryanne O'Hara

FOUNDING EDITOR
DeWitt Henry

FOUNDING PUBLISHER
Peter O'Malley

PLOUGHSHARES, a journal of new writing, is guest-edited serially by prominent writers who explore different and personal visions, aesthetics, and literary circles. PLOUGHSHARES is published in April, August, and December at Emerson College, 100 Beacon Street, Boston, MA 02116-1596. Telephone: (617) 824-8753. Web address: www.emerson.edu/ploughshares.

EDITORIAL ASSISTANTS: Gregg Rosenblum, Amy King, Samantha Myers, and Tom Herd.

FICTION READERS: Scott Clavenna, Monique Hamzé, Tammy Zambo, Emily Doherty, Leah Stewart, Michael Rainho, Andrea Dupree, Karen Wise, Jeffrey Freiert, Mary Jeanne Deery, Jessica Olin, Gregg Rosenblum, Holly LeCraw Howe, and Billie Lydia Porter.

POETRY READERS: Brian Scales, Renee Rooks, Michael Henry, Tom Laughlin, Charlotte Pence, Jennifer Thurber, Paul Berg, Jessica Purdy, Michael Carter, and R. J. Lavallee.

SUBSCRIPTIONS (ISSN 0048-4474): $21 for one year (3 issues), $40 for two years (6 issues); $24 a year for institutions. Add $5 a year for international.

UPCOMING: Winter 1998–99, a poetry and fiction issue edited by Thomas Lux, will appear in December 1998. Spring 1999, a poetry and fiction issue edited by Mark Doty, will appear in April 1999.

SUBMISSIONS: Reading period is from August 1 to March 31 (postmark dates). Please see page 246 for detailed submission policies.

Back-issue, classroom-adoption, and bulk orders may be placed directly through PLOUGHSHARES. Authorization to photocopy journal pieces may be granted by contacting PLOUGHSHARES for permission and paying a fee of 5¢ per page, per copy. Microfilms of back issues may be obtained from University Microfilms. PLOUGHSHARES is also available as CD-ROM and full-text products from EBSCO, H.W. Wilson, Information Access, and UMI. Indexed in M.L.A. Bibliography, American Humanities Index, Index of American Periodical Verse, Book Review Index. Self-index through Volume 6 available from the publisher; annual supplements appear in the fourth number of each subsequent volume. The views and opinions expressed in this journal are solely those of the authors. All rights for individual works revert to the authors upon publication.

PLOUGHSHARES receives additional support from the Lannan Foundation and the Massachusetts Cultural Council.

Retail distribution by Bernhard DeBoer (Nutley, NJ), Ingram Periodicals (La Vergne, TN), and Koen Book Distributors (Moorestown, NJ).

Printed in the U.S.A. on recycled paper by Edwards Brothers.

CONTENTS

Fall 1998

Cover painting: *Street Scene I* by Nancy Mladenoff
Fabric paint on fabric, 34″ x 40″, 1995
Courtesy of Dr. James and Dorothy Stadler
& Dean Jensen Gallery

Ploughshares
Patrons

This nonprofit publication would not be possible without the
support of our readers and the generosity of the following
individuals and organizations.

COUNCIL: $3,000 for two lifetime subscriptions,
acknowledgement in the journal for three years,
and votes on the Cohen and Zacharis Awards.
PATRON: $1,000 for a lifetime subscription and
acknowledgement in the journal for two years.
FRIEND: $500 for a lifetime subscription and
acknowledgement in the journal for one year.
All donations are tax-deductible.
Please make your check payable to
Ploughshares, Emerson College,
100 Beacon St., Boston, MA 02116.

Introduction

Not so long ago, in trying to dislodge a student from some writing that—due to her fear or complacency—was overly safe and conventional, I experimented with a bit of pedagogical brutishness. I looked her in the eye, held up her story, and said, "*I* could have written this." Now I didn't say, "A baboon could have written this." I only said that I, the teacher—the writer and writing professor—could have written it. Nonetheless, she burst into tears and ran from the room.

Did I have a banana in my purse to snack on right then and there? I believe I did. I'm afraid I did.

Of course she was right to be upset. "I could have written this" is an anathema to both a writer and a reader. It inserts the alleged skills and the boastful-if-deflated ego of the reader into a conversation where they have no place. It is the knuckleheaded reader-reply that every writer prays never to hear—and every avid but busy reader hopes never to feel inclined to utter. (It is also the typical response of writers at the movies, squirming or dozing in some cineplex of mutual disregard.) Though it is usually assumed, usually goes without saying that readers are looking for something that they could never have written themselves, such a standard is no flimsy thing. It may be simple and basic—but it's simple and basic the way gold is. When readers think "I could have written this," they have not been successfully distracted from the stupidest fact of themselves (or from making unfortunate remarks). They have been told nothing interesting and taken nowhere convincing, new, or newish. They have been shown only the obvious physical and moral surfaces of the world, the cheapest, most available experiences and perceptions—all set forth in possibly stale or unfeeling or mistaken or ham-handed and perhaps commercially mediated language. Consequently, such readers encounter only their own irritation and a disheartening idea of collective mediocrity.

So let me say of the amazing stories in this issue the thing that should go without saying, the thing that sounds like the faintest, feeblest praise: I could not have written any of them. I, who have not had a suntan in fifteen years, was in thrall to the narratives of bright, wounded women traveling in Chile, Ecuador, and Barbados (Vicki Lindner's "To Cole Cole," Pam Houston's "Three Lessons in Amazonian Biology," and Debra Spark's excerpt from *The Ghost of Bridgetown*). I was moved completely by the lyrical stories of boys orphaned through terrible accidents (Howard Norman's chapter from *The Museum Guard* and Max Garland's "The Land of Nod"), as well as boys living through other kinds of violence (Robert Boswell's "Guests" and Bradley Owens's "A Circle of Stones"). Two comic stories by Alice Adams and Meg Wolitzer begin in a therapist's office, surely a gloomy place made funny only by the most spritely of minds. Meditations on fraught but holy marriage (by Charles Baxter and Michael Blumenthal), tales of the bourgeois aftermath of Asian-American assimilation (Gish Jen's "Just Wait") or of struggling rock musicians in San Francisco ("17 Reasons Why" by Paul Leslie), I could not, on my own, have imagined my hobbled way toward. Wayne Harrison's enraged and melancholic auto mechanic, Sheila Schwartz's endangered and passionate young mother, Mona Simpson's twenty-eight-year-old already in a condition of pre-nostalgia for her quickly passing life, all concentrate their narratives on states of mourning I feel I've known. But they are contained in very specific dramatic circumstances or richly nuanced settings that show off each writer's particular genius; and so, the stories startle, remind, refresh, take aback, and powerfully engage the reader.

The sequence I've imposed on the stories is the result of the same irrational process I have in the past imposed upon my own story collections. I have tried to make an unruly assortment resemble, well, a book. Some instinctive or mysterious aesthetic takes over— one juxtaposes color, mood, size, as in flower arranging; one lumps, then separates, then steps back and squints. At times, I aimed for a kind of ragged emotional arc: from adventure/misadventure, through catastrophe and reminiscence, toward grief, and, finally, to love. It is a trajectory that lands on the only note worth landing on. Sheila Schwartz's "Afterbirth" contains that entire arc within its own narrative, and so I have started there. If one cares to read the stories in order.

My apologies to the authors of the many fine stories I was unable to include. And to my student who dashed from the room, but who eventually returned with brilliant new work.

Afterbirth

A t first when the captain's voice came on over the intercom and made the announcement, she felt almost glad. Not gleeful exactly, but a sudden ching! of recognition coursed through her; events fell into place. She was glad she'd had her weekend at the hotel, glad for her swim in the hotel pool, for sleeping late, for the free hot coffee available in all the lobbies, tables laid out formally with linen napkins and china trimmed with gold leaf. She was glad, most of all, that she was flying alone; her husband and children hadn't come with her as they'd threatened to at the last minute. She was glad to be so selfless knowing that they were safe on the ground.

The captain's voice echoed her mood. It had a cheery lilt to it, like someone in a cartoon with a bubble over his head. It was his sightseeing voice he used as they passed over the runway then abruptly surged upward again into the clouds above the lake. His tone seemed to imply that this just might be a Christmas miracle, the kind in a made-for-TV movie about the yin and yang of self-sacrifice, as the engines churned forward, then picked up speed, the wings hovering and dipping like an uncertain insect. "Ah, well, folks," the captain said, "it looks like we've got a little problem here. Our landing gear light is shining red, and we don't know what it means. That's why we did that little dress rehearsal back there." He paused to chuckle at his own wit for a minute, dryly, then turned sober and reassuring. He banked the plane again for emphasis. "Now don't worry yet—it may not mean a thing. We'll just fly around for a little bit and check out some systems. Try to be patient with us, if you please."

Donna looked around to see what her reaction should be. No one else seemed to be panicked yet. An elderly couple across the aisle exchanged a look with her, a grim little smile that said, "We go through this every day." Other passengers, seasoned business travelers, were pretending to read their newspapers, thumbs paging casually, tenderly, through *The Wall Street Journal*. They were pretending to read computer printouts, legal briefs. Two seats up was a teenager who hadn't even heard the announcement. He had his Walkman on, turned up high enough for Donna to hear the bristle of drums, the angry thud of voices protesting some teenage issue—bad drugs, bad sex at the multiplex, exams without curves. She wondered if she ought to tell him, tap him on the shoulder gently and mouth it, "Honey—could you turn that down a bit? We're going to crash." (Donna had called everyone under thirty "honey" since her children were born, as if she'd suddenly and irrevocably catapulted into maturity, responsible for the frail moods of all souls. She practiced smiling when people were rude and ill-tempered, understanding for the first time how these were linked to a yearning for innocence, for the brick wall of mother love that would accept them).

The boy swung his head back and forth, "No...no no no..." His smile was squeezed tight in a sullen orgasm of rebellion. "No...no no no..."

No no no no..., Donna mouthed to herself, but the captain interrupted, this time twinkling. "Yep! Still here, folks. Now just sit tight. We haven't found anything specific yet, and things are stacked up over the airport, anyway, as per usual. So we'll keep cruising. If you'd like another beverage, our personnel will be coming through the cabin to serve you."

At this cue the flight attendants broke their huddle at the cockpit. They clattered trays and carts, hoisted coffeepots, sprang soda tabs with a merry "Pffft!," jingled changed for beer and whiskey, all the while smiling as if they were just here to perk up a weary office party. They moved quickly to fend off questions. They handed out extra bags of peanuts, as if this were one of the perks of crash landings. Their eyes were a geometry of evasion.

"And what would *you* like?" The flight attendant smiled, acting her part flawlessly—grace under pressure. "Coffee or tea? A beer, maybe? We're not charging for alcoholic beverages." And though Donna wanted to ask her, What do you *really* know? What did the captain tell you up there?, she did not want to be the one to ask nor to undo the carefully composed mood of the cabin. "Diet Pepsi," Donna said, "if you don't mind."

"No bother." The flight attendant nodded gravely as if it were not only appropriate but wise to choose, as one's last beverage on earth, something low-cal. Her gestures were a ballet of calm. "We're here to make you as comfortable as possible."

Donna had heard of masquerades like this one before. She'd heard of captains like this. Their bravery put ordinary humans to shame. In times of catastrophe, they could sound like a training manual. They could go through all the niceties of protocol as if death didn't mean a thing. They followed their procedures. They enunciated their last words clearly into the black box. There was a captain like that a couple of years ago she'd read about—somewhere over Iowa—who saved the lives of more than half the people on his plane by his expertise, his presence of mind. He was able to speak about the crash moments after the plane landed in a cornfield, able to explain how he'd decided on that particular site based on wind velocity, angle of engine failure, forward thrust and momentum, air to ground time. The empty field was a miracle, though, the God-given aspect of the situation. It opened up like a mirage just in the nick of time.

Of course, Donna thought, everyone knew there was nothing *but* cornfields in Iowa—what else would open up there? What interested Donna was how quickly the captain refocused the disaster into something positive. He didn't exactly gloss over the ninety-seven people who'd been killed, but he made it seem as if they'd beaten the odds, anyway. Two hundred and twelve people had been saved in a crash that might have killed everyone. He didn't bother to describe the burning bodies, entire families wiped out in one fell swoop. He didn't describe the particular horrors she'd read about later, the passenger accounts. One woman in particular had written an article for a parents' magazine, pleading with readers to pay for an extra seat on a plane trip to transport an infant in a carrier that could be secured with a seatbelt. Donna wondered if Captain Marvel had read *that* article, if he'd read the mother's description of her child's trusting look as she tried to soothe him before they crashed. "I love you," she murmured to him, her hand poised across his brow, as if to check for one last fever. "I love you, little Bobby, little dear one. You've had a beautiful life." Then she kissed him over and over until the end. She wasn't able to hold on to him when they struck the ground. He'd hurtled forward through time and space, a frail illustration of the laws of physics, the rest of his life condensed to a few brief seconds of fear. Donna wondered how a mother could survive such a thing.

She was glad that she might not have to. That was one of her greatest fears, the possibility of outliving her children, imagining the hundred different ways she could lose them: fire, car crash, inhaled balloons, the impervious marble of bathtubs, the magnetism of empty electrical sockets. The thought of a knife too close to the edge of the kitchen counter sometimes made her gasp right out loud.

Now she might be spared all these—though there still weren't any clear signs of doom from the flight attendants. They were hurrying through the aisles like precursors of the Christmas rush, balancing cups and trays, swinging sprays of tiny liquor bottles that chimed succinctly into the trash.

The plane itself seemed quiet as it plowed through the muffled darkness of clouds. The engines had smoothed to a hum, not loud and grinding like the plane she'd taken on the trip out to St. Louis. That one had needed a tune-up, she'd joked with a fellow passenger after landing, a man about ten years older than she. He had a tiny crease in his ear from a long-gone rhinestone, like a fossil imprint of his wild youth. She watched the discreet cascade of emotions that rippled across his face before he answered her: surprise, boredom, curiosity, lust, and, finally, lethargy. "Yeah. Well, that's what you get for flying a bankrupt airline," he said. He faced forward into the crowd of departing passengers and made his eyes glaze over.

She hadn't meant to pick him up or anything. It was just a remark to make while deplaning, her face pressed into the wool of someone's back as everyone crowded to get off. A thought like that hadn't occurred to her in years—she was a woman so thoroughly married, she'd lost all gender. Though she didn't mean that with any special bitterness. It was just the inescapable result of being married, of being a mother, of parading nakedly through the streets with a double-stroller.

And since she thought of herself that way, as a bad mystery ("The Case of the Revolting Mother"), it seemed ironic how this trip itself had come up. An old college friend had offered her a chance to be on a panel: "How Images of Women in the Helping Professions Have Changed Since the Feminist Movement of the '70's." She didn't really qualify for the panel—she had no image. She'd been a literacy volunteer before the children, had quit five years ago when Jackie was born, but she hadn't ever been a professional anything, had never done anything with vehemence or discipline except maybe waiting. She'd made a profession of that—waiting to grow up, waiting to leave home, waiting for her first love affair, her first husband, house, child. Her own mother had taught her to do this, had made her understand that happiness always seemed like a distant hill, just far enough away to look pleasant at twilight.

Like this trip. Something she'd anticipated for months, since her third child, Michael, had been born. It was an anniversary present from Tom, but she'd waited almost a whole year to do it, to be sure that as she walked out the door to the taxi, Michael's cries wouldn't draw her back. They circled her, but she shrugged them off, shrugged off the rationale behind Tom's gift—time to "rediscover" herself. *His* words. What could she find in a weekend? What could possibly be left?

She shivered now to think how eager she'd been to leave home, how it all might turn out to be a bad omen in a few short minutes—Tom's offer, the conference, her reunion with her friend, the man on the plane who'd snubbed her, the man at the conference who didn't. It had seemed like an opportunity at the time. Now it seemed like a mirage, a trap; it was her fault because she'd been so happy to leave her family. The plane was going to crash because of her, because she couldn't stand how much her children needed her, how they screamed every time she left the room, even if it was just to get their pajamas from the linen closet.

When she'd slammed the front door, departure day, it made an airtight seal. On her side, there was cool, clean air, trees as light-hearted as ghosts. On their side, sealed in amber, three despairing faces. Abandoned forever? Time was like that for children. A few minutes seemed like a lifetime.

She wondered if they'd gotten to the airport yet, Tom and the children, whether they were already waiting, her babies with their noses pressed to the glass, caroling: Mommy! Mommy! Mommy! They'd be wearing their new snowsuits, their tender faces haloed in bunny fur. She wondered how long they'd stand there watching for her plane before Tom dragged them away to check the board, what the word DELAYED would signify to them except that Mommy hadn't kept her promise; she was supposed to burst through that door right away like an angel and save them. Life for them was one rescue after another—from boredom, broken toys, premature bedtimes.

Someday they'd be too old to want her, and that would be worse. They'd be like that boy in the next row, oblivious, uncaring. His headphones were still on, and he was sound asleep, the static at the end of the tape whirred on and on, the mantra of all electrical equipment. Why didn't anyone wake him? Even the flight attendant speeding by, the jolt of her hip, an inadvertent nudge to his lolling head, didn't rouse him.

The flight attendants were gathered again at the door to the cockpit, waiting for further instructions, whispering the way nurses do outside the door of a terminal patient. Predictably the captain's voice reappeared again, not quite so cheery this time. It sounded strained, muffled, as if he'd placed a handkerchief over his mouth to hide his true identity.

"Sorry to keep you waiting," he sighed. "We're still checking our systems and coming up blank here, so we're going to try something a bit different. We're going to come around again over the airport and buzz the tower. They'll check us through their binoculars to see if our landing gear is intact. If it looks okay, we'll make one more pass again then proceed with our landing." The captain's voice dwindled. Even now he was unwilling to say what they'd do if their landing gear wasn't intact. "Sorry to keep you," he added.

Of course that was what the red light meant—no landing gear. Donna felt a chill yawn open inside her, a mouth to a secret cave. She tried to remember any similar cases she'd read of—a plane landing in that condition, what were their chances of surviving?— but all she could picture was an explosion, their plane, pregnant with passengers, bursting open, trailing fire as they skidded down the runway, plowing red searing scars into the tarmac.

Now everyone else seemed nervous, too. They tucked their heads down and checked their seatbelts. They stared out the darkening windows to grapple with fate, with clouds shifting form, disappearing into the night. Donna heard a rush of air that might have been the engines accelerating or the sudden whispering of everyone around her, lips forming wishful prayers. "I've been in worse situations," she heard someone say, but who? Not the teenager. He was as still as the moon. Not the old couple across the aisle. They were holding hands, peering at one of their tickets, maybe rereading the provisions for sudden death. What sorts of allowances would be made in such a case? Who would benefit?

Only the businessmen three rows back seemed to still be taking this in stride, though at a slightly higher pitch. They shook their heads as if this were just another part of their job description. They were swigging beers, rattling bags of potato chips, their faces flushed with scorn for the other passengers. It was as if this were an office party they didn't want to break up, a Xerox of other near-tragedies that could be averted by a loud voice, a jovial attitude. They were laughing to keep the mood from changing, telling stories of near-misses they'd had, crashes they'd avoided by accidental rebookings, malfunctions that didn't pan out, emergency landings.

"I've been on a lot of dud runs," one of them said.

"And I've been drilled in shit," said another, "and lived to do the deed!"

"What deed?" his friend across the aisle asked. "What the hell does that mean?"

Who knew? What did it matter?

They rambled on rapturously as if these were war stories or tales of sexual conquest. There were mountainous fogs they'd braved, shorn engines, battered wings, smokers in lavatories who set off alarms, were caught shamefaced with their pants down around their ankles stubbing out the evidence of their pleasure into their palms. There were baggage holds that split apart and cabins that lost pressure. There were drunken captains, incompetent ground crews who de-iced windows instead of wings. There was wind shear in their voices, tailspin in their eyes.

Of course all three of them had ordered several rounds of whiskey from the flight attendant on her last trip through. And then chasers. A few more chasers. All three wore London Fog raincoats buttoned and belted, ready to bolt when the plane came down. Their briefcases were poised across their laps, though the flight attendant chided them now to stow these safely in the overhead until they landed. (*When* they landed. *If* they landed.)

"Let's not get too grammatical," one of them said.

Which reminded his friend of another story which he told as soon as the flight attendant flickered back up the aisle. "I knew this guy once who boarded his live snake in the compartment in a lunchbox of all things. What an incredible jerk! I told him not to do it, but he claimed he didn't want to freeze it in baggage—it was a tropical snake! When we hit some turbulence, the compartment sprang open and out fell the snake—it had been crawling around in there loose the whole flight. A constrictor or something—long as my ass, long as a witch's tit." (*What* is that expression?) "At any rate, all hell broke loose. Somebody yelled, 'Help! Snakes! Terrorists!' One lady peed her pants—I swear! She wet the seat. You could see this big dark stain. That was one landing we made over water!"

The other two laughed uproariously, but Donna suddenly wanted to cry. What if they were really going to be killed? What if the last thing she heard was some horrible stupid story? What if she never saw her children again? Or Tom? She should concentrate on remembering them, press her feelings and memories into thumbprints, leaf stains. They probably had at least a half an hour left. Fifteen minutes, anyway, before they circled all the way over the airport and found their landing gear definitely gone.

Donna tried to picture them—Tom, with his arms around the children like a family portrait, grinning his gigantic smile, so sure that life was just right, that things would work out eventually if she wouldn't worry so much. Then she tried to review each of her children separately, their perfect limbs, their subterranean smiles, but they seemed to streak right past her without stopping, too small to be held. All she could clearly remember was the moment of their births, feeling them gush from her legs in a waterfall of pain, their tiny heads pushing, pushing, pushing her aside. Those were the only real moments of her life, it seemed, for the last five years. If not forever. The three births. Jackie. Allen. Michael. One right after another. Her life with Tom was over as soon as her life with them began. It was horrible but true—why bother to disguise it now? They both knew it, though they were too polite to say so. She would never think of Tom first ever again, would always feel that the best nights of her life were those first nights spent with each child, alone in the hospital room, their tiny lips pressed to her skin, soft as flowers; all night their infant moans of pleasure as she nursed them. They were perfect children untouched by memory. Perfectly safe. Perfectly hers.

Donna wondered if the other passengers were having thoughts like this. Weird thoughts. Desperate thoughts. What exactly were you supposed to be thinking at a time like this? Something profound, no doubt. Something that would change the course of your life forever, brief as that course might be. Dwelling on old sins, maybe. Or new ones. Maybe that's why they were so quiet.

She certainly had enough to keep *her* busy for the rest of the trip. That man at the conference, for instance. As different from Tom as she could make him. A lot like the businessmen behind her. A complete stranger. Horrible to her in most ways, frightening, even, with his briefcase filled with monetary funds and annuities, his eyes set thirty years ahead on retirement, as if what happened in between was neither principle nor interest.

They'd met at the pool, where she could see his skin stippled with scars, pockmarks, maybe. His white legs underwater thrashed as if there were a strong current. They grappled desperately with unseen forces. Donna had been a swimmer all her life and scorned people like this—hellbent on the rituals of exercise. They bought expensive swimsuits, put plugs in their ears, showered with gusto, strode to the edge of the pool, and peered down as if it were Niagara Falls. Then—plunge!—dove in with such a splash, the waves knocked everyone else out of the water. It was people like this who broke their necks diving into the wrong end. That was their idea of real get up and go.

Predictably he surfaced heartily, thrusting up an array of water, gulping air. His backwash dislodged her goggles. "Nice dive," she told him, and he was pleased.

"Thanks much," he said. His great round head nodded with slippery satisfaction. He was the least desirable man at the pool, so she chose him, to punish herself for what she was about to do.

"How about a drink?" he asked her, waiting around and waiting around until she'd showered and dried her hair. She didn't believe in saunas but lingered to try out the free soaps and lotions in their tiny bottles, neat as family heirlooms. It fascinated her, a bathroom like that, with carpeting and silvery wallpaper, silk flowers nodding in crystal vases—a locker room decorated for an assignation.

Like the restaurant where they went to grab a bite beforehand. No time to waste. Part of the hotel's package deal. Though it was only nine-thirty in the morning, the bar was already open and fluid with customers leaning over candles in red glass jars flickering knowledgeably, without warmth. Maybe it was the management's idea of romantic, implying checkered Parisian tablecloths and tree-lined boulevards from some bygone era. That was the meaning of the red carpet, the crystal chandeliers and brass sconces, a timeless bar for timelessly tacky love.

She didn't mind that they went there. She wanted it to be tacky. And fruitless. She planned in advance that he'd disgust her, to prove to herself, maybe, that touching someone other than Tom would make her sick. It was good that his arms were too thin, his chest was too hairy. She hoped that when it happened, after these last hollowed-out years of her marriage, his lips would feel sticky, like pieces of a burst balloon. He would kiss her too long here. Not long enough there. He'd hold her afterwards in a noncommittal way as if this were a demographic—the average length of post-coital grip. Wow! Wow!

That's what he said at the end but in a voice that rang of sex manuals. Do this. Do that. Express urgency.

There was no real way to explain what she'd done (what excuse could she possibly give? "At least I didn't have to pay for a babysitter"?), and now, maybe no need. When she looked out the window again, they were lowering through the clouds, coming closer to the airport once more, waiting for their moment of truth. Donna recognized features of the landscape they'd just passed a while ago, an hour ago maybe? Who knew how long it was when your mind was wandering free of responsibility, of logic. They passed over the usual grids of suburban neighborhoods just like hers: tree, lawn, house, tree lawn house, treelawnhouse—a series of what must be golf courses with tiny perfect ponds, miniscule flags waving, roads that looped around like elegant, handwritten O's. They crossed the marshy discarded fields that surrounded the airport, the glowering highway filled with rush-hour cars staring up as the plane roared over with the unreal magnitude of a blimp. So close. Donna could feel the magnetic pull of the landing strip (a battery of twirling lights from fire trucks already waiting for the crash), as they approached, the desire to kiss earth drew the plane downward, but they resisted; the plane rumbled over the tower slower than gravity, then shot upward again, expelling a loud groan.

The engines demurred, showed fear for the first time. "God-dammit," the captain muttered, "goddammit to hell," then real-ized the intercom was on and revised himself, "Oops!" as if this were a program for children and he might have to be recast. His voice wavered up and down a notch, searching for the right key. He cleared his throat. "Well, folks. Ahem," he said. (A-hem. Two syllables.) "I have some good news and some bad news. The bad news is—we're missing something. Part of our landing gear must have fallen off somewhere along the way. Folks over Des Moines probably thought they saw Kahoutec." He paused as if to let his audience recollect this forgotten comet of the seventies. A mur-muring filled the plane, but not of recognition. "Also, the tower has figured out the runway here is too short for a gear-up landing, and we've now burned up too much fuel to go to another airport. The good news is—there have been many successful landings over water."

Water? A water landing? A shiver ran through them, a collective ripple of terror and reluctance.

The teenager two rows up screamed finally, but in his sleep, of all things, as if their bad karma had jumped ship and ignited him, made him dream his tapes were all snarled, unwinding for no rea-son into thin shining slivers that rustled onto the floor. Words tumbled from his mouth: *Help! Help! I hate you!* like an echo to all their thoughts.

Even the businessmen seemed unnerved for the first time. Puz-zled. Their deadlines were tangled. Their calendars were really bol-loxed up. A checklist of disappointment welled up on their faces: Death. Water. Death. Water. Death. Jesus Christ—not Death!

Death.

Clearly they weren't made for crash landings, though the flight attendant seemed to think so. She slid up the aisle smooth as glass to tap two of them on the shoulder, the two in the aisle seats, as soft and lightly as an angel, and pointed to the third in the window seat, her finger outstretched, serene, granting them pardon, or grace.

These men, her gesture seemed to say, were in the exit row—that was a privilege and an honor. These men were potential heroes—from where she stood, they were still neatly ironed. They could be guardians of the water slide, masters of the emergency chute *and* life rafts. The flight attendant warned them she'd be back in just a minute to give them further instructions, but they could reread their passenger safety cards in the meantime. They could hold themselves steady. Keep their heads up and look chipper. Smile those brushed white smiles.

Her words were light and frothy, much lighter than the air holding the plane up, still heavy enough to lift all three of them partway out of their seats. They leaned forward in unified protest, their smiles frozen in overdrive. "God Almighty," one of them muttered—the snake charmer. He screwed up his lips as if to spit, but nothing came out, just words made plain and grammatical by fear, "God Almighty—did she really mean that?"

"We're going to be pretty busy up here for a while," the captain announced, jumping in to divert their panic into smaller, more manageable streams. "It's going to take us some time to position ourselves, and the emergency ground crews are consulting with the Coast Guard about the best possible landing sites." He made it sound so simple, like a car pool, but he wasn't really fooling anyone.

All up and down the aisles there was motion, an animated universe of gestures like branches suddenly tossed by a hurricane, thrashing to get away, though the flight attendants warned them to stay in their seats with their belts fastened. The captain signed off again and left them alone without giving them any specific notion of time. Would he be back again? Did "some time" mean five minutes or two hours?

How much fuel did they have left? Maybe they would just cruise around until everyone had made his separate peace with

God. Well—why not? She'd once been in a plane with engine trouble over Peru. That was long before she'd met Tom. She'd been a different person then high above the clouds, someone with a sense of mystery, who believed in magic beads and the advice of tea leaves. She'd gone to Peru on a whim to learn to "see," a phrase she'd borrowed from a popular mystic she barely understood. She'd had a couple of ambiguous moments (maybe spiritual, maybe not)—chewing coca leaves with an Indian on the train to Machu Picchu, again at the peak of a volcanic mountain she'd assumed was extinct until it rumbled. (She hadn't bothered to read her guidebook.)

Then there was that *real* moment, the one she'd thought was real, flying over the Andes, above a lake of clouds, when she was sure it was all over, felt the shining pinnacle of her body dissolving into the sun, had thought how light and casual it felt, like snow melting on a bright winter's day, pleasant almost—the way she'd repeated her own name out loud, several times, as if it might survive her. It had thrilled her then that no one knew she was on that plane, no one at all had the slightest idea where she was. Her entire history could be erased in a single minute, and there'd be nothing left to remember her. She was twenty-five years old and hadn't accomplished a single thing.

This time it was a completely different story. What *wouldn't* she leave behind? Everything she'd ever touched would become an artifact. Every word she'd ever said to her children would be a mystery.

If they could even remember what she'd said—words beyond "No, no, naughty!," words beyond "Don't touch!" Had she ever said anything meaningful, something they might remember as the years went by that would still glow for them like the birthday ring Tom had given her, a sapphire with rays of shifting light?

She tried to think, but space seemed to be roaring around her, as if it weren't infinite and desperately wide but small and crushing, shutting her in. She could only think of one conversation she'd had verbatim, with Jackie, her oldest boy—at Christmas, a year ago. They'd been walking around the neighborhood together looking at displays of lights when suddenly a meteor had fallen, had moved across the sky slowly and deliberately as if pushed by an unseen hand. Donna had gasped and exclaimed, "I can't believe it! I can't believe it! We saw the Christmas star!" Though Jackie had no idea what that was, he smiled for her, then exclaimed back, "That's nice, Mommy!" He still was young enough he'd say anything to please her. She tried hard to explain to him the star meant they were lucky; they were special. Maybe it meant they were blessed.

Now she saw it was just another crazy moment in a long line of them. It lifted her out of her skin for just a glimmer, and that was it.

All up and down the plane, they were remembering their own crazy moments as they stowed away their last belongings—books, magazines, extra jackets, needle-pointed pillows that whiled away the time. They wouldn't while away the time now. Barely time to remember who they were, where they'd been for the last twenty, thirty, sixty years. No way to define it except in glimmers, as she had done.

What were they thinking? What last memories? The old couple—were they remembering their grandchildren? What medications they'd forgotten to take that morning? Were the businessmen thinking about statistics? Or that special lunch at the Four Seasons, how lucky some of their clients were to eat caviar as casually as Spam?

It was bad to be bitter in one's last moments—that's what Tom would say. But how would he ever know? Nothing in the clouds to tell her what her attitude should be. They were a gray shroud, a thick, indecipherable tissue. They were still as an x-ray, silent as ice. As were her fellow passengers, riveted in their seats by expectation, facing straight forward, not speaking, not even swallowing. No one looked to see if there were life jackets underneath their seats; no one felt to see if their seatbelts were properly fastened. No one looked to find the nearest emergency exit, as if, even at this late hour, that would be the grossest possible lapse in taste, to seem as if you were wondering how you could be the first person to leave the plane.

Not that Donna had ever been much for good taste. She didn't care much if her children were muddy, if they used their forks and spoons to eat. Tom blamed her for things like that, for socks that never matched, for the tone of voice she sometimes used to yell at the children, and him ("I feel like a dog that just peed on the carpet—"); sometimes she thought he blamed her for everything, right from the moment they met, years before, at a barbecue to celebrate the summer solstice. It was two months late because the hosts had been too stoned to organize on time. As if that were *her* fault. The party was held at their farm, a never-say-die commune that had long since collapsed into private ownership. The members believed in total honesty, and that was how her friend had introduced her to Tom. "Now *this* is a woman worth sleeping with." That was marriage brokering in those days. It didn't seem to deter him. They went off to pick buckets of blueberries that stained their hands and lips dark as ink, a tribal rite— "We're marked for life," Tom had said.

This was clearly romantic, but later there was a pig roast, despite some vegetarians who objected, who took their tofu burgers and set up camp in another part of the field far away from where the pig smouldered in a deep pit plowed over with leaves and mud. Like a murder victim unearthed by accident. They dug the body up to eat it, subdivided the parts with a huge carving knife, waved forelegs, hindquarters. Donna and Tom sat next to each other and giggled at how weird it all was.

Though not as weird as the little 8mm film of a home birth brought along by a newlywed couple to celebrate the first harvest and offered proudly as a follow-up to the dessert of blueberry pie and ice cream. What was it supposed to be? Entertainment? Erotica?

That's how Tom had labeled it afterwards—"porno lite," though this really missed the essence. But so did the barbecue crowd, chanting: "New life! New life! Go! Go! Go!" as the screening progressed.

Still, the couple was proud. Their timing couldn't have been better. As luck would have it, the birth coincided with their wedding day—the film was still rolling from the ceremony when the bride felt the first contraction. She took off her wedding gown to labor right there in the field, got down on all fours to push the baby out into the billowing mess of her veil. Donna couldn't believe how the woman's haunches had clenched, unclenched, clenched, unclenched, in a demonstration of sheer animal fury. There was no sound, thank God, to explain her wide open mouth, but Donna could feel the screams as if they were her own as the woman swayed from side to side, grinding her belly into the earth.

Donna and Tom left before the placenta came out, after the top of the baby's head had popped in and out several times like a shy woodchuck peeping from its hole. That was one of the few times Tom was ever at a loss for words. Even at the birth of their own first child, he'd been composed, had whispered something into her ear about launching a new ship. Back then, though, he'd said, "Is it *me*, or is this the most disgusting thing you've ever seen?"

Back then Donna had agreed, but she didn't think so now. What could be more disgusting than dying before you were ready to?

That's what everyone else was thinking, she was certain, except for that crazy, comatose teenager still sleeping up there. Donna leaned forward in her seat, ready to wake him, just as the flight attendant passed by, already in the act. She ran one bright red fingernail across his forehead, then shook him by the shoulder for good measure. "Wake up, sir," she said firmly. "You can't sleep now. We need your attention."

The boy opened his eyes and cursed. "What the hell?" but she was already gliding away to another destination, another crisply performed task. "Damn," the boy muttered again, as if she'd interrupted something truly special—a memory of rollerblades or a bright green Mohawk, maybe the first time he told his parents to go screw themselves.

Nothing sentimental in *his* face. It was a map of pain and boredom—bored to be alive, bored in the U.S. of A., bored by the sound of rain pattering along the drainage ditch in his suburban cul-de-sac. A boy with just one parent. Or maybe four, six, eight. The wrong number, at any rate—all his exponents were mixed up. He was the kind of boy she was afraid her sons might grow up to be, the kind she always saw at shopping malls, too tall and skinny to be handsome, bent like a praying mantis over the record rack, worshipping the latest dance mixes, the type of boy who'd sit on the floor of a coffeehouse in the dirt and cigarette butts, enthralled by the sound of the espresso machine (hissing, hissing...); he probably liked to have his tongue vacuumed at the dentist, any sensation as long as it was unpleasant. A plane crash wouldn't bother him at all. He shrugged when the flight attendant warned him of what was to come. "Who cares?" he asked with such bitterness it was almost touching. "We're all gonna crash sooner or later." Then, bolstered by his own wit, he readjusted his headset, tucked the spongy earpieces tenderly back into the hollows of his ears, and closed his eyes, breathing deeply, face tilted to his airjet as if it were glue.

They were handing out final instructions, holding up the laminated cards that looked so simple. There was the plane cruising midair. There was the plane nestled in the ocean, waves lapping gently. There were the merry passengers taking their turns obediently, zipping down the chute like a great water slide adventure.

"This is your flotation device," the flight attendant said. She held up a seat cushion and waved it. "You'll want to take this with you on your way out. After we're safely in the water, you'll need to dislodge it and take it with you down the emergency slide. Don't take any belongings. You'll want to get out as quickly as possible. This is the only thing you'll need—it will help you to remain on the surface of the water while we wait for rescue."

The flight attendant moved backwards several rows to give her spiel again. As she passed by, heat rose from her uniform like steam. (She was really nervous after all, despite the look on her face of frozen glee.) Her body trailed perfume—rose or lilac? She moved forward in a cloud of goodwill and determination. "Now *these* gentlemen," she said heartily when she reached the businessmen, "these fine gentlemen—" She waved her hand across them like a magic wand. "They're going to help you," she explained as she rotated a half-circle to face them. Her voice had a bright glare to it as she said, "You. You. *You.*"

She pointed to the one in the window seat. "You will open the emergency door when we land. And you," she tapped the middle one with her long fingernail, "will help him place the door in the row behind you. Don't throw it outside, or you might puncture the evacuation slide, which will deploy automatically." She nodded to the snake charmer across the aisle. "*You* will move to the window seat, and you will remove the door yourself and deposit it in the next row. After you do that, jump down the slide. The three of you, don't stay and try to assist people. You'll only block the passage for the other passengers."

24

She paused there, as if this were a moment in her script that deserved some thought. Donna marveled at her composure, the way her voice balanced on the ledge of a tall building. Her lipstick still gleamed thick as a layer of frosting. She could be dropped underwater, and she'd keep right on ticking. Though none of *them* could. They'd be at the bottom of the lake in just a few minutes, enshrined beneath the fierce upswellings of cold, of industrial waste, an occasional algal bloom. Their mouths would be clogged with ice, or fish, or stones. In summer the beer cans would rain down on their skulls, boats would roar across them, suntan lotion would seep towards them through the water slow as tears.

There was silence in the plane now, as if they'd all just shared the same bizarre fantasy, but the flight attendant didn't miss a beat. She treated this silence as if it were a loud and drunken outburst, as if she were waiting for the man to say, "Hell, no, lady—I won't do that. You're some crazy bitch if you think I'll do that—crazier than a witch's tit!" but he just shook his head—once, twice. His mouth was screwed up as if to spit, but nothing came out.

Donna felt sorry for the man. She nodded in sympathy like everyone else on the plane. Who was the flight attendant kidding? Even assuming that a safe water landing was possible, gentle as Icarus tumbling into the sea. She thought of a father watching from shore, his son burning up like a meteor, then of Tom shielding the children's eyes as the plane exploded. Luckily they'd be too far away to see her. If they saw anything, it would be like fireworks, like a far-off sparkler.

"This is a very important job," the flight attendant tried again, as devoted to her job as a mother. "It entails a great deal of responsibility," she added, as if this were something to add to a résumé later: 1) Dispatched rescue equipment. 2) Saved face in plane crash. She bent towards the man to pat his shoulder, but he turned away and pressed his face to the window. This made the flight attendant nod once more, agreeably. "Okay," she said. "That is perfectly all right. If you feel you are unable to perform your duties properly, then will you please change seats with someone who feels more confident? Can I have a volunteer?" She peered down the aisle expectantly, a glimmer of a smile on her face. Be brave, the smile said, be noble, be the kind of person you've always wanted to be! "We haven't much time," she chided.

As if to reaffirm this, Donna saw the lake appear below them, waves as sharp as fingerprints, the tiny festive dots of boats crawling over the hard surface of the water. She knew just how hard it would be when they hit, like iron, like Tom's face if she lived to tell him what she'd done that weekend, how she'd betrayed him as an experiment to see what it would feel like to do something absolutely wrong, to take on the shape of another life, a shadow that would glide between them, silent and dark, filling in the space her children had made that couldn't be explained, not the moments of crisis, not the moments of ecstasy, but those absolutely plain moments that were sheer as ice—tucking them in at night, washing their hair, pulling up their pants, their little socks that fell around their tiny ankles, pouring corn flakes into their bowls each morning, tenderly, measuring their sleep in hours, weeks, sometimes in seconds, reading them the same books over and over again ("Spot likes to chase his bouncy red ball..."), careful to vary the rhythms of her sentences, the pitch of her voice, patting a piece of bread with a smidgen of butter, a smidgen of jelly, smoothing her palm across each forehead as if she could instill something divine in them, make them healthy, better than she and Tom had ever been, better than they ever would be. "My children!" she thought. "My little babies." As if this were the most complete idea she'd ever had, the most enlightened.

"Okay," Donna said. "I'll do it. *I'll* do it. I'm willing," though the flight attendant didn't hear her. Everything was suddenly out of order, shaking to pieces as they went down, tipping over towards one wing, and then the other, unsure of gravity, where it might take them, the captain calling one last time over the intercom, "Hold on now, folks—this is a little sooner than we expected!" the teenager in front wagging his head back and forth as if this were some far-out beautiful rhythm, plane crash as performance art. He was shaking his shoulders. He was beating the armrests with both hands. He was yelling, "Yes! Yes! Do it, Mama! Do it to me, do it to me *now*!"

"You be quiet," the old lady across the aisle leaned over to glare at him. "Have some respect, young man," as if they were in a church, a reverent movie theater, and suddenly Donna knew it was okay. His craziness would save them. This was *his* crash, not theirs; he was the only one who believed in it. Everyone else still believed it couldn't happen to them, not today, not with so much unfinished business, so much misunderstood, not with a husband and three babies waiting down below, their lives not yet unfolded, crushed up in cocoons of adoration, still wet with joy and love.

Three Lessons in Amazonian Biology

The River

I'll admit I picked Ecuador for its symbolic possibilities. I wanted a place where things were reliable: twelve hours of darkness, twelve hours of light. It was the end of the old year, two weeks before my thirty-third birthday, the age my Catholic friend Tony said all things would be revealed to me. Thirty-two's highlights included three busted friendships, two bogus photography assignments, and a lover turned stalker. I wasn't holding my breath.

Balance, I thought. New Year's Eve at the equator. I called every magazine I'd ever shot for until somebody paid me to go.

My guide's name was Renato, and he was Catholic, too, sweet and serious, a broken-in Pittsburgh Pirates cap on his head, fresh out of guide school, and looking for plants to identify, rare butterflies, tropical birds.

First Renato took me to Mount Cayambe, a hairsbreadth short of nineteen thousand feet above sea level, its summit smack dab on the equator and covered always with ice caps and snow.

"This is the highest point on earth along the equator," Renato said, "and the only place in the world where the latitude and the temperature reach zero degrees simultaneously."

I framed Cayambe in my camera and snapped the shutter. Renato and I were going to get along fine.

Renato said he would take me to the north coast to see the remains of the ancient culture of Agua Blanca, to the Isla de la Plata to see the blue-footed boobies, to the cloud forests near Mindo to see the Atta ants by the hundreds of thousands, each one carrying a piece of a leaf over its head like a parasol.

I told him I wanted to lay my eyes on the Amazon Basin, wanted to feel her dark waters underneath me, figured she might have something to tell me that I needed to know.

"The jungle is a magic place," Renato said, "like a temple. We will waste the trip if we go too soon."

"It can't be too soon," I said. "Not for me."

"Going straight from your America to the jungle," he said, "is like going from the brightest sunlight into the darkest cave. If you don't take time to adjust your vision, it doesn't matter what the cave holds for you, you will never be able to see."

The rivers had been my place once, Colorado Plateau rivers that tumbled through the Sawatch and the San Juan mountains, that carved through deserts of slickrock and sand. But I hung up my oar blades over a year before, moved myself to a city next to an ocean, saying, *Water is water,* as I drove toward the coast. I traded in my life jacket for halogen sensor lights and an electric garage door opener, told myself that one life story was as good as the next.

I thought if I went to enough art museums and unrated movies, I'd stop thinking about the sound the river makes when a hot June day has brought a foot of snow down from the highest peaks and I'm lying in my sleeping bag beside it, listening to the boulders roll.

I'd heard, too, that city men were different, that I might find one there who read books and cooked with spices and didn't save all his passion for class-five rapids and narrows and chutes. What I found when I got there was the same man with different excuses, enough rancor in him to bring me to my knees.

I'd sworn off the whole species for a while after that, at least till I knew how to pick one better. When I went to Ecuador, I hadn't had anything resembling a date in six months.

I had an idea in my head about going home for the first time to the biggest river system of them all, more massive than all the Colorado Plateau rivers I'd been on at high-water put together and then some, a river as thick with life as the Colorado was barren, as torpid as the Colorado was fierce. I wanted to remember what it was like to float down something that wouldn't try to swallow me. I wanted to see if after a yearlong flirtation with tidal pools and breakers, Big Mama River would take me back in.

"I will take you first," Renato said, "to the river of riches, Aguarico, which flows into the Napo, which picks up the Curaray, and then becomes the Amazon that you see on the maps. But you must understand it is all the Amazon, in the same way that every part of the cow is beef."

"I do understand," I said. "I told you I know about rivers."

"I will take you to the Lagarto," he said, "to Imuya, the place of the howler monkeys." He fingered the bill of his ball cap. "I will take you," he said, "to the Filet Mignon."

But first we went to the ocean, to a town called Puerto Lopez, where we ate ceviche for lunch and dinner and slept in window-less rooms above the Spondylous Bar. We drank pitchers of Caipi-rina, made from vodka, sugar, and lemon, listened to the music of Eros Ramazotti and Franco De Vida on old vinyl disks. Renato taught me how to dance salsa, cumbia, and ballinato, and when the music allowed it, which wasn't often, I taught him how to country swing.

The bar was run by three Colombians—Alberto, Abel, and Jimez—three of Peter Pan's lost boys who danced all night with the local girls and swam in the ocean all day. I was the first tourist in the bar since the end of October, and they went out of their way to show their appreciation, to make me feel at home.

"Woodstock," Abel, who knew no English, said, pulling another battered album from behind the counter. "Eric Clapton, Crosby, Stills & Nash." He pronounced each syllable like a class in English diction. "Janis Joplin," he said, "Steppenwolf, the Byrds." Jimez traded me my belt buckle for his switchblade. I was the only one Alberto had permission to dance with other than his wife.

"There are 3,800 vertebrates in Ecuador," Renato said, after our third pitcher of Caipirina, "1,550 birds, 400 reptiles, 2,500 fish, over a million insect species, 25,000 varieties of vascular plants."

"Biodiversity," I said. "Do you know that word?"

"Of course," he said, and frowned a little. He always said *of course* when the answer was no.

The next day we went by boat to the Isla de la Plata to see the nests of the blue- and red-footed boobies, the flight pattern of the frigate and tropic birds, and a crab called Sally Lightfoot, who made her ghostly way across the beach's rocky dividers and ran across the surface of the water like Jesus when the tide came in.

"A woman like you," Renato said, "pretty and smart. Why do you come to Ecuador without . . . someone."

"How I can't get that right," I said, "is almost uncanny." I saw the frown crease his brow. "Do you know that word?"

"Of course," he said.

We watched the sea urchins wave their spiny selves back and forth in a tidal pool.

"In the Amazon," Renato said, "there is a tiny catfish called a candiru that will swim right into a man's penis, and lodge itself there by erecting sharp spines."

"And you are telling me this..."

"To amuse you," he said, "to give you something to wish on all those bad men." He held out a picture of a dark-haired woman holding a child. "Anyway," he said, "it amuses my wife."

"She's lovely," I said. "They both are." I handed him back the picture. "So I can swim in the river, then, worry-free."

"Yes," he said. "Except for the piranha...and the six hundred volts of electric eel."

"You won't scare me off the Amazon," I said, "so don't even try."

"I want to go there even more than you do," he said. "But you mustn't think it is all pretty birds and lily pads. There are things that will hurt you there, like here," he said, and a stingray jumped from the water as if in service of his words.

"Like everywhere," I said. "It isn't paradise."

"That's where you're wrong," Renato said. "It *is* paradise." He shook his head. "Is this what they tell you in your America," he said, "that paradise is a place without pain?"

"Tonight," Renato said, "Carmita has something very special for you to eat."

"Steak?" I said, because I knew that was his favorite.

"Only in your country," he said, "do they eat steak near the ocean. This is better than steak. You wait and see."

We were back from our boat trip, sitting on the porch of the town's only restaurant, watching Alberto and Abel run into the water with inflatable rafts and ride the small waves back onto the beach, their skin glistening with salt water, their hair slicked smooth and black. They tumbled together like porpoises, like harbor seals, laughing like creatures born in the sea.

"They are amphibious, those boys," I said to Renato. "Do you know that word?"

"Of course," he said.

"Like the grand cayman," I said, and snapped my arms together like jaws.

"Amphibious," he said, trying to save the word in his mouth for later.

The sun hovered on the horizon, unsure whether or not to set. Abel ran up the beach and made his hands into a megaphone; "Blood, Sweat & Tears," he called out, "Procol Harum."

I gave him the thumbs up.

"In my America," I told Renato, "there is more light in the summer than there is in winter. The days are shorter now than they are in June."

He squinted his eyes first at me and then at the sunset. "I think," he said, "that this is not possible."

"No," I said, "it is. In Alaska, in fact, there is a town called Point Barrow that is so close to the North Pole that the sun goes down one day in November and it doesn't rise again until February 1st."

"You have seen this place?" he said.

I shook my head.

"Then you do not know if it is so."

"I *do* know," I said, "because it happens where I live, too, just not as dramatically. In the summer, our days are fifteen hours. In the winter, they are only eight or nine."

"No," he said, shaking his head, frowning, "It is not as you say."

"It isn't something *I* made up," I said. "There are reasons for it ... theories."

"I do not know these theories," he said.

"Then you have to take my word for it," I told him, "until you go and see for yourself."

Carmita's husband came to the table and set a plate in front of us covered with something that looked a lot like the creature from *Little Shop of Horrors*. A crusty brown body with no head and a dozen gray spongy legs, all of them ending in black and red claws.

"*Percebes*," he said proudly. "You must have *cajones* to catch them. Do you know this word *cajones*?"

"Oh yes," I said.

"It is *mucho* dangerous," he said. "The *percebes* live in the place where all day long the ocean pounds into the rock." He slapped his left hand against his right palm, hard.

When he'd gone back to the kitchen, I picked the thing off the plate by its largest claw, let the body and the other claws dangle. "This is a test," I said, "to see if I'm ready for the Amazon."

Renato smiled. "It is not a test," he said. "It is a delicacy."

"Okay," I said, "then you take the first bite."

On our last morning in Puerto Lopez, I woke up to find the balcony next to the Spondylous covered with papier-mâché heads. There were at least a hundred of them, some black-haired, some brown, some male, some female, some pink-skinned, some brown-skinned, some mustachioed, some with glasses; a whole town full of people cut off at the necks and stuck on wooden pegs nailed to the balcony's rail.

Renato came outside to find me in the street taking pictures.

"On New Year's Eve," Renato said, "Ecuadorians burn life-size puppets in the street . . . loved ones who have died, failed politicians, sports heroes who have let us down."

The biggest pig I'd ever seen in person was making his way toward us on the street.

"It is not a happy new year, like it is in your America," Renato said. "On New Year's Eve, we are crying. On January 1st we are happy again."

The pig walked right up to me, rubbed its bristly hair against my bare leg.

"We will be in Quito on New Year's," Renato said. "Thousands of puppets will be burned, even George Bush, even Lorena Bobbitt." He scratched the pig behind the ears, and it made a noise like a cat purring.

"Perhaps," he said, "you should make a puppet or two of your own."

On the way back to Quito, we stopped first at Agua Blanca, where excavation had begun on the ruins of a culture that thrived in 500 A.D. and whose people are remembered first, Renato said, for trying to become more beautiful by deforming their skulls and removing their teeth.

From a boy on the street, I bought a necklace of tiny clay human figures, half of them pregnant, the rest of them men, turned on.

Then we went to Mindo, and got the van stuck in the cloud forest mud along the side of the road. While Renato dug with the shovel, I walked two miles to town, drank a *cerveza* with the local boys while the bartender ran around trying to see if the one truck in town would start. In the end, the bar crowd pulled us out with an ox so thin, his rib cage looked like a weapon. That night we stayed in the Hostelria El Bijou for a dollar per person. The rooms had mosquito netting, and not much else.

I was watching the biggest spider I'd ever seen in my life systematically devour giant mosquitoes by candlelight when Renato knocked on my door.

"How's your netting?" he said.

"Absolutely nothing bigger than a small dog will get through," I said, sticking my head through one of the bigger holes to smile at him.

"Mine's no better," he said, "or I'd trade. Did you hear them say there is no water?"

"To drink?" I said.

"To drink, to flush, to wash your hands." He started to close the door. "I'm sorry about this, Lucy," he said. "We should be in Quito by now, eating steaks and drinking good Chilean wine."

"But I'm getting extra credit for this," I said, "aren't I?"

"Two days in Quito," he said, "and the Amazon is yours."

In Quito he took me to the Church of the Basilica, where all the gargoyles were water creatures: turtles, iguanas, dolphins, and snakes.

"No *percebes*," I said, pointing to the decorated buttresses.

"As you can see, the church has not been completed," he said. "They obviously haven't gotten to the *percebes* spire yet."

Inside, the altar was decorated with coral and sea stars and mother of pearl. The bells pealed in loud, rapid halftones, a gentle waterfall reaching the sea.

"For the people of my country," Renato said, "water is everything: love, life, religion...even God."

"It is like that for me, too," I said. "In English we call that a metaphor."

"Of course," said Renato, "and water is the most abundant metaphor on earth."

* * *

Outside my window in downtown Quito, a hundred thousand people were burning puppets in the street. Renato had gone home at ten p.m. to be with his family. It was the first time I'd been alone in nearly a week.

"Happy New Year," I said when Tony answered.

"Where the hell are you this time?" he said.

"You have to guess," I said, "but I'll give you good hints."

Tony and I had been friends for years, lovers one brief weekend in the middle of them. He was a triathlete, and he read poetry; to my friends, I called him the most beautiful man in the world.

"Australia," he said, after two hints; "Thailand," he said after a third.

He'd been an alcoholic, had stopped drinking long before I met him; his sobriety day the same as my birthday: January 8th. He told me once that New Year's Eve was the most difficult day on his calendar. I called him each year, from wherever I was.

Ecuador was his fifth guess; the clue: *"Here it's the equinox, every single day."*

He said, "Lucy, I want you to stop in Ann Arbor and see me on your way home. We've never been together when we're both single. We ought to do it this time, see what we've got."

I felt the last lonely six months change in my head from an eternity to an instant. I counted all the ways Tony was different from the others.

"It's your day, angel, and mine, too," he said. "I want to show you my house, want you to meet my great new dog. Let's lavish a little affection on each other to start the new year. Come on, Lucy, what do you say?"

The distance hummed in the line between us. "Did you say ravish?" I said.

"Yeah," Tony said, laughing his easy laugh. "That, too."

"I'm going to the Amazon in the morning," I said. "I might not be able to change my plane."

"Just try," he said. "I can feel it this time, Lucy, it might just be our year."

I walked out into the streets, where heaps of half-burned puppets and garbage smoldered. It was only a few minutes after twelve, but the city was deserted. All the Ecuadorians had gone home to have a midnight feast with their families. The only people left on the street were the foreigners, the homeless, and me.

An old woman in rags handed me a shot of something that tasted like rotten peaches and made my head spin right after it went down. I threw the paper cup onto one of the fires. Across the flame I saw another woman sobbing, holding her sides.

I went back inside and called the airlines. It cost six hundred dollars to make the change.

Renato and I raced down the Rio Aguarico all day in a speed boat to get to a camp called Zancudo—mosquito in Spanish— that doubled as a border base for the Ecuadorian army. The Peruvian army was stationed on the opposite bank, not a hundred yards downstream.

"When we are not at war with Peru," Renato said, "we play football with them on Sunday. But now we are at war, so you may hear gunfire in the night."

He was walking me to my cabin, making sure I could find the bathroom in the dark.

"We have an informal agreement with the Peruvians not to aim at the tourist cabins," he said, "but I wouldn't sleep in the window bunk, even so."

When the shots came loud and close and in the middle of something good I was dreaming, I sprung awake so fast I nearly hanged myself in my mosquito net. I hit the floor and crawled under my bed, pulling the netting down with me. There were five or six more rounds of gunfire; then the night went silent again.

The next morning we took a canoe with an outboard motor farther down the Aguarico and made a hard left turn up the Lagarto River, which was smaller and clear and the color of weak coffee. Everything else, from the banks of the river to the top of the canopy, was a rich and relentless green. Jungle sounds were all around us, the wild music of lunatic birds.

"Today we go to Imuya camp," Renato said. "Imuya means place of the howler monkeys in the language of the people who have always lived here."

"Will we see them?" I said.

"We will see all manner of monkeys today," Renato said, "spider, woolly, titi, capuchin, squirrel, tamarins, marmosets, three-toed sloths. No one ever sees the howler monkeys. But when they call, you can hear them from five miles away."

We saw a flash of pink just under the surface of the water, and then again just above.

"Pink-bellied river dolphins," Renato said and shut the motor off. "You can swim with them if you want."

One dolphin surfaced and rolled over slowly. The skin on his back was brown tinged with pink, the same color as the boys from the Spondylous Bar.

I slipped over the side of the boat and into the water.

"They are shy, you know," he said. "It won't be like . . ."

"Flipper," I said.

"Yes," he said, laughing, "that's right."

The water was warm and turned my skin chocolate. The dolphins made big arcs, keeping their eyes on me from some distance away.

I tried to imitate their dives, and Renato laughed harder.

"Stay away from the edges," he said. "There are cayman, fer-de-lance, water moccasins . . . did I tell you about the candiru?"

"Yes," I said, "and don't tell me again."

We walked the two-mile boardwalk across the floating rain forest to Lake Imuya carrying our gear, our water, our food. The jungle around us was thick and green and brimming with life sounds, teeming with them. Every time we took a step off the boardwalk, I thought, *I am killing at least a thousand different species at one time.*

When we got to the lake, two Siona Indians, Rojillio and Lorenzo, were waiting in a rough-hewn canoe, hand-carved from a single tropical tree. Renato puffed out his chest, carried his load a little higher.

"You will take my picture with Rojillio," he said, and I did. "He is a wise man," Renato said, "has learned every lesson of the river."

Renato sat in the very front of the canoe, then Lorenzo with a paddle, then me. Rojillio sat in the very back, holding the big paddle he used to steer. Rojillio spoke in a language that was not quite Spanish. Lorenzo grinned, started to laugh.

"He says the last few days they have seen a grand cayman near here," Renato said. "Thirteen feet long. He says she may have babies. He says we mustn't make her mad."

Rojillio made a noise in his throat three times, a low guttural croaking like a frog. Lorenzo giggled again, but soft this time, like a breeze.

"That is the noise," Renato said, "of the baby cayman."

Rojillio made the sound again, didn't even get to the third croak when the big cayman's head popped up above the surface of the water.

"There," Lorenzo said, his first English word spoken.

I got the cayman in my viewfinder and clicked off a couple of shots. She was coming toward us slowly, toward the front of the canoe, not making even a ripple in the water, her eye fixed, it seemed, only on Renato.

She came closer and closer, till I had to back off from my zoom to get anything but her eye in the shot.

I backed it off as far as it would go, realized in that split second that the lens distance had met reality, dropped my camera to my chest just in time to see the cayman rear up and out of the water, propelled by the muscle that was her tail like nothing I'd ever seen before and silent. Her two front legs and eight or nine feet of her thirteen-foot body were in the front of the canoe, and she was snapping her three-foot-long jaws hard at Renato.

Rojillio barked out a command that in any language could only have been "Don't fall into the water," and Renato made a move around Lorenzo, out over the water on the opposite side but somehow not in it, prettier than a wide receiver with the goal line in his sights.

The cayman stretched her neck at Lorenzo and Renato, who were now more or less both in my lap, and we all high-sided to keep the boat from tipping toward the cayman, till she got tired of the balancing act and slipped back down into the water.

Her head stayed above it, though, her one eye fixed on me this time, so close I could have scratched her head without extending my elbow.

For several minutes we floated that way in the dead silence of Imuya's high noon. Then Lorenzo took his paddle and put it in the water as smooth as a spoon in fresh whipped cream, and pushed us, just slightly, away from the cayman.

We were twenty yards past her when Lorenzo and Rojillio

exploded into laugher. Renato smiled, but I could see he was still shaking bad.

"In guide school," he said, "they told us grand cayman are non-aggressive."

Later that day I took Renato's photo with his head inside the jaws of a skeletal cayman, the camp's biggest trophy, nowhere near the size of the one that had jumped in our boat.

"I keep thinking," Renato said, "of my wife, my son, my mother, how they would be feeling right now if things had gone the other way."

He scraped a speck of dirt off one of the teeth of the cayman with his nail. I stared off the dock down into the dark water, then up into the thick canopy of green above. A tree frog dropped from a branch onto my upturned neck, and I brushed it away without so much as a squeal.

"It must be strange for you, as well," he said, "to think that no one would be grieving."

"It's not quite as bad as all that," I said. "I do have friends."

"Still," he said, "to be alone is unnatural. Look around you." He motioned to the trees above us, the lake below. "There isn't an animal in the jungle that doesn't have a mate."

A pair of scarlet macaws flew past us at eye level chattering to each other.

"How do you do that?" I said. "Is the entire animal community at your beck and call?"

"No," he said, "I am at theirs."

"Besides," I said, "finding a mate is no problem; finding a good one is where I go wrong. I guess I'm a little fussier than a scarlet macaw."

"And why do you think she is not fussy," he said, "just because she knows how to choose better than you."

Something big crashed in the water, and Renato flinched more than he wanted to.

"Why haven't you been paying attention?" he said, touching first his eye, then his earlobe. "Why haven't your rivers taught you how to live?"

I thought about the rivers I'd left behind in my America, remembered their golden mornings, the delicate surprise of a midsummer frost. I remembered how from above the desert, rivers gleamed like emerald necklaces, the only green for hundreds of miles of driest buttes and steepest mesas, of broken rocks and blowing sand. I remembered thinking that if the Amazon were flat and green, it would have no way to hurt me. I had forgotten the first lesson I ever learned on the river: the place that makes you vulnerable is the place that makes you strong.

Just then we heard a sound like the wind through a culvert on the coldest day of an inner-city winter, though the temperature in Imuya couldn't have been much under a hundred degrees. It was the most hollow, the saddest, the loneliest sound I'd ever heard.

Renato motioned with his head to the rope ladder, and we climbed to the camp's thatched lookout spot. The sound was louder up there, but the trees weren't moving. Even the top of the canopy was still as the first breath of dawn.

"It is the howler monkeys," Renato said, "calling from four, maybe five miles up river."

"It's the wind," I said. "An animal could never make that sound."

"It is the monkeys," he said, "and they are no bigger than well-fed parrots." He held his hands together to indicate their size. He said, "I told you the jungle is a magical place."

"How do you know it is not the wind," I said, "if no one ever sees the monkeys?"

"It is like your three months of night in Alaska," he said. "You have to take my word that it is so."

Renato drove me to the airport as the sun rose on my last morning in Ecuador, as it always did, at precisely six a.m.

"My head is swimming," I said, "with all the things you've shown me."

"It is my country that has shown you," he said. "I only drove the car."

At the airport he adjusted his cap and stood straight, almost at attention.

"I feel," he said, "as though we have become *compañeros*." He grinned like a boy. "Do you know that word?"

"Of course," I said.

"More than friends," he said, "less than brothers. It is"—he shook my hand—"almost uncanny."

"Yes," I said, smiling, "it is."

"When you come back to Ecuador," he said, "we will see how much the river has taught you."

"And if I come back alone?" I said.

"Then next time we will give your eyes even longer to adjust."

The Lessons

The traveling time to Ann Arbor was seventeen hours, counting a mad dash across the parking lot at Kennedy, several de-icings, and fifteen circles in a holding pattern around Washington, D.C. Tony wasn't at the gate when I got off the plane at Detroit International. Nor was he at baggage claim, nor in the parking lot, nor in his office, nor on his cellular phone.

After two hours I called my friend Henry in Chicago because he was in the next time zone and that was as close to human contact as I was going to get after midnight.

"You've come all the way today from a different hemisphere," he said. "Go get yourself a nice hotel room and call me in the morning."

I was on the phone to the Marriott when Tony walked in.

"I'm sorry," he said, "I must have gotten the times confused."

Back in Ann Arbor I admired his new furniture. I petted his handsome and young black dog. It was three in the morning in Michigan; in Quito, I knew, the sun was about to rise. I said, "Tony, I've got to go to bed."

"We need to have a little talk first," he said, patting my hand like I was an old person. "I'm sorry, Lucy, but I've met someone new."

My eyes felt like the insides of a clothes drier. "Since Friday?" I said. "In only five days?"

"Yeah," he said, "I guess I should have called you. Her name is Beth"—he let go of my hand when he said it—"I saw her in a shop window on Tuesday, and it feels really healthy so far."

"It's okay," I said, and meant it. "I'm fine right here on the couch."

"Well, that's the other thing," he said. "Beth has kind of a problem with you being here. I guess I should tell you it caused our first fight."

"I'm sorry, Tony," I said, "I'm not going anywhere till I get some sleep."

When I woke up, Tony was sitting on the couch looking down at me. Outside the window everything was glazed with a fresh ice storm, blinding in the sun.

"I don't think I handled last night very well," he said.

"I've slept," I said. "Now you can take me to the airport."

"I don't need to," he said, stroking his dog. "I went to Beth's last night and patched everything up and now she's dying to meet you."

"Tomorrow's my birthday, Tony," I said, "and all I want to do is go home."

In the car on the way to the airport, Tony said, "You know I could still turn this car around at any moment."

I looked out the window at the frozen trees, the branches heavy with icicles ready to snap.

"I would probably do the same thing you are doing," he said. "Of course later I'd feel like a total jerk."

Lesson #1

"Monarch butterflies," Renato had said on our first day in Imuya, "make blue jays throw up. That is how monarch butterflies keep from being eaten. But over the years, by a process known as Batesian Mimicry, several other butterfly species have learned how to color themselves to look like the monarch every time a blue jay comes around.

"The problem arises," Renato said, "when a blue jay's first experience is with an impostor butterfly. If the blue jay doesn't throw up that first time, he will spend the rest of his life not knowing which are the safe butterflies and which are the ones that will make him sick."

I put my head against the little window while they once again de-iced the plane.

"Whoever the hell he was," a voice said above me, "I'd bet my front teeth he wasn't worth it." She was small and black and sexy, stuffing her bag in the overhead bin above me and pulling her skirt down, adjusting her thirty or forty gold rings.

"Ecuador," she said, eyeing the tag on my carry-on. "Now there's a place I've always wanted to go."

"I just got back," I said.

"And the guy," she said. "Was he in Ecuador?"

"No," I said, "Ann Arbor."

"Well," she said, "if you'll excuse the expression, then fuck that shit."

She settled in next to me, stuck out her hand. "My name's Charisma," she said. "What's yours?"

"Lucy," I said, "Lucy O'Rourke."

"Well, let me ask you something, Lucy O'Rourke, do you know where I'm going tonight?"

"Oakland, I guess," I said, "if you're on the right plane."

"That's right," she said. "That's where my ex lives...my first ex...God knows where the second one is...but the first one called me up last week and said, 'Charisma...you just fly yourself out here and bring an empty suitcase cause we're going shopping.' That, my girl, is what to look for in a man."

A boy of eighteen or nineteen paused in the aisle beside us, held up his ticket, shrugged, said to Charisma, "I think you're in my seat."

"Another pick of the litter," she said, and then to the boy, "This is a great big plane, darlin', I know you can find another."

The boy hovered there for a minute, shifting his weight from seatward to backward, then he moved on.

Charisma said she was a writer, and a painter, and she ran an antique store her third husband bought her, and she also sang on weekends in a Detroit club, blues and a little jazz, though I couldn't tell which thing she did for pay.

"Do you write novels?" I said.

"Novels, lord no," she said. "I can't even stay married." She pulled out a nail file, scissors, polish, decals of tiny gold stars.

"Now you tell me all about Ecuador or the man in Ann Arbor," she said, "whichever you need to talk about more."

When I got home there was a phone message from Steven, a carpenter turned massage therapist and tantra expert I'd met back in the summer, when I'd sat in Oakland's Café Roma drinking my first macchiattos and looking for friends. At that time Steven was stinging from a breakup with a woman who he said was so uptight she wouldn't talk about her bowel movements. Going to India for two years, he said, had forever changed his life.

He said that if Capricorns would only embrace their goatish nature, they could be the most successful people on earth. He said Mercury was coming out of retrograde soon, and then everybody's problems would be solved.

I hadn't heard from Steven since that day, but he had remembered my birthday all that time, had called to see if he could take me out. I looked at the pile of bills and the empty refrigerator, took a shower, and called him back.

He took me out for sushi, said that because it was raw and because it was art, it was food in its purest form. I drank enough sake to choke down even the flying fish eggs, even the shrimp heads. He said there was no bad karma with sake as long as you drank it out of a box.

Back at my apartment, on opposite sides of my couch, he gave me a coupon book for five free massages. He told me about his family, his Mormon roots, the years he spent on the Big Island, how he and his second wife took sex to such an art form that sometimes the neighbors came by to watch.

Then he said, "I think I'd like to give you a big birthday kiss."

"That would be nice," I said.

When we were finished, he said, "That was a little bigger than I anticipated."

"Oh," I said, "I'm sorry."

Then he said, "Tell me something, Lucy, have you ever thought about you and me having sex?"

"No," I said, because I hadn't, and I didn't tell him the rest of it, that I hadn't thought of him at all since that day at Café Roma when we met.

"Perhaps," he said, "you could think about it now."

I fingered the coupon book and tried to imagine it; I thought about his Hawaiian neighbors, how I didn't even know what tantra was.

"Well," I said, "It's been a lovely evening...and I feel like we're becoming friends, and everybody says that's the place sex should come from..." His eyes wouldn't let mine wander. He nodded like he hoped there was more. "I do have a kind of a passion for men who can build things," I said, "and I know you can, though you don't anymore."

"But I could...," he said, "if we were together and there was something you wanted."

"So I guess," I said, "it might be nice, it being my birthday and all."

Steven lifted his hand off the place it had fallen, between our knees. I counted off through thirty seconds of silence.

"And what do you think, then," I finally said, "about you and I getting together."

"Well, frankly," he said, drawing a big cleansing breath, "I just don't think you are spiritually advanced enough for me."

Lesson #2

On the second day in Imuya, we saw all the hummingbirds: the green-tailed golden throat, the fawn-breasted brilliant, the amethyst-throated sun angel, the spangled coquette.

"The spangled coquette," Renato had said, "got its name because the males of the species are pugnacious and territorial and they won't let the females get close to the flowers to drink the nectar they need in order to live. So the female has learned to go into a false heat, a false blush of her mating colors. When the male hummingbird sees her, he becomes very generous, he lets the female eat whatever she wants. When she has stuffed herself sufficiently, the female hummingbird turns dull again, and flies away."

A week after my birthday I broke down and picked up a copy of the *Bay Guardian* just to look, I said, through the personal ads. After spending the better part of the night reading them, I settled on a man named Mitchell Wagner whose ad was benign and funny, focusing mostly on his six-year-old son.

We made a date for the following Friday—Mitchell, me, and Willy, dinner at his house, trout with lemon and parsley, broccoli, potatoes, and German chocolate cake for dessert.

I negotiated the six-year-old well, I thought, watched *Snow White and the Seven Dwarfs* with him, and played teepee under the table until my back was sore.

Mitchell fired one question after another at me: what was the best and the worst thing about me, what was the character of the last three men I dated, where did I expect to be living in five years, and in ten.

In between questions he talked about his ex-wife, her addictions, how he'd left her in Baltimore one middle of the night, taken Willy with him, got ready for the police or the FBI to find him, for the investigation that never came.

"She didn't even call my friends to see what had happened," he said, "not even my mother." He moved his hand around Willy's head in giant circles. "I mean, does that sound like natural motherhood to you?"

"No," I said, though I knew nothing about motherhood, natural or otherwise.

"You wouldn't ever pull a stunt like that," he said, "would you?" and his eyes got narrow like he was expecting me to lie.

"No," I said, "I can't imagine."

"You know," he said, when I told him it was time I should be leaving, "I was going to say this to your answering machine, but after some reconsideration, I think I'll say it to your face."

I braced a little against the arm of the couch.

"Never before," he said, "have I spent three hours with anyone who took less of an interest in me."

"I'm sorry," I said, "It was all I could do to ..."—*keep up with the questions,* is what I was going to say, but then he had his hands around my neck in something I at first believed was strangulation, and only later, when his tongue went down my throat, understood to be a kiss.

"I'm having a hard time," I said, backing to the door, grabbing my purse as I moved down the landing, "keeping up with the turns this evening has taken." I moved my eyes back and forth between Mitchell and Willy. "Thanks for dinner," I said.

Willy made tiny fists at me inside his too-big pajamas, and said a soft "Bye-bye."

Lesson #3

"The loudest bird in the jungle," Renato had said on the third day, "is known as the screaming pehah."

He stuck two fingers in his mouth and made a sound indistinguishable from a wolf whistle on a construction site. A few seconds later, the bird answered back, almost as loud.

"The screaming pehah is an interesting bird," Renato said, "because he spends over seventy-five percent of his life looking for a mate."

"Not like anybody else we know," I said. Either Renato didn't hear me or he decided not to smile.

"And the reason he has to scream so loud," he said, "is because he is just a plain bird, small and brown ... and living in this jungle with so many beautiful birds—blue and yellow parrots, ruby-throated hummingbirds, scarlet macaws—he knows he is made superior only by his scream."

The phone rang at two a.m., and it was Mitchell Wagner.

"I can't stop thinking about you," he said in a voice that was half croak and half whisper. "In one night you've changed everything I'd come to believe about women."

"I don't know what to say," I said.

"Say you'll see me again," he said. "Say you'll come for dinner tomorrow."

"No," I said, "never," and hung up the phone.

Long before daylight, the phone rang again.

"Darling," the voice said, "this here's Charisma. I was just calling to see if you're feeling as beautiful as you are today."

"Yes," I said, "thank you, Charisma. I think maybe today I am."

"There are two basic kinds of birds in the jungle," Renato had said on our last day in Imuya, "the ones who eat fruit and the ones who eat bugs."

"You make it sound so simple," I said.

"It *is* simple," he said, taking both my hands so I'd listen. "The ones who eat fruit have more time to sing."

On the 747 from Quito to Miami, I'd been amazed by the graceful curve of the South American continent, by the way the biggest waves shimmered before they crashed on the impossibly long virgin shore. *In the beginning,* Renato had said, *all of the world was America.*

I stayed awake until the sky started to lighten. Even in Point

Barrow the sun would be rising soon. I fell into sleep and dreamed about taking my life back to the river. For the rest of the morning, the howler monkeys cried in my dreams.

Carol and Tommy

Right in front of everyone at Two-Bit's Worth, my last girl-friend called me unfit to drink in public, and I told her she was heavyset and that, after three months dating, I had come to realize she would *always* be heavyset. In this ugly way she walked out of my life for good. I was twenty-seven. After that I was single for two years straight. I'd had troubles before holding a steady job, and I'd scraped with the law under circumstances that result-ed in fines and community service, but nothing can hollow your soul like spending dark hours with a radio you're reluctant to turn off, imagining a night deejay as being exactly too beautiful for the man you are. Old romances that should have amounted to something I'd think through backwards, from last fights to pre-fucking, like starting a pencil at the end of the maze and tracing to all the possibilities in the center.

When Carol's Tercel pulled into the lot of the repair shop where I was working, its front rotors worn to the thickness of two quar-ters, I was at the bottom of a cruel and lonely place. Carol was thirty-six and alone in the world except for a son named Tommy, who was five years old. There was a crazy ex-husband recently out of the picture—a refrigerator and air-conditioner repairman out west—and in the space of an afternoon, Carol had fled with Tommy, from her home and the people who embodied her life, in the hopes of never laying eyes on the man again. All this she'd told me a few hours into our first date, while Addicted to Sacrifice was between band sets. Shaking my head gravely as I listened, what I was saying was, "It disgusts a normal guy like me that this whacko loser son of a bitch poisoned love for you—let me show you better." But there was also an instant when I might have understood the guy. Carol was a slender, attractive woman with shimmery auburn hair and expressive eyes whose purple some-times blew your mind, though I imagined her a different kind of attractive ten or fifteen years earlier, the kind that could set your heart on fire if you tried to love her.

We were on her bed one night while the ten-o'clock Creature Double-Feature finished up on the small rabbit-eared set across from us. There was a metallic funneling sound behind the walls from air-pocketed radiator piping, whose fluctuating heat had left me under a sheet in my boxers and Carol on the spread in her terry-cloth robe. We were holding hands and had been like that for some hours, resting.

Carol had just finished telling me about a car accident on I-84 that morning in which one of the men involved pulled the other out of his car and beat him with his fists all around the median. "What you realize," she was saying, "what breaks your heart is that people can kill each other over spare change. You could see in the way the first one circled his car that he was psyching himself up to be so pissed. Like he needed to concentrate on it."

"It helps you win," I said. "You work off an adrenaline fix."

Carol finished her beer and set it on the nightstand. "It's because hating someone isn't a natural feeling. It's not something we're born with. I love you without having to try, and I love Tommy that way. But hate is different. You have to teach yourself to feel hatred. Or get driven to it, I guess."

Love was something we hadn't spoken yet, and hearing it now I felt the first sensation of doubt, a light sweat, a tickle in the gut. It was old, suddenly familiar. And it involved leaving someone for the false notion of someone else, a woman younger or prettier, like a sure thing on the rim of your life. Though now the feeling passed more quickly than it ever had and I was slightly exhilarated. "Tell me that again," I said.

"You mean love?" She tilted her head, exposing a soft curve of white neck. "It doesn't bite, Jerry. I love you. There. And if I held back because I was worried how you'd take it, I'd be a bullshitter." She placed my hand next to me, clicked off the TV, and got out of bed. At the far end of the room, she opened one of the bifold closet doors and brought out a golf club. "I don't know what other virtues are intact," she said. "But no one can call me a bullshitter."

"That's the virtue worth keeping." I considered my beer on the nightstand, but the buzz I'd established had a resilient attitude so I let it go warm.

Carol set down a handful of dimpled white balls across from a rubber putting cup. Her first shot nicked the side bank, mostly the fault of a stretch of floor whose boards, worn rough of varnish, pitched in the centers. The ball floundered back out and stopped. Carol had this way of smiling suddenly which always surprised me. She said, "Because you're a mechanic, I think. You understand the inner workings, the tiny triggers that get the big results. It's that you think with patience."

"I love you back," I said, and it occurred to me that the people around I knew, some even that I felt inferior to, were bitter at heart and lonesome.

"I'm newly in love with a man who can speak," she said. Her fingers closed like falling dominoes around the club grip. "Now there's a blue-moon idea." Behind her the bedroom door rattled with sudden force and startled us both. The knob was loose in its stile, and couldn't twist enough to open. When Carol saw me about to say something, she held out her hand. "Get in the closet."

"Carol."

"Jerry, please. I can't think."

I pulled on my pants absently and lumbered across the room, heavy with knowing the night was about to last longer than I wanted-ed. In the closet I steadied myself between her hung blouses, breathing air congested with vanilla perfume and static, and watched through the middle louvers. When the bedroom door opened, Tommy burst across the threshold and latched onto Carol's leg. He was wearing maroon sweatpants and no shirt. He coughed and shivered, tears spraying from his lips. "Screamed...," he said. "Screaming at me, Mommy..." In the narrow rectangle of what I could see, his face was sunken and bloodless, the sideways figure-eight of his mouth tremoring. And I thought then that nothing can ready you to see such a look of terror on a boy. I'd seen that look once before, on the face of an acquaintance I'd been drinking with who was my age or possibly older, a few minutes before he went to the police to turn himself in. Like things can somehow go worse than you imagined.

Carol received Tommy's face in the crook of her neck and stared across the room. There was an ease about her like she'd known these nights before, though I couldn't say, since I'd been sleeping at her apartment only once a week, and for less than a month. As I adjusted my footing, a plastic hanger scraped my neck, and I fought it off without turning. Her eyes stopped at points along the floor as if measuring distances. I wiggled my finger between two louvers and scratched the paint just a little. It seemed like enough sound for someone who knew I was in there, but she didn't look in my direction. And all at once I felt laughed at or as though my manhood had been challenged. I pulled my finger back and counted to five. Then I opened the closet door and stepped out.

Carol closed her eyes for a moment after she'd seen me, and when she opened them, her look was vague, though I didn't think angry, and I said, "It was just a bad dream." Tommy jerked violently away from his mother and tried to break free, but Carol took a firm hold around his waist. "Look, honey," she said. "It's only Jerry."

"It's only me," I said. His face was wet with tears, sticky tracks of them down the bell of his midget pot belly. His red hair matted dark across his forehead. "Let *go*," he screamed, writhing against his mother's grip. He slapped the fat bottom of his hand against her side. "I hate you, Mommy!"

"Easy, partner," I said, and his shoulder blade moved and stiffened when I touched it. When he looked at me, his expression seemed dazed, as though only now he'd woken from the dream, as though I were his first piece of what was real but he didn't know where to fit me in. "How come you came here, Jerry?" he said. I smelled urine on him and in reflex drew my hand away. Carol frowned and took him in a loose hug. Tommy watched me step back as he lifted his hands around his mother's neck, and I was pinned inside long embarrassing seconds. "I don't want him," he said, his voice easier now. Something had calmed him. "Let's take me back to bed," he said.

When Carol came in and closed the door, I was back under the sheet. She went to the window and lifted it open. From the chain-linked courtyard outside, white December air curled in in a thin wave, and somewhere nearby a car chirped its tires and tore off.

"It was a nightmare about before, wasn't it?" I said. "It was about your ex-husband."

From the top drawer of her bureau Carol found a black tube, the kind used for camera film, and brought it to the window with a pack of matches. She sat on the floor and pulled her robe tighter. "I asked you to stay in the closet."

"I'm a stranger around here," I said. "You know what I'm saying? Hell, the kid doesn't even like me." I thought about going in the living room and turning on the TV. I thought about cracking a few beers. "I'm not going to worry about it," I said.

Carol took a marijuana joint out of the tube and lit it, closing her eyes with the first hit, and though a few tokes would have done me no harm, she wasn't offering any. She let the smoke out the window. "His face is so peaceful when he's sleeping," she said. "You'd wish the demons could just stay away." She hit three times then tapped the end of the joint and dropped it into the tube. "You can never outlive your past. Didn't somebody have that carved on their gravestone?"

"I couldn't tell you."

When she came back to bed, I could see that the thing we'd ended up on different sides of was over for her now. There didn't have to be more unless I was starting. She untied her robe and compressed her shoulders so that it fell all at once to coils around her ankles. "Here I am," she said, her voice soft and matter-of-fact. I smiled because it was something she'd said before, the night after our first date, when from the bathroom she paused in the bedroom doorway, unexpectedly naked as I bobbled off my jacket and shoes. She was a small woman, petite, spare and bony in the hips, though she'd gone through childbirth. There was a dryness to her skin I associated with age, and her breasts dimpled into all their freckles under a light touch. On the inside of her thigh she had this tattoo of a swan, a simple, stringy figure, black-green like an old bruise.

Carol spun the alarm dial of the clock radio and a split-second's lead guitar blared. Then she lay beside me and took my hand and placed it near her navel, over a crescent of stretch mark like rough wood to the touch. She turned off the bedstand lamp so that light from a pole on Connecticut Avenue lipped in over the ceiling and gave us silver outlines.

"It won't get easier later on," I said, intending that to be the last word of it.

Carol was quiet, though I could feel her nodding slowly, and the thing she was staring at, which I trained my own eyes on, was a funnel of cobweb riding drafts in a ceiling corner. For entire minutes it wouldn't connect its sticky reach or let go. She turned to me, and we made love with exhausted minds and bodies. After, she touched my lips with a finger. "Give us a while," she said. "We're still okay." And it seemed too late by then to tell anything but the truth. I closed my eyes and drowned in heavy sleep, thick with the kind of insignificant dreams I hadn't known in years.

Carol liked to call me at Doc's Motorwerke during her half-hour between work and picking up Tommy from daycare. I planned my lunch break around this time, in the parts room where there was a swivel chair and a desk to put my feet on. Our shop had an arrangement with a halfway house on the north end of Bridgeport, and the mechanics they sent us wore gold studs in their noses and knew more about breaking into cars than fixing them. I pulled them off commission jobs for warranty work, and they cocked me the kinds of looks you'd be a fool to turn your back on. So when one of them came in for a computer sensor or spark plugs, I'd say something sweet to Carol over the phone. It was cheap, I knew, but in a way it made me feel lucky. She would call from Sikorsky's, where she inventoried gears and fasteners for military helicopters. I knew the factory only as background noise, but as she told me her small plans for the night, I imagined massive ceramic vats behind her, catching red fountains of molten iron.

On the day of the first real snow, Carol put together her Christmas tree and invited me over to have a look. It was a white hemlock imitation with spiraled wire for a trunk, the kind stores will buy in bulk for their own decoration. The balls were solid blue and solid silver, which gave the tree an ordered look not very friendly or cozy. But the dark imitation paneling in the living room was better for the blinking lights, and I told her it was pretty. I'd brought a quart of eggnog that turned out to be rotten, so I ran across the street to Larry's Liquor Locker for a six-pack of beer.

After dinner Carol needed to make a few phone calls, so I went out into the living room with Tommy to watch TV. Usually he was set for bed by the time I came over, and all I really knew of him was a tired face stamped by upholstery creases, blinking indifferently at me while his mother carried him off to bed. I volunteered a comfortable distance of sofa between us, and Tommy married himself to the screen, to the dentist elf setting out for the

Island of Misfit Toys. Two Christmas cards were butted together over the TV, and I noticed that one of them was the same wish for peace and prosperity People's Bank had sent me. On the wall across from us were two framed photographs of white-tail deer, antlered bucks poised in haughty stances over rugged, snow-blanketed country.

"That's what I want," Tommy said at the television, where a toy commercial ran. "Only the green kind with the other buttons." He didn't seem to have anyone in mind he was saying this to, though after a while he looked at me. A beer rested between my legs, and I had been peeling off pieces of the label and setting them on the coffee table. "Okay," I said. "What's that, a squirt pistol?"

Tommy stared at me vacantly until my question lost meaning, and we were involved in the kind of complex quiet where if one of you doesn't smile soon, some meanness will probably come out of it. A tightrope quiet, you call it. So I smiled. Tommy waved me near, and I leaned in. "You should have a dog," he said into my ear. And then with his cold hands, he pulled my face closer and kissed me in an area under my eye, a small, wet kiss. It made me awkward, the way you feel in a public place catching a woman breast-feeding, like it's innocent enough but just the same. Tommy opened his hand over my forehead, pushed me lightly back.

"A dog," I said, ticking my tongue with nothing else to say. I cleared my throat. "Did you have a dog?"

"Roxy first. We got Ginger after." Tommy stood on the sofa, the back of his hair lifting with static. Then he laughed a mighty shout of a laugh. "Once Daddy put Ginger in the bathtub with me and my mommy. Cause she was mudd-eee. Mudd-eee!"

A door clicked shut down the hall in the direction of Carol's room. I took a drink of my beer. Tommy was watching me. "Where is Ginger now?" I said. "Does your daddy have Ginger?"

Tommy climbed onto the armrest and in his alligator slippers steadied himself. He bounced knees-down off the cushions, and then he got up and did it again. It was like he'd gotten into rocket fuel. "Ginger drinked antifreeze," he said, fidgeting now with a throw pillow. He heaved it high over his head and slammed it against his thighs. He did this a few times until he was red in the face, and just before he hurled the pillow at the TV screen, he yelled once for each slam, "Ginger—drinked—anti—freeze." And that was it, he settled into this agitated idle, like someone trying to outlast the shakes, and his program had been running, but both of us were staring with surprise and curiosity at the dust-blown place where the Christmas cards had been.

"Do you need your mom now?" I said. I wasn't angry and didn't want to come off as if I were. I guessed he'd just had some sort of episode. Tommy hesitated a moment, then shook his head no. He wiped his mouth on his wrist. Solemnly he said, "Ginger sometimes bited Mommy." He looked at the tree while opening and closing a small fist to the pulsing of the lights, and then underneath, at the shaggy cotton skirt without any presents on it.

"It's okay, Tommy," I said. "It's okay for dogs because the secret is they can't really feel it." And as he nodded, all his flat little teeth shown in his smile. "Here," I said, taking his hand in a shake, a modest up-and-down, and handling his random squeezes with light but steady pressure. I was teaching this to him. "That's it," I said. And I thought about his father then, the man Tommy may have resembled, who through jealousy or greed or something worse had lost his family and a future worth believing in.

When Carol stopped in front of the television, the snowbeast was toothless and unoffending as a lamb. She surveyed the room and looked at Tommy. "I'm mixed up with a couple of crazies," she said, and Tommy laughed and said, "Crazies." Carol gathered the fallen cards in an unhurried manner and set them back. "I thought I was getting a cold before," she said. Her eyes were pink-rimmed and a little swollen, though she may have been smoking in her room. "You look run-down," I said without thinking.

"My prom queen days are behind us now," Carol said and smiled in her surprised way. She picked the throw pillow off the floor and sat between us. Tommy crawled half into her lap, and she tousled his hair. "And you've got a voice that could drop a mountain, mister," she said, and she made him laugh, squeezing at his sides. "God, Mommy. Oh God, Mommy," he said.

I finished my beer and went into the kitchen for another, and one for Carol, and I thought about running out for another six-pack. Through the sink window, dense snow leaned in sideways and a primered Monte Carlo wound for traction up the small hill Carol lived on. Police sirens began weakly, as though they were in my head, then peaked distinctly in wide rolling pulses. A few blocks in the direction of Father Panik Village, they dropped off, and I watched the stormy night with a satisfied sense of being far removed from the cold city.

Tommy was riled again when I joined them on the sofa, and I don't know, it had an effect on me. His frenzy now, dancing beside his mother, his hand gripping at her shoulder, wasn't any less enthusiastic than his frenzy before with me. "*There's* that caterpillar," he said at another commercial. "If you have him you could walk him like a doggy. I knew it. I knew that was him." When his foot caught between cushions, Tommy lunged forward, tearing the gold chain from Carol's neck. I thrust an arm between his head and the coffee table just as Carol pulled him back into her lap. My beer foamed over, and I hopped up. "Shit." I scraped icy lather from my jeans onto the braided rug. "Rotten kids don't get presents," I said. "Look at this crap."

Tommy saw something in me that made him reel back. "I am a good boy," he said, his eyes darting and glistening. "We're running away, and not you, Jerry. You can't come."

He opened his arms to his mother, and when she took him against her, Carol narrowed her eyes at me. "Just steal his Christmas away from him," she said. With Tommy in her arms, she began rocking slightly. He said something in her ear, and she nodded and whispered something back.

"I apologize," I said. "I was out of line. I'm sorry to both of you."

"It's by your foot," Carol said. I scooped the small gold cross from her necklace off the rug and handed it to her. "Listen," I said to Tommy. He hesitated and finally loosened from his mother, and I took a moment to remember things right. I told him about the time my father's Christmas present to me was two fifty-cent pieces. Only the way he did it was he put them in a small box, then that one in a bigger one, on and on. He handed me a package the size of a Tyco Ferrari racing set. Smaller and smaller I went, tearing the boxes open in a rage, and my father had been drinking and thought it was the funniest thing ever. "So there I was," I said, "all these boxes around me, and a dollar to show for it." I took a long sip of my beer, and Carol shook her head in a pleasing way that said I was forgiven.

But Tommy had frozen, his mouth agape. "It was a gag," I said. He crawled over Carol, got to his feet, and touched me on the shoulder. His eyes found mine and waited there like he didn't know how to tell me something awful. "But when," he said.

"I was a kid. Little."

He slapped a hand at the air between us. "When did he give you the race cars?"

Carol and I were out on the porch of her duplex smoking ciga-rettes when the subject of Tommy's father came up. We were just talking, one thing to the next. It was colder than hell.

"He had some nice Chevelles," Carol said. "They used to race. For money, pink slips, whatever. That was the thing in California."

"Was his name Tom?"

"Rick," she said. "That's Tommy's first name. Richard Thomas McLean." She rubbed her arm, and a small bouquet of sparks shot off her Winston. "He gave me this tattoo," she said, pointing her chin to where it was under her jeans. "He did it himself."

Leaning against the railing, I tore strings of wood from a rotted baluster. After drugging her up, he scribbled that sloppy mark, his mark, I thought, like a mutt staining its territory. I took a few long drags of my cigarette. "He raced pro?"

She smoothed a small pouch under her eye and shook her head. "He liked to run them out in the desert where he could hold it right to the floor. Past the red line. You could smell them burning up, oil or rubber, that kind of smell. Like any minute it would all just explode."

"Sounds like a winner," I said. I imagined him in a bandanna cap and Harley-patched leathers, enterprising in a weight room, quiet around men but intense. Someone, though, who had his limitations like anyone else on God's green earth. What keeps a man from acting out of his dignity is the capacity to know this when the dangerous moment finally comes. "Sounds like a real Boy Scout," I said, the skin of my throat coppery in the thin air.

She shrugged and dropped her shoulders. "Life had a different set of rules back then." From somewhere not far beyond us, a woman sent a child's name into the night. Carol turned toward the sound, to ashy darkness over brick-face, to the escape ladder across the street, and after a few moments, the calling ended. Between cloud cover, a patch of stars hung upon us like chips of ice. Then Carol said, "Do you think it's funny the way I am with my son? Peculiar, I mean. Do you think I raise him in a way that's peculiar?"

"No," I said, and shook my head to make it definite. It wasn't something I'd given much thought to. I flicked my cigarette into the street. "Let's go inside," I said.

Carol scooped her hair back with one hand so that her face seemed narrow and drawn, and she paused, watching me watch her. "Sometimes you worry about our ages, don't you, Jerry. You worry it will reach a point where you don't find me attractive anymore and you won't be able to say it."

"Jesus, Carol."

She dropped her cigarette and ground it into the scabby paint of the porch floor. "I want you to know that I'm brazen to that, to that and about anything else you could throw at me. It's all right. And if you were seeing someone else right now, that would be all right, too."

"What the hell does that mean?"

"I never asked for commitment, Jerry," she said. "Just even-temperedness." She pulled her hands back in the cuffs of her jacket, and the funny thing was that right then, she looked younger to me. Girlish. She looked like someone I'd never met.

I went back inside. Tommy was belly down in front of the TV, cheeks on palms on elbows. I had on the Brotherhood of the Right silk-screened jacket I'd won off a retired member in a card game, and Tommy turned to watch me take it off. He liked the smell of leather, and I knew he wanted to hold it. "What?" I said, and without looking at me again, he got off the floor and ran down the hallway toward his room. "I'm not in a mood," I said after him. His door slammed. "I'm not in any goddamn mood." I threw the jacket on the couch and went into the bathroom.

The exhaust fan droned as I paced and finally opened the medicine cabinet over the sink. I didn't know what I was doing. Mint-Flavored Fluoride Gel, Band-Aids that said Adhesive Strips for Cuts and Scrapes. On the top shelf were two prescription bottles, Erythromycin and Tranxene. NO REFILL was typed under her name on the second bottle, and I could judge by its weight it was almost empty. Two things suddenly came to my attention: the cabinet's contents I'd been lining on the edge of the sink and Carol at the open door.

She took the bottle from me, knocked one of the blue pills onto her palm, and brought it to her mouth. "I wonder," she said, opening her eyes from swallowing, "if that day at your shop, I should have just paid for the brake job and drove away clean. Or maybe I should have told you to give me love in small increments."

"I didn't deserve that," I said. I folded my arms and looked at the brown grout between the tiles.

"You didn't," she said. She closed the door behind her as if she had some further action in mind, but she seemed to lose purpose. Her hands found her front pockets, and she sighed. "I waitressed at a truck stop for three years," she said, "and I thought that was the lowest point of my life. I still think that. And what I remember is that you won't spill coffee if you don't watch yourself carrying it. Isn't that a telling thing? Three years of my life, and that's where it got me." She looked at me, and I realized I'd been waiting for her to. She opened her arms. "Will you come here?"

And we hugged then in a way we'd never done before and didn't again after that night.

Four days before Christmas, Carol was making dinner for us. I'd come over late, and Tommy had already eaten. He was sleeping in the living room, which was pretty much the routine, as was her carrying him to bed while I set up a movie. Some nights, she would stay with him for half an hour. I'd get up and start walking toward the door, to peek in on what was happening, but the wooden hallway flooring creaked like crazy. I'd soft-foot back to the sofa and wait it out.

Carol shook chicken legs in a baggy while I sat at the table with torn-out pages of K-Mart and Bradlees circulars strewn around me. I had an assignment. She'd circled pictures of toys—a talking Barney doll, a preschool tape recorder, that sort of thing—and my part was to scissor out each picture. She planned to leave them under the tree Christmas morning for Tommy to find with notes from Santa. The next day they'd take the clippings to after-Christmas sales and get everything half-price or better.

We were in the middle of dinner when the phone rang. Carol answered it and thanked the other person for returning her call. She brought the phone to the counter by the sink and went through her purse. When she found her credit card, she read the numbers out loud, and then said what I assumed to be her mother's maiden name—the security code for inquiries. "Who did?" she said. "Where did you send the bill? The address." Her resulting silence stretched long minutes, and I set down my fork and came behind her. The phone receiver shook slightly in her hand, her thumb pressed against the button to end the connection. She set the receiver down on the counter.

"Rick?" I said. Carol faced the kitchen windows that against the night had become mirrors. "He had my bills sent to him," she said and turned on the sink faucet. "Jesus, what an idiot thing. Anytime at all he could have taken my card numbers." The water started running out of the pot, taking all the soap with it, but she didn't shut it off.

"So he knows the state you live in," I said, thinking through it. "Maybe the town." The phone started buzzing, and I hung it up. "All right. We're just going to hang fire and see what happens. I'll run home and get some clothes packed."

I waited for a reaction from Carol because I was excited then and felt this development would connect us in a positive way. In the window reflection, I could see the strange white of her eyes as she looked down into the sink. I grew aware of a cool lightening through my chest and upper body. Suddenly it was easy to think in terms of violence. "He won't stop if he thinks he can get away with it," I said.

"I don't need a hero's trouble, Jerry."

I went back to the table and slammed my chair. Still holding its back, I saw the tendons in my wrist swollen like wires. "This is shit," I said.

"Maybe I don't understand you," Carol said, turning from the sink, looking at me point-blank. "Maybe you know just what to do if he found you here. I guess it doesn't matter." She crossed her arms and after a few moments let go of a breath. "Tommy told you about Ginger the other night—he screamed it for half of Bridgeport."

"The fucker poisoned your dog. There you go."

"It wasn't any antifreeze," she said. "Rick hung Ginger by the throat off a garage rafter. And it was because I told him to get rid of her. Me." She shook her head and sniffed sharply, as though she'd been near tears. "I married him once," she said. "I used to love him, and I was a monster myself. That's what I have to live with. You're not a part of that."

"Running away is letting him win. Do you understand that? Someone's got to teach him what he is."

Carol pinched the bridge of her nose. She closed her eyes and slowly opened them. "I'll run," she said, her voice now flat with resolve. "If it comes down to that, we'll run." She looked at the doorway, and Tommy appeared. It was like she knew his mind. I went over to him, and he squinted at the kitchen light. "We need a couple minutes," I said. His eyes were shiny and small, and he didn't move. "Go on, now," I said.

Tommy touched the helmets on his 49ers pajama bottoms, and there was a dark triangle of wet down his leg. "It's warm, Mommy," he said.

"Terrific," I said, "just goddamn terrific. What the Christ."

"Let's get you in the bathroom," Carol said, and she turned off the sink water. "I'll be there in a minute." Tommy did what he was told, and when he was out of the room, Carol said, "I want you to leave."

"Nobody's leaving."

"Don't turn it into a big thing, or I'll hate you."

"Listen a minute. He's a stalker, for all I know. He'll break in a window."

"Don't make me hate you, Jerry."

I knocked over a chair and swore at its crash. I grabbed my jacket in the living room, pausing just short of the door. Carol had followed, stopping as I did, ticking her nails once over the television, and in her face I could see that she was only there to make sure, to throw the bolt behind me. And taking the knob then, I felt the way you do in a plane lifting off, when you're between gravities and no one can tell you what will happen. As I stepped out into the steely slap of winter, I promised myself it was over. I'd had enough.

Christmas fell on a Wednesday that year, and at noon when I pulled myself out of bed, it could as easily have been any other day. I mailed a card off to my mother and her new husband in Florida. Nothing but church services on TV. I drank to Jesus, and

I drank to Mary. I drank to the doughy, black-bearded priest who warned against losing faith in the new year. Outside, the air was damp and rotten with the Sound at low tide, and I walked the block over to Two-Bit's Worth. Behind the bar, Dex was eating soup out of a can, and his face lost expression when he saw me. Dex had been to prison in New Haven for stealing a snowblower, a crime enough to foul his record with the world but not one that afforded him any special respect from the rest of us.

There wasn't anyone else in the bar I could see. "Somebody forgot to deck your halls," I said. He set his soup can on the bar and aimed his good leg in my direction, following with a dragging bad leg. As he neared, something took shape along his jaw, tobacco somehow or food, but when he was right before me, I saw it was four black stitches. "Who won?" I said.

He shook his head. "With the pool cues, last night. Christmas friggin' eve." Then he cracked a Heineken under the counter and dropped it in front of me. "Where the hell you been?" he said.

One night I drove out to Carol's. The streetlight coned out over her front porch, but the living room was dark. I parked two houses up and listened to the engine tick cool. I looked through my cassettes, straightened the glove box. I waited for inspiration.

I didn't need a black knit hat and shoe polish to sneak behind the place. There were no stars or moon. I looked first in her bedroom window. All the golf balls were gathered in the plastic cup. Empty boxes from grocery stores were stacked against the closet by her dresser, and her bed was made and empty. I tried to imagine us in there, holding each other, and when the vision came to me, a cold space opened in my chest. I moved on, through an elm sapling brittle as toothpicks. Tommy's room was visible in an orange tent of nightlight, and in that soft place, he slept with an arm slung loosely over his new Barney doll. Carol knelt by his bed with her hands laced at his feet. In a moment she looked across at him, and her lips formed words I couldn't make out, words, I thought, that I had never heard her speak. And if she had cheated or had been otherwise to blame, it would have been all right with me then. I wanted to feel wronged and better for how things had turned, but the truth I couldn't get away from was that in some important way I had only proven myself insufficient. She dropped her face a little closer to her hands, and I stayed watching until my breath misted everything away.

I went back out front to her Toyota and wormed my fingers in through the grill. I found the plastic-coated cable, traced it up to where bare wire was exposed, and pulled. The hood popped up to the latch. I didn't know exactly what I wanted to come of crossing her ignition wires. When you've had everything and lost it, and when the process could have been changed by opening your mind or your heart in a difficult way, wishes diminish to the smallest things that can get you by. I thought maybe she would call me at the shop the next morning, and that was the best I could hope for.

When I clicked the hood down, Carol was on her front porch with a cigarette. She didn't look surprised to see me. She must have been there awhile without letting on.

"I hope you didn't fuck things up too bad under there."

"I'll go fix it," I said, but instead walked toward her. "Where are you going?"

"Key Largo, if anyone asks, or Madagascar," she said, and shook her head. "I'm not even sure we're going yet. It seems like a smart thing to be ready if we have to." She stabbed her cigarette against the doorframe and flicked it away. "I'm not going to ask you in tonight, Jerry. So you might as well get any of those ideas out of your head. But I've got something for you."

She went inside, and I stayed on the porch. I wished there was a present in my car I could give her. I'd bought a pair of women's cabretta golf gloves but returned them the day after Christmas. When she came back out, she handed me a card, its width the closest we'd come to touching in eight days. It was homemade out of heavy red paper. Inside was a crayon drawing of a blue-haired man in a leather jacket standing by a Christmas tree.

"He made a bunch of them," she said. "That one surprised me."

"I didn't bring his present," I said.

She pulled opened the door and stepped through. "I'll tell him you got the card."

The door closed, and I was alone with my steaming breath under the streetlight. I looked at the card again. The tree held three different crayons' worth of ornaments. In the picture I was smiling.

A Circle of Stones

In 1967, when I was ten years old, my mother married Harlan Frame, and we moved that summer to a house he'd bought for us in Slaughter, Texas.

Harlan was a farmer, a word my mother found too plain; she'd tell people Harlan ranched, though he kept fewer than a dozen cows on a patch of scrub land that was too poor to support a crop. Mostly he farmed wheat and cotton. He would put some acres into sorghum if he thought a booming cattle market might push up the price of feed, but he called sorghum his casino crop because if he guessed wrong he'd lose what he put into it. It was not like wheat or cotton, he said, where insurance and the government made sure the farmer didn't get too badly hurt.

My mother could have done a whole lot worse than Harlan, and probably would have, given half a chance. As far as I know, Harlan is the only man who ever courted her, besides my father. Harlan overlooked the fact that she was divorced and had a child, which was to his credit. In the 1960's such things mattered more than they do now. Also, my mother was a knockout. She had pale blue eyes and dark hair, and she kept herself thin by eating only every other day. If Harlan hadn't come along, someone else would have, and then who knows where we'd have been? Worse off, most likely. My mother was easy prey for the unscrupulous because she believed herself to be more knowing than she was. Harlan Frame was the first man to want to marry her, and she said yes.

I felt no regret or hesitation about leaving Amarillo, where I'd grown up, for a farm town where I didn't know a soul. The apartment that my mother and I shared was in an ugly duplex that was set at one end of a parking lot, in a part of Amarillo where there seemed to be a murder, rape, child-snatching, or assault a week. The man who lived behind us sometimes got drunk at night and argued violently with his wife, and a few times I'd awakened to the sound of someone quietly turning the knob of our front door, trying to get in. When that happened, Mother would call the police, and we'd lock ourselves inside the bathroom until they came.

I thought that one bad chapter in our lives was ending, and that we would start off fresh in Slaughter and have something like a normal life again.

The house we moved into had been let go, and Harlan had to have the roof patched and the outside painted. Mother stripped the bedroom walls of old wallpaper and painted her room mint-green and mine yellow. She lined the kitchen shelves and drawers with new tack paper, put new curtains up, and cleaned the pinewood paneling and cabinets with lemon oil. She and I spent all of one day cleaning windows with potato halves and crumpled pages from the newspaper, a method she'd learned from some women's magazine she'd picked up in the beauty parlor.

"New carpet," she said, bending down and squinting through the pane of glass I'd just cleaned. "That's the next priority." Then she straightened and gave me a quick, appraising look; I imagined I was being added to her list of items that could bear sprucing up. "Well," she said, crumpling another sheet of newspaper, "Rome wasn't built in a day."

I had never seen my mother work as hard as she worked on that house. In the three years since my father left, she had started to take on the habits of an invalid, staying in her bathrobe all day, sleeping in the afternoon. She complained of feeling worn out, and sometimes she'd lapse into silences that could go on for days. Now she was like a different person, energetic and determined, as if she'd left that old self behind, for good. We had done without for too long, she said, and now she meant to make up for some part of it.

"I was young and stupid when your dad and I got married," she said. "What we've got here is a second chance."

My father got interested in visitation rights about the time we moved to Slaughter. By the terms of the divorce, he'd always had the right to see me two weekends a month, but he had rarely claimed the privilege. I saw him at Christmas or Thanksgiving and the few times he showed up on impulse at the duplex, saying that he wanted us to be a family again. One time he broke down the front door when my mother wouldn't let him in, and when he asked me if I wanted to come live with him, I said yes. We spent two days in the Starlight Motel in San Angelo, swimming in the motel pool and having food delivered to our room. When he brought me home, a sheriff's deputy was parked in front of our apartment, waiting for him.

My mother asked if I was all right, and I told her yes. Then she slapped me, hard, across the face. "That's for worrying me to death," she said.

When we moved to Slaughter, I hadn't seen my father in a year.

He called the second week we were down there. It was the first time we had heard our new phone ring, and I happened to be standing next to it. I picked it up.

"Hey, tiger," he said. "How's the new digs?"

I was too surprised, at first, to say a word. "Hi, Dad," I managed to say, finally, and that caught Mother's ear. She took the phone away from me and told me to go wait outside.

When I came back in, ten minutes later, she was grimly polishing a coffee urn, using toothpaste and old panty hose. She knew I was waiting, but she kept on like I wasn't there.

"Well?" I asked, at last.

She set the coffee urn down and turned to look at me. I could see the faint lines that the conversation with my father had brought out around her mouth and eyes. "Weekend after next," she said, "you're going to go see your father. You can ride the bus to Amarillo; he'll be there to meet you."

Harlan was an only child. The fact that he had married a divorcée broke his widowed mother's heart, and she cut off contact with him. Mother and I would see Mrs. Frame creeping down our street in her green Valiant, wearing white gloves and a feathered hat. She'd let the car drift to the wrong side of the road as she leaned across the front seat to gape at the house. Mother kept the blinds closed so she couldn't see inside.

"That woman's going to have an accident," Mother would say. "Or cause one."

I spent most days inside, out of the heat, watching TV or reading. Harlan left early in the morning and stayed gone until suppertime; the land he farmed was twenty miles away, too far to be driving into town for lunch when there was cotton to be stripped, and winter wheat to get into the ground.

Sometimes I'd stand in the window in the living room and look out on the street. Nothing moved on still days but the heat waves shimmering above the asphalt; other days there would be dust storms. Inside the house, on those days, I would hear the wind throw sand against the house, like it was rain.

One afternoon, when I was standing in the window, Mrs. Frame drove by. She lifted one white-gloved hand off the wheel and wiggled her fingers at me, tentatively, as if she were afraid the gesture might provoke me. I waved back.

Mother and I would go downtown for groceries twice a week, and we'd stop at the library to get more books. Her tastes ran to John Steinbeck and Harold Robbins, while I liked ghost stories and anything to do with flying saucers, the Bermuda Triangle, or the Loch Ness Monster. Slaughter didn't offer much else in the way of entertainment: there was one movie theater that played the same movie for a month at a time, and a bowling alley that was only open in the winter. There was a pretty green park downtown, lush with walnut trees and cottonwoods, that had a fishing pond, two bison penned up in a corral, and a "Whites Only" swimming pool. When integration came, in 1964, the town fathers had the pool drained rather than let Negroes use it, and in 1967 it was still shut down. If we got tired of being in the house, we'd go for a drive, and maybe stop at May's Drive-In for lime Cokes with shaved ice.

There was a comic book store next to May's, where comics with the covers torn off sold for five cents each. I was afraid of the old man who ran the place, and would make my mother come inside with me while I picked through the bushel baskets full of comics, looking for the ones I wanted. The old man never greeted us. He sat on a stool up front, with his elbows on the counter, grumbling to himself and running his spotted hands through his yellowing white hair. When I took the comics I had chosen to the front, he would quickly count them, take my money, and hand back any change, all without a word. He seemed to be as eager to get rid of me as I was to be gone.

"Goddamn snakes," I heard him say one day. I looked up to see who he was talking to, but no one else was there. He was sitting at the counter, pulling at his hair as if there were some pain inside his head that he was trying to get hold of. He didn't see me looking at him.

Harlan and I were elaborately polite with each other, as if we were strangers who had moved by accident into the same house and spoke only fragments of each other's language. We'd squeeze past each other in the hall, muttering, "Excuse me," and at night, if I was in the bathroom too long, he would tap lightly on the door and clear his throat. It was rare for us to speak directly, beyond courtesies. He was taller than my father, with thick, roughened hands and knobby wrists. I had noticed how he'd stand when he was talking to another person—with his weight on one foot and his other hip thrown out to the side—and I realized he did this in order to seem shorter.

"Harlan isn't used to being around children," Mother said. "But he'll get used to it. You'll see."

My father had moved into a new apartment complex, where there was a clubhouse and a swimming pool. His apartment had a small back patio; the first night I was there, we grilled steaks and baked potatoes on the barbecue.

"Tomorrow," he said, "I thought we might get kites. We could take a picnic lunch out to a park and fly kites. How's that sound?"

"That sounds good," I said.

"We could ask Dana if she wants to come along," he said. "But only if you want to meet her. This is your weekend. We'll play it any way you want."

"Sure," I said, "she can come."

He had started telling me about Dana at the bus station, before we'd even made it to the car. He said they'd been dating six months and that she had made him take a hard look at his own life. "I was to the point," he said, "where I just didn't give a shit. I really didn't. Dana changed all that."

He also told me that he had a new job, keeping books at a meat packing plant. That's where he'd met Dana; she was the boss's secretary.

The next day Dana came over, and we got picnic stuff and kites and took them to a nearby schoolyard. She wasn't what I had expected: I thought my father would have some kind of bomb-shell girlfriend, but Dana was skinny and had a face like a rab-bit—big front teeth and little eyes, set wide apart. Her fingernails were chewed down to the nub, and her fingertips were stained from all the Kools she smoked. She had beautiful red hair, but that was about the best that could be said for her. I thought she was plain old homely.

She called my father "sweetie," and tousled his hair with her fingers while he drove. When we'd parked in the school's parking lot, she said, "No, sweetie. Over there," and made him move the car so we would be five yards closer to a picnic table.

After we'd unpacked the car, she had me hold her kite while she played out the string for twenty yards or so, and when she told me to, I let go, and she took off running. My father and I whooped when the kite shot straight up in the air. Dana turned around and let the string run off the spool until the kite was way up. She knew how to make it dip and dive, and when she'd helped me get my kite up, she showed me how to maneuver it, and then we had a mock fight, each of us making feints and lunges at the other's kite. Every time we came close to colliding, she'd shout, "Hold on, Harold!" and let out a squawking, surprised laugh.

"I have three brothers," she told me. "That's how I know this stuff."

She had me take her kite while she ran over to the picnic table to get another cigarette, and when she came back, she said, "Your dad says come on and eat a bite, but I told him we're not ready. Unless you feel like pulling the kites in?"

"No," I said. "Not yet."

"All right, then. He can just cool his heels."

That night we grilled more steaks, and we made peppermint ice cream in an ice cream freezer Dana brought over. Later we put on our suits and played Marco Polo in the pool.

"I'll let you in on a little secret," Dana said to me, while we waited by the pool for Dad to bring towels out for us. "But you can't tell."

"Sure," I said.

"Your dad's about to get a big promotion. He doesn't know it yet, but he's going to be making a lot more than he makes now."

Dad was on his way across the pool deck with the stack of towels, and so I nodded, not wanting to say anything that he might overhear. Dana leaned closer to me. "You should be very proud of him," she whispered.

Sunday afternoon Dad drove me to the Continental Trailways station. We got there early, bought my ticket, and went back to wait in his car.

"I have done one piss poor job," he said, "as far as being a good dad goes. But I promise things are going to be different from now on."

We sat in silence for a minute, and then he said, "I know your birthday's coming up, and I was wondering if there's something special that you'd like to have."

"A telescope," I said. I had found a book about astronomy mixed in with the comics at the comic book store, and had flipped through the pictures before putting it back. The idea about the telescope had just formed in the instant.

"Okay," he said. "All right. A telescope, it is."

When it was time to go, he walked me across the street and hugged me before I got onto the bus. He smelled like the hairspray Dana had got him started using on his hair. "Next weekend you're up, we'll go see the motorcycle races," he said. "Dana's brother races a Ducati."

When the house was cleaned up and refurbished and all our belongings were unpacked and put away, Mother went out to buy some new things. First thing, she had wall-to-wall shag carpeting put in. Then she bought new appliances, all of them a color she called "avocado green"; the refrigerator had an ice maker that made ice shaped like half-moons. She bought me a French Provincial bedroom suite, which was more to her taste than mine, and, as an early birthday present, a small color television set.

"You need an air conditioner in your room more than you need a TV set," she said. "But that will have to wait. I knew you'd rather have the TV."

For the living room she bought a new couch, a recliner, and an armchair, all upholstered in crushed velvet, and a walnut console stereo with an AM/FM tuner and a turntable.

Harlan showed no sign that he begrudged the money she was

spending, or that he felt strapped. He took off his boots and socks and walked around in bare feet on the new shag carpet and admired it. He sat on the new couch, and the new armchair, put his feet up in the new recliner, and said that it was heaven on a stick.

But a few years later, Harlan chopped that stereo to pieces with an axe, right there in the living room, and when he finished, he broke my mother's records, one by one, in pieces, and threw the pieces in the fireplace. She had Sam Cooke records, Ray Charles, Joan Baez, and Barbra Streisand. Harlan said he never wanted to hear another piece of music by a nigger, or a nigger-lover, or a Jew in his house again.

A package arrived on my birthday, but it wasn't from my dad. The address was written out in blue ink, in a trembling, old-fashioned hand. I tore off the paper—brown bags from the grocery store—and inside the box I found a Quaker Oatmeal carton filled with marbles, the locomotive from an electric train set, and three silver dollars. I poured the marbles out onto the carpet and looked through them. I could tell that they were old: glass tiger's eyes, steelies, blue and white milk glass, several chalkies. There were seven or eight larger marbles, shooters, mixed in with the others.

The card inside was meant for someone younger than I, with its drawing of a small boy in a fire engine, a Dalmatian sitting on the seat next to him. It looked like it had been saved in someone's dresser drawer for years; the edges had frayed and were starting to turn brown. Inside it said, simply, Happy Birthday. It was signed by Mrs. Frame.

Later that afternoon Mother and I went to the drive-in for banana splits, and then we went into the comic book store. The old man was there, as usual, behind the counter, grumbling and combing his hair with his fingers. Mother looked through old copies of *Life* magazine while I went through the baskets.

The book that I was looking for was still there—the one about astronomy. I brushed the dust off of it and took it to the front.

"How much for this one?" I asked.

The old man picked the book up, turned it over, and then set it back down on the counter. "Take it," he said.

I just looked at him.

"It's your birthday, isn't it?" he said.

I nodded.

"Then you don't have to pay."

Back in the car, I asked my mother, "Did you tell him it's my birthday?"

"No," she said, "I didn't. I have no idea how he knew."

That night Mother asked me to show Harlan the presents Mrs. Frame had sent me. I brought them to the kitchen table. He took the top off the oatmeal box and scooped some marbles out with his hand.

"These were mine," he said, "when I was your age. The train, too. I don't know what happened to the rest of it, but my parents gave me that train for a Christmas present. That was just about the best surprise I ever had."

I hesitated for a moment, then I said, "They're yours, then. You should keep them."

He shook his head and poured the marbles back into the box. "No," he said, "they're yours now. Someday you may want to give them to your son."

Harlan said he had a present for me, too, but that I would have to wait to get it. He said he would let me know when it was ready.

Before I went to bed that night, I tried to call my dad, but the telephone just rang and rang, and no one answered.

I spent hours studying the pictures and descriptions in that book. There were color plates of galaxies and nebulae and planets. I had never seen a picture of the Horsehead Nebula, in Orion, or the Veil Nebula, with its pink and blue glow. The Milky Way, the book said, was made up of a hundred thousand million stars; the red spot on the planet Jupiter was actually a storm that had been raging, now, for several hundred years; the craters on the moon were astroblemes, a word that means "star wounds."

At night I went into the backyard, watched for shooting stars, and picked out the planets and the constellations. Mars was red; Venus bluish white. I thought about the light that had left the stars a million years or more before, and was just now reaching my eyes. I was looking at a picture of the way the stars were, way back then, and not how they were now. The sky we saw was an illusion, everything had long since changed, but we went right on believing we were seeing things as they are.

The week after my birthday I got a postcard from my dad. It was a photograph of him and Dana that they'd had taken in Las Vegas. They were standing, arm in arm, in front of a display case that contained a million dollars. Dad looked groggy and disheveled; at his side a bottle of beer dangled from his hand. Dana's smile was tense and grudging, as if she'd been forced to pose. She gripped my father's elbow with both hands and looked directly at the camera, her small eyes narrowed in anticipation of the flash.

"We decided to come out here and get hitched," the postcard said. "Which looks better, do you think—your new stepmom, or that million bucks? Ha! Will call when we get back to Amarillo. Love, Dad."

Harlan came into my room one morning that same week and shook me by the shoulder. "Get up," he said, "I want you to see something."

I got out of bed, put on my clothes, and went into the living room. Harlan was standing by the front door with his hat on. "Come on," he said.

The sun was not yet over the horizon, and the sky was just beginning to turn light. But when I looked into the sky, I saw a shooting star, and then two more. Then I saw three and four at one time, some no more than a brief flash, others a long streak across the sky. I thought, at first, that this was what Harlan had brought me outside to see, but he had already climbed into his truck.

We drove south, and as we drove I rolled the window down and put my head outside to watch the shower of stars.

"They were saying on the news last night that this was starting," Harlan said. "They said it was a once-a-year deal. The Perseds. Something like that."

I brought my head back inside. "Perseids," I said. "They're named for one of those Greek gods."

Harlan leaned over the wheel to get a better look. "It's something, all right," he said. "Never seen so many at one time."

The meteors, I knew, were chunks of rock, debris, that orbited the sun and burned up in our atmosphere when their orbits intersected ours.

We pulled off the road eventually, went through a gate, and drove across a rutted pasture towards a rusting tractor shed. Harlan's cows were huddled there, waiting for the sun to warm them before they wandered off to graze. There were eight or nine cows, Herefords, and one Angus bull. As the truck approached, the cows jostled one another nervously, and I saw a tiny black and white calf, suckling.

Harlan let the truck roll to a stop and then shut off the engine.

I wasn't sure why Harlan had brought me out there. He saw my confusion and said, "That calf is your birthday present. Remember I told you that you'd have to wait until it was ready?"

"Thank you," I said. "Thanks."

Harlan leaned his head out of the window and yelled, "Soooeee!" The cows began to walk towards us.

"I thought it would be good for you," he said, "to raise something as your own."

We sat there awhile and watched the cows. They looked at us with big, wet eyes, dreamy and expectant, as if they'd been promised something for their trouble. My calf shivered by its mother's side. Then we headed back to town. I looked out the window at the fence posts whipping by along the roadside, the long, green rows of cotton stretching to the far horizon. Meteors etched white lines in the milk-glass sky. Harlan spoke, but I did not hear what he said. I put my head outside and turned my face into the wind. It made my eyes tear, and I had to close them. An alphabet of lights flared in the dark behind my eyelids, and then faded, and my head filled with the empty, rushing noise. I stayed like that the rest of the way home.

Arabel's List

W as this your first, uh, infidelity, Mrs. Kennedy?" asked the
somewhat prissy, prurient marriage counselor, to whom
Arabel and Bertram Kennedy had gone after her teary confession
that she loved another man—a very young man, Richard, not
only unemployed in a gainful way but a poet, whom she meant to
marry.

A pause, while both the counselor, who was small, and large tall
Dr. Kennedy, a college dean, waited for Arabel to say yes, and perhaps to cry a little more.

But instead her head went up like a horse's, scenting something
special in the wind. "Well, no," she said. "As a matter of fact—
quite a few," and she went on to specify.

Or, so I imagine the scene. But Arabel has recounted it almost
exactly in that way both to me alone, when we were first becoming friends, and later once or twice to a group. I think she
couldn't resist the drama of that moment, her own moment, of
confounding expectations.

"There was Bob, and then George. You remember Kenneth?"
she said to Bertram, who paled, as the counselor's breath quick-
ened. And Arabel went on, and on.

By the time I met Arabel, at Lathrop College, in Marin County,
California, she had probably been through—fucked, screwed, or
simply *had* (that last would have been her own word, I think)—
she had had sex with most of the male faculty, especially in the
English department, the department that this particularly self-
conscious, upscale party was meant to welcome and to introduce
to each other. In which my own husband, Kevin, was to teach.
Meeting Arabel, there was no evidence of such adventures; I only
thought and later said to Kevin that she did not look like the wife
of a dean.

Arabel was tall and rangy, with striking gray-white hair that
looked premature. Smooth, tan skin and big, clear, sky-blue

eyes—Montana eyes, which is where she was from; when I learned that, she began to make more sense to me. To an Easterner, especially from New England, Montana was far more exotic than California was. Arabel dressed violently, her style was carelessly dramatic: big sweeping skirts and randomly bright scarves, over well-worn cotton T-shirts, a shade too small. Everything could have been pulled at the last minute from a tangled closet floor. ("Is that what you're going to wear?" I could imagine Bertram, the dean, asking this. "Sure is!" Breezy Arabel, barely looking at him.)

This party, given by the president of Lathrop, was at his house, a glass-and-steel structure on a steep hillside in western Marin, near the coast. The view was ravishing; now in September, lovely spreading live oaks cast their wide lacy shadows on yellowed grassy slopes that here and there were creased with dark ravines. And in the distance, the shining flat Pacific, stretching out to a thick wall of fog.

So beautiful, it should have beautified the room, but it did not. The room simply failed to live up to that view. High and narrow, crowded by impossibly tall bookcases, that space turned a party into a traffic jam. It was rather like being in a drugstore, a postmodern show-off drugstore, with a giant Kodachrome "view" on one wall.

Kevin and I had come out to California from New York and New England, respectively. And I think New England may explain the extremity of some of my reactions. In my old schools and colleges, the wives of deans wore proper suits and pearls. As I should have said, all this took place in the seventies, when many people longed for a return to the conformity of the fifties. Recovery from the sixties had been hard; it was felt to be generally incomplete. Kevin the New Yorker was less judgmental than I; also he was busier, he had his job. I had planned to work in San Francisco, but the commute was intimidating, almost two hours. Besides, in an essentially non-publishing city there was very little work for a book designer. I would find something, I knew, but it would take a while.

That afternoon, along with the Kennedys, we met the local English department and their husbands and wives (quite a few of Arabel's former lovers, it later turned out). No one, I thought, was especially memorable—except Arabel. The food was interesting, though, to me: a lot of goat cheese and mussels and crab, in what were then innovative combinations.

At some point I asked someone for directions to the bathroom, and then made my way down several high, narrow passages. Arrived at a closed door, I knocked.

"Come on in," urged a friendly voice. "I'm just finishing off my nose."

Arabel.

"Oh, it's you. Great." But she added, "I was afraid it might be Bert, pestering me to come on home. He's got a really short rein for parties." And then, "Go on and pee, and then we can talk."

Then, as I was washing my hands and she was still brushing that beautiful unruly hair, she said, "Lord, these parties almost stifle me to death. You'd think I could manage by now. Well, I guess I do manage, in my way." She looked over at me and gave a sudden, complicitous, small laugh, with a matching grin.

"I guess this is my first one," I told her.

"I thought. Well, you'll either get used to them or you won't."

"Do I have a choice?"

A long look which I felt to be of appraisal, and then she said, "Well, that depends."

Kevin had been my English professor at the University of Northern Iowa, in Cedar Falls, whence I had gone to escape the Vassar fate of my sisters and many cousins, all Bostonians. Kevin was there because, despite a Harvard Ph.D., it was the only job around. We were excited about Northern California, so much change, along with his divorce and our instant subsequent marriage. California seemed a marvelous achievement, both exciting and propitious. And Kevin to me seemed endlessly exciting, with his curly gray hair and serious blue eyes. "A typical Irish," my Boston mother had said, thus ensuring my marriage. We felt that our passion and our daring, our love, were both brave and unique—as almost everyone does, at some time or another, I guess.

But after that first department party, when I said to Kevin that Arabel did not look like a dean's wife, his response was disappointing. "Looks like a typical aging hippie to me," he said. "I guess some of them did marry deans."

"I thought she had a lot of style."

"Oh, Kate, come on to bed."

Willingly enough, I forgot about Arabel for that moment, and went off to bed with Kevin.

Our romance, Kevin's and mine, had mostly taken place in a Holiday Inn just outside of Cedar Falls. I would go and take a room and wait for Kevin, who lurked in his car, in the adjacent parking lot. And those tacky rooms with their ghastly paintings seemed progress indeed from Kevin's messy office, the paper-strewn desk on which we had first made love.

All of which is by way of saying that when Arabel first began to hint to me that she had put in some time in motels, of an afternoon, I knew what she meant—although I also experienced some lessening of my own sense of high and original adventure.

And unrelatedly, perhaps, I began less and less to like the small house that Kevin and I had rented on the edge of some woods. It was just too small, a motel of a house, one story, stucco, with its kitchen-dining "area," its diminutive one-sofa living room, its one-bed bedroom. In both rooms there were large picture windows that showed the enormous grove of redwoods and eucalyptus that dwarfed the house—and dwarfed, too, our sense of ourselves, of our own importance in California, *to* California.

Everything had looked better on paper, especially the house: such a bargain, so near the campus. And Kevin's salary had looked better before deductions and alimony shriveled it to a barely living wage. For every reason it began to seem essential that I get a job. Bookstore work would have been ideal, I thought, though I knew that probably dozens of people at that time had the same idea. Aware of the sheer unlikeliness of getting what I wanted (though, after all, I had got Kevin), I nevertheless began to comb Marin County.

And one afternoon, in a parking lot in Corte Madera, I ran into Arabel.

"You can't have been where I just was, can you," was her greeting, not really a question.

"I was at the bookstore over there," I told her. "I'm out job-hunting. It's pretty discouraging."

She looked in the direction I'd pointed, and then at me (an

appraisal). "Oh, Sandy's store. He'll hire you, I'd bet on it. He's very horny, and he loves little blondes with big tits."

Too embarrassed for any response, I certainly did not ask what she was doing there.

But she told me, ten minutes later, over the coffee that she insisted we have, in a handy non-Sanborn coffeehouse.

"The most terrible thing," she began, and her blue eyes pooled with tears as she spoke (but of course I didn't know her at all; maybe she cried a lot?). She went on, "It must mean something, your being here just at this moment. And you look like a person to trust," she said, carefully scanning my face. "Well, this is going to sound funny but it isn't, not at all. I've fallen really in love, I mean for real. For good. I really think that, and he's only thirty. And a poet; that's the supposedly funny part, but it isn't. The really funny part is that he's crazy about me, too—at my age! I think I'll have to tell Bert. God, if he doesn't kill me—"

I had no idea what to say to all this. None.

Arabel continued, though with less intensity, more in the tone of someone musing to herself. "God, after all the guys I've had, and known not to take seriously. God, I hate to think how many motel afternoons. Years of those." She laughed briefly. "Well, it's the only way I've found to get through the days around here. Does 'hoist on your own petard' apply, do you think?"

Because she was calmer now, I saw fit to ask what I had wondered from the start: "Bert doesn't know any of this?"

"God no. Though sometimes I've wondered how he could not know. And there have been a few near misses." She raised her chin, and focused her eyes on some distant prospect. "But this time I'll have to tell him."

"You weren't in love before?" I asked. A bold and sentimental question, but Arabel had a sort of anything-goes style that permitted—anything.

She laughed. "Of course not. Well, maybe the first time out, a little in love, or at least pretending to be. Pro forma, so to speak. But the ones after that, I was just amusing myself. A fun way to kill time, kill boredom, as I saw it. But with Richard, this is a whole new ballgame."

"Oh."

"Really. I think I want us to get married." She sat up taller, and straightened her shoulders. "I'm going to tell Bert tonight."

Which is what she did, I guess. The next story I heard, over more coffee in the same Corte Madera coffee place, was that of the marriage counselor who had managed to make things much worse with his question. "Tell me, Mrs. Kennedy, was this your first infidelity?"

"Well, no. As a matter of fact—" And so on. Arabel's list.

Arabel was right about the bookstore. I had been hired by Sandy, and if he was horny, he was restrained and polite about it. ("So far," said Arabel, with her smile, when I interrupted her story to make this observation.)

And the fact that the bookstore was almost adjacent to the motel most favored by Arabel and Richard was certainly a factor in our developing friendship, Arabel's and mine.

"What will be interesting will be this Richard's reaction," said Kevin, as we discussed the situation over cheap California wine and pasta. "He may be a little less than totally delighted."

"On the other hand, suppose he is?" I argued. "He could be mad for her, too, she's really attractive. Even if you don't see it."

"But twenty years older? He may not be dying to support an older wife."

"Kevin, he may not have to. Maybe Arabel will get a job and support him. She thinks he's a wonderful poet." I added, "So does Sandy, we want to give him a reading at the store."

I was surprised to see Kevin bristle a little at this. "Wouldn't that be sort of taking sides?" he asked. "In a not very tactful way?"

"How many people from around here go over to a bookstore in Corte Madera? It takes a goddamn forty minutes. I should know."

"That's just the point. You work there."

"Oh, Kevin."

This was a side of Kevin that I had either not seen or had ignored in Iowa: the conformist, yielding to authority (deans). One could put it more crudely, which to myself I did. But the truth is that in Iowa I had only been aware of a nice voice, great eyes, and later on, in that awful and unforgettable Holiday Inn, great sex. Also, since Kevin was considerably older than I was, not twenty years but a close seventeen, the subject of Arabel and

Richard was a little touchy, and became more so. There could come a day, we both knew, when for reasons of age and retirement I would be the one supporting Kevin.

Arabel had been wrong about Sandy, I decided. He wasn't horny, especially; just a friendly, slightly depressed, and intelligent guy in his middle thirties, married ten years or so, with two little kids and a heavy mortgage, and a mania for books. He also felt strongly about independent booksellers, one of the last of which he felt that he was.

We shared wildly promiscuous tastes in literature; we both loved, with passion, Robert Musil and Alice Munro, Turgenev and Trollope, Iris Murdoch and Anne Perry. Carl Hiaasen. We spoke with happy enthusiasm of all these writers, we tried to sell their work. Sandy did nothing with me that could be construed as "coming on." Or maybe, I thought, Arabel was wrong about that and I was not his type.

In a way he was my type, though not at all like Kevin. Sandy was tall and skinny, gray-blond, nearsighted, a little stooped. He smoked a pipe, an old-fashioned bookish touch that I found endearing.

Richard the poet lived in San Francisco, where he drove a Yellow Cab. But he often came to Marin, for solitary hikes on Mt. Tam, or the headlands, near Inverness. And that is where they had met, he and Arabel, at adjacent tables in Barnaby's, a dockside restaurant specializing in seafood. Local oysters. And there they were, Arabel and Richard, side by side at separate tables, out in the sun, scoffing down oysters, washed with white wine.

"Very sexy, really, oysters." Arabel laughed as she recounted this meeting. "We must have both thought of that at about the same time. We looked at each other and we sort of giggled. Although he's not the giggling type, more a melancholy Dane. Big and blond and serious, sad-looking. We talked, and then, as they say, one thing led to another."

Everything led, eventually, to the marriage counselor, and his ill-advised question. "Was this your first infidelity, Mrs. Kennedy?"

"Well, no—"

Leading to Arabel's list and, a short time later, to a nasty, explosive divorce.

That explosion, like a small, lively, and unexpected fire, sent sparks to scatter at random, singeing spectators. Couples took sides, and quarreled. The side-taking was not always along gender lines, as one might have expected. Some wives felt that Arabel had been "terrible," she should and no doubt would be punished: Richard would leave her flat for someone at least his own age. And some husbands avowed, in private, that "old Bert" had always been the most colossal bore; how could a lively and attractive woman put up with him for so long? A spectrum of other opinions was also expressed—self-righteously, drunkenly, lengthily. Former *amours* of Arabel, who did not know that they formed part of a list, all tended to be loyal. They were grateful, Arabel was a warm and generous woman. They remembered kindness, and wit.

We go now to about five years later. Kevin and I are still married, though somewhat less thrillingly so; however, we have two small children who are, to my amazement, quite agreeable, on the whole. I still work in the bookstore, though now on quite a new basis: Sandy and I, though once intense and furtive lovers, became good friends (I was "seeing" someone else by then, and so was he). Also, when Kevin's very old father died and considerately left a sizeable chunk to each of us, I invested my share in the store, so that now I am an equal partner.

Arabel and I remain friends, although she and Richard (married) live in San Francisco, and we don't see each other a lot. Also, Kevin was one of those husbands most censorious of Arabel and very pro-Bert, of course he was.

Richard never gave a reading at our store. He was scheduled for what turned out to be the week of Arabel's divorce proceedings, and her lawyer felt that for Richard to read at that moment would be "provocative." ("And God knows you've done enough to provoke the guy," she, the lawyer, lightly scolded, and Arabel agreed.) However, Richard is doing better and better, poems accepted here and there by quarterlies, almost enough for a book, very soon. And instead of driving a cab, he does house painting, something else that he is very good at.

It is my impression that they get on very well, although Arabel does not discuss the relationship in detail. But then she never did. Once, when we met for coffee in Sausalito (she is doing substitute teaching, which sometimes brings her to Marin), as we sat in the warming sunlight and watched a weather-beaten seagull who watched us from a piling, Arabel said, "You know, I'd never, never be unfaithful to Richard. Isn't that odd? Or is it?"

I laughed at her. "No, not particularly." For I knew what she meant.

As for me, between the store and the children, and sporadic love affairs—sex affairs, really; not much to do with love—I keep busy. Sometimes I wonder if there's another Richard somewhere down the line for me, someone to make an honest woman of me, as they say. But if not, that's okay, too. As Arabel used to say, it passes the time. And it's fun.

To Cole Cole

She knew she would not reach Cole Cole even before she started to walk, knew she could not do twenty-five kilometers in the sand with this pack. These new boots, she had learned on her last hike with Freyda, were a half size too short, had bruised her big toenails on the Towers of Paine in wind that tossed her body against rocks. Worse than the bruises was the raw blister that oozed into grit trapped beneath its loose moleskin plaster. She was determined to do a minimum of fifteen kilometers, but how far was that? Eons dispersed into the sky's opaque membrane—she had not worn her watch—and she had no idea how long she'd been walking, or if darkness would strand her on this wild beach overnight.

Just a few days ago, she was camped in a filthy trekker's *refugio*, still stuck with Freyda, hundreds of miles south. There, far from the blue ice leaves of the unattainable Gray Glacier, a thin French guide had drawn her a map. At what then seemed a turning point in a meaningless journey, he had advised her to go to the Free Zone, buy a cheap *mochila*, then take the ferry to this insular island from Puerto Montt. The line penciled from a dot he had labeled "Cucao" ran up her notebook to "Cole Cole," representing, she'd imagined, a short uphill hike. He had said six kilometers, she was fairly certain, not six hours; but *seis horas caminando*, six hours walking, was what all the locals, including Pedro, and the bored guard at the CONAF kiosk, had told her, their arms flung indifferently north.

She'd informed the French guide that she had left her own knapsack at home because she was traveling with Freyda, who'd once ruptured disks heaving sacks in Africa, and couldn't carry ten pounds, much less a pack. He'd stared at her acutely, as if to imply that this, as well as other shortfalls, could still be remedied. "Next time you must come here with someone who can carry fifty-five kilos," he said, his voice private, intense, like the muffled birdcall of an Andean flute. He pointed to the Japanese woman he had guided on a ten-day tour of The Circuit, cheerfully inhaling a bowl of steaming four-grain porridge. "She is carrying thirty-five kilos, and she is fifty-four years old," he exclaimed, italicizing *fifty-four*. How old does he think I am? she had wondered hopefully. Despite Freyda's compliment about her "good aging genes," she no longer deceived herself about looking younger. After that, the apotheosis of Cole Cole, "next time," and what could still be changed was a secret that she shared with him, this guru of the International Female Mid-Life Crisis, whoever he was. (He revealed only that he'd come to visit this country and stayed forever.)

"Good luck," he whispered as Freyda clumped down the stairs. Even her footsteps managed to sound pissed. She wore a pancaked safari hat, a leftover from Kenya, and a purple rubber wind suit that stuck to her body like a wet plastic bag and made her look fat. Her dry, lipstick-less mouth was ratcheted into an upside-down Y by her anger (about what?). She would ferret out a minor injustice—a different exchange rate than the teller had said—and snap like raw electricity from a cut wire in places like banks. Freyda had asked the French guide if he would donate some of his boiled water for tea, pressing her palms into a praying formation, singsonging, "Oh thank you thank you," before he agreed. She hated watching her old friend, not fat, but thicker, almost humped, trying to look cute to get a young guy to take care of her. Perhaps Freyda was the same as she had always been—they hadn't seen each other for a couple of years—and it was she who had changed, living with Jack in the unfinished cabin so far from Manhattan. "He's pretty!" Freyda whispered about the French guide, honing his Swiss Army knife in the window's dusty sunset light. "Hey, remember what's-his-face in Ecuador?"

She instantly recalled (although she'd just as soon not) an image of a slender, long-haired boy with skin the color of wet Bentonite, framed by a ragged stone archway—of what? A ruined convent? She couldn't dredge up his name, it had been twenty years, but oddly the name of the German guy that Freyda had met in Colombia came back. (*Franz*. He'd never joined her in Cuzco as he'd promised he would.) That was the summer she and Freyda had hooked up on a third-class bus to Latacunga, two solitary women adventurers, never married, and discovered that they both lived alone in Lower Manhattan, free spirits, more or less, who traveled abroad whenever they could. In Latacunga, they had bought a pile of sugary pastries heaped in baskets at a market bakery, and eaten them all as they obsessed about love, or, in their cases, lack of it.

This was supposed to have been the anniversary return to South America, a celebration of a twenty-year friendship forged in wanderlust, a difficult one—they were too much alike, bossy, controlling—but after the scene over the penguins she had been positive that the trip wouldn't work. She should never have come to this country with Freyda, ditching Jack on New Year's Eve, a mistake. Freyda had argued that her office closed for the holidays on December 23, why should she cut her vacation short by a week? She had acquiesced, changed her flight to the day after Christmas, succumbing to the memory of a no-strings attached freedom, when she owed men nothing but desire, not to Freyda's self-centered demands, she thought.

The penguins had turned their relationship tense; but they agreed to be polite, instead of arguing nonstop, to continue to Torres del Paine National Park together, and see how it went. At the garbage-strewn *refugio*, infested with mice, without a shower or electric lights, they learned that the boat that crossed Lake Esmeralda to Gray Glacier had sunk. Their itinerary was shot! Burdened with Freyda's oversized suitcase mounted on wheels, they were unable to go anywhere without public transportation, or at least a horse, and horses cost fifty dollars a day in the National Park. Instead, they resolved to store the suitcase, sufficiently massive to qualify as "trunk," and her own aqua duffel in the Visitors' Center, bungee-cord the two-man Tadpole to her medium-sized daypack, cram it with food, strap their sleeping bags to their belts, and hike to the Gray Glacier; but then, a chaotic Patagonian wind had blown up.

The thin French guide had taken her aside, intoned in his lyrical voice, "You cannot walk there with your face in this wind without a good pack." He'd glanced at Freyda, unpinning her faded underwear from the portable clothesline she'd strung over the dirty foam mattress and stuffing it into her king-sized valise. He ought to know, she thought; his T-shirt, baring his sinuous vine arms to the chill, revealed tight muscles shaping his chest. Freyda was right: twenty years ago, who could say what might have happened with him, but looking good for your age, she understood, was not the same as looking good to young men. Jack had worried that she might "take up" with someone—touchingly, he saw her as universally attractive. She'd located a Lacdel phone booth on New Year's Day and called him; he wasn't at home at seven a.m.; ominous, as the cabin must have been snowed in.

While Freyda futzed with her embarrassing laundry, the Japanese hiker pointed to the black and yellow striped suitcase, flung open on the *refugio* floor, revealing its complex stuffing of plastic bags, a heavy, supportive car seat, and a portable umbrella with broken ribs. She shouted, "You go with all that?," grabbed her big round stomach, and laughed.

The sea at Cucao belonged to an age before the entire world was discovered. Its waves gathered energy from the transparent moon's ghost and blasted forward as if there was no shore to catch them. The relentless curls of white foam that dissipated without changing velocity or shape were making her dizzy, or maybe the Korean-made *mochila,* not as comfortable as her backpack at home, was aggravating nerves in her neck. This iconic dream of a beach, unmarred by resort hotels, thinned to a shiny vibrating tine then vanished. There would be no way to capture its endlessness in a photograph, but she could imagine eulogizing its unspoiled beauty to her academic colleagues when they asked, without interest, "How was your trip?" or to Freyda, who might not have come to this island after their Air Passes took them in different directions.

Like a petulant child, Freyda had refused to say where she was going, or even goodbye, after she lost the coin toss for the laminated map of the south. The next day they'd bumped into one another in an ecclesiastic museum featuring dusty stuffed albatrosses; Freyda was coughing with a severe bronchial cold, holed up in Casa Mochiladero, the same type of seedy, two-dollar youth hostel she'd favored the summer they'd met, sharing a room with six adolescent male rock climbers, all smoking cigarettes and dope. She'd felt sorry for her old friend then, trapped in her miserly concept of youth, despite a decent job, an inheritance. Getting to Cole Cole would prove she'd had a moral imperative to jettison Freyda's moving van of a suitcase, her neurotic fury, and cheapness, her dowager's back, although this no longer seemed a good reason to plod so many kilometers in pain, *agony,* she had to admit.

In the end, Freyda had been the one to suggest that they separate. On their last hike up the steep trail with views of Cambrian granite dikes, she had said, "Let's face it, even when we aren't battling over every little thing, this isn't good." They had argued childishly about whose fault it was: *You and your pronouncements!* Freyda exclaimed, and she had retorted, *You're always projecting anger at me. Whatever I may be doing to you, I'm not doing that.* Then Freyda said, sensibly, that if they didn't stop this, they really wouldn't be speaking to each other by the end of the hike. They'd agreed never to travel together again, but to keep in touch. At the top of the boulder cascade, where the wind flattened the air into dust-laden sheets that flapped through the gorge, moving the surface of the diaphanous lake that roared beneath the towers' oblique fingers of rock, their resentment did dissipate. Yet as she descended the rough path, she secretly planned to take the French guide's advice, buy the Korean *mochila,* and backpack to Cole Cole, transforming the failed reunion into an important adventure she could one day tell Freyda about.

Twenty-five kilometers in one day was pushing it, though, she should have known that. *Seis horas?* More like six years, she thought ironically. She wished she'd taken a chance on the weather and left the tent in the *residencia.* The mimeographed CONAF map did show a shelter at Cole Cole, as the French guide had said, but none of the trekkers coming from there had seen it. To be on the safe side, she had fastened the Tadpole plus metal stakes, seven and a half pounds, under the straps on the front of the pack instead of sticking them under the flap on the top where she had stowed the heavy water bottles. As a result, the tent was dragging her backwards like a claw hooked into the tendon between her shoulder and neck. There was no point trying to repack unless she dumped most of the water and drank from the river at Cole Cole, which, according to Pedro, was clean and safe.

The joints in her hips were beginning to ache. Her powers of concentration should have enabled her to blot the *tavernas,* black horse flies the size of newborn mice, if not the pain, from her consciousness. These whining insects, materializing in the late morning heat, pursued her denim shirt to cool breezes emitted by the surf. They would have eaten Freyda alive, like the fleas in the infested hotel on the beach in Ecuador the summer they'd met. She had refused to give the poor Indian girl who gently bathed the infected bites the blue bandanna she'd begged for. *I need it,* Freyda kept insisting. At the time she'd believed that her new traveling companion's refusal to bestow a trivial gift signified more than pure selfishness; the girl's maternal tenderness was pressing warped psychic buttons, perhaps. *Oh, just give it to her,* she'd said. *You can buy another in New York for twenty-five cents.* The scene over the penguins had reminded her of that long-ago incident; Freyda, the self-acclaimed world traveler, had always viewed the citizens of foreign countries as servants.

She had met the Ecuadorian boy at a drunken carnival in that town on the coast. Within minutes, it seemed, they were fucking on the beach. Twenty years later, the memory of the sex eluded her, but the cans and bottles beneath their bodies, the other couples passing behind a curtain of salt-infused darkness, the music strained through the Pacific's lapping, came back with visceral clarity, as if her pain on the beach she was now on recalled them. She couldn't remember speaking Spanish with him. Surely they spoke? That's right, he had been an exchange student in Canada and learned some English.

When she'd returned to the hotel, Freyda was lying on the cold tile floor, thin, wiry curls propped up on a pillow, playing Bach on a recorder, her face still inflamed from the bites; her back had collapsed again, she said with stoic cheer; she hoped she'd still be able to trek to Macchu Picchu with Franz. *That's really wild!* Freyda had exclaimed with admiring wonder when she told her about the boy on the beach. Freyda could always give back the excitement of semi-crazed trysts that she herself would too quickly forget.

Before they'd flown down to Punta Arenas at the beginning of this trip, they had sat in the *zócalo* in Santiago, watching gypsies, drums attached to their backs, whirling dizzily to their self-imposed beat. "Catching up," as Freyda called it, they had strayed to the risky subject of the future, growing older. Freyda complained about her poor circulation; her legs had always been lumpy with purple varicose veins; now they were worse. *They don't see your legs unless they're in bed with you*, she had said consolingly, aware, as the words left her mouth, that her own legs were all right. Freyda had rambled on, as she often did, about Hank, her favorite ex, dead of a brain tumor at forty-nine; she imitated his buoyant Swahili greeting when they'd traveled in Kenya decades ago, shortly before he went back to his wife. She continued on to the subject of that fat, crazy lawyer who'd crashed at her place when he'd come down to the city to fight for custody of an illegitimate son. As the loud gypsies danced, Freyda had said with a calm acceptance, *I think he was the last one; I don't think there will be any more men.* Then she'd exclaimed, with cheerfully exaggerated envy, *I want a Jack!* This comment, intended to be flattering, had made her feel guilty, both for having the man her friend wanted and for abandoning him.

If she'd known she would end up backpacking without Freyda, she'd have brought her MSR water filter, her Whisper Lite stove, and light freeze-dried food. She wouldn't be schlepping four greasy *milpoa*, fresh tomatoes, six rolls, cheese, and two weighty cans of *sardinas desmenuzados*. Few provisions were available in Cucao because the dirt road to the small settlement had been half washed out. Even in dry weather the town was remote. The woman who ran the *residencia* where she'd spent the night told her that until last year, when electricity arrived, there was no ice; when one family slaughtered a sheep, it shared the meat with other families. There was still no television or hot running water; Pedro heated buckets on the woodstove for baths. He had looked at her, a deliberately neutral expression on his long, sour face, suggested that she take a guide—him—and a horse to Cole Cole. He must have seen the weakness she had hid from herself. Why hadn't she hired him? She had the money.

She stopped to rest—for the second time in half an hour—on a white driftwood log hurled out of the sea. Immediately the horse flies were on her, injecting venom into the back of her neck. Before she left the *residencia* this morning, she had raised the pack plus herself to a standing position by slipping her arms in the straps and crouching on all fours while bracing her hands on the chair next to the bed. *I'm not going to get there,* she had thought. As she'd trudged toward the wood-slatted suspension bridge, a back-lighted streamer of evaporating moisture laddered up along the pale sticks of a fence. Pedro's Arabian horses wheeled, snorting, through moon-colored grass and ignited tendrils. Vines rubbed magenta flowers into the blur of fresh sun. She could hear the ocean beating drumrolls on its sliding skin. She followed the broad backs of two Mapuche women, mounted on mules, parading ahead. A small Indian man wearing a formal blue suit, vest, and fedora galloped by on a chestnut gelding, crying, *Cole Cole! Seis horas caminando!* enthusiastically to her. She had felt exhilarated then, glad to be attempting what she believed she should do, and for a little while, the pack had felt carryable.

A male figure emerged from the mica haze of the primordial beach. The young man joined her on the log; his dark eyes shy, yet intently inquiring, followed her finger as it attempted to trace the route on the lousy CONAF map. He said, casually, that he had not arrived to Cole Cole; it was *difícil* to walk in the sand with boots. (His were not Goretex, but black leather military castoffs.) He had camped by the lake instead. She gestured toward a faraway point, extending rocky knobs into the ocean. "To Punta Denai?" she asked him. No, he said, squinting at the map; the place where the trail left the beach was not there, but *más lejos,* beyond that; you must cross two rivers, using the bridges if you did not miss them, climb a small mountain, thick with jungle; the path was easy to lose because it was not marked. They talked for a while; he was a student from a small town near Temuco.

Solita? Alone? he questioned, like everyone else from this country. She had developed a snappy retort, *Sí, como no?* (Yeah, why not?) She didn't use it with him (his brown eyes, shining with the self-involved sincerity of the idealistic young, deterred her), or mention that she had started the trip with a friend. People from this country reacted negatively, almost with fear, to the revelation that she hadn't gotten along with her traveling companion; perhaps in Spanish she was saying more than she meant. (*No one goes alone here,* a sophisticated woman from the capitol had told her.) Now she replied, "Yes, solitude is better sometimes." The student nodded doubtfully; he was alone, too, but he was not a middle-aged female American tourist.

She looked at the sun, said *adiós,* and struggled to her feet, like a camel unfolding its legs to leverage a burden attached to its hump. Her ankles were killing her. The student watched her go worriedly. As she felt herself disappearing down the beach's platinum funnel, she realized that instead of hurrying on to a place that she wouldn't get to, she could have stayed on the log and talked to him. She could have asked about Temuco, the birthplace of Pablo Neruda.

The Ecuadorian boy had the same long, dark hair, scraped back in a ponytail, receptive eyes, and wet clay skin as the student did. She remembered his last name—*Aguilar,* or was it *Aguilar-Lanza?*—but not his first. Twenty years ago, she had flown from Cuzco back to Quito, leaving Freyda still waiting for that German shit. The boy had managed to meet her at the airport (she hadn't told him the time of her flight), and carried her duffel to a cheap hotel. That night he led her through a cobblestoned back street to an unsigned rooming house that must have been a brothel where unmarried couples also went to have sex. After twenty years she could picture the bed, a narrow cot, with one thin, gray sheet that bunched up to reveal a blood-stained green mattress. Flimsy partitions concealed the owner of a continual wet cough. Doors banged all night. He had gasped, *Dios,* with grateful amazement; then translated, *"My Got,"* knowing she spoke enough Spanish to understand *God.* She remembered telling Freyda the story in the Café Dante when they got together for cappuccino in New York. *Do you think you'll ever hear from him?* her friend had asked, interpreting, as she always would, any male-female encounter, however ephemeral, as legitimate romance. She had never imagined she would hear from him, although she had given him her address, watched him read it, sounding out the English words with careful attention, button the paper into his breast pocket, then happily pat the place where it was.

All morning she had encountered other hikers, mostly young couples, returning to Cucao from Cole Cole. When the hot sun dried the flare of her shadow, she saw two men and a woman, walking briskly, as if their cumbersome packs were loaded with bubble wrap. "It was beautiful there, all right," one of the men, an American, told her. "Great views of the bay... I have no complaints except for the flies." The way to drive them all off for a nanosecond, he said, was to injure one, badly, by bashing it with your hat. He took off his hat, and swiped a buzzing *taverna* to demonstrate, revealing faded red hair and a lined, freckled forehead.

He looked at her closely, recognizing, she knew, the type she was—an aging hippie, like himself—hiking alone with a useless pink backpack. She told him she was headed to Cole Cole... probably wouldn't get there, though; this Korean pack was junk; she should never have put two liters of water in it. She'd heard you could take water out of the river, but she was a coward... The trekkers at Torres Del Paine were using the trail for a bathroom, and that really scared her.

"My Argentinean friends here will drink anything," the sunburned man said, gesturing toward the silent couple that gazed at her curiously, "but the water in that river didn't look too good. The drought has made it awfully muddy. You were supposed to drink on one side of the bridge and bathe downstream on the other. I let it settle, then boiled it."

"See, and I don't have a stove."

He stared at her. "How about a pot?" he asked. "You're alone?"

"Yeah." She explained that she'd started the trip with a woman friend, but it hadn't worked out... This guy, a hip American, would understand what she hadn't said; then, inexplicably, she felt as if she were betraying Freyda.

"She left you in the lurch, huh," the American stated. He looked at his watch, noted that they had been walking for four hours. "You could still get to Cole Cole before dark. What time does the sun set? Ten, ten-thirty?"

"Actually, I'm considering bagging it. Cole Cole can't be much better than this," she said, circling her head to encompass the here and now, the Zen of the glittering, undiscovered beach. The American looked at her sorrowfully, and she saw herself through his blue eyes, nested in crow's feet, a crazed hag, limping alone, face clenched in torture, and realized that she wasn't carrying enough food, water, or the right equipment for a four-day trip into the heart of a jungle. "I might camp at the lake instead," she said, remembering that the student from Temuco had mentioned one.

"Lago Cucao. It's about half a mile back, inland a ways. You already passed it," the American informed her.

Had Freyda gotten rid of her? Perhaps, she thought, as she continued on. (She hadn't wanted to give up, turn around, in front of an audience.) She had tried to control her irritation, to be kind, to comprehend that her furious friend must be going through a dark night of the soul she hadn't confided. After the absurd scene over the penguins, she had lost it, though; rage dredged her voice in a whisper, *Ugly American! You made a fool out of yourself and me!*, and immediately regretted the cruel word *ugly*. That night, alone in the room on New Year's Eve, she had written to Jack, a letter, it turned out, he never received.

She reached the point after circumnavigating an inlet the breadth of a dead sea that refused to part. The sand sucked her blistered feet into it. Sobbing feebly, she threw down her pack, picked it up again, howling. She heard her cry waver through the loud air like an imaginary spear and vanish. Now she sat, weary, her shoulder knotted in a painful spasm, on a baklava of shale. Thick ropes of a rubbery orange seaweed plopped over the chewed rocks where hand-shaped fronds gestured, oblivious to the absence of soil. Birds she couldn't name, wings blackened by the late sun into charred silhouettes, cruised overhead. The oasis's flowing tide streams pooled into clear eyes of water on scalloped white shells, a miniature world of extravagant beauty, offering her a truth her focus on Cole Cole, a destination some French guide had inscribed in her notebook, might have caused her to miss. Could Cole Cole, whatever it was, be more inspiring that this? She knew she lied to console herself, not for failing to reach the goal, but for not having the strength.

She took off her boots and peeled away the waterlogged moleskin. The broken blister had been bleached by wet, wool socks to the color of drowned flesh. *Rene.* The Ecuadorian boy's name was Rene. When he'd walked her back to her cheap hotel the following morning, the friendly maid, ironing sheets, had projected a scorn she could feel brushing her face like a spider's web. Then the maid had looked the other way, pointedly, as if she were shunning a prostitute. (That she had not told Freyda about.) A few months later the boy had written a barely literate letter, *Hello,*

Babe! I am here thinking to you, and included a flash-bleached photograph of himself, lounging on a sunken blue sofa, wearing an unbuttoned candy pink shirt. *I want to come for to visit you in United States of America.* He had desired, not her, but her prosperous country; from the perspective of her real life in Manhattan, she realized that she'd known this from the start. After that, she had avoided thoughts of their depraved rutting, two dogs on a beach, although only Freyda knew about it and had never judged her. Now she wondered if she had damaged Rene by altering the path of his expectations while forgetting his name.

As she soaked her feet in the opal stream, the ancient Mapuche she'd greeted at the beginning of the journey, still wearing a formal blue suit, galloped up on his horse, leaped off, and cast a homemade reel into the surf. *"Corvina!"* he exclaimed gaily. She watched him with dull amazement; he was a hundred years old, yet his eyes, blinded by the cooked egg whites of cataracts, did not stop him from riding, fishing, recognizing her. *Cole Cole?* he shouted again, confident that she was still headed to the same place as the rest of her kind. She nodded dumbly. As he remounted he threw his arm, like a lariat, north. *Seis horas caminando,* he cried, and rode off smartly, spurring his steed into the dense, drought-bleached jungle.

Could she be no closer to Cole Cole than she was this morning when she set out? Had she walked all day and gotten nowhere? It was possible. She had never seen the lake, the rivers, or the bridges that were supposed to cross them. She stood up, disoriented. She wanted to call, "Wait! Where is the path?," *Donde está el sendero?,* but the monotone thud of the sea, her desolation, swallowed the words before she could speak.

She sat on the point, gazing into the tide pool's eons of layered white shells until the hard pink sun expanded, fraying at the edges, and dropped. When she arose she dumped most of the water and turned back to look for the lake.

An animal will steal her food that night. The Mapuche woman, manager of the crude campground near Lago Cucao, will open her mouth wide, laughing, and exclaim, *Sí! Perros! O gato cholo!* Before she leaves this country, she will ford a rain-swollen river, risking hypothermia, to get to El Encanto, because she never made it to Cole Cole. There she will eat the *sardinas desmenuza-dos* in a water-logged rowboat as multiple waterfalls steam down boulders. On the Esplanade in Puerto Montt she will meet a gypsy woman, *del Norte,* maybe a thief, who knots the hundred pesos she gives her in the ruffled hem of her long, flowered skirt, saying, "Because you have given me this coin, I will answer one question." After she asks it, the gypsy will reply, flat pale eyes gazing past her face to the port, "You will suffer much sorrow and disappointment in this life." Forest fires will burn underground on the insular island of Chiloe, where, in the time of Darwin, torrents of rain fell. Blue glaciers in Puerto Natales are melting beneath the ozone hole; she and Freyda had seen that for themselves. Home in the unfinished cabin, she will feel confused and lost, although Jack will be there, resentful about New Year's Eve, but glad she is back. She will tell him the news her lost letter contained: Freyda castigated the driver from the agency they'd booked to take them to the Pingüinera because he was late. *It is New Year's Eve; I meant no harm.* "Freyda, will you shut up!" she injected. Freyda had cursed her then, with a hatred so venomous, so long-stifled, so Biblically intense that she had immediately repressed the exact words her friend said. *You know this woman long?* "She can't tolerate schedule changes," she'd apologized to the driver, who understood English, wondering why she was defending this selfish crone, a stranger she barely recognized. Young, coarsely handsome, the driver recited a proverb: *It is better to go alone than badly accompanied.* He offered to give them their money back, but together they traveled to the end of the earth, to an unfrozen bay, where the ancient tuxedoed birds twirled stunted wings and poked their heads out of burrowed nests. When she tells the story of her lonely, dissatisfying, final adventure, as she often does, the scene over a penguin tour seems insignificant, a weak denouement, a poor reason to hike twenty-five kilometers in pain, to abandon an old friend. She will realize she had known she would not get to Cole Cole even before she started to walk. Why did Freyda carry a broken umbrella all the way from New York?

Août

The note was slipped to me on Wednesday, July 20th, at two minutes before three. I know the exact time because I happened to be staring at my watch, wondering if Dr. V. would be running late today, as she sometimes did, when the double doors burst open, and Peacock Throne walked out. I called her that because she had the darkly imperious ethnicity of an Iranian princess, and also, of course, because I didn't know her name. Sometimes she was crying when she came out, her mascara softly running, but today she seemed actually giggly, as though she and Dr. V. had been in there exchanging amusing stories about bad dates. Usually, Peacock Throne threw me a cursory smile when she left, the smile of a princess to a subject. But now she seemed to veer toward me as she walked through the narrow waiting area littered with old copies of *Gourmet*. I swung my knees to the side to let her pass, like someone at the movies, but as I did, she let something tumble deliberately into my lap. I was shocked. In thirty seconds, Dr. V. would be poking her head out of the double doors, having done her little preparations for the next patient, which apparently consisted of ripping off a single sheet of Viva paper towel and placing it over the headrest of her couch. I've never understood whether that piece of paper towel was supposed to be for my protection, or for the protection of her couch, a beige Jennifer Convertible covered with a thicket of woolly nubs.

Peacock Throne just kept walking, leaving the waiting room and heading outside, the front door clicking quietly shut behind her. In my lap was her carefully folded, slightly used-looking note. I opened it. The note read: "If you are interested in discussing Dr. V. with her other patients, please meet outside this building on Monday, August 1st at 12:00. Also, kindly pass this on to the next patient after your session. Whatever you do, don't tell Dr. V. about the existence of this note. And please don't break the chain. Thanks!!!"

The three exclamation marks after the last word gave me pause; they seemed such a young and girlish garnish to this forceful letter. Had Peacock Throne written this herself? Or had it been lobbed into her lap by Lighting Booth, the heavy, melancholy man in the rotating collection of Broadway show bomber jackets (*Carousel* had recently replaced *Miss Saigon*). Or maybe it had been thrust at her by Learner's Permit, the kinetic teenaged boy with the blurry bad skin and beautiful eyes, whose therapy probably consisted of tentative pontifications on whether death really is final. Before I had a chance to sift through the possibilities, the double doors opened again, and Dr. V.'s head appeared: the quick smile, the scarf, the big blue-framed glasses. I dropped the note into the pocket of my shoulder bag, then walked into her office, where I carelessly tossed the bag over a chair, as always, and headed for the couch.

She always made me start. If I were lying there choking on a sourball, she would not say a word until I managed to emit some guttural, farm-animal sound first. Dr. V. seemed so passive that at times I felt as though we were two polite strangers occupying different corners of an otherwise deserted subway car, looking everywhere but at each other. On July 20th I kept quiet about the note, and instead began the session by dredging up a minor dream from a few nights earlier, which I had almost forgotten. I would often leave a single dream in reserve, one which I wasn't sure I even wanted to mention, so that if there was another subject lurking which seemed too mortifying to discuss, I could always sigh and say, "So I had this interesting dream..." The spiral pad and pen would dutifully appear; I could hear them, the paper asserting itself as it crackled on its spool of wire, the Bic pen clicking into readiness. Dr. V. loved dreams, especially dreams about her. As soon as I said, "And *you* were there," like Dorothy after she returned from Oz and lay in her bed surrounded by familiar Kansan faces, Dr. V. instantly perked up.

"Oh?" she would say. "Tell me."

On this particular day, I launched easily into the dream, something about my father secretly being the real person responsible for the Salk vaccine. Soon I stopped thinking about the note entirely, and when the hour was up, I was reluctant to go. What if I didn't get up? What if I just lay there, ignoring her suggestive

rustling? Usually, when I stood up and looked at Dr. V. at the very
end, I would be reminded of how shocking were the things I had
said to her only moments earlier. "The mole on my great-uncle's
shoulder made me sick!" I had cried one day. I told her everything, while she remained a cipher to me. I could not even imagine her going home at night. If I pictured her putting a key into a
lock, the door would lead only into a dark, empty stockroom, not
a home. She would never tell me anything about herself, of
course: whether she had a husband, or children. She wouldn't
even say where she went every August when she closed up shop.
Did she stay in the city like I did, sitting in front of the air conditioner blast, eating take-out kung-pao chicken and doing the
Jumble in the newspaper? Or did she migrate up to Wellfleet with
her husband and their two or three children, the family car
packed with the belongings of the family V.?

On my way out of the office on July 20th, I slung my bag over
my shoulder and closed the double doors behind me. There in
the waiting room sat Game Show Host, his hair high and blown. I
could not imagine what men like this discussed with their psy-
choanalysts. He was so carelessly handsome; he seemed the kind
of man who would do better committing himself to one of those
bursts of expensive, faddish therapy that involve hundreds of
people and take place in the conference rooms of midtown hotels.
But here he was, under the quiet, fairly traditional care of Dr. V.,
just like me. I tossed him the note, while gazing into his clear and
startled eyes.

"Hey, wait," he said. "What *is* this?" But I was out the door.

I said goodbye to Dr. V. on the last Thursday of July. I admitted
that I would miss her during August. I said that no doubt I would
call her answering machine once or twice during the month, just
to hear her recorded voice, and then hang up without a word. The
session ended now, and I stood awkwardly. She actually smiled—
a slight wince, as though she'd located a tiny chink of glass in a
mouthful of food—and then she reached out to shake my hand.
"Goodbye, Susan," Dr. V. said, and then our hands were touching,
warm palm to warm palm. I was standing close enough to get a
more thorough look at her; this happened every August. Last
summer when we shook hands, I noticed that she had a widow's

peak, which I have, too. My whole life, this widow's peak has been a problem, causing my hair to remain jaggedly parted. I wanted to say, "Look, look!" and pull a hank of hair back from my forehead in solidarity, but I didn't. I glanced at her face now, trying to notice some new detail for future use, but all I could see were the things I already knew. She was a middle-aged woman in a scarf and big-framed blue eyeglasses, not unlike the women in my mother's book discussion group. I used to see them whenever the group was held at my parents' house; they arrived with their copies of *Middlemarch* or Anaïs Nin's *Diaries*, the text of the book feverishly marked up. "Symbolism?" they would write in the white space, or "How true!"

I am not proud of what happened on the first day of August, of what we did and said, or of the damage we caused. But it was as though, once we started this, we had to finish it one way or another, like an analysis itself. Shortly before twelve o'clock, I stood alone under the awning on East 83rd Street. I assumed that we would all meet here and then go to a restaurant. I pictured the bunch of us crowded into a big wooden booth, nervous and jangly as strangers at a singles' brunch. I looked over at the lineup of brass professional nameplates nailed to the outside of the building, the catalogue of psychiatrists, psychologists, and the occasional, proud M.S.W. who were housed in the first-floor offices inside. Now, though, the offices were silent, and even the white noise machines had been unplugged. Every August, it was as though a virus had wiped out the entire New York population of people in the helping professions.

Peacock Throne arrived, and to my surprise she smiled warmly at me, so I smiled back. Next came Learner's Permit, in his high-tops and backpack. Then I noticed that, a few feet away, Lighting Booth was approaching, humming a song I knew from *Fiorello*. By ten past twelve, there were eight of us in front of the building, several whom I recognized from occasional schedule changes over the years, a few whom I did not. There was a man who I was pretty sure played a young father in a Bell Atlantic commercial, and an ethereal woman carrying a battered edition of Proust—Volume II, I glumly noticed. I myself had never been able to get beyond Volume I. I imagined that this woman and Dr. V. spent their sessions in gentle contemplation of literature, not to mention language itself. She was probably a graduate student who read late into the night, subsisting on bowls of ramen noodles. A couple of patients were still missing, and we gave them a few more minutes' leeway until finally, a dark, compact man carrying a strongbox arrived and said, "Shall we?"

"Shall we what?" Lighting Booth asked.

"Well," said the man, "this whole thing was my idea, and I thought we'd just, you know, go in." He turned and walked into the vestibule. We followed him, watching as he squatted down, snapping open his box and removing a few small, serious tools. "I'm a locksmith," he explained. "This shouldn't be very difficult." Within three minutes he had worked open the door to the lobby, then the door to Dr. V.'s anteroom. We others followed sheepishly behind, stunned at the illegality of this, but undeniably thrilled. The locksmith popped the lock on Dr. V.'s double doors, and we filed in without saying a word. The room felt as warm and close as the stage set for a production of *No Exit*. At first, no one could bear to turn on a light. Then Proust Woman began to laugh nervously, and a bony woman in a Laura Ashley sundress switched on the halogen lamp, which flooded the office with that familiar yellow light.

The room was orderly, with very few changes. The paper towel on the end of the couch was gone, and so was the plant that usually sat on the windowsill. Learner's Permit went over to the couch and flopped down hard. "Feels good to sit," he said. "I'm sick of lying down. The ceiling is boring."

"Did you ever notice," said Lighting Booth, "the way the cracks in the ceiling above the couch form the shape of a baker's hat?"

"Not really," said Peacock Throne. "And can we just get started?"

Then she actually sat herself down in Dr. V.'s chair. We all just stared. It was one thing to break into the office of your psychoanalyst, and another thing entirely to sit in her chair. She swiveled the chair from side to side; it made a very slight creak and scritch, which I realized I had heard many times before during sessions. "First of all," said Peacock Throne, taking over, "does anyone know where Dr. V. goes in August? I mean, really know. Not just a guess."

"How would we possibly know?" asked Laura Ashley. "It's not as though she tells us anything." She paused, then added suspiciously, "Why, does she tell you things?"

"No," said Peacock Throne. "Not a word. But my brother-in-law found out that *his* analyst spends August in a house in Dutchess County, because his friends, who also have a house up there, were talking about this couple who have a house down the road, a psychoanalyst and his wife, and they mentioned that the husband's name was Nathan, and my brother-in-law started shouting, 'Not Nathan Kantor! Not Nathan Kantor!' And the friends said yes, their country neighbor was Nathan Kantor the psychoanalyst. And they told my brother-in-law all these unflattering things about his analyst, like the fact that he has raspberry shrubs growing all over his property, but he never lets the neighbors' children pick raspberries."

Then Proust Woman said in a small, trembling voice, "My theory is that Dr. V. goes to France every August. She and I have discussed certain aspects of French life before, and she's always struck me as very sensitive on the subject. I asked her if perhaps she and her family rented a home in Provence, and she didn't disabuse me of the fact."

"Fact?" said Lighting Booth. "It's not a fact. It's a fantasy, that's all."

But I thought to myself: I can see her in France. Tooling around the countryside with her family in a rented Citroën, wearing her big blue eyeglasses, using her rusty Seven Sisters French language skills. It made sense to me that even as we all sat here in her office, she and her husband and children were standing with their passports splayed open at the Air France desk at JFK.

Suddenly I noticed that the locksmith was starting to go through the drawers of Dr. V.'s desk. He took out a few papers, and we all grew excited, but they merely turned out to be fliers for the annual " 'Fling into Spring' Blowout" at the Karen Horney Institute. Then he reached deeper inside a drawer and fished out an opened pack of Trident, followed by a pen that read PROZAC on the side. The objects were passed around for inspection, and Proust Woman discreetly pocketed the pen, but these little details brought us no closer to knowing who our analyst was.

Just as I began to think that this whole adventure was misbegotten, Laura Ashley suddenly said, "Did you ever notice the way Dr. V. really starts to pay attention only when you talk about *her*? I mean," she continued, "I can be telling a story about the day my father walked out on us, and Dr. V. doesn't say a word. But as soon as I say, 'This reminds me of how angry you make me feel sometimes,' she always says, 'Oh? Tell me.'"

Several of us laughed bitterly. Oh, that "Oh? Tell me." We knew it well.

"The thing is," said the locksmith, "I have no idea whether my analysis is helping me, but I'm very sexually attracted to her, so I enjoy coming here. She has a wonderful body, under all those big blousy things she wears, and those scarves. You know," he continued, "many people in my profession undergo psychoanalysis in their lifetimes. It's quite common."

"Really?" I said. "I didn't know that."

"Oh yes," he said. "Two of the other guys at Keys Plus have been in treatment for years. Something about the image of the key in the lock fills us with dread and intense longing. I suppose it's like being small boys and spying on our mothers in the bathroom, learning their intimate womanly secrets. It's all very interesting, of course, and I've been coming here forever, but you know something? Lately I've been thinking that I could find better ways to spend my ninety dollars."

A shocked silence fell over the room. *Ninety dollars!* I paid a hundred dollars a session; when I first came for a consultation, Dr. V. had said that her usual fee was one hundred twenty-five dollars, but that she would lower it to meet the needs of my budget. I had felt special, chosen, tapped for Skull and Bones. Yet now, many years later, I was learning that all along she had been charging the locksmith less. Maybe if I had pushed her a little more, I could have talked her down. But how could I have known that you could treat a degree-holding psychoanalyst like a Florentine street-merchant?

We went around the room, telling one another how much we paid. Most people were squarely in the ninety to one-twenty-five range. I felt relieved that mine wasn't the highest fee; that honor went to Learner's Permit, whose parents, he admitted, paid their son's analyst one hundred and fifty dollars a session. "What can I say?" Learner's Permit said, shrugging lightly. "My dad's a big fat art dealer." The only person who hadn't revealed the amount she paid was Proust Woman. She looked very nervous now, as though hoping that everyone would forget about her. But I had to know.

"You didn't tell us how much she charges you," I said mildly.

"That's kind of personal," she answered.

"Come on," said Lighting Booth. "Nothing's personal here. We don't even know one another's names."

The woman uneasily plucked at the spine of Volume II. "Well, actually," she said in an apologetic whisper, "she charges me fifteen dollars a session."

We all gasped. I thought there might be an uprising, everyone encircling her in rage, yanking the Proust from her small, pale hands. "Fifteen dollars!" said Lighting Booth. "How could she do that to me? I give her all my money. I can't even afford cable!"

"While she waltzes off to France for the month of August," added the young father. "Or should I say, off to France for the month of *Août*. Oo-la-la, renting a villa, sitting and eating *les brioches*."

"And you know what else," said Learner's Permit. "I really don't like her eyeglasses. They make her look so average."

"Exactly," said Laura Ashley. "So undistinguished. Why should we give all our money to such a person? And her answering machine, can you believe that message?"

Lighting Booth sprang up and went to the answering machine, which sat on its own low table. He pressed a button, turned up the volume, and in a moment we heard that familiar voice over-enunciating into the room. We all laughed, agreeing that this was the lamest message ever recorded. When the beep sounded, the locksmith announced that he was going to erase her message and replace it with a new one. We listened, impressed and appalled, as he rewound the short tape and recorded a new message in its place. "Hul-lo," he said in his husky baritone, leaning close to the built-in microphone. "This—is—Dr.—V." In the background, despite our disapproval, we all began to hoot and cheer. "I cannot come to the phone right now," he continued, "because I am spending August in the South of France, on *your* money! Having a great time without you, far away from your disgusting little homoerotic fantasies—"

"—and your boring dreams," added Peacock Throne.

"—and," I found myself piping up, "the oil from your hair on my paper towel!" The others screamed with laughter.

There we were, all eight of us hunched around the answering machine, talking into it and howling, when the door opened. We turned, and there in the doorway stood Dr. V. We were silent. Behind her stood Game Show Host, bobbing up to peer over her shoulder. "You see?" he was saying with triumph. "I wasn't making it up."

For a long time she stood and looked at us. "What am I going to do with you?" she asked us sadly. I can't quite remember what else she said, so shocking was it to hear her voice. I only know it had something to do with the bonds of trust that we had broken. Proust Woman suddenly interrupted, asking her why she wasn't on her way to France, and Dr. V. just looked puzzled. "France?" she said. "What gave you that idea?" No one could answer. "So, did you find out what you wanted?" Dr. V. asked, and her voice was almost kind. None of us could say that we had found out anything. We stared down at our hands, or at the rug, and we apologized over and over. Finally she said that we could go, and that we would sort this all out individually in September, but I knew that that would not happen, at least not for me. I could not imagine that my analysis would be strong enough to withstand the shame I now felt as she looked us over. We said our goodbyes to Dr. V., then we left her office and walked back out into the sunlight, like the stunned survivors of a massive wreck.

My new therapist does not need to be referred to by only one initial. "This isn't Kafka," she said cheerfully. Her name is Linda Manzini, Ph.D., and her office is located downtown in the West Village, in a brownstone that also happens to be her home. The edges of her personal life are occasionally revealed to me by accident. There is a gray, elderly family cat that sometimes makes a brief appearance in the waiting room, and once a package lay in the front hall when I arrived, a delivery from Williams-Sonoma that bore the shape and heft of a cheese board. I always notice the details, but it's really out of habit, not curiosity.

Mostly, I am relieved not to be in analysis with Dr. V. anymore, but sometimes I do miss the mystery of it all, the pointed silences, the sheets of paper towel, the strange, inarticulate understanding

that lived between us. I now sit upright, once a week, in the palm of a big leather chair that has a slight fall of cat hair on it, and when I speak, Linda Manzini always meets my gaze. She is a motherly and sympathetic woman who wears caftans year-round. I know exactly who she is, and I have to say I am disappointed.

from *The Museum Guard*

On the morning of July 23, 1921, my parents, Cowley and Elizabeth Russet, died in the crash of a zeppelin at the fairgrounds in Fleming Park. They had each paid fifty cents to ride in the gondola, to float and drift over Halifax, the harbor, then back to Fleming Park.

That day, I had been sitting with my uncle on the porch of The Lord Nelson Hotel. My uncle was already living there. We had chosen the porch, because he had read in the newspaper that the zeppelin's route included the sky directly above the hotel. It was a hot day. Coffee after coffee, my uncle was working off a binge, and I was having a sandwich and root beer float. He was just about to scoop a bite of my float with his spoon, when a man—I remember he had a handlebar mustache, and the sleeves of his sweat-soaked white shirt were rolled up to the elbows—ran up the steps and shouted, "Is there a Dr. Moore here?" Across the crowded porch, Dr. Moore stood up, removing his cloth napkin from his collar. "Here!" he shouted back, his hand raised like a schoolboy's. "Is it my daughter?"

The mustached man stood on a chair. He choked up mid-sentence, but managed to say, "You're needed at the fairgrounds. There are bodies everywhere!"

What happened next, I can never forget. I yanked at my uncle's sleeve. "I want to see! I want to see!" But he lifted me entirely out of my chair. At age eight, I was a slight boy, and he stood me right on the table. He embraced me so hard, I thought that he would break my ribs. He held on, and it frightened me. I felt the plates and silverware under my shoes, heard the near and distant pandemonium of voices, saw people running from the porch, which was empty of everyone but us in a matter of seconds. My uncle then held my face a few inches from his and said, "Do *not* move, DeFoe. You wait right here. You'll be fine. Sit down, and don't move an inch, understand?"

My uncle ran into the hotel. I kept standing on the table; it

afforded me the best view of people fanning out along South Park Street, into the Public Gardens. I saw a few men and women wave down horse-drawn carriages, all but tossing money at the drivers. With all the commotion, all the people zigzagging and shouting, two horses reared, whinnied hysterically, and one started backing up its carriage, the carriage tilted, and both driver and woman passenger leapt out. I remember thinking, "Something terrible is happening to all of these grown-ups." The horse actually backed the carriage up the remaining length of the park; the driver was chasing it, waving his arms, which may have made things worse. An old pastry chef, Dunsten Brooking—my uncle often got him to concoct rum-filled cakes—wearing his chef's hat and spattered apron, hurried right past me, then into the street. I followed his hat bobbing among the rosebushes, until it disappeared across the park.

In a few minutes, my uncle came back. There was a woman with him. I had seen her at the hotel. On occasion, my parents would drop me off, and I would do my school homework at a corner table, while my uncle played cards with the bellhops and kept an eye on me. I had seen my uncle kiss this woman near the electric lift. She was very pretty, with red bobbed hair. But awfully nervous now. My uncle set me down on the porch. "Now, DeFoe," he said, "this is Altoon Markham. We're good friends. She's going to be your good friend, too, okay? And she's going to stay with you while I— Grown men and women are needed at the fairgrounds. Do you understand?"

"I'm going with you."

"No, I'm afraid you can't."

"We'll get along just fine," Altoon Markham said. She was squinting hard, forcing a smile.

"At the fairgrounds some people fell down," my uncle said. "I'm going to help pick them up."

"Okay. I'll stay here. But tell Mother and Father where I am. I don't want them to think I'm alone. You know what they're wearing, Uncle Edward. You'll find them. My father has a new haircut."

"I know he does," my uncle said. He kissed me on top of my head.

"Sweet darling," Altoon Markham said. "I'll get you some ice cream. The cooks and waiters have all left, so ice cream's ours for the taking. We'll go be ice cream robbers, this one special time, all right? Cake, too."

"It's your birthday, isn't it?" my uncle said.

Altoon's expression changed quickly from puzzlement to exaggerated agreement. "Why, yes. In all this excitement, I almost forgot my own birthday. And wouldn't you like to celebrate with me, DeFoe? A little party, just the two of us?"

"Don't let him out of your sight," my uncle said.

He pushed a number of wadded-up dollar bills into Altoon Markham's hand. He looked at me sternly, lovingly, and with a hint of pity, which I noticed because I had never seen quite that look before, and it made me want to hold Altoon Markham tightly, even though she was a perfect stranger. "Altoon has a short-wave radio in her room," my uncle said. "It gets London—all sorts of faraway cities. Ask her to show you how it works, okay?"

"If I like it, will you get me one?"

"It's a deal. I promise."

"Okay," I said. But by this point both my uncle's and Altoon's faces betrayed enough to let me know that something very, very wrong had occurred. My uncle ran from the porch.

"Edward has nice shoes," Altoon Markham said, a statement so at odds with every emotion I felt at the moment that I relied on it.

"I was with him when he bought that pair," I said proudly.

"Which shoe store, Kerr's?"

"Yes, ma'am."

"My, my—well, I'm sure you helped pick them out. And don't you and Edward both have good taste, then? Now, let's sneak into the kitchen now, all right?"

She took my hand, and we walked through the abandoned lobby into the restaurant. She pushed open the white swinging door into the kitchen and walked to the freezer along the back wall. Opening the freezer, she took out containers of three different flavor ice creams. She glanced around and found what she was looking for. "And there's my cake!" she said, pointing to a chocolate cake that already had candles on it. Of course, it was not her cake, there were only half a dozen candles. It was not her birthday. All this occurred to me much later. But Altoon and my uncle had promoted this lie in order to make the distraction more intimate. It worked, because when Altoon said, "Dunsten Brooking especially put so few candles on it, to make me feel better about getting older," I believed her. My uncle had often intimated that everyone who worked at The Lord Nelson Hotel, bellhops, waiters, laundresses, chefs, desk clerks, cleaning ladies, were one big family. They knew secrets about each other, but the secrets never went beyond the porch steps, never got out into Halifax at large. So I felt that Altoon Markham had confided in me. I put my finger to my mouth and said, "Sssshhhh," like I would never tell anyone, ever. Holding the cartons of ice cream, she walked me over to the cake.

"How about we sit at an indoor table?" she said.

"Fine by me," I said. I looked over the flavors. "I'd just like vanilla."

She returned the other two cartons to the freezer. "I'll carry the cake, you take the ice cream. Pick any table that's neat and clean."

A few tables had abandoned lunches on them. I chose a table near the park-side window. Altoon set the cake down, scooped out ice cream onto each of our plates.

"It's the custom that I make a wish," Altoon said, "but guess what?" She reached into the pocket of her white smock, took out a matchbook, and struck a match. Lighting the candles, she said, "I'm going to let you make the wish, DeFoe."

"My stomach hurts."

"Why, DeFoe, and you haven't even had a bite of cake and ice cream."

"I know. But my stomach hurts. I don't want to make a wish."

"Well, eat an eency bit of cake. Then we'll go up to my room. I'll let you find all sorts of countries on the radio." She closed her eyes. "I'll wish something for you, how's that?" She blew out the candles. She cut a slice of cake for each of us. By this time, my stomach was cramping; I actually clutched at it, and Altoon bent over me and said softly, "Come now, darling. Let's go upstairs, all right?"

"I want my mother and father."

"Edward's gone to find them."

We went up to Altoon Markham's room, which I remember to this very day was number 43. I saw the big radio on top of her bureau, but had lost interest in it. I lay right down on Altoon's bed. It had a quilt, rather than the standard hotel chenille bedspread. I noticed right away that Altoon kept her room homey. I was suddenly exhausted and fell asleep. When I woke up, Altoon was ironing a shirt. "Sleepyhead," she said, smiling. "I've brought my work up here, from down in the laundry. I was out of the room just a few minutes. I wouldn't have left you alone for too long. The bellhops helped me lug this stuff upstairs."

There were four or five baskets of laundry on the floor.

"You were out like a light," she said.

"Is my uncle back yet?"

"Not yet, I'm afraid. I mean, I'm not afraid, and he did telephone to say he'd be a while longer. Are you hungry?"

"It's dark out."

"It got dark while you were sleeping. You slept like it was already nighttime, DeFoe. It surprised me. I thought maybe you were sick. I felt your forehead, but no fever."

"My parents were out late last night. I stayed up in the hotel lobby till all hours. My uncle was playing cards. It might have been the latest I ever stayed up."

"That explains it, then," Altoon said, humoring me.

"Probably my mother and father are still helping to lift people up. They're like that."

"Are you hungry?"

"No. And I'm sorry I ruined your birthday party."

"You didn't ruin it at all, young man. This is nice for me. Just the two of us. I think this is nice, don't you? A birthday party, just minus the cake and ice cream, is all. You're very good company, DeFoe. Asleep and awake."

"My mother and father would like you."

"Thank you. Do you help out with the ironing in your house?"

"Not with ironing. Not yet."

"You're old enough to."

"I guess you're right."

"How about this as an idea? You give me the birthday present of letting me teach you how to iron? You might need to know someday."

"That's what you want for your birthday?"

"Good practical know-how. Someday, a woman will admire that in you."

"My mother will, I bet. She'll be surprised I know how to iron."

"Actually, I meant when you were much older."

"That's a lot of clothes you have to iron."

"I do this much every single day, six days a week. But I have some seniority. I can choose which day of the week I'm free. It doesn't have to be on the weekend, either. I like walking around Halifax on a Thursday, for instance."

"You must do my uncle's clothes, then. Since he lives in the hotel."

"Yes, in fact that's how we met, Edward and I. He came downstairs to complain about how I'd ironed his shirts, and I told him they were ironed perfectly well. That was our very first conversation. Quite romantic, eh?"

"My stomach feels much better."

"Strong enough for a lesson now?"

"I think so."

Altoon stood behind me at the ironing board. Mainly she taught me shirts, at first guiding my hand, as I ran the steam iron over a sleeve, back, between buttons. "You learn by doing it," she said. And within half an hour, I had taken over. Though Altoon kept adding detailed instructions, depending on the type of shirt. "Always check for missing buttons," she said. "Sprinkle on too much water, you can actually get deceived and singe a shirt." Things like that.

"How old are you today?" I said, folding a shirt like she had just taught me, setting it in a basket. She was sitting on the bed, paging through a magazine, but still looking distracted.

"Well. I'm thirty-one."

"My mother is thirty-three. My father is thirty-three."

"Oh, dear," Altoon said. "Excuse me." And she hurried into the bathroom, shut the door, ran the water in the sink, trying to drown out her crying. But she did not. I kept on ironing a shirt. It was a blue work shirt, the kind my uncle wore at the train station. Hearing Altoon's sobbing, I did not forgive myself for asking how old she was. My own mother had warned me, "Don't ask a woman her age."

When she came out of the bathroom, Altoon's face looked dreadful. "Can I just lie down on the bed with you, DeFoe? Darling. We've only just met. But I know your uncle Edward quite well. He wouldn't mind. There's nothing shameful about it, really,

is there? It's like I'm your aunt. You can think of it that way. Worn
out after so much ironing, aren't we? Come over here, all right?
It's nighttime. Time to sleep. If you can't sleep, just lie here with
your eyes open."

I crawled over the bed to where Altoon had laid down, and she
turned off the bedside lamp and embraced me. In the pitch dark.
Then, in a short time, by the way she was breathing, I knew she
had fallen asleep. I lay awake awhile. But finally, I think I had
made myself sick and exhausted with nervous premonition, was
why, a few moments later, I so readily slept. And when I woke
again, my uncle was lying asleep crosswise at the end of the bed. I
shook him awake by the shoulders. "What took so long? What
took so long?" I said. "Uncle Edward—"

He sat up. "Oh, DeFoe." Altoon was sleeping soundly. "Nephew,
I've got some bad news."

And then he told me.

I sat in the same place on the bed for at least an hour. I could
not stop shaking. Not crying, shaking. I had the quilt wrapped
around me. It was not cold in the room. It was a summer's night.
The only thing I remember saying was, "I ironed all those shirts."
My uncle went downstairs and returned with a hot cocoa; he
added a healthy dose of rum, which helped knock me out. The
three of us slept with our clothes on, there, on the bed. I woke up
once in the night, groggy, alarmed, and thought, for an embarrassed moment, that I had crawled into bed with my parents the
way I used to when I was three or four. The radio woke me up
early the next morning. "...the zeppelin fell in flames to the
ground about 12:25 p.m. Terrified spectators—" I turned it off. I
saw that my uncle had moved to the rocking chair. He was still
asleep. Altoon was gone. The ironing board and iron and folded
laundry were nowhere in sight. I went downstairs to the lobby.
The newspaper, on its metal stand, had blaring headlines:

ZEPPELIN CRASH KILLS 18 PASSENGERS
AND 5 ON GROUND
CAPTAIN AND CREW PERISH IN ACCIDENT
AT FAIRGROUNDS

The funeral was a week later. I remember that across the cemetery grounds, another victim of the zeppelin crash was being

buried. And when I walked with my uncle and Altoon Markham past that funeral, a boy about my age, standing in front of the casket, caught my eye, and we just stared at each other a fleeting instant. It is odd to admit, but I named him. From that day forward, in my memory, I called him "Paul." I do not in the least know why. The name just flew into my head. That night, lying in my bed—and maybe this is just how an eight-year-old would think—I wondered if he named me.

from *The Ghost of Bridgetown*

A duppy by default, he was drowned, but he came out of the sea. *Never dead*, he said, though who would believe him? *Life raft*, he explained, but his employers—a graying pair, nondescript Anglicans who already spoke of the Will of God to describe his disappearance—now spoke of that same Will to describe his appearance.

He was an unlikely, sunburnt ghost, white-teethed and island-bred. At the request of the local clerics—and for the general benefit of the public—he was installed on a stool and behind a bottle at the Breadfruit Bar. The whole arrangement—bar, stool, man, bottle, beer—sat on Farhall Street. By day, the Breadfruit was a failing bar, an eye in the storm of activity of the street. By night— who knew? The place had a reputation, and each evening, it earned its changeable identity, only to be scrubbed clean in the morning of peanut shells and beer, events and personality.

Charlotte was standing in the airport customs line when she first heard tell of the surprisingly good-willed ghost. She craned her head back to eavesdrop on two women, huskily whispering about a man who spent his evenings laying hands on the ill and blessing children. Apparently, he would tell the story of his life, his time at sea, only if you told your own story, whatever that might be, first. He accepted payment in cigarettes and liquor and an occasional flying fish sandwich.

Charlotte turned to hear more, but the speaker gave her a look, blank with hostility, so she swiveled her head back around, pretended to be deeply engaged in a "You Are Welcome to Barbados—Drugs Are Not" sign.

Later, Charlotte's youthful cabdriver continued the story. "The ghost's age," he started. No one could guess what it was, though his parents, or so the reports went, had specific numbers to offer. He seemed to be, alternately, craggy sage or soft-lipped infant, and sometimes both at once. If you slit your thumb open on a knife, he might heal the wound with a wisp of the tobacco smoke he blew from his mouth.

Charlotte, already wilting in the day's soggy heat, nodded at this. Around her, the island sped by: coconut palms, bamboo, hibiscus. She couldn't name the other trees: one covered with gaudy orange-red blooms, another dark and wispy, smudged against the sky like a charcoal drawing. There were goats tethered to posts, cement-block homes painted pink, turquoise, or peach but weathered into colorlessness, the flat hue of decay. Everywhere, rusted galvanized tin was pieced together to form crooked backyard fences, and there were bars—really no more than shacks built over counters—with reveal-nothing names like "Hideaway" or "T&P." And churches, of course. Moravian. Church of Christ. United Church of Holy America. Salvation Army.

The road the cab was on narrowed and angled towards the water. The first sight of it was a shock, such a vibrant turquoise, and Charlotte allowed herself a pointless exclamation: "Oh, the water." Yes? There was a pause in which the driver waited to hear more. Charlotte offered the required sentence: "It's beautiful." And it was, though otherwise the landscape—both Third World and all too familiar—disappointed. The taxi passed two strip malls, filled, as malls with sixties and seventies architecture were invariably filled, with unglamorous banks and laundromats. The street's gutters were rivulets of papery trash, highlighted with the signature yellow of M&M wrappers.

At a stoplight, three bare-chested men, wearing crocheted wool caps, puffy as popovers, crossed in front of the cab. "Hey," one waved to the driver. *"Hey."* The driver stuck his arm out to grip his friend's hand.

"I tellin' her 'bout da duppy." The driver gestured with his thumb to Charlotte.

"What duppy?"

"Ah, you doan know, mahn?" the driver said, but the light changed color, and he had to wave goodbye without enlightening his friend. It was hard to tell if the exchange was meant to mock her in some obscure way. The pure embarrassment of being white, Charlotte thought, especially here, where it was clear white people were tourists and black people had real lives.

"You doan believe me 'bout da ghost." The cabdriver laughed. "Da ghost a Bridgetown."

Charlotte was about to answer, "Sure I do," when he interrupted to say, "But issa fact." At least, he reported, it was what everyone was saying, and they were saying it often and loudly.

Charlotte smiled and sunk deeper into her seat, hugged her arms, as if that might hide her skin color from the general observer. "I'm here on business," she wanted to announce. And it was true: she was using her art history background to do some research for Howard, her lawyer-grandfather, trying to help him settle a repatriation dispute about a menorah. It was unclear to whom it should be returned: the island Jews or the island blacks who'd originally fashioned the piece. But Charlotte's true purpose hardly mattered; she'd have said anything to convince the driver she wasn't who he took her to be. "For Christ's sake, why do you care?" she could hear her sister, Helen, say. And she'd be right to ask. This desire to be above reproach was dumb for a thousand reasons. But even Helen—breezy, loud-mouthed Helen—had felt it. Just four months ago, in the hospital, at the end, she'd said to their mother, "But I'm a good girl, aren't I? Aren't I?"

Inside the Hilton, Charlotte's room—pleasantly cool with air-conditioning—was standard issue with a few tropical touches: a bamboo headboard on the bed, a gift basket of fruit on the dresser, a sliding glass door that opened onto a small concrete patio, overlooking a white, spacious beach. Below, black women wearing brightly colored headdresses dunked themselves into the sea. There was something oddly ritualistic about their play, as if they were actually baptizing one another. As a girl, Charlotte had been on family vacations that seemed to require the same false cheer as this hotel. Disneyland, she remembered, had made her sick with grief, a guilty depression padded after her as she shook Pluto's hand and pretended to enjoy riding a dumb little boat through a world of singing dolls. The only fantasy that could engage her was of *working* at Disneyland, sitting in an overheated booth and dispensing tickets. Even now, only work—or the illusion of it—appealed, so she stepped back out of her room with a self-imposed assignment: She would find the synagogue before dark.

She walked, along the crumbling edge of a road, into Bridgetown. Narrow, toy-like cars chugged past her. At intervals, a white van—some sort of bus?—gave a double-noted beep, and a black man, early twenties at the oldest, emerged from a passenger-side window to make a "Ride?" gesture with his forefinger. She shook her head, No and No, but came to regret it. The heat only increased with her distance from the hotel. After ten minutes, her clothes—none too roomy in the first place—were slicked to her. And what with the sunscreen she'd slathered over herself, she felt filthy. She'd had sun poisoning as a teenager, spent a full week before college lying on the cool tiles of her family's bathroom, rising only to vomit or gross her sister out with the large pieces of tissue she pulled from her back. An experience she didn't intend to repeat, so even with the sunscreen on, she darted from one side of the street to the other, keeping, best as she could, to the shade from the second-floor porches that hung over the narrow sidewalks. Occasionally one of the buildings would open on a small market, selling little more than soda and chips, but most of the places she passed were sealed up. On the buildings' second floors, signs stuck out like file-folder tabs: Bayview Jazz, The Club, 'Round Midnight. Once things got dark, she supposed, the street would be hopping. "Don't," the hotel's desk clerk had warned her, "walk back here at night." And Charlotte saw how what was now harmless could feel seedy without sunshine: something about the slight sag of the buildings and the semi-secrecy of an upstairs club, the vague feeling that what *really* went on here happened in places that were hard to find—there being no clear map to the illicit.

Eventually, she came to a harbor and then a bridge, which led to the rush of activity that was the city: New York's 14th Street meets the tropics meets St. Moritz. She passed a glittery watch store, then an alley littered with cardboard boxes and coconut husks, only to run into two schoolgirls, neatly dressed in their pretty blue pinafores, looking into the window of House of Deals. A familiar, greasy smell wafted past her. A Kentucky Fried Chicken.

She was ambling, but heading—more or less—toward the synagogue, though the building eluded her. Finally, Charlotte stopped at a stand to ask for directions.

"What you like?" prompted the vendor.

"Oh, nothing, nothing," Charlotte said, "but..." She held out her map. "Can you tell me where this is?"

"You're right there."

"Really?" Charlotte looked around. "Do you know where the synagogue is?"

"The what?"

"A..." Charlotte stopped. Suddenly "synagogue" seemed like the most exotic word in the world. "A temple. You know, like a church for Jewish people?"

The man shrugged but kept smiling at her in a vaguely lascivious way.

"Hmm," Charlotte said and pulled her top from her sweaty chest. "It's supposed to be around here somewhere. Well, never mind," she chirped, happy to wander farther if it would remove her from the man's stare.

Charlotte was soon lost again. Not that she didn't know where she was; she knew exactly where she was. And according to her map, she should have been within arm's reach of a stack of yarmulkes, kissing distance from a Torah. But she wasn't.

Of course, Howard might just have neglected to tell her that this particular synagogue was invisible. As a girl, Charlotte had had a recurring dream about an invisible clubhouse, a place that only revealed itself once you went inside, but then you discovered it wasn't a place where you wanted to be; it was strewn with the remnants of a desperate fight, clothes and broken furniture and, most horribly, a chunk of someone's hair with a bit of the scalp still attached.

"Miss," a voice called as Charlotte stepped off the curb. Charlotte turned to see a straggly fellow with one of those never-trimmed beards that makes a man look insane. Was he talking to her? Apparently sensing an opportunity in her hesitation, the man rocked forward, like a clown punching balloon. "Can I have some money?" he said, bobbing back.

"I'm sorry." Charlotte turned abruptly and crossed the street, but the man followed, coming right up to her ear and pleading, like any disappointed child, "Please. Please. Pllleaasse." He was so close, a drop of his spit landed in her ear. Charlotte stopped short, slapped at her ear, and said, firmly, both words quick and hard, "Sir, no," before she continued on.

Behind her, the man whined, in a hurt, baby voice, "You don't have to be so sell-fish."

At a different point in her life, Charlotte might have considered the charge, but now she turned and said, "You don't know anything about my life. So fuck off, mister."

But the man was already out of earshot.

A vendor, sitting in a sagging lawn chair, under a blue umbrella and beside a cart lined with plastic syrup bottles, looked up and said, "Don't trouble yourself. He a bad man. These people," he gestured with his chin in the direction of the beggar, "there's a greediness to them. They eat too much and beg too much. Just enjoy yourself. Enjoy your time in Barbados."

Charlotte flushed. This was somehow worse than the beggar. "Okay," she said, "I'm sorry," and hurried away.

Back on Broad Street, the city's narrow main thoroughfare, she stopped for juice in a tiny, overly air-conditioned mall. Inside, a line of men were waiting to play something that looked like the Lotto. Her creepy drink in hand—sorrel juice, she shouldn't have experimented again—she sat down on a sticky bench and studied her map, trying to figure out where she'd been. Her eye settled on a street name. Farhall. Why was *that* so familiar? A cigar brand? But then she remembered: the street which housed the Breadfruit, the bar which claimed the duppy each night. It was only a few blocks away. Why not abandon the search for the synagogue and pay a visit?

True, Charlotte wasn't a believer, never had been, but ghosts. They...attracted her. Or, belief in ghosts did. What enticed her was the metaphysics of the matter. Wouldn't it change your sense of what death was? And why didn't people ever talk about *that*?

Charlotte shivered. It was freezing in this tiny mall. Her juice was repulsively cold. She looked for a place to toss it, but there were no bathrooms anywhere, so she placed the full cup on top of a garbage can. As she turned to leave, a young man called something at her.

"What?" Charlotte said.

The man stepped closer to repeat himself. It was the beggar from before! He brought his face so near Charlotte thought he might kiss her. She jumped back. His lips were chapped and bleeding. Was he reproving her for buying a juice, a drink she didn't even want, instead of giving him her change?

"Don't be scared of Barbados," he laughed, darting his face towards her again.

"I'm not," she said, jerking her head back and walking purposefully out the door and into the early evening warmth, a comfortable blanket after the chill of the air-conditioning.

Everyone, she thought foolishly, as if a horde had just descended on her, *leave me alone.* She was on the edge of tears, not because the fright from the man had been so serious, but because she felt dreadful for still being capable of fear. The worst had already happened. What right did she have to flinch at anything else?

The sun was starting to lower. Charlotte checked her watch. It was only 5:20. Back home, it wouldn't darken for hours. So Farhall. Charlotte didn't need to believe the duppy story to check it out. No one else seemed to. *Rumors, rumors:* they entertained but didn't persuade. This was an Anglican island, after all, and in these first few hours meandering the streets, Charlotte saw that there was a reserve to people here. They didn't meet your eyes, and the evidence of those to whom she had talked aside, they seemed to have the kind of British propriety that Charlotte associated with the eminently sensible. Still, she couldn't help but want to find the people who weren't, those who really did believe, even if they were, like palm readers in Manhattan, a slub in the regular fabric of island life.

She pushed down the street, past "Amen Alley," a tiny passage, cut off from the light of day. Charlotte could just make out two men filleting fleshy fish on a lopsided wooden table. The image pleased her into wishing she was the woman waiting to receive those fillets, to fry them up. A simple dinner, the end to a simple day. But then a spider hit her arm, and its frantic scramble as she brushed it away depressed her. Fish, bugs: everything wanted life. No surprise there, but still, she didn't want to be reminded. Only last night, while she was half-watching late-night TV, the hysterical cowering of some bad guy in front of a gun made her feel like disintegrating.

The streets led to increasingly narrow roads till she came to Farhall. She walked the length of it, but no Breadfruit Bar appeared. How irritating to be stumped, twice in one day. But she was also relieved. The city's atmosphere had changed perceptibly in the last half hour: things closing up, groups of men clustering around sidewalk domino games. And all the stores, as if by some agreement with the hour, seemed to have become betting places or bars, each an entirely male province. She could hardly imagine entering one. But then, as she was turning for the harbor, she looked down an alley and saw a pile of sand. So the bar *was* on Farhall, but on the alley side of the street.

Earlier, Charlotte's cabdriver had told her that every morning, locals came with plastic buckets and created a virtual sandbox in front of the Breadfruit's door. A duppy, he explained, wouldn't enter a building without first counting all the grains of sand at the door, and, math whiz or no, your average duppy couldn't do that before daybreak, the hour when all duppies are due back at their graves. But the ghost of Bridgetown . . . apparently, he hadn't so much as flinched at the sand. He'd stepped right over the pile and into the bar. He'd ordered himself a beer and insisted, once again, that he'd never died.

Charlotte hesitated before entering the alley; it felt too private, like someone's backyard, though halfway down, there was an "Open" sign poking out like the flag on a trick gun. Below it, a child's shovel, fluorescent pink, was upended in the ineffectual sand hill. The toy gave Charlotte courage, but then at the bar door, she faltered again. Perhaps the "ghost" wouldn't be around? And what did she want from him, anyway? Some confirmation that her skepticism was faulty, that death was a pleasure, and that the community of the dead was so chummy that when he returned to the grave, he'd be able to greet Helen? Stupid, Charlotte thought, and yet she peeked into the bar with something close to expectation.

It was a single room, unadorned, save for a handful of wooden tables to the right and a bar to the left. It didn't seem to be a frightening place, which is to say it looked more like a sandwich shop than a place for hard drinkers, honeymooners, or men on the make. At one table, two women fanned their babies with menus.

Charlotte pulled a *Time* magazine out of her bag, thinking she'd pretend to read while she eavesdropped, but she didn't have to wait long for information.

"It's the duppy," the bartender said as soon as she took a stool at the bar. He gestured to the room's only other white person, a man sitting two stools away.

"Oh, really?" Charlotte lifted the damp hair from the back of her neck. Above, a ceiling fan creaked noisily but offered no real relief.

Next to the white man, a patron with a closely cropped beard, linen pants, and narrow red suspenders leaned back on his stool to call over to Charlotte, "He's no duppy."

The white man reached up to pluck at one of the red suspenders, as if it were a bass string. "Sit down, Greg," the white man said cheerfully. "Sit down and shut up." He rolled his eyes at Charlotte, as if she were in on the joke of Greg.

Charlotte smiled and looked back at her magazine. Greg came over to see what she was reading. "News," he said dismissively. "I'm a reporter," he added, swallowing a burp. "And I'll let you in on a secret. I'll give you a lead. Here's news." He pointed at the white man. "It's the Will of God." He laughed once derisively.

"Just call me Will," the white man said, rolling his eyes once again, as if he'd already identified Charlotte as someone who could appreciate foolishness, without engaging in it.

"Will. Hi." Charlotte turned to the bartender. "Could I get a . . . ?" she pointed to a glass of whiskey someone had abandoned at the bar, and he nodded.

She tried to take Will in without appearing to look. There was a delicate roundness to his face, a cap of dark hair. He was a handsome man . . . almost pretty in that long-eyelashed, slim-bodied way that some men had. "You're?" he asked.

"Oh, sorry," she said, as if waking from a doze. "I'm Charlotte."

"This is Greg," Will offered, pointing to the reporter at his right, "and Winston," gesturing to a third man, silent all this while, sitting next to Greg. Charlotte nodded a hello. Greg offered a goofy, absentminded grin, but Winston did nothing. Reserve or hostility? Charlotte couldn't read his studious silence, so at odds with his dress: black pants and vest, a white shirt open to just above the navel. He seemed about Will's age—somewhere in his twenties. Greg had to be older. The hairs at the bottom of his beard had begun to whiten. He almost looked like an elf who'd dipped his chin in a vat of milk.

"What you looking at?" Greg barked at her, his fingers playing quick little trills on the bartop as he waited for an answer. The question didn't seem rude, exactly, but some mixture of authoritative—*he* knew what was going on—and ironic—he knew what he thought about what was going on.

"Nothing," Charlotte said. "Sorry," and then she took several quick sips of her drink.

She glanced down at her magazine then back up at Will. It seemed clear that all the stories about the duppy were a joke. Anyone could see he was no sage. He was a kid, despite the patch of hair thinning in the back and the high rise of skin at his temples. She guessed he was a fisherman or a day laborer, because he had the body for it and also the clothes, the nondescript blue jeans with the plain blue shirt.

"Yes, I heard you were a duppy," Charlotte offered tentatively. She still wasn't sure she wanted to get drawn into conversation. "But you look—what can I say?—decidedly corporeal to me."

"It's a case of mistaken identity," Will shrugged and slipped a cigarette out from the cuff of his shirt. "Like one? They're wrinkled, but..." He palmed one over.

She took it but said, "No, no, I don't smoke," and turned the cigarette over, tapped the wood of the bar with it. Her head hurt slightly from the day's sun, and she felt a little odd, as if she were playing at being sophisticated.

"Okay." He reached over to take the cigarette back, carefully returning it to his shirt's sleeve. Charlotte thought of someone replacing a vein. He was Frankenstein, building himself up after a temporary loss of a part.

Charlotte couldn't figure out where to put her eyes, so she looked back down at her magazine, tried to find a hard-news article to read, though normally she worked her way from the gossip through the arts before pushing herself through the economic and political news. It would help if she had a man with her. He'd be like protection, declaring her interest to be decidedly nonsexual, though, in fact, Will had the manner and look of the men on whom she always had crushes. "Working-class heroes," her college roommate used to call them, then laugh at Charlotte, who was so clearly an urban intellectual, destined for the professions.

"Hey," Greg shouted, and Charlotte looked over, as if he were going to reprove her again for staring, but his words were directed elsewhere—at a second white man, just entering the bar. The newcomer sported a broad-brimmed cowboy hat and a leisure suit jacket, both a pale eggshell brown. He had a substantial "generosity," Helen and Charlotte's term for the prominent belly that some men wore like a pillow strapped under their belts. For some reason, this particular distribution of fat always seemed arrogant to Charlotte, though she knew that wasn't fair.

"Hi, all," the man said.

From Texas, Charlotte decided. There was a slight twang to his voice. The man called out to Will. "So you're back from converting the heathen."

"You know I was just along for the ride," Will said. He used the thumb of one hand to move across the back of the other, cracking each knuckle along the way. "Nothing wrong with a little gainful employment." He turned to Charlotte and explained, "I was a cook on a charter boat. I had a little accident, and now I'm okay. That's why everyone's saying I'm a duppy."

"Where are they?" Charlotte said. "I mean, the people from the boat."

"Oh, other side of the island. They put in a call. 'Glad to hear you're alive,' and so on."

"But you've seen them?"

"No," Will said. "I've only been back for a couple of weeks."

"I'm sorry," Charlotte said.

"What's to be sorry about?"

Charlotte shook her head. He seemed, suddenly, very young to her, perhaps because he appeared so unaffected by his brush with death. It made her think she'd better be going. There was nothing to learn here.

"Hey," Will started, as if something had just occurred to him. "Do you play poker?"

"Sometimes."

"Fantastic, then we've got a game," he announced to the men surrounding him.

"Let's do it." Greg slapped the bar then stepped unsteadily to the back of the room. Charlotte watched him disappear through a wood door.

"We were going to play," Will explained to Charlotte, almost apologetically. There was something odd about the way he was talking to her, as if she weren't a stranger, but someone whom he had in his care for the evening. "We set up a little table on the patio." He cocked his head toward the door.

"Oh," Charlotte began, gripping her magazine to indicate that it was something she needed to get back to, "I'm not much of a card shark."

"Why don't you play, anyway?" Will said. "Game's starting, and we'd never forgive ourselves if we left you to these jokers." His head jerked back. "You can quit whenever you want."

Charlotte considered this for a moment. She had come for Will's story, yet here she was hesitating. For a brief while in college, she had thought she'd be a journalist, but it was this very sort of timidity that stopped her. She knew she'd always be too frightened to get the scoop. But what was there really to be frightened of here? Or anywhere? she reminded herself, thinking of the man with the bleeding lips and then of Helen, lying in the ICU and noticing, for the first time, a huge bloody bruise that had been on her arm for days. She'd jumped when she'd seen it, startled by how painful it looked, then nodded back into sleep.

"Okay," Charlotte said. Perhaps she had decided too hastily that there was nothing to learn here. Didn't her first impressions tend to be untrustworthy? And anyway, it wasn't late. She could play a few hands without destroying her plans for the evening—which were, essentially, to sleep, so she could get an early start tomorrow. "Why not?"

Out on the patio, Greg was turning over a bucket to use as a table. He could have dragged in any one of the tables from the barroom floor, but, Charlotte supposed, this made the gathered feel makeshift and grubby in a way that proved they were men, stubborn people with no use for arrangements. Card sharks...no less skillful and conniving for the sandwich-shop atmosphere, the lushness of the vegetation growing by the peach-colored patio walls.

"Let's leave this open," she said and slid a rock under the door to the bar. If she was going to be the only woman on the patio, she wanted easy access to those inside, particularly the middle-aged mothers rolling dewy Coke bottles over their foreheads, the ones with T-shirts that proclaimed "150 Years of Witness: Greenbay Moravian Church."

Silent Winston and the man in the hat stepped onto the patio. "This is Edward," Will said. The man in the hat gave a half-bow.

"What this?" Winston pointed his chin at Charlotte. "I don't want none of this."

"Put a cork in it," Edward snapped, his Texas twang even more pronounced than before. "Put a couple corks in it."

"I don't want none of you no neither, brother."

Charlotte looked at Will, but he was busying himself with the poker chips. Charlotte supposed she should get angry, not on behalf of herself, but on behalf of her sex, but she didn't feel like a worthwhile representative of her sex at the moment. She wasn't very good at cards. She wasn't going to upset all stereotypes about women with her hard-assed poker game.

"Don't pay him no mind," Greg said.

"I think we should let her play," Will suggested, almost sweetly. "What do you think, Winston?"

" 'Kay," Winston said sullenly and slid into one of the five chairs that Greg had drawn up to the bucket. " 'Cause she friends with the duppy."

"He isn't a fuckin' duppy," Greg said.

"Thank you," Charlotte offered, ingratiatingly. She could feel herself focusing on Winston. She always wanted to win over people who didn't like her.

"Cut," Winston said and placed the pack of cards in front of her. Charlotte took the chair opposite him and did as he said. Winston leaned back and ran his fingers along a gold chain that he had fished out from under his white shirt.

"Let me sit by the lady," Edward insisted and installed himself between Charlotte and Greg. At her right, Will smiled. It was a suspicious smile, and Charlotte suddenly wondered if she'd been drawn into an elaborate con, but then that seemed stupid. It wasn't like they were going to get any money out of her. She was a conservative player. She'd fold if she didn't think she could win.

Will started dealing the cards, quickly shooting them into five stacks.

"Let's see, let's see," he said. "Seven-card stud. High-low. Deuces wild."

"This a joke?" Winston snapped.

"No joke, sir."

"The woman, and now this."

"He thinks," Greg said, apparently by way of explanation for Will, "the wild-card crap is for sissies."

Winston gave him a long look and said flatly, "He read da mind."

"My deal. We'll play my way. Your deal, we'll play yours. How's that?" Will said.

Winston shook his head and looked at the floor, mumbled, "Some duppies is rude, mahn."

"Okay, okay," Greg said edgily, "I give the sun only about ten more minutes till it completely disappears." He gave an appraising glance up at the square patch, the blue-gray ceiling, that capped the patio. "So, let's go."

As they played, Will talked up the hand. "Looking like two sweet cousins, two jack of all trades for my friend here," he chimed once Greg had two face cards up. And later: "Those cousins still leading. You going to make your bet?"

"Yeah," Greg said and lit up a cigarette. The chips went in, clink, clink, clink. Charlotte was used to playing for peanut M&Ms with Helen and her parents, back when she was a kid, and always stayed in the game, if only to be a good sport, to make it more fun; back when the loser wasn't the worst player but the person who couldn't keep from eating the profits.

The first hand went to Will.

"Hmm," Charlotte said as Will gave her the pack of cards. Her deal. "It'll be five-card draw."

"No fun," said Will.

Winston just snorted, and Edward said, "That's the way."

Charlotte shuffled clumsily. When she was ten, it had been enough to simply scramble the cards all over the table then gather them up.

"Look at that," Edward said now as she awkwardly smashed the two halves of the deck together.

"I know, I know," Charlotte nodded. "Let's see ... most people could do it better with one hand, right? Most people could do it better with two feet? How's that?"

"Couldn't have said it better myself," Edward allowed.

Charlotte took a sip of her drink. She was a little drunk and grateful for the feeling. Already she could hear herself, back home, at some party, bragging about joining the locals in a poker game.

They played a few hands in relative silence. When there was conversation, it focused on the game. Finally, a gap-toothed woman with the round, too-large head of an infant came out and placed a large candle on the ground by the bucket. Ominous shadows licked Will's face. "Ah, I can see the cards now," he smiled at the woman. A spidery blood clot floated in the white of her right eye.

"I'll sit out a few hands," Charlotte said, and when no one acknowledged her words, added, "I need another drink." She could see it was the only acceptable explanation for getting up. Inside, she paid the bartender and asked, "How do I get a cab?"

"Oh," he said, waving his hand, "no trouble. I call you one." He said he'd let her know when it came.

Back outside, in the candlelight of the patio, Charlotte tried, unsuccessfully, to bluff a hand. This made the men hoot with laughter.

"She keepa da straight face," Winston punched Will to say.

"Oh, shut up," she said, exasperated.

This was even funnier. "She tell me to shut up da mouth."

Charlotte brushed a fly from her ear. All she could think about was how wonderful a bath would be. She tried to focus back in on the game. Who was winning? Who losing? she wondered with little real concern, then a pattern seemed to be developing. She got interested. Was it or was it not true that Will won every hand he dealt? Surely, Charlotte couldn't be the only one who noticed this.

"What you want?" Winston suddenly demanded.

"What?" Greg said.

"Drink," Winston spit.

Greg tapped his temple and said, "Okay. Okay. I'm drinking gin." He palmed over a large bill.

Winston hadn't touched a drop of liquor all evening, but he seemed to have a fascination with making sure everyone else had what they needed.

"You?" Winston asked Charlotte. It was the first time he'd spoken directly to her.

"I'm through for the night," she said.

"I'll come with." Greg stood.

"Yeah, Winston can't be trusted with change when he's losing," Edward said and followed the other two men into the bar.

Will pushed his chair toward Charlotte's. The inside of his knee knocked against hers. Accident or not? she wondered and left her knee pressing his. Her cab would be here soon. She could do what she wanted.

"Let me teach you something while they're gone," he said conspiratorially. Charlotte thought she'd like him better if he faltered a bit when he spoke, if his hair were longer and fell sloppily in his eyes.

"I *know* how to play," she said.

"Oh, I know you do." He shuffled the deck slowly.

"I just have bad luck." It was true; she never won at games of chance.

"And I . . . ," he fingered the deck, "have good luck."

"I don't need your kind of luck, thank you," Charlotte said.

"What's *that* supposed to mean?"

"Nothing," Charlotte breathed softly, willing herself all the courage to spit out the word *cheat*.

"Don't you believe in luck?" he said.

"No, I guess not. Not really. Unless it's bad." She laughed, though she was thinking that she reminded herself of the sort of cynical women who sit late at bars, talking of old husbands, old hurts, who sit and lick their wounds. A contest. Whose wounds went deeper? Who could add cancers and rapes, muggings and untimely deaths, peculiar accidents, exploding pumpkins and crazed, man-eating guppies to the rest? In fact, Charlotte had never met a woman like this. And yet she was driven in fear of becoming one. The whole cartoon catalogue: shrying bitch, whore, ice cube, prima donna, just-one-of-the-guys girls, fag hag. Stupid terms, all of them. She knew that, but it didn't matter.

"No, no, I'm serious," Will was saying. Where *was* her cab? "I'm talking about luck. Do you or don't you believe in it?"

Charlotte shrugged. Maybe *this* was what she'd come for.

"It's a matter of concentration. Let me tell you a story. When I was a kid, I could fix broken clocks. All sorts of clocks. Grandfather, cuckoo. I'd just concentrate and . . . there it was. One day, I'm sitting in the back seat of my dad's car. He's driving around with this lady in the front. I still don't know who she was. We've got this clock in a paper bag that we're taking over to the Salvation Army."

Charlotte wondered for a moment what it could possibly be like to have a childhood on this island.

"I'm thinking, 'Sure, we'll have to fix it right up or the army won't want us.'" He laughed. "I don't know what I was thinking. I was a kid. So, I set to thinking about fixing that thing, and soon enough, there's a tic-tic sound along with the steady hum of the motor, and this woman in the front starts screaming, 'What're you doing? What're you doing? How'd you do that?' And then I see that what I've done is out of the ordinary, and that very knowledge... it's like a loss of innocence, if you see what I mean. I couldn't do it anymore."

Charlotte nodded. What she thought was *Simpleton*, but what she said was "I see."

"You believe me, don't you?"

"Well, I—" she hesitated. "I guess I don't. But I believe that *you* believe."

"Oh, well, *that's* flattering." He pushed his chair back a few inches. Charlotte looked down at her hands. "Well," Will leaned forward again, "don't you believe that there are things we humans don't know about?"

"Of course." Charlotte straightened up in her chair. Here it was. The other person acted stupid, you acted smart. They acted smart, you fairly drooled a reply. Can't have two people in power. Everyone knew that. Also, can't have two people out of power... a lesser-known fact. "Obviously, I know we're limited by our way of perceiving the world. We've only got our eyes and ears and hands to go by, and, who knows, if we had something else, there probably would be a whole other world, a whole thing outside even our limited notions of worlds or..." Now she was getting lost in her own thought; she tried to start again. "If we didn't need our bodies to receive all this data for us—"

"I didn't *go* to college," Will interrupted. "What I'm asking is," he paused, "don't you think there are unspoken forces?"

Charlotte felt a sudden panic. What she thought was: *He's asking me to go to bed.* But, then, that seemed ridiculous.

Before she answered, she twisted her long hair into a rope and pulled it across one shoulder. Was she neatening herself up for him? "I don't think you can make a clock work by concentrating... or win poker, for that matter."

"But, come on. Don't you think sometime, there's just this thing—" Will looked up and searched the sky, now freckled with the night's first stars, for the thing, or word, for which he was looking.

"I'm sorry," Charlotte said, and she was, sorry she couldn't agree with him or pretend to agree. His enthusiasm, his desperation for convincing her... there was all that to appreciate. And if she could honestly assent, the world wouldn't be what she thought it was; Helen would be, somehow, okay, deeply okay. She'd be in the afterworld, having a ball with all the virtuous dead: her grandparents and a childhood friend who'd died of leukemia. But who could buy this?

"Come on," Will whispered.

"Let's stop this," Charlotte said, almost frightened.

"No, wait." His chair screeched against the floor as he moved it nearer again. "Don't you believe that there are forces between people? Don't you? And you can't see them? And you can't hear them, but they can make things happen?"

"Yes, but..." He looked at her. "Emotions aren't magic," she said flatly.

"So, you do admit it, that there's something there?"

Please, she thought, *please.* If he went just a bit further, she thought she'd cry.

"Or maybe you don't believe in it?"

Love, she thought he meant now. It was hard to hold on to what they were talking about. *Passion.* Or maybe you're *one of them.* Senseless virgins... that's what she'd have to avoid seeming like now.

"Don't you believe in *that*? Don't you?" he whispered one final time, then snapped his back into his chair. Winston, Edward, and Greg had returned.

Charlotte pulled at the skin of her lower lip. He was saying, *Don't you believe in love? And passion? Don't you? Or maybe you believe I didn't fix that clock in that car?* But it was an either/or situation. She was Dickens's Miss Havisham, Faulkner's Rosa Caufield. Or a believer. There was no in-between.

"A cab came for you," Edward said.

"Oh," Charlotte started to stand.

"Sit, sit." Winston patted the air, as if it contained an imaginary dog.

"We told it to come back later," Edward said innocently. There was no apparent sense, on his part, that this might be read as a hostile, even threatening action.

"I need to go," Charlotte said but didn't stand.

"No trouble," Winston said.

"It'll come back," Edward coughed. "When the game's over." He placed a whiskey in front of her. "For you. It's on me."

"God," Charlotte said. "What time is it?" Her watch—she knew she'd checked it earlier—wasn't on her wrist.

"Early still. We're almost through," Will said.

"I'm going to sit a few more out," Charlotte decided. But no one seemed to much care. For a while, she thought about phone calls she might make tomorrow, then she tried to concentrate on the game. Will had folded, so he looked up, raised his eyebrows, then reached behind the bucket to drum his index finger lightly on the back of Charlotte's hand. She looked down. He was pointing, very slightly, to her left. At once, Charlotte saw what he was trying to show her. The ornate, ivory handle of a handgun was peeking out of Edward's suit-jacket pocket. Charlotte started.

Helen, if she were here, would whisper, "He loves it. Thinks it's a second dick. You should see how he's decorated the first one."

Responding to Charlotte's movement, Edward looked up and smirked. "Ever been to Montana?" he asked.

"Once, yes," she said. "Once I was in Bozeman." This was a lie, but Helen had been there. Charlotte found herself doing this a lot lately, appropriating Helen's life. Only last month, she'd cut her finger while slicing a carrot. At the emergency ward, squeezing her hand in a dish towel and answering the intake nurse's questions, she'd given her age, automatically, as twenty-six, then said, "I mean, thirty." The nurse had given her a queer look. "Wishful thinking, I guess," Charlotte grinned queasily.

"Well," Edward folded his hand and turned purposefully to Charlotte, "Bozeman, that ain't real country. Where I'm from is real country. Up in the mountains. Bozeman..." He turned from Charlotte and spit at the floor.

That, Charlotte hoped, would say it all, but then he turned back to her and said, "You can hear mountain lions up there. Ever hear a mountain lion?"

"No, I guess I haven't."

"It sounds like a woman screaming, if you know what I mean, just like a woman screaming, if you see what I'm saying."

Charlotte looked at her knees. Her skin felt too sensitive. Yes, she knew what he was saying.

"What I mean," he said, in case it was not entirely clear, "is it sounds like a woman screaming at the height of passion. You see?"

"Ante up," Will said in a disapproving voice. It was his deal.

And then a shot fired; Charlotte jumped at the sound, imagining she could hear it, even after the initial shock, ringing through the narrow streets outside, bouncing from building to building to the street, and never once finding the sky to escape.

"My God," Charlotte said, tears springing embarrassingly to her eyes. *I want to go home,* she thought. *Right now.*

She picked up her drink to hide her reaction, but her hands were trembling, so she set it immediately back down. She'd had way too much, and her drunkenness descended on her quite suddenly, like some dirty, gauzy garment she now had to wear.

"It's only a firecracker," Will said.

"Some festival," Greg explained. "It starts at midnight. You walk backwards into the water for good luck or to clean your soul of sins or something like that. A religion thing," he added dismissively.

"I've never heard of that," Will said.

"I saw some people," Charlotte offered, and tried to talk very carefully, clinically, to prove to herself that she wasn't drunk. "Outside my hotel room? They were doing something in the ocean. I mean, it looked like they were baptizing people in the ocean."

"Probably the Tie-heads," Greg said. The reporter. He would know. "Colorful clothes?"

Charlotte nodded. Too broadly, she thought, and pulled her chin to a halt.

"The Spiritual Baptists. I think they do that. Right?" Greg turned to Will.

He shrugged. "How the hell would I know?"

Water made Charlotte think again of a bath. How nice it would be to get clean. She really felt terrible now and had that vague sense of her skin as being insufficient, as if she couldn't count on it, not tonight, to hold her together. If she stood, who knew what organs might drop to the floor?

"Okay," Will said. "Another game of seven-card stud." Charlotte didn't even look down at the cards Will dealt her. "I'll be right back," she said to no one in particular. "Nope, nothing there," she heard Will say as she stood.

She knew she had to step carefully now. How had this happened? Greg had brought her a third drink, and she'd sipped it, even though she hadn't wanted it, because she couldn't figure out what to do with her hands. Or had it been a fourth?

Inside, she again asked the bartender to call her a cab. "Please don't let him leave," she smiled. She wondered if he could tell she was drunk. She felt suddenly exhausted by everything—the traveling, the conversation with Will, even her own embarrassment.

"Bathroom?" she asked, and the bartender pointed to a door in the corner.

It was small and old, but, thankfully, clean, with those brown paper towels that smelled so horrible when they got wet.

She set the water running. Her face, in the tiny mirror above the bathroom, was pale and twisted into a mask of pure irritation. Charlotte tried to settle her face into expressionlessness. Even so, she saw that there was something hopelessly stupid about the fatuous flesh that ran along her jawbone to her ears. The unnecessary softness seemed greedy. *I want, I want.* Even her cheeks were petitioners. *You don't have to be so sell-fish. Oh, God,* she thought. *I hate myself.* She leaned her forehead against the wall and started to cry.

When she stopped, she looked up at her stained face and thought of something she'd heard, years ago, when she'd seen a production of *The Dybbuk.* In the play, the water stains on the synagogue's walls were the building's tears, its sorrow over the sad moral state of the Jews.

Charlotte burned herself when she went to test the sink's water. The short, sharp pain almost set her to crying again, but she added cold water, and when it felt right, she scrubbed her face with a small bar of white soap.

Okay, she thought to herself. She was settling down. *Okay.* This was how she always ended her crying jags, with the sense that she'd just retreated from a fistfight and found, despite her breathlessness, that her wounds weren't so bad.

She stepped back to look at herself in the mirror. Her top was pasted with sweat to her breasts, each nipple clearly outlined in white cotton. She groaned and pulled the fabric off her chest.

The door to the bathroom cracked open. "Someone's in here," Charlotte called, but the door continued to open, and she quickly brushed the back of her hands over her cheeks, as if some tears might still be there despite her fierce scrubbing. It was Will, pushing the door open with his blue-jeaned hips, then elbowing it closed.

"You okay?" he asked. "You all right?"

Her eyes had started to tear again. She turned from the mirror, and, in that watery space between them, it seemed he was swimming to her.

"Are you all right?" he asked again and put his arms on her shoulders. "We're all your friends here. Don't worry."

"Thank you," Charlotte sniffed and crossed her arms over her breasts.

"It's okay," Will said. Next to her, he was just her height, smaller than he'd seemed before, and she found this frightening. How could she have expected answers from someone who was so negligible in the flesh?

"Thanks, Will," Charlotte said cheerfully, to undercut the intimacy of the situation. She knew she should ask him to go.

Will laughed. "I've got a real name. It's Henry."

The water was still running in the sink, and Henry reached behind her to wet his hands. He rubbed his palms over his face. "This what you doing? Washing up?" Charlotte nodded. He dipped his hand into the water again and said, raising his eyebrows, "I could help."

"Oh." Charlotte felt too panicked to say anything more. So he had been flirting with her, after all. "I," she started, leaning her hip against the edge of the sink. She felt flattered. If someone as attractive as Henry would consider her, then maybe she wasn't so bad. Naïve, Charlotte knew, but there it was. Maybe her problem wasn't that she was a female type but a male type; the guy who thought a beautiful woman on his arm signaled his own attractiveness.

"This okay?" Henry said, and she nodded her head yes. He moved toward her. "You're really...you know, you're..." He waved his hand. She saw she was supposed to fill in the blank with a compliment. So what? Beautiful? Special? Vertical?

Charlotte laughed and rolled her eyes. "You, too."

"Me?" Henry said, placing a wet hand on her neck. "Naah. I'm a dime a dozen."

He leaned in to kiss her.

"Um," Charlotte said, pulling back. "What's your last name?"

Henry smiled, and before he answered, she let herself imagine their life together, self-deception of this sort being her prerequisite for sex. The future, as she saw it, involved an alarming amount of sunburn.

"Lazar," Henry said.

Jewish? Charlotte wondered. That might be awkward, given her reason for being here. But he didn't *look* Jewish.

"Well," she said, mock-satisfied, "*now* I know everything." He leaned forward again to kiss her, placing his warm lips on her own and his tongue, quickly and deeply, into her mouth. A kiss that wasn't a prelude to sex so much as an assumption of it. Charlotte felt this was the moment for a decision on her part, but all she thought was that she probably tasted like alcohol, even though her earlier dizziness was subsiding. Tomorrow, she couldn't blame this on drink.

She felt her blouse being pulled from her skirt. And then Henry's warm hands, his chapped fingers, moving on her waist, her stomach, and finally under her bra, damp with the day's sweat, and onto her breasts. His thumbs were slightly scabby, as if they'd been cut up by fish lures.

Henry edged her around to the side of the sink, then pushed her carefully back over the porcelain. "Cold," she said and almost giggled.

"Condom?" she thought to add.

"Oh, yeah, yeah," he said, reaching into his back pocket, and Charlotte flashed on the day she'd thrown out Helen's diaphragm. She'd been squatting on the bathroom floor of the apartment they shared, going through a cabinet and pitching Helen's lipsticks and headscarves into the trash. When she came to the diaphragm, she felt compelled to open the case. The diaphragm itself was virginal, never used. Charlotte already knew that. She'd spent much of the past year reassuring Helen about the man she'd eventually meet, the one who wasn't going to care about her lumpy reconstructed breast. One night she'd even said to her old boyfriend, Lawrence, "Well, you wouldn't, you know, care, if it was someone you loved," and he said, "I hate to be horrible, but sure I would." "Wrong answer, bucko," Charlotte had said, then pulled her pillow out from under her head and clobbered him. She had thought of all this as she had clicked the diaphragm container shut and tossed the whole thing in the bathroom's plastic waste bucket, registered the light thud of plastic hitting plastic, and then... and then nothing. That was that.

Once Henry had the condom on, he pushed into her with such ease that Charlotte imagined she had been doing this all her life, wandering into restrooms and having men she wasn't even sure she had been flirting with follow her.

She felt she was going under, and she was, sort of, slipping sideways over the low sink as he rolled onto her. Her feet, crossed at Henry's back, left her toes to tickle the string of a light cord, her hair to graze the dirty linoleum. Henry whispered, for no apparent reason, "Oh, hey, I'm sorry." And then, "You believe me. Don't you?"

She didn't answer. His skin was lovely. Perfect, smooth, save for a spot where it was peeling at his back. Why hadn't his days in the lifeboat done more damage? She envied the hardness of his thighs against her own. *God,* she mouthed, blood rushing to her head. Lawrence had never been this... this what? "Yes?" Henry said, as if she'd spoken aloud.

"Just, just," she stopped. "Do it"—dumb pornography, the truth was she relied on it—"as hard as you can."

He smiled, like he'd figured her out, and said, "Oh, so it's like that, is it?" But he did what she wanted, saying—and she winced at the words—"Here you go." And then the liquor she'd been drinking took another lap through her circulatory system. She felt woozy, her brain—for once, for once—abandoning her to her body, only she was completely aware of that abandonment. The bathroom cartwheeled around her, and then she thought, as if she were a third party in the room, an outside observer, *Hey! I'm doing it with a spectral being.*

Henry reached around her side to turn off the faucet, to stop the water from streaming below her. "No," she closed her hand around his. "Leave it." Everything was so unlikely that she assumed, in a distracted way, that this was it; she was finally having the nervous breakdown she craved. The release of a collapse. Didn't all grievers want that?

Water swooshed under her. "Okay," Henry whispered, while Charlotte imagined the drain stopping up, the sink filling, and then water running over the lip of the sink, building up on the floor, crawling up Henry's legs, over his hips, then reaching her back and rising farther. She couldn't help it. She was one of those women who liked a flood.

Just Wait

1. Those Absent

Any reasonable baby shower would have properly culminated in the videocorder with the instant playback feature. The present was addressed to The Formerly Thin Addie Ling from her three tactless brothers, and arrived suspiciously wrapped in a brown paper grocery bag. There was no box or warranty card. If the camera was hot, nobody said so. As for the bag, this was fastened with an antique diaper pin courtesy of Addie's number two brother, Billy, who was Mr. Flea Market in the family as a result of having gone to prep school. No one could explain it, but that's what had happened. He had gone in wearing Nike everything, thanks to money he had made with his paper route, and had come out a 1930's North Woods type who read Herodotus by lantern light. Billy could ice fish. He talked suddenly slowly. He left off talking after making his point. That proved the most dramatic change, and the most unnerving, especially as he kept it up all through college and on into what was apparently his adulthood. Now he was forty-two and still doing it.

To be fair, Addie thought that the outdoorsy persona was about embarrassment. He was embarrassed to have turned even more thoughtful than he was before. He had always been a guy who sought the bottom of things, as if there were a bottom that could be found—as if people could do more in life than paw down through one viscous reality into another mess. Addie found this charming. She herself knew what it was to wade into a field full of lupine and be filled with wonderment. Once, too, in a rogue storm on a mountaintop, she had dropped to her knees and prayed—not knowing what else to do in the onslaught of water and wind—and the extremis of that moment had stayed with her. She recalled the cold press of the hard stone, and the rain running from her clumped hair; she remembered the sky—brutal, power-mad, dead to mercy. And recalling those things, she understood Billy's hunting and fishing clothes. They were his way of saying he didn't belong to the quotidian world. He belonged to the world of transcendence, like a priest.

But Addie's stepbrother, Mark, liked to say that Billy—Will, he called himself now, had in fact called himself for some twenty-odd years—looked as though he had lent L. L. Bean his first tent. And wasn't that some trick for a nice Chinese boy from the wilds of a Boston suburb? In contrast, he, Mark Lee, the youngest of the boys, was Mr. Real World. He had gone from a public high school to a state college and lived, being the last son, the dumb son, his father's son.

These days Mark wore blue jeans and T-shirts and drove a red Ford station wagon with a factory third seat he had liberated from a car wreck in a junkyard. This he had installed himself, much to the delight of his kids. Mark once explained to Addie how he figured the third seat had to be a feature the dealer popped in, rather than was factory-installed, and, of course, he was right. Mark was always, well, on the mark. This was how he had come to head the family building business. Mark could predict which streets would get plowed first in a snowstorm and how long the whole cleanup would take. He could make sure their street was plowed early—not so early as to attract attention, but early. Mark was the brother who had arranged for, and possibly fixed up, the videocamera, loading and charging it in the meantime, so that it would be ready for immediate use.

As for the card, Addie was amazed to see that Mark and Billy had gotten Neddie, her number one brother, to sign it himself, in that chicken-scratch handwriting that Mark used to call positive proof he was headed for a padded cell, until Neddie went into the hospital. Then for once Mark didn't say anything at all, prompting Billy to remark how heartening it was to see that Mark sometimes knew when to shut up. Neddie himself was not physically there at the shower, but so familiar was his absence that it had become his presence. In this, he was unlike their father figure, Reynolds, who in his absence from the shower could be considered more authentically missing.

2. The Shower Proper

Now Addie panned around the room. To zoom or not to zoom? From the casbah comfort of an upholstered rocking chair, Addie tipped forward, touching her feet to the floor to steady the shot.

Forward—*voilà*. There was her beaming husband, Rex, looking as though he had just won a Nobel Prize, the first ever given for paternity. He called himself a mongrel Mongol, and indeed had the romantic slashing brow and broad planar cheeks that evoked a wind-blown life chasing sheep on the steppe; never mind that he was half Japanese. Addie zoomed back. Now you could see how he was flanked by females. These were friends of Addie's, around whom Rex had looped his arms playboy-style. Actually he was a sensitive intellectual engaged in good works, as were Addie's friends. Nevertheless they all waved little flat babe waves before Rex disengaged and leaned forward, elbows on his knees, with a serious look. "I just want to say," he announced, "now, and for history, that you, Addie Ling, are the love of my life. My harem is nothing to me."

At this everyone laughed, even Addie's women's studies friends, who had over the years practically come to appreciate him. "That's good, since I'm sure you are nothing to them," she managed—not the best reply, but people did laugh at that, too. After all, it was her shower, and they loved her. Addie had always thought Rex should have married someone with a gift for the comeback line rather than someone who felt pressured by banter, as she did. But he claimed it was hard enough being married to someone who was always right, he needed to at least know the good lines were his.

Next in her viewfinder were her brothers Mark and Billy, the study in contrasts who nonetheless looked surprisingly alike. Mark's hair was short, Billy's in a ponytail. But both wore shorts that showed off their surpassing fitness and sparsely hairy legs. They both seemed to be idling about, awaiting suitable challenge. And they waved with similar nonchalance—as if this was yet another thing they could do one-handed.

"Try the date button," said Mark.

Billy turned toward some veggie dip. "Billy," said Addie. "You have to say something."

He turned around with a largish spear of broccoli, and wielded it like a microphone. "This is Billy Ling, reporting live from the shower of the century," he said. Then he turned back sideways to the camera again.

"Come on," said Addie.

"Some party," he said.

"Billy."

"Some camera."

"Billy."

"I'm going to work for Mark," he said. "Starting tomorrow."

"What?" said Addie.

"He'll be a real asset," said Mark.

"It is my deepest ambition," intoned Billy. He wielded his broccoli mike once again. "I have always yearned to be an asset."

Beside them chattered Addie's five sisters-in-law, none of whom knew what irony was. Mark's wife seemed to have modeled herself on the late Princess Diana of Wales; this involved headgear and a vaguely tragic air. Then there were Addie's roommates from college and graduate school, some of whom had updated, but others of whom you could pick out in a lineup as ex-hippies. Emma Rose, for example, wore all natural fiber; Mark said she looked like a model for a burlap store. The one buddy Addie had kept up with from junior high, Jessica, likewise still did a gypsy look, with a matching manner that involved clasping people's hands as she talked; she was full of exaltation. In general, though, updated or not, most people looked surprisingly happy for their age. Still young, as opposed to plain young, they no longer talked about Life as if it were the next city on a walking tour. They were knowledgeable about knee procedures and dental work, and wary of what came next—either justifiably or needlessly, Addie had heard both. For now Addie saw in her eyepiece that apprehension gave rise to a special clear happiness—magical as the pane of blue ice that let a wavery square of light into modern-day igloos.

That pane was broken, thankfully, by only one unhappy mother, hers. Addie swept guiltily past Madame Lee, as Rex called her, vaguely hoping that Rex had not put her on wrapping paper duty. For even after forty years here, Regina was ambivalent at best about pitching in American-style to events like these. She took offense at the idea that anyone would expect her to help like a servant. And asking is expecting, Addie explained to Rex, who locked eyes with her as she spoke and, in a manner he had learned in a sensitivity seminar, received her words. "I hear you," he said. "You have spoken."

Yet there was Regina, balling up the paper with the nobly suffering air of a movie star in a labor camp, while Addie's mother-in-law on Prozac fairly beamed with the honor of keeping a gift inventory. Doreen waved enthusiastically at the camera lest it miss her and, when Addie zoomed in, advised for the ages, "Lists are important. Believe me. You simply cannot rely on your mind." A nisei from Hawaii, Doreen had more foundation on one cheek than the other, and had once told Addie that Japan was the most amazing place she had ever been. The women there, she said, put on nylons to go to the grocery store. The men get perms.

Behind Doreen stood Addie's friend Lorna's books—beat-up seminal tomes subsumed by bright volumes of Brazelton and Leach. Nearby, world travel artifacts commingled with a wide selection of educational toys and stuffed sea creatures—a family of orca whales, a dolphin, a manta ray—and what appeared to be a token teddy bear. In front of them stood the automatic baby swing that Lorna had said used an unconscionable number of batteries. If she had to do it over again, she would get a windup, but anyway, she hoped Addie would accept the loan, which she accompanied with a crate full of batteries of every size. This, in addition to the shower, was her present to Addie, who had exclaimed with real surprise when she opened it. "Everything takes batteries," said Lorna. There was another box, too, from Lorna's husband, Ken, to Rex. This, it turned out, was full of scotch tape. "All will become clear in time," said Ken. "Just wait."

Addie filmed these things thinking how glad she was that, like Neddie and Reynolds, she was not going to be in the picture. She wondered, too, whether she could have avoided gaining forty pounds with this pregnancy; and whether anyone only gained twenty-five who was not under twenty-five. These thoughts were so retrograde that she could hardly believe them hers. She had read *The Second Sex* in high school, and underlined everything. All her adult life, she had refused to be objectified. Yet the thoughts seemed to have a life of their own, like her body, potent and miraculous, yet big as a submersible, and on a mission she was most notably not directing.

The baby began an aerobics routine; Addie flexed her turgid feet. People called summer pregnancies the worst, but at least you were spared having to wear real shoes. And if your body seemed a spectacle, at least everybody else was a body, too, all armpits and skin moles. She was hardly the only one with an inelegant appendage. Addie sneakily recorded for the ages several inelegant appendages, then more sweetly continued on to not only the batteries and the scotch tape, but the more traditional presents. These Addie made her friends hold up and explain.

"This is a wipe warmer, for to pamper your child's tush."

"This is a rattle, designed to encourage early grasping."

"This is a breast pump, for comic relief."

Inspired, it seemed, by their testimonial, Regina produced from the next room one last present. She moved slowly, as if, though the same age as Rex's mother, she were far more elderly. She had had her hair done in a petrified dandelion puff for the shower, and she put her hand up to it from time to time, as if to be sure it was stage-ready.

The present was not wrapped. "I explain for you," she offered; and so Addie filmed as Regina held up a stuffed sailfish.

"This fish your father give to me for last year anniversary present," she said. "This year I give to you. We are getting divorced after thirty-five years marriage, I have no place even to stay now."

At this Addie put down the camera, leapt out of her chair—as best as she could leap—and of course offered her mother sanctuary with her. She took the sailfish from Regina's arms, attempting to embrace her mother at the same time. This was not quite possible, but the intention was clear. Her stepbrother, Mark, picked up the camera and caught the rest of the exchange. "I am your difficult mother. Our whole lives we fight. How can I move into your house?" Still Addie insisted, trying as she spoke to put the sailfish down. Its sail was so high that she could barely see over it. She made her heartfelt offer into a shellacked ribbed fin. But it was heard. By the time a friend rescued Addie from the trophy, other friends had chimed in encouragingly.

"Perfect!" proclaimed Jessica, predictably ecstatic. After all, Addie and Rex were going to need help, and how nice for the baby to get to know its grandmother!

"No help." Regina waved her wave of flat refusal, her palm adamantly prominent. Her beautiful fingers were stiffly splayed in a no-nonsense manner; only her pinky arched back coyly with a slight crook. (This was the same pinky that reared like a prairie dog when she picked up a teacup.) Her manner, correspondingly, was despairing in an alert sort of way—edging, like the cry of a child, from a wail of sheer pain to something more artistic. Addie watched as the wave of flat refusal became a wave of polite refusal, then of pro forma refusal. By this time Regina's predicament had inspired a kind of call and response.

"No help, no help," said Regina.

"Of course you'll be a help!" said the crowd.

"Addie has no room."

"Addie will make room!"

"Who wants an old lady come live with them?"

"They do, they do. They welcome you! They want you!"

Finally, Madame Lee agreed to be welcomed. The crowd burst into applause, as if on a TV show. Then Doreen moved to congratulate Regina while Lorna and Ken brought out dessert—a cake with a jogger stroller drawn on top. The jogger stroller held a big question mark.

3. Pillow Talk

"Shh. See? It's moving."

Rex successfully connected with a kick, but then drew Addie's T-shirt back down like a shade and continued his miracle appreciation through the cloth. In principle he adored her belly, her taut and mottled, veiny belly, with its popped-out navel like a gag from a joke shop. But in practice he did not adore it. In this way he was out of step with his times. He dimly recognized that the body had in fact snuck in, mid-century, to dominate contemporary thought. No truth but in things. No ideas but in hormones. Yet how was he supposed to feel about Addie's avid interest in their neighbor's dog's new litter, for example? A year ago it would have been Frank Stella's mid-career crisis that elicited that kind of deeply involved reaction. The switch to the Indian Birds, and what Caravaggio would have thought of these aggressive steel constructions projecting a foot out from the wall. Now Rex watched, aghast, as Addie and the bitch exchanged soulful glances of mutual understanding. The bitch was a dachshund, no less. And what did Addie talk of now, endlessly, but her body? This twinge, that twinge, a funny fullness, a distinct soreness. Stretching, rumblings, gas. Her entire belly sometimes lurched from one side to the other as the baby sought to get more comfortable.

How uncomfortable they all were! He least of all; and yet it was no small, poignant, delighted terror he felt as he watched Addie grow larger than him and sexually voracious. More, more, more. This wasn't in any manual he had read.

"My mother," she said.

He shook his head sympathetically. "We can only hope she'll come to our senses."

"Very funny. The scoop is that Reynolds's new woman lives right here in town. My mother ran into them at the club, can you imagine? A redhead wearing that kind of bikini where the top doesn't even match the bottom."

"No wonder your mother's upset."

"Where are we going to put her?"

"In the nursery, of course. Where she belongs."

"It'll be like having twins."

Rex thought this over. "There's always murder," he concluded. "Smother her with a pillow."

"Don't you think that would be ethically problematic? If we didn't at least first try to discourage her from moving in?"

"We'll smother her with a pillow and see if that discourages her."

"That fish wasn't even an anniversary present. I mean, Reynolds gave it to her, but not for their anniversary."

"Did he at least catch it himself?"

At this, Addie sighed deeply. "I don't know why I married you," she said, closing her eyes firmly. She had an air of utter resignation. "You are truly hard to talk to." All the same, she cagily advanced a hand onto his waiting thigh.

4. *The Problem*

Their condo, on the second floor of a three-family house, was not large. Their condo was, in fact, small, as befitted two people with meaningful professions. Rex did low-income housing in the inner city. This represented a personal victory of sorts, as it had been a struggle for him, the firstborn of his family, to become this variety of do-gooder. Not that there had never been a family do-gooder before. In fact, his mother's father had been a Buddhist priest in Japan. He had had his own temple, via which he had made a fortune mumbling sutras at funerals.

The trouble was that Doreen thought Rex should find himself a similar monopoly situation. For example, as a doctor in some remote area. He could open his own clinic, etcetera. Rex had explained, explained, and finally given up explaining. Finally he had turned deaf ear, as Doreen complained—an achievement, to his mind, in itself. He had felt sorry for his classmates with better hearing who had gone to medical school. The ones with immigrant parents in particular seemed to do nothing but perform, perform, only to be pronounced still lacking. If they were practitioners, they weren't researchers. If they were internists, they weren't surgeons. Rex had realized that you had to live your own life. He had broken with his family's expectations—realizing, as he liked to admit, that he could use all the nobility he could get.

But more recently he noticed that, parent-plagued or not, his doctor friends were certainly most comfortably trapped. How easy it was to get burned on second houses, they lamented. Whereas, what with the baby coming, he was beginning to wonder whether he couldn't trade in, say, half of his unimpeachable integrity for cash. This was to keep from qualifying to live in one of his housing projects himself.

In this regard, Addie, a garden designer, was no help. If she would go back to school, she might at least someday bill at landscape architect rates. But she pointedly did not because, she said, she liked the humbleness of her work as it was. In her twenties she had aspired to achieve immortality as a sculptress; she had even had a flirtation with marble. But in her thirties, she had come to realize that all her ambition was about death. It was about defying death. It was about denying death. It was about death, death, death! A friend had given her a book about this; the friend later asked for the book back. But it was too late. Addie was working then in primitive materials like soap and felt, and achieving some recognition for her work. She had in fact just had a piece of hers hung at the Museum of Fine Arts right opposite a Lucian Freud when she realized, she said, that art was over for her.

That's when she became first a hospice worker, and then an artisan—a person who took small spaces and simply made them beautiful. Sometimes her efforts were nontraditional. Once she made a pergola of Coke bottles; once a mossy swale; once a garden of tennis balls on stakes. But she also planted tree hydrangeas for children to run under, coneflowers to attract butterflies. She did reliable, joyous gardens for Rex's city projects. Everything was addressed to the humans living in the shadow of the large mountain, and not to the mountain itself.

5. Addie's Room Becomes Regina's Room

It wasn't until Regina and the baby that Addie wished her practice a less modest activity. For as the site of a modest activity, Addie's workroom became an irresistible topic of discussion.

"I don't know how comfortable I am, your books and paper everywhere," said Regina. "Where am I going to put my clothes?"

Regina said, "Once the baby comes, you will have no time for gardening, anyway."

"Gardening, she called it," grumbled Addie to Rex.

Luckily, Mark, hearing of their dilemma, offered to help. "We'll convert that kitchen closet of yours into a home office," he said. "Put in a pull-down desk with some built-in storage. I've got some exotic wood trim from another job—beautiful stuff, you can have it for free. Billy of the Northlands can supply the labor; it's his chance to learn how to hold a hammer. I'll charge you cost."

Rex and Addie pondered this offer. Would it simply encourage Regina never to move out?

"Of course he wants her to be comfortable here," said Rex. "He's afraid she'll be looking next at his beautiful place, with the renovated kitchen and the pool in the backyard. He knows if she could stand his wife he'd be sunk."

"Billy says she made all that up about Bloomingdale's," said Addie.

"How interesting," said Rex.

"I can't work in a closet," said Addie.

Addie said, "The kitchen is noisy."

All the same, the next Saturday, they were looking at plans, with Mark, in the kitchen, when the first of the contractions came. Was it a Braxton-Hicks? thought Addie. But it was nothing like a Braxton-Hicks.

"It's happening," said Addie. She stood up; then sat back down.

"What's happening?" said Rex, looking at the drawings. Rex loved drawings.

"Nothing," she said then, and leaned over the drawings, too, as if deliriously absorbed. Once upon a time, Neddie the Absent used to look around at them all and announce, *You see me not,* to which Regina would reply, *What you talking about?* and *You must be crazy!* Now Addie was going to a hospital, too. For a different reason, thankfully; and how much more likely it was that she would have too many visitors than too few. Yet as Mark talked of a board that could be easily unhinged, she thought of Neddie and of Billy, and of their father, so long dead she had no memory of him. Had Neddie ever held a newborn before? Probably not, she guessed; another contraction gripped her; she looked at the clock, her mind turning, fearfully, toward labor. But even as it turned, she thought for just one more moment of what a treat it would be for him to meet the baby. She could picture his face already, soft with delight, yet crying—he cried at everything, poor Neddie. She could picture him trembling like an old man at the very prospect of visitors. *This is my child,* she would say. He would say, *But of course.* Then he would open his arms with the sudden strength of the happy. *How very bald,* he would say. *How very red.* And, *How nice to have a new stranger in the family.*

Guests

Bobby Bell's fingers numbered four to a hand. His thumb and pointer were identical to God's, but the other two were just fleshy stubs, stunted and fused on each slender paw. He was a dumb kid, besides, if progress in school is a fair measure. He sized me up my first week in town, then came by my locker to demand a fight, the fall of 1967.

We'd moved to New Mexico from Illinois because my father was sick. How the change was supposed to help, I didn't know. When I asked, he removed his glasses as if the problem were with the black-rimmed lenses. His head tipped slightly on its thin scaffold of bone. I felt a corresponding tilt in my senses. "I'm host to a disease," he said. A smile flickered across his lips.

I began to tremble.

He continued. "You could say it's a landlord and tenant affair." When he focused on my expression, his attitude shifted. He slipped the glasses on again, which made his eyes the wrong size for his face. "You're worried." His hand lighted like a butterfly upon my head. "All right. I'm host, but there are no tenants, just uninvited guests, too small to see." His lips crinkled, a modest grin. "Too small," he assured me, "to even imagine." His head tilted once more. "You won't worry, all right?"

I promised.

I had inherited my father's slight build, which must have cheered Bobby Bell, to think he'd found a frame, at last, more flimsy than his own. I colored easily as well, which provided him a hope even he knew to leave unsaid: blood that surged so close to the surface would wet his wrinkled shirt, spatter his shoes, and saturate the dirt where they paced. From the moment I met him, even before he required a fight, I understood that his world was neatly cleaved into those who could beat him and those he could enslave. The division, extravagantly uneven, presented him his quest—to find someone over whom he could have dominion—all of this written upon his face, as the truth of my father's condition was written upon mine. Which might have been why Bobby Bell thought he had an edge, as I was taller and only barely thinner. Why would he think my eyes were asking to be blackened but for a father frail as a child's pledge?

During that time, my mother came to my bed every night to take from me whatever book I was reading and point to the ticking clock above my head. She'd sit on the mattress and tell me how well my father was doing, how this move could make all the difference. "Friends will come," she said the night before the fray, meaning that I would make some eventually, that perspective was the larger test—we were here to save a life, to protect him from the guests that lived within.

What a good boy I was, wanting to believe, and then, after I no longer could, willing to pretend. When she left, shutting the door and light, the room drifted away in a darkness that knew no end, which I would close my eyes against, and wait for the smaller dark of sleep.

Later that night I woke and stumbled into the hall—disoriented, still in Illinois. Light at the far end of the house drew me. My mother knelt by the easy chair to fit a pillow beneath my father's sleeping head. He wore the top to his striped pajamas, the dark hair on his thin legs exaggerated like the carbon filaments I moved with a magnet to whisker a cartoon face. Mother's gown rose up her legs as they straightened, covering her to the hips, the tan of her legs ending abruptly in the buttocks' white exclamation. I retreated to the hall, watching her float a flowered bedsheet over him, then touch her lips to his temple, her solemn nakedness like a holy garment—in itself a kind of prayer.

How distant I lived from Bobby Bell.

The fight I remember with a clarity that defies time, as if I had more than lived it, as if it had not yet happened. We met at the bus stop, two stupid, savage children, enveloped by a crowd of onlookers I sensed more than saw. Bobby Bell pointed at my narrow chest. "Fairy," he accused, a rage in his throat, an evil passion in his eyes. I had no decent reply, but spoke what first popped into my mouth. "Pixie," I said, wanting to laugh, but the finger, that deformed hand thrown out at me, seemed a kind of reminder, like the mechanical voice in the underground that reminds you you're on a train, like my father's dry cough even on a morning following rain, the sky pristine with sunlight and the cleansing smell of creosote.

We wrestled on a patch of ground made bare by children's shoes, exhaust from the school bus lingering in the air. We lunged and grappled like things less than human. A friend of Bobby Bell's invented a jeer. "You fucking Mr. Happy," he yelled, his breath close and bitter, as if he might not be well.

Did my mother choose my father for his weakness, as Bobby Bell had chosen me? Is it cruel to suggest that she loved him most when he was his weakest? What of the girl, a few years later, who claimed to be drawn to my silence? Was she Bobby Bell in feminine guise, her white thighs holding me with such gentleness that I wept? What of the women I later met, who picked me less as a man than as a mission, and who I treated like guests who'd overstayed their welcome? I don't understand the first thing about love, especially that first thing, when passion inhabits your body before you're aware, a passion you come to detect by the symptoms that remain.

As it turned out, I was weaker than Bobby Bell could suppose, and quicker, too, throwing him to the dirt, shoving his nose against the hardened ground, the blood that colored his shirt his own. I can still hear his single cry, as I bent his arm beneath my knee. His skull, I tethered by his hair to my fist, and I might have gouged a hole with it, but his arm escaped. I had to make a dive.

Shall I attempt to describe the feel of that inhuman hand in mine?

"You've made your point," another boy said, as if it were a debate I'd won.

I climbed off Bobby Bell and backed away, studying the crowd to see who might be pleased I'd won and who might jump me if I turned. That act of accidental compassion—my world, like Bobby Bell's, cleaved—caused in me a peculiar response. I could see Bobby Bell, his body in a twisted sprawl, but I could not see the others. As if my vision had grown too small, I could not hold them in a single frame.

"That don't make no nevermind," consoled his friend, touching the place on Bobby Bell where my knee had pinned his knobby spine. The others huddled—or hovered—about the fallen boy, but they were impossible to take in, the many guests, witnesses to that unfortunate accomplishment.

To be truthful, I've never had trouble imagining the small. I pictured the microscopic company my father kept with a clarity that was almost scientific. And I could see how, in Bobby Bell's eyes, each thing claimed only the value of its use to him: a tool, or not a tool. Viewed in this fashion, all of creation could be made minuscule. How unlike Bobby Bell was my father, who always saw the other side even in his own slipping away. "Such beauty," he said to me, gripping the rail of the bed. "I might have missed it otherwise."

We're forty-three now, Bobby Bell and I, wherever he lives, whatever small place he now calls his. We have our own uneasy children. And still, I can't retreat far enough to see them all, those bodies assembled about the fallen one. How, precisely, do they gather? How, exactly, do they stand? I think it matters. Are they stooped or standing erect? Has one covered her ears, another closed his eyes? Does that head swivel to miss the farce? Or is she laughing, giant that she has become, at the grappling of such silly and malignant boys? I carry them all with me—a fist that rises in what might be fear, shoulders that turn in what might be submission, hands that rest on what might be knees.

He told me what threatened him was too small to imagine, as if, given this, I could be spared the rest, but it wasn't the microbes that troubled me after his death. He had it wrong, my father and his tiny beings. The guests that stubbornly remain haunt us because they're larger than visible things.

The Land of Nod

The organist pumped out the blurred tones of "Just as I Am," the song sinking like a rusted hook in Jack's chest. Jack locked his ankles, clenched his knees to the underside of the slick oak pew as his grandfather, Emmett, snored quietly beside him. *Stop it. Please stop it,* Jack said to the whirling in his body. He stiffened, as if he might somehow bolt himself in place. His grandmother, Ruby; his aunt Agnes, Miss Abigail, the whole choir launched into the second verse—

> *Just as I am, and waiting not*
> *To rid my soul of one dark blot,*
> *To Thee whose blood can cleanse each spot*
> *O Lamb of God, I come! I come!*

And you were supposed to come then, to rise and walk straight down the aisle and let the blot be washed away by the blood of Jesus. Nine years old was old enough. Jack had seen eight-and-a-half-year-olds already born again. Late last summer, some seven-year-old twins had even been saved, though the girls had been from up in Illinois, and tall for their ages. The washing of blood and the rinsing of baptism. And there you were—clean as a dish in a cupboard.

Jack held on to his pew. He looked up at the choir, and though they were dressed in robes like apostles or angels, their garments as slick and bright as Christmas ornaments, he tried to keep them who they really were: his overpowdered aunt Agnes, who shook his hand like a politician and wore an asfidity bag to ward off illness; his own grandmother, who would stand at his bedroom door that very evening. *Night-night,* Ruby would say, just as his mother had said before she died. *Off to the Land of Nod,* his mother's words coming from his grandmother's shadow at the door, and then the door closing and him falling asleep to the muffled sounds of TV gunfire.

* * *

As the choir repeated the verses, Brother Dannon descended from the pulpit to the altar to greet whomever might be called forward by the invitational hymn. Since it was Easter, there were pots of white lilies lined up around the altar rail—tall, slick, polished-looking flowers. A smaller bouquet sat atop the organ where June Dannon, the preacher's second wife, fretted and pumped at the keyboards and pedals as if sewing a huge invisible dress. Above the altar and pulpit and tiered choir, the milky portrait of Jesus hung, his face lean and kind with disappointment, his left hand raised in front of his chest like a shy man bidding at an auction. The robes of Jesus were the same purple, like a vein or the inside of a wet rose, as the stage curtains at Jack's school, Morgan Elementary, the same heavy waves and folds. It was like a wave, the motion inside Jack now, the part right before it crests and falls. In fact, as Brother Dannon stood there between the pots of donated lilies, his arms spread wide as the planks of the cross itself, Jack felt his own backbone go watery, as if it might somehow come apart, the segments of his spine unlocking like soggy puzzle pieces. Behind the preacher, the choir members stood in their robes, a slightly glossier purple than the robes of Jesus. The choir robes were loose, and swept against each other so that at times they appeared as a single rippling garment, or a series of continuous purple waves threatening to drown their inhabitants. It was no use trying to think of the choir members as they existed in their ordinary lives then—beautician, insurance agent, grandmother, mailman. The hymn and the waves of the robes had driven them upward, and in their places now were these holy shapes, shining white hairdos and moving mouths, as if angelic ventriloquists were perched among the rafters.

Jack felt a blaze of inner heat that reminded him of the onset of chicken pox. He had stood on his bed, his mother had told him, had cried and whooped like a flamingo. "No more idea who you were than the man in the moon," she had said, and Jack had felt a welling pride, like a second fever, at the extravagance of his illness.

But the thing inside him was racing now, almost certainly alive. Jack tried to concentrate on something else. He looked at the woman sitting directly in front of him. *Where your treasure lies, there will your heart...* But that wasn't the thought he needed. *If thine eye be single, the whole body shall be full of light.* That seemed closer. It was hard to know which verse of the Bible to aim at a particular part of life. *Judge not, consider the lilies, behold the fowls of the air, ye are the light, the salt, knock and it shall be opened*—so many of them already stored in Jack's memory, little holy snippets, oracular phrases and commandments. *If thine eye be single* seemed fairly pertinent, almost scientific, in fact. If he could just concentrate on one ordinary thing, the steadying light would stream in, the agitation stop. Jack looked at the woman, really only inches away. From the back she seemed vaguely familiar, like any adult. Her hair was stiff and perfect, done up for Easter tight as a snow cone. He examined the clasp of her necklace and the dark freckle, possibly a mole, between the silver clasp and the neckline of her dress. There was an abrupt snuffle, almost a snort from his sleeping grandfather, but even that didn't help. The thing inside, blot or cleansing spirit, was truly racing now. Whether it was heading into the hymn or away from it, Jack couldn't be sure. Could it possibly race both ways? But that made no more sense than the words of the invitational hymn—*O Lamb of God, I come! I come!*

Jack knew it was only poetry, but still, *Lamb of God*? Jesus hung in his portrait above the choir, no lamb at all, but more like some kindly bearded lady.

In the stained-glass windows, several apostles were moping; paired, jigsawed animals spilled from a grounded ark, plump cherubim swarmed like bees about the wimpled head of Mary. The colored light from the windows was cast everywhere, not only soldered in the glass, but beamed and scattered in bits and pieces across the floor, altar, and across the blocked shoulders and tilted Easter hats of the congregation. In the middle of all the scattered light, Jack thought for an instant he picked out his grandmother's quivering alto. It was odd that her voice would be there, in the wrong realm, among colors instead of sounds. Or maybe it was a little of both. He listened, tried to push the drone of basses to one side, the papery sopranos to the other. It was like weeding a garden, he thought, hunting for the rickety flower that would be his grandmother's voice, that would calm him, help anchor him to the wooden pew. He studied her lips, but it was hard to tell. Ruby's lips opened and closed from so far away, Jack found himself trying hard not to think of a fish's moving mouth.

It didn't help that the hairdo Ruby had come home with the day before shone on her head, gleamed in the church window light like the rose quartz in his empty aquarium.

Jack bit down hard on his lower lip to stop the shaking and jittering inside him. He had felt it before, of course, the quivering lure and pull of salvation, even before his mother's death six months earlier.

His mother had been returning from a visit with his father down in Oak Ridge, where he had been transferred to work at the uranium plant. Just four miles from home (at the funeral, people had seemed fascinated by the number—*just four miles*), from the trailer where she and Jack lived, the jet-black 1961 Impala he had helped his mother pick out slipped or skidded, veered or didn't veer, but somehow managed to miss a downhill curve. The car tumbled down a ragged embankment, and by the time the first farm truck passed, the fire had splashed outward in an arc that eventually blackened a quarter-acre of corn stubble.

But even before that, Jack had felt the preacher's eyes upon him in church, felt the blot of his own soul swelling up in his chest like a bull's-eye. Every person was a sinner, and the wages of sin was death. It couldn't help but be your fault. And today was even worse. It was Easter now—the stone rolled away, Jesus loose and free as a bird. The woman in front of Jack was no anchor at all, no place to put his heart, to make his eye be single and still. He stared at the mole or freckle on her neck. It *was* a mole. Would there be others? On her shoulders? Her belly? But even that was no distraction. The woman may as well have been a pane of glass, no more substantial than the translucent Mary in the window.

Wasn't this the feeling of being saved, then? The terrible flutter and motion of the Holy Ghost? Or much worse, was it the squirming of demons like the ones Jesus cast out of the swine? Or was it *into* the swine?

Jack drove a fingernail deep into his palm and held it there as he had at his mother's funeral. If he could just do that, if he could just hurt himself enough to stay put, to stay *Jack*. "You have the name of a president now. How about that, Jack?" his mother had said just after President Kennedy's election. When he was younger, she had read to him all the stories and poems full of

Jacks—Jack Sprat, Jack Horner, Jack and the beanstalk, in-the-box; Jack be nimble, be quick. *Jack,* he spoke his name very softly now, like a stifled sneeze. He wanted to say it much louder, to repeat his own name over and over with a sound as sharp and plunging as an arrow.

Suddenly, from somewhere in the choir, a soprano launched a wild string of notes. The notes fled north of the harmony line, ascended into a wheezy teakettle sound that seemed to lose its balance and blow crookedly among the rafters of the choir loft. Oddly enough, it was a relief to Jack, even more help than the lip biting. The mistake was embarrassing, yet comical, and Jack felt a small hitch in his fever, a tiny breath of calm, though he was careful to keep a corner of his lower lip tight between his teeth.

As Jack searched the faces of the choir for the wayward soprano, a man he had never seen before rushed down the center aisle. Jack turned in time to see him pass. The little man wore a plaid jacket that resembled wrapping paper, a tie as wide as a circus clown's. He was already weeping (*weeping,* not *crying,* was the word for it; *Jesus wept*), and when the man reached the altar, Brother Dannon quickly laid a hand on his shoulder, then both hands, as if to keep him from floating away like the false notes of the soprano. The plaid man wept in heavy, gasping sobs, and Jack thought suddenly of rusty mechanisms, sorrowful old engines cranked up after long storage. As the weeping continued, Jack wondered if, in spite of the preacher's hands, the sport coat might actually leap from the man's shoulders. The mole lady in front of Jack went for her handkerchief, and Jack could hear the unsnapping of purses all around him.

Was it the same hook? The same rusty hook Jack had felt in his own breast now snagged into the little man? Had the man sensed it hovering, baited with the Easter sermon, had he felt it happening before it happened? All sermon long, during the part about Jesus thirsty on the cross (*"And who did He thirst for, friends?"* Brother Dannon had asked), and the part about the empty sepulcher and the linen garments unoccupied, and during the part about the terrible angel whose countenance was like lightning—during all of it, had the plaid man been sitting, trying desperately to remain in his pew, safe in his familiar self?

It was exactly what terrified Jack, this tugging and tugging and
then the clean outright jerk, and Jack would find himself trembling at the altar, crying like a baby, or *weeping* like Jesus, the slick
smell of lilies and the odor of Brother Dannon's aftershave and
breath mints washing over the straw-like smell of his own panic.
It had happened to the plaid man, and it could happen to him.
Jack thought of the twins, saved in their identical dresses. He
thought of Saul, struck blind and knocked from his horse in the
Bible. God's eye was on the sparrow. His hooks were sweeping
down. One minute a boy could be safe, locked in his pew, his
grandfather snoring peacefully, unconscious as a clock, and the
next minute he would be swept down the worn trail in the aisle
carpet like somebody's bride. *Poor Jack who has no mother,* the
congregation would think in unison, although the absurd
thought sprang to mind that they might actually sing these
words, work them right into the sagging tune of the hymn.

That was what the song already wanted, wasn't it? That was what
the donated lilies wanted and the pale raised hand in Jesus' portrait wanted. To reel Jack in, to fish out the blot. To make him lose
his grip on himself until a spectacle for Jesus was what he would become, blatant as an Easter egg, repeating whatever vows or promis-
es the plaid man in the jumping coat was now repeating. But at
least it would stop then, wouldn't it?—the trouble inside, the frantic vacant thing, that, while no longer racing, still rocked and wob-
bled as if Jack's heart had been replaced by a spinning jar lid.

Jack pressed his fingernail into his palm deep enough to bleed.
He didn't care. He hoped it would. Even if he had no mother, he
wasn't budging, not for any Lamb of God or bearded lady Jesus.
He knew it was wrong; it was stubbornness. Or worse, it was the
sin of pride, the very first one, the one the devil had fallen from.
The women's handkerchiefs daubed and fluttered before their
faces now as if they were trying to catch the bits of colored window light. The more they fluttered, the deeper the nail, and the
more Jack wasn't budging. The choir slogged through the verses
of "Just as I Am" as the first rows of the congregation began to file
up to the altar to shake hands with the saved man.

"Wake up, Grandpa." Jack nudged his grandfather, then gave
him a second jolt, this time with his elbow. "Wake up, church is
over," Jack said, just above a whisper.

"Now, then," his grandfather muttered from his sleep, and raised his hands so that Jack feared he might actually applaud. Instead, he came awake, noticed his hands poised in the air in front of him, studied them briefly, then seemed satisfied, as if they were the very tools he had been searching for in his sleep.

"*The Lord bless you and keep you...*" Brother Dannon was reciting the benediction. "*The Lord make His face to shine upon you...*" The preacher's right hand was raised, fingers spread wide. "*The Lord lift up His countenance upon you...*"

But the words seemed distant to Jack; they seemed oddly adrift, almost confectionery, like icing on someone else's cake. Jack saw his grandfather draw back his cuff and begin winding his wristwatch, an activity that somehow allowed Jack to release his lower lip and even ease the fingernail from his palm. The watch winding made a small crickety sound, a ratcheting of gears so faint it was possibly imaginary among the words of the benediction, the hymn, the creaking and stirring along the pews.

Nevertheless, time was back, it seemed, and Jack was in it. In a matter of minutes, his grandfather would offer Brother Dannon a single stiff handshake at the church door, and he and Jack would wait in the Rambler while Ruby changed from her choir robe. They would pass through the quiet neighborhood of city houses near the church, the Easter sun too bright on everything, almost painful, so that the houses themselves seemed to squint and want to be shadows. There would be the two traffic lights, and then, through a break in the distant tree line, the glimpse of the Ohio River bridge. They would pass the peach orchards already in full bloom, the blossoms a very pale violet, like the sheen inside a mussel shell. And then Mount Moriah, the actual cemetery where Jack's mother was buried—the older sections, weedy and chaotic, with mossy, tilted angels and rained-away names; the newer graves with their tidy stones standing at the heads of loaf-like mounds where bluegrass was still trying to grow. There would be the seven slow miles home then, and maybe, *probably,* no one would utter a word. It didn't matter.

Jack sat in his pew and listened to his grandfather's watch winding. He thought for a second he might even walk up and shake the saved man's hand, but decided not to press his luck. Maybe there would be a Godly hook or two that could still snag

him so close to the altar. He looked over at the stained-glass windows, all the broken colors there. He said his own name very quietly, the way his mother at bedtime would have. He thought of
the highway and the rows of peach trees, and suddenly wished he
could find, among the colors in the glass, the exact shade of their
blossoms.

Unidealized, Twenty-Eight

The young woman in 15F stood looking out her window. Thousands of other windows—wavy rectangles, shaken towels of light—seemed to signal in code, *You are not alone.*

Of course, she was not alone, anyway. Margaret turned back to the living room, where her Nebraska mother was sitting up very straight.

"Twenty-eight is not old," Margaret said, correctively, to her mother, who was already nodding in agreement.

Her mother agreed too easily. It was a habit she had always had with men, and, now that they were grown, she was doing it to her own children.

Didn't she think anything at all?

"No," her mother began, "oh no, not now. Twenty-eight is still young. You're just getting to the beginning of your real life."

Not that, either, Margaret thought. In her grim assessment, she had been living a real life for some time now. She considered herself to be right in its brown middle.

Four years ago, Margaret had begun a novel about her great-grandmother, who'd come to Nebraska on a covered wagon. Although, when asked, Margaret frequently said she expected to finish *Horizon Farm* within the calendar year, truly, she saw no end.

Her mother was talking about marriage. Marriage was what Margaret was or was not old for. Marriage was what her mother meant by real life, although she herself had now endured more than four decades without it. This was her after-real-life life.

There had been an article in the newspaper. *College-Graduate Spinsters on the Rise, Study Shows.* Mothers in fifty states had clipped the piece out and sent it to their daughters. The study, conducted at Stanford, said that American women were not marrying later, as many of these mothers had hoped, they were marrying less. As a teenager, Margaret's mother had been admitted to Stanford, but she'd not gone. She'd stayed in Tulsa, to Get Married.

If a woman was not wed by thirty, the paper said, she'd most likely not get married at all.

Margaret's friends, the spinsters themselves, read the article, too, but they didn't clip it out or send it anywhere.

"No one I *know* is married!" Margaret had screamed at Harold, her running partner, "none of our friends!" Harold was also twenty-eight, also single, but not of the marriageable variety.

'Course I'm *only* twenty-eight, she was thinking, as she listened to Harold's not-quite consolations. That gives me two more years.

Now, when her mother tentatively mentioned the article, Margaret said, "I don't want to get married, anyway."

Thousands of girls told their mothers long-distance they weren't sure if marriage was for them. But in Manhattan, these same young women, including Margaret, sat in the offices of therapists whose fifty-minute hours strained their budgets, and spoke of why they weren't meeting "anyone" or of what had gone wrong so that now, they found themselves not in love or loved, alone.

In the case of Margaret, there was not absolutely "no one." There was a Bob.

Everyone was trying to make the best of him.

The amazing thing was that he seemed entirely oblivious of the huge effort these courtesies were costing and seemed to strain to accept them.

Because of the newspaper article, Margaret's mother had come to New York in August. She'd taken her vacation here in the city all vacationers had left. The corners of Margaret's eyes stung when she saw her mother's suitcase open a little, like a clam, on the five-o'clock-made bed. (Margaret had promised herself her normal Friday. She'd worked all morning in the office, and when everyone left for the jitney at three, in old but somehow immaculately clean sneakers, she closed her door and turned to *Horizon Farm*. Then, she hurried home, hid things, and got on the train to the plane.)

"Well, I didn't know where all we'd be going," her mother said.

Parties, she'd imagined, judging from the chiffon packed in tissue. So much.

Margaret chose the nicest restaurant they could walk to from her apartment, but as she watched her mother's carefulness, sipping the bad wine as if it were fragrant, she felt sorry. It was not only that the city's good restaurants were elsewhere (this was a poor-ish, student neighborhood), but that these restaurants hardly seemed to be restaurants at all—they seemed to be fronts pretending to be restaurants, while actually functioning as something else entirely. Periodically one would close, and its replacement would offer a different cuisine, another shabby decor, and a menu newly minted at Kinko's, but still it would be not quite credible.

"I thought you'd be tired," Margaret said.

"Oh, I'm not tired." Her chin raised slightly to the city's possibilities.

What would they do for four whole days?

They'd lived together for eighteen years once, and now four days seemed an outward-bound-scale challenge. They'd lived together, but they hadn't recreated, exactly. They'd eaten dinners, Margaret had done her homework. Her mother moved around the house picking up.

Museums, Margaret thought. That was just the kind of thing they had never done together.

Why?

Saturday morning offered a typical New York summer day: moist, warm, with rising winds blowing debris against your ankles, the sky not clear but white.

It was unmistakably a weekend, when the rich and even the enterprising were somewhere else already. There was a time Margaret's mother believed Margaret would become one of those people; now she wasn't sure.

And for years, Margaret had been trying to make weekends feel like other days—a Tuesday, perhaps, or a Friday. She needed the time away from her job for *Horizon Farm,* but there was something about the span of Saturday afternoon that seemed overarching. The very bells of Sunday morning sounded to her like a summons calling out pairs to the street cafés for brunch.

"I don't brunch," she said to her mother. "I've usually eaten one, if not two meals by then."

Margaret showed her the museum listings. There was a traveling show of Dutch paintings. Years ago, on her ten-week charter flight college summer backpacking trip through Europe, she'd seen two paintings by Rembrandt, *(Idealized) Portrait of the Artist at 27* and *Portrait of the Artist at 27.* The two small paintings were different enough that twenty-year-old Margaret could imagine falling in love with the idealized one but not the other. She'd wanted to see them again when she was twenty-seven.

Of course, she was twenty-eight now, not in love and with her mother in a cement-floored croissant shop that would have been crowded if it weren't August. Though the streets felt deserted, everything was still open. They tore the airy morsels with their fingers, standing up.

Her mother looked around nervously for what was not here.

The city was a way Margaret liked it, the air soft, wet, warm, a little sooty, like a bundle of damp wash in your arms. Everyone leftover fit together like people at a singles' dance.

"Where is the good shopping area?" her mother said. "I'd like to buy you some new clothes."

Margaret glared at her as if she'd said something nonsensical. Even tragic. Wasn't it obvious this was something she didn't know? Did Margaret look like someone who shopped?

Her mother had been the sweetheart of Kappa Kappa Gamma and had never tried hard enough to get over it.

Then what had happened to Margaret all her life began; she felt herself softening, dissolving on one side to join her mother.

She was offended, but perhaps she could also be intrigued. Even tempted. Maybe some new clothes would be nice. There was a girl at work, her boss, sort of, whom she would have liked her mother to meet, except, of course, Caroline didn't stay in town summer weekends.

But Caroline was fluent in clothes. Last week a girl had called her from Texas asking to borrow a certain dress, and Caroline FedExed it, right from the magazine office.

Last week, Margaret had been in a store with Caroline. They were on their way to an appointment, and Caroline wanted to pick up a skirt from alterations. While they waited, she ordered Margaret, her sort-of assistant, to try on a shorts-suit, something Margaret had never known to exist. The outfit was made entirely out of seersucker.

"You need something like that," Caroline declared.

Margaret mimicked that with hilarity to her friends. As if anyone ever needed a shorts-suit.

Even besides the money, which was more than the balance in her checking account, Margaret knew she had a gravity, some largeness of face and asymmetry, that was mostly a misfortune but in her better moods could seem like the beginnings of a style. Even Caroline was a little intimidated, so that as much as Margaret annoyed her, she also knew she would never be fired. Caroline was the managing editor, but Caroline had a Reading Block. She saw a psychoanalyst four times a week, connecting the meaning of the word bin—what they used at the magazine to keep manuscripts in—to the word Ben, her father's name. Caroline depended on Margaret to read for her and often repeated Margaret's comments as her own.

Margaret didn't mind. She wasn't trying to work her way up. For her, this was a job to support *Horizon Farm*.

Now that everyone else better at these things was away, it felt easier to enter stores.

Margaret's mother was intrepid. She'd lived long enough to understand that the membranes of snobbery in stores and restaurants would all dissolve at the touch of money.

She was worried about Margaret, clearly. Sometimes Margaret thought her manners caused her mother's consternation; at other moments, she was sure it was her nose.

Her mother marched through department stores as if conducting a mandatory inspection. At one, Margaret spotted the shorts-suit and started her mimicry.

"Now *that's* becoming," her mother said, hands on hips.

It went on the *take* pile.

Margaret's mother took full charge. She seemed to regret Margaret's taste. "That? It's dull as dishwater."

"You look like a little schoolmarm," she said, opening the buttons of a blouse.

Sex seemed to be switching on Margaret, in a way that made her sit down dizzy on the velvet padded bench of the changing room. After a whole lifetime of whispered threats—*They're going to want, he will try, take...from you*—now it seemed no one was trying at all, and her mother wanted to gussy her up.

It had been only a game, after all.

Margaret followed mutely into the various departments: lingerie, stockings, shoes. Her mother became imperial, a general. She told Margaret to go try on this skirt, and Margaret did.

Margaret asserted herself only once, over a pair of black pants, the item she wore every day, the item most young women in New York wore almost every day.

"Let's buy two," Margaret said, when her mother discovered a pair that fit, after making her try on thirteen and examining them from behind. Then that would be done, for a long time.

"But everybody'll think you have on the same thing all the time."

At lunchtime, they sat in the exact center of a waving, murmuring, many-tentacled restaurant, surrounded by shiny shopping bags.

Her mother was talking about how her dentist met the girl he married.

"She's adorable. And they rock climb *with* the baby."

Why was it that marriage still seemed to her the high bright thing? Margaret's father had been killed in a sailboat accident when she was three. She did and did not remember him. She hadn't ever known her mother married, unless you counted three harrowing years with Martin Brody, a Tulsa banker who'd turned out to be mean.

"Mom, why do you care so much if I get married? It didn't work for you."

"No," her mother said, suddenly shy, perhaps offended. It embarrassed her to be unmarried. "No, but having children did. And I would have liked to have that, too. I want you kids to have it because I didn't."

"But you have friends. You always worked. That's a good life, too."

"Oh, yes, a very good life. But I'd like you to have both."

Who could argue with both, whatever it was. As if both was just what you had now, and the other, neither shaved down or changed. Double the Fun.

"Should we go look at paintings?" Margaret said, as they walked out of the restaurant, into the hazy mid-afternoon heat.

Margaret felt glints of her mother's pleasures, if she were Margaret's age, here, now. Her mother would have found a share with five other girls in the Hamptons. They'd catch rides out, meet one another's buses, share blouses in the flurry before dinner dates.

And there was nothing wrong with it. It probably happened in the Roman Empire. It will be happening in a hundred years.

But a man passed them in a raincoat. He looked as if he were on a mission to some used bookstore or a place which sold ancient toy lead soldiers. I would rather be here, Margaret thought, in the sluffy day.

Her mother was nervous because there was still time, time to push Margaret up onto the bus, the way she'd tried all her life.

"I don't know if I feel like a museum now," she said. "Let's just go home for a while, if we're going out tonight."

In the taxi, Margaret began to sift back into herself, and she cried with exasperation at all the shiny colored bags and the loss of that second pair of black pants. "This isn't my life," she said, half standing in the checker cab. "I should take it all back and just get the other black pants. That's all I'll really wear."

Her mother looked at her with utter, innocent incomprehension.

"Get them. We'll call and have the girl put on a hold."

The doorman jumped up. "Mama take you on a shopping spree! I know. I know. Let me get."

Margaret was truly tired, the way she'd been tired as a child, after a tantrum. She lay down on her old couch and fell fast asleep.

When she woke up, the window was open, a phone was ringing somewhere, in the steady New York air-noise outside, her mother was in Margaret's old clothes, it was almost dark, and then she understood the ring to be her own phone, alarming, and sat up straight. It was Bob.

"Can I call you right back?" she said. "I fell asleep."

"You're asleep at five in the afternoon? Is your mother there?"

"Mm-hm."

"What's *she* doing while you're asleep?" There was the sound of a snicker, but that was just Bob, Margaret reminded herself.

"Cleaning, I think."

"Well, are we on tonight?" She had told him tonight or tomorrow.

"I'm not sure. Can I call you back?"

"Well, when? You were going to call me this afternoon."

She was. "I am. Five minutes," she said, overpromising again.

While Margaret slept, her mother had noticed everything she'd deliberately decided not to worry about until later.

"I ran out to the hardware store," her mother said. "I'd just as soon stay here tonight and organize a little, but it's up to you."

The way she saw it, the girl was fine, the job was enough, the problem had to be *décor*.

Because of course there was a problem. Twenty-eight. Only a Bob.

As Margaret went through the bags, she found six cans of paint. Her mother, it turned out, had spent almost three hundred dollars. She'd already begun reorganizing. She'd moved bookshelves and taken down torn rice paper blinds. Perhaps this was the eternal work of mothers visiting daughters in city apartments.

After the first surprise, she would never say *shock*, no, just a little taken aback, that was all, she pitched in, trying to help her child in this foreign world.

At the bottom of one bag was a Kleenex box holder, made out of some type of woven reed.

"Mom, I don't even *use* Kleenex."

"I noticed," her mother said, carrying in two rolls of toilet paper she'd collected from the bedside table and floor, picking up another from the desk.

They decided to put off Bob until tomorrow.

"Then he can see what we've done a little," her mother said, opening paint cans with a butter knife. "See which colors you like. Never pick a color without putting it on the wall first."

These were the koans of Margaret's home education. *Never let anyone cut your cuticles, just push back.* It was all enough to make her cry. She was so behind.

It appeared that Margaret's kitchen/hallway presented problems. For one thing, it was a kitchen/hallway. The majority of the sink was tucked behind a structural pillar. There was very little cutting room, but Margaret's mother had found a bracket that would allow a chopping block to be pulled out and then folded down flush against the wall. The hardware store would be delivering the butcher board before seven.

By the time it arrived, all the furniture was pushed to the middle of the room, and they'd begun painting. The New York sky out the window was deep blue. There were no screens.

"I love these summer nights with no mosquitos."

"They're in the Hamptons," Margaret said. "We're too high up."

The walls teal blue with yellow trim, Margaret was sorry to put her own furniture back. Her couch was inoffensive, though there were coffee stains, but her chairs were ordinary, and her desk dominated most of the living room.

She looked to her mother. "Should I move it?"

"This is where you are most of the time. You might as well have the view where you work. Besides, if you have people over, throw on a cloth, and it'll be your dining table."

Margaret was grateful to her mother for recognizing the small temple. Her mother had never worked at home. She liked getting out to her job, the way Margaret did, but there was never something else her mother wanted to do more. Except this. Her and her brother.

They stayed up all night fixing. Her mother had such stamina. This was what they'd done together, been good at. It had been difficult when they'd been trying to find New York's pleasures, but, working, they both felt easy.

"I don't know about you, but I'm starving," Margaret's mother finally said. "New York has to have some all-night eatery."

"It does. The Empire Diner. Let's go."

They took a taxi just as the sky was getting light. "Wait a minute, what's this? Stop, please, sir."

"It tis a flea market," the man said.

Margaret's mother found two lace panels that would be drapes in the bedroom and a throw to cover the splotchy couch.

They ordered large plates of eggs at the diner and then walked the ninety-four blocks home.

Bob's call woke them again. Flake by flake, the sky outside the windows devolved to twilight, ashes mixing into gorgeous color.

"Well, where should we go?"

The apartment, always a treasure, at $460 a month, with its fields of view, punctuated by steeples and water towers, now seemed loved inside, too. "We painted everything, you should come see."

"You want to eat up *there*?" It was a joke with them, already, one of their few agreements, that there was nowhere to eat north of 60th.

Bob had an actual income. Usually, they went to modest places, anyway, but for her mother he would probably splurge.

"How about come here, and then we'll go down to dinner."

"Let's eat up there, then. I don't want to come up and then go down again."

But that's what he would do, anyway, it was only a matter of when. She knew, though, that there was no arguing or he'd be silent all night, with that glittering edge.

She had to pick. Already the rope sagged. She wanted her mother to have an elegant New York dinner. Bob seeing her apartment, with its clean corners, wasn't worth Upper Upper West Side food.

"He can't just come pick us up?" Margaret's mother said.

Margaret shook her head. Nothing looked right on her, either, none of the new clothes. In the dresses, she looked dressier, but no more and possibly less pretty. Less because they called attention to her trying. This was an argument Margaret and her mother had had forever. Margaret thought a really beautiful woman looked best in just anything, old jeans, a T-shirt, hair back in a rubber band. Margaret's mother believed anyone, beautiful or not, looked best in a well-cut dress.

Margaret tried on each new item, shaking her head. A girl in such a dress shouldn't have this nose, she decided. Finally, she put on the black pants. The other things exposed parts of herself to a lineup, as if she were entering her knees in a contest.

"You're not going to dress a little?" her mother said.

"I just can't."

The restaurant was a place Margaret had heard of. Published writers ate there and editors who were more famous than the writers. Of course it was just a restaurant, and so many other people went, too. Caroline came here with dates who were not the guy she lived with. The one she lived with and loved, for whom Margaret composed grand, carved letters, Caroline kept hidden the way you might keep a cat if your building didn't allow pets.

Many people seemed to be speaking foreign languages. They sat at the front, where the doors opened to the street, and in the trees outside, someone had strung lights.

Bob was an occasional oasis in her general poverty, when it came to meals.

He was, as always, polite, at least on the incoming side. He was capable of great silence. Most of their time together seemed to be spent with Margaret teasing words out of him, by means of shock. Sometimes she became more and more audacious, to shake him as if some penny inside would rattle.

But to her surprise, her mother's soft, beckoning questions seemed to elicit more. He was already embarked on a long amiable conversation about the vagaries of foreign investment. He and her mother seemed to exchange some signal, every minute or so, to confirm their agreement.

All this made Margaret sullen.

Who was Bob? Anyway.

A nice man. Not someone unkind or unreliable.

Could she love him?

In a way, perhaps. Truly, she didn't know.

Did he love her?

He had an interest, a certain grudging respect. But no, not love, wouldn't say love.

"The woman wanted a rest after ten years of hard work! Reasonably enough," he said, "so now they're making a huge general case about it."

His argument was often that the world, Margaret included, made too big a fuss.

Could she do better? Was there more to be had in the world?

Yes, but she did not know for sure. She had an inkling. But sometimes it seemed that all happiness would be temporary, followed by pain.

Was it only a matter of attitude?

She understood that she had not been blessed with a good disposition. She had better hair.

"I know it," her mother was saying emphatically.

Margaret became even more silent. In this kind of conversation, there seemed no place for her. She excused herself to the ladies' room.

There was some grinding, endless quality to their sex. Often she wanted to stop halfway through and go to sleep. She would look at

*the clock and remember her morning hours were her own, the hours
she devoted to* Horizon Farm. *Bob himself was an insomniac. It was
disconcerting. Sometimes she'd wake up, and he'd be staring at her,
propped on an elbow. She immediately worried that she'd been
sleeping unattractively, maybe with her mouth open.*

She had been in New York now five years. Her mother had visited once before, near the beginning.

Margaret had been in love then, the way she imagined people
are. She believed for a while she held a portion of that true thing
which was at once rare and altogether common. The boy had
seemed a little too good for her, she'd been amazed he liked her,
grateful and always nervous. He talked a way she just loved and
always made himself sound average.

Yes, she had been in love once, but it hadn't been the same for
him, she knew that really, even from the start, there was something slippery about his feelings for her, he could easily slide off
them.

She'd tried to play his affections a bit, lift them. Taking counsel
from her running partner, Harold (who often gave the same
advice she rejected from her mother), she tried to NOT CALL.
Once, Harold instructed her to send a postcard from her vacation
with no message on it, only her name.

The thing about really being in love was Margaret understood
her mother then. Because she would have done anything for that
boy. Her work seemed a front, like those fake restaurants, the only
real business was trying to keep him.

"Narrow escape," Harold called it.

And since that first important boy in New York, Margaret had
made many tries. There had been a handsome sculptor, talented,
but not verbal. He hadn't liked *Lawrence of Arabia,* at one point
calling it *Attila the Hun.*

There had been a pointy-faced collage photographer, who
turned out to be dangerous.

There was a bisexual high school teacher, too. All she remembered of him was making out on her couch, everything feeling
jagged and mushy, his elbow in soft parts of her, his mouth wob-
bly and unstable. There was a stagnant, never-ending feeling to
the afternoon. She needed to get outside for air desperately, but
when they took a walk, there was still no air.

All of their names went unmentioned in her Sunday phone calls home.

As Margaret had grown up, in Nebraska, her mother had had several Bobs. There was real-estate Bob, machine-part-salesman Bob, and Bob the ex-Jesuit, who was still her friend.

Her mother hadn't married any of them, either.

Bob never drank, only Diet Coke, and never touched dessert, but tonight he ordered a piece of pie and actually refilled Margaret's mother's wineglass.

Once, Margaret's mother reached over and touched her forehead.

"Are you feeling all right?" she asked. "I'm not used to my girl so quiet," she said to Bob.

"I'll say," he said, with a choking laugh, and this became another of their agreements.

"I'm fine," she said.

Her mother looked down at her ice cream dish, and Bob glanced away, beyond the trees to the dark Village apartments and streets.

When they said goodbye at the front of the restaurant, she felt a way she hadn't even remembered—like a girl with her mother, at the age she just began to wish her mother was not there, because whoever she was was not possible in the presence of this larger force.

Monday morning, Margaret took her mother on the bus she always took, and they walked the seven blocks together she usually walked by herself. It was quiet, commerce closed for the holiday.

No one else was in the building, but she had keys. She took her mother up the grand elevator, down the winding, cluttered halls, to her office. Her mother stood looking. "So this is it."

It was a small job, deliberately (she'd passed up one promotion), but it was enough for her mother to squeeze out of it many things: glamour, purpose, even accomplishment. All her mothers' friends knew that Margaret was a New York Magazine Editor. She'd bought them subscriptions for Christmas. Margaret understood that, for her mother, succeeding as a writer or just staying the editor she already was seemed just about the same, equal—

both good. Sometimes this exasperated Margaret (what she was trying was so hard, she wasn't good enough yet, far from it), and her job was just her job, which she'd felt too good for for years, though some days it gave her relief.

Those days, when she got out of the office at six o'clock and walked out into the blast of warm, solid air, she tried to feel like the hundreds of other people wearing New York clothes and sneakers, walking out of offices, carrying take-out cups. She was making her own living. She wasn't hurting anybody. That was something. Even if the main thing, the invisible thing she lived for, came to nothing.

"What a view!"

"At night I can see the bridges. Chrysler Building's there."

"I can see why you like it. What a place to bring somebody after a date."

Margaret's own suspense was not her mother's. Her mother really didn't agonize over Margaret's hope of success. She just wanted her to get married.

And that was a far easier thing to do, if you really wanted. There was a guy in San Francisco who'd been her boyfriend in college. He said he'd marry her if nobody else turned up. Last Christmas, when there had been a blizzard, he sent her a down coat for Christmas.

No, it wouldn't be hard to get married. To get that feeling she'd had once, that was what was hard. And as the years went on, she decided it was not, anyway, that desirable. There was this one person she'd felt that way about once, and there were all the Other People. She supposed if you wanted to get married enough, you'd go ahead and marry one of them. The trick would be deciding which one. Because it would be a choice. Unlike with him, that first important New York boy. They would have different qualities, hard to measure against each other. Bob, for example, was consistent. And very neat. No, better than that. He had integrity.

She thought maybe if she kept going to her therapist long enough, she would cease to think of the male population as Him and Other People. The way to make it honorable was to just forget about him and start from scratch with the Other People. To take them one at a time.

Right now, to imagine marrying Bob was depressing, but so was being in love again, with shaking misery.

"Life is exhausting, when you can't even have a good fantasy without the wires short-circuiting each other." She tried explaining to her mother but ended up just shrugging.

So she showed her the place where she spent most of her day, a huge square chair in the corner, and felt grateful her mother didn't say anything about slip-covering. There were splits in the fabric where yellow foam poked out, but the firm broad arm supported her morning coffee. That was where she sat all day and read.

This was her job! Someday, she would die, and she would have made her living, watching the snow sew steady seams on brick buildings between heaven and earth, reading.

Much that she'd talked about to her mother was here. On a shelf sat the bin/Bens full of manuscripts.

Margaret showed her the case of champagne in the refrigerator, sent to Caroline by one of the young men at a publishing house. In reply, Caroline had ordered an ice chest from *Better Homes* and had it messengered to him with a card that said *Cool it, Brad.* Margaret led her mother to the appliance he'd sent back with no message: a huge toaster oven they all used now, which was a mess with poppy seeds from a month's worth of bagels.

Margaret's mother found it incredible how much money Caroline and her friends spent on flirtation. "Ridiculous, really," she said.

And yet, all those young men were, to Caroline, only Bobs. The one she really loved was addicted, hidden.

"Still, a little romance is a nice thing to have. More than Bob, maybe."

"I thought you liked him."

"Oh, I did. I do. But I don't see him with you, really. This project of yours. When do you think you'll be finished? I want to give a party."

Maybe after last night, after Bob, her mother was finally giving up on her. She was asking her about her work, acquiescing, at last. Maybe from this day on, she would accept Margaret's own notions of suspense, foreign as they were, as if she'd been given a sheet of pronunciations. She'd never insist on shopping again.

Perhaps she would no longer think of her daughter as stubborn but as unfortunately handicapped. She would send her pens for gifts.

When other people asked Margaret how close she was to finishing, she lied. In fact, she almost always felt she was lying when she talked about her work. When she'd been in love, she was lying when she sat down to work. The lie then was that she wanted to at all. But now, she liked to go in her sloppy, loose, spill-marked clothes into the easy room, the playroom, the cry room, the curl-on-the-floor room, but she didn't really want an end. She could go on like this longer—being in the somewhere middle.

She said, "I don't know if I can."

Margaret understood how hard it was for her mother to have her. To her mother, it was unfathomable, the way Margaret always liked the foggy days, when everyone else was sorry to miss the beach. She seemed amazed that Margaret wanted to keep on like this, never proud, never celebrating, always living for the something she would still do. Margaret had an aversion to drama. The normal high points of life meant nothing to her.

As a girl, she'd seemed dumbfounded when people tried to celebrate her high school graduation.

"As if it's some a*chieve*ment?" she'd said.

It had been the same with college. Her mother sat in the front row, clapping, though Margaret hadn't even gotten around to renting a gown.

But Margaret wasn't really such a moper. She just didn't know how to prove it. How to explain a preference for the normal hours?

She truly loved New York's blowy days, the round air leaping into her lap like a light child. Men in raincoats, hands in pockets, scouring the street on missions to arcane stores.

Her mother was a sailboat used to being herself, tiny, manning ropes inside, but being watched from far away on the shore. People saw not her steering, but only the big bright billow of white sails.

It was one thing to reject the life your mother had. It was another to turn away from what she'd wished for.

But then again, except for the boy in San Francisco who'd sent her the down coat, who was offering?

Even that boy had a girlfriend now. Actually, that was why he'd sent the coat. A soft apology.

That night, Harold called, wanting to run.

"Go," her mother said.

"Well, we should probably get dressed if we're going out." This was her mother's last night, and Margaret had already made the reservation.

"Do you have any vegetables? We've been eating such rich food, let's just steam something here," Margaret's mother said.

The phone wilted down from Margaret's wrist.

"I mean it," her mother said.

Margaret and Harold ran, as they always did, in the darkening dusk of Riverside Park, downhill toward the Boat Basin. They passed the gated subway tunnels, where they saw a flicker of fire. Margaret assumed hobos lived there, homeless men, and the kisses of flame were them lighting their cigarettes or joints. It was strange to have a subway tunnel, all caves and darkness, under such a populated treed and flowered park, but it was New York, and even the entrance to those caves was arched, gated in art-nouveau black metal.

"WPA," Harold said.

Tonight the flame was insistent.

"Have you ever been in there?" she asked.

"No. Always sort of wanted to."

"Hope the poor guy doesn't burn himself."

"Not burning himself. That's a signal. Somebody wants a date." She looked at Harold sideways, as if a door had opened, just a wedge, to the mystery of his suspense.

After, they stopped at the Korean market and bought Diet Cokes.

When they walked into the apartment, Margaret's mother's suitcase was waiting neatly by the door, and the apartment was shining with lit candles, the summer windows open. Her mother had set the desk/table for dinner by the view.

On the suitcase, Margaret banged her knee, and her breath started stuttering. It was their last night, and only now they'd found their ease, she felt again their old love. But the plane was booked, the suitcase packed and buckling.

Margaret would have to sit through the after-ride for days in an aching way that resembled the demolition of a breakup. Less acutely because it was not a new breakup. It was just a reminder of what had been once, for a long time, and was now over. And maybe love like that, where you lived with someone and they cared about you every day, maybe that would never happen again.

Harold came out of the shower in his black jeans and shirt, his wet hair combed. He bent down to kiss Margaret's mother, whom he called Janine, and asked about her office friends by name.

She made Margaret try on the new dresses for him.

They sat in the long, slow twilight, Harold and her mother around the desk/table.

As Margaret stepped out of the tangling clothes in her large bathroom (somehow the square footage lost from the narrow kitchen/hallway reincarnated in this pink and black bathroom), she heard her mother's somber voice answering, and she leaned back against the cool tile.

It was easy to try on clothes for her best audience out there laughing, from whom there was nothing to gain or lose.

Margaret looked in the mirror at her uneven but still young face.

Maybe the *(Idealized) Portrait of the Artist* had been what Rembrandt really looked like at twenty-seven, only he couldn't see it himself then.

Perhaps on the eve of a late wedding, at thirty-six, say, she would look back at tonight, an average night, one of millions, the way a girl who marries a prince from a faraway land might remember the friendship she'd had with the boy in her castle as real life, though it had nothing to do with the word love.

17 Reasons Why

I was living in San Francisco's Mission District, at Valencia and 14th, across the street from some projects and a Gold's Gym and above the Lady Luck Candle Shop. On the corner was a dusty convenience store run by two Lebanese brothers. You could get loose cigarettes there for a nickel. Up 14th Street, half a block, was Kate's place.

She had a fairly big studio, nicer than mine, on the second floor of a clean white building. There was no furniture except for a folding table with a typewriter by the kitchen, two lamps, and an end table, a futon in the big walk-in closet, beneath a small window, and various books and chunks of candle. There was nothing at all in the main room. The drapes were large swatches of burgundy cloth, tied open most of the time; light from the streetlamps poured into the apartment and turned it a kind of dark amber. We could see into the places on the other side quite easily and guessed the same was true for hers, but only the main room was really visible. I would wait on the futon when she went to the bathroom, and she would hurry back along the wall, as if the shadows were deeper there, one arm folded across her breasts.

Kate worked half days as an assistant at a Montessori school on Dolores, a couple of blocks away. I would walk her there in the mornings, before the fog burned off, and she would pull me into doorways and kiss me, and we would say ridiculous, sweet things. I would walk down to 16th Street and get coffee and write her long, rambling notes which I would leave under her door (we did not exchange keys) before heading off to practice or to my job.

I was waiting tables in Hayes Valley four days a week at a place, several years gone now, called Way Out West that served American cuisine: basic farm breakfasts with a little unconvincing vegetarian fare—garden burgers, three-bean chili, cream of broccoli soup made with chicken stock—thrown into the mix. Though the crowd, especially on weekends, was made up mostly of artistic types, bikers and skate kids who coasted down from the Lower

Haight and Western Addition, the owner, Mr. Bong, routinely fired waiters and waitresses for getting their noses pierced or dyeing their hair. In many ways, he behaved like a man who woke up one day and suddenly found himself in charge of a faltering restaurant with unreadable menus. He was always shouting in Korean at his half-brother (whom we referred to as Baby Bong) and drawing up battle plans to improve business, the first step of which often involved getting physical with the bums who propped themselves up against the wall outside the restaurant. He would give a broad you-can't-fool-me smile to certain hippies and blacks who came in for lunch before bluntly asking them, "You got money?" He distrusted me, too, because I had an earring, and, after almost a year, he would still get on my case from time to time. "You stink," he'd say when I came back after a cigarette break to find him clearing one of my two-tops. "You not professional." But I was making at least forty dollars a shift; and if I did my side-work as I went, I could always cash out by nine, and that was key because of the band.

I played bass in a power trio along with my friends Blue and Jack. Things were starting to happen for us. We were headlining all over town, and we'd made our own record: *BAM* had liked it, the *Guardian* had liked it, and Michael, our manager, was sure it would get distributed.

We took a fairly straight-forward approach: power chords, big initial hits, lots of fuzzy harmonics developing in a wide way. I wrote some of the songs, but most of them were Blue's, and his tendency was always toward two- or three-chord, overdriven, crunchy punk riffs. The structure was sometimes so simple that calling it verse-chorus-verse would have been an exaggeration (it was more like verse fast-and-loud followed by verse slow-and-soft). But Blue had a knack for coming up with interesting melodies, and his voice was a beautiful sound, careening and confident; he could wrap a dozen notes around a single chord. The simple progressions gave me a lot of freedom, and my bass lines had gotten way more complex. I had a 200-watt Ampeg head, a matching cabinet with four 12's, and I played a black Fender P-bass. I'd have my hands all over the frets, playing eight notes to every two coming off Blue's guitar, doing descending fills, arpeggios. In a lot of ways Blue's voice was the most dynamic element in our sound, and whenever possible I followed *it*. Onstage, under that real high sound-pressure for which there is just no substitute, with all the secondary reverb scrabbling across the floors and up the walls, you would get this weirdly delicate counterpoint; this pretty, bridgeless thing.

We'd gone on some short tours: down to Santa Barbara and L.A. a few times, and twice to Eugene, Portland, and Seattle. I was never crazy about those tours: you're driving so many miles...and when you finally do reach the city, you're tired and disoriented, your hands smell like gasoline and ketchup, you're just a few more goofs out walking in the rain. We trudged our equipment from the van into clubs, past kids our own age in whose faces I saw the arrogance I myself could work up for bands I didn't know. What was unnerving was that you noticed it: you only did when you were down. And you never mentioned it to each other; you said things like "Let's kick some ass."

I'd met Kate during the winter at a party. She was living with a guy in another band, a drummer named Neil. For a short time, Neil's band had shared our rehearsal space in the Lower Haight. They were an acoustic-electric blend, sort of art-poppy and moody: no real setup or climax, lots of minor chords (Jack said listening to them practice was like looking at a lava lamp); and they would do things like hand out fliers at their shows quoting Borges and Nietzsche; but we liked them, had recently played with them. Neil was a good drummer and a kind of big, smart, quiet guy. Neil and Kate had gone to school together in Michigan. She was a writer. She'd written a novel that was going to be published, and with the advance they had come to California in the fall. She wasn't sure if she liked San Francisco yet, she told me. Her father lived in Long Island; she had thought about moving to New York instead.

At the party she seemed to run into me quite a bit. While we were both waiting for the bathroom, I was in the middle of saying something to her when she cut me off. "Your eyes are like little Earths," she said. "Little planets."

I said, "Thanks a lot, I guess," and we laughed.

I knew Blue had met Kate previously. When I mentioned her, he said, "I don't like that girl. She's a bitch."

"What's wrong with her?"

"She's so proud of herself. She wrote a novel. Big fucking deal."

About a month later, I ran into Kate at a café on Mission Street. She was reading a book I'd never heard of; she told me about it and had me read a paragraph: it was some novel about God and horse thieves. She and Neil were living near Alamo Square at the time, but that night he was playing a private party at the Crystal Pistol, a few blocks from the café, and she planned to head over there later. I asked her if she wanted to get a beer, and we went down the street to Uptown, somewhere I liked to go after gigs and rehearsal because it was mellow and you could sit down. With an ashtray between us, we talked for an hour or so.

Kate was tall and thin, and her long neck seemed to hold her head in a dangerous balance high up over her shoulders, like a marionette's. She had thick brown hair, cut straight across, and a stunningly beautiful face that was nevertheless drawn, and very pale, and intense. She laughed easily and seemed very sure of herself: she would look right at you when she talked.

She acted like she knew me well. At the bar she told me that she wanted to be famous.

When I laughed, she said, "People don't like to talk about that, I know."

I said, "Yeah, well. It's not exactly my favorite sport, either."

She seemed a little embarrassed, and we moved on to another topic, but it wasn't that I thought she'd said a horrible thing. I just didn't know what you could really say.

We left the bar in time to get her to Neil's show. The blocks near Mission were always bleak and poorly lit, uriney, strewn with garbage. It was cold and windy. Kate wore a thin leather jacket over a light green cardigan—a wino sweater, she called it. The jacket didn't sit right on the sweater, and her jeans were loose: I couldn't tell exactly where her body was inside her clothes. She had a graceful, determined, somehow unathletic way of walking. As we stood at the crosswalk on Mission and 17th, she said, "So, Dean, does this go on a lot, or...?"

"Does what?"

"I don't know...rocker boy, knocking around, 'Wanna grab a beer with me?' sort of thing." She was smiling. "Isn't that...pretty much...?"

"Oh, *that*."

"I mean, I like it—" She touched my arm and pointed almost straight up. "I love that sign," she said.

There were a lot of cars on Mission, and people hanging out on the sidewalk near the porn store and donut shop. Across 17th, some were already curled up with blankets and cardboard in the darkened storefront of an old retail warehouse with empty upper floors. The sign Kate was talking about was on its roof: a gigantic frame without lights, and empty except for enormous old letters in stark relief, like cutouts, against the sky. "17 Reasons Why!" That's all it said. In daylight you could see it from blocks away, looming like a marquee for an outdoor theater.

It was a cool sign, but at the moment I was thinking of other things. I said, "Kate, you're giving me a hard time. What's up with that?"

I took her arm and turned her around to face me, and I kissed her; she leaned back against a dark store window, and we went at it. After a minute or two we pulled apart, and I looked away from her, down at the ground, and my hair dropped over my eyes. I let it hang there. My heart was pounding. I could see her right foot propped against the glass, and she was swinging her knee very slowly, bumping it against the outside of my leg. Two of her fingers were hooked into the cuff of my jacket. She said, "Well, then." When I looked up, she was staring at me—an impatient, solemn expression that surprised me. But she was trembling, and she stayed where she was, and I started kissing her again.

Sometimes, during the murky six weeks that followed, Neil would answer the phone when I called for Kate, and we'd shoot the breeze for a minute or so; eventually I'd ask if Kate was there, and he'd say, "Yeah, sure, hang on," and that was that. Not that I thought he was actually happy to hear my voice: Kate had told him she was looking for her own place, and I was sure he knew it had something to do with me.

But I wasn't pressing Kate for details of their home life. I was running between pay phones in Hayes Valley after work trying to reach her; I was waiting on her for half an hour by the canned cat food in the back of a corner store on a rainy night and kissing her goodbye behind the big tree in Alamo Square Park at three in the morning. For me, the thing was so intense and was happening so rapidly—she called it "our collision"—that it was easy, when I thought about it at all, to see in Neil's laid-back attitude a cool acceptance of the facts. It seemed possible that everyone involved would emerge safely on the other side, away from the wreck.

By March, Kate had left Neil and moved in down the block from me. Now if I happened to see Neil, walking down the street, he would ignore me. When I first saw him after their breakup, I addressed him directly and he just kept going. He was growing a beard.

That first time, I was truly caught off-guard when he didn't say hello, and I felt like an ass. It was as if, strolling past, he'd held out his share of our phony phone conversations and by reflex I'd taken them off his hands.

Kate met Neil for coffee several times that first month, and they talked on the phone quite a bit. If she was on the phone when I came over and mouthed that it was Neil, I would hold up my middle finger and she would smile—but she wouldn't just hang up; she wouldn't say, "Neil, I have to go, Dean is here." And if I spoke out loud, she instantly looked furious. "Have a heart," she would say, when she finally did get off the line. "Jesus." Sometimes I apologized: I knew she felt guilty for leaving Neil; but I didn't see what good it did to pretend I wasn't there. Late one night, not long after the move, we were lying in bed when her doorbell rang, and she jumped up in alarm: she thought Neil was down at the gate with a box of her things. "So go down and get him," I said, sitting up. "I'll pick up some of these condom wrappers."

She said, "That's not funny, Dean. Please. You've got to—would you just get dressed and, just for one minute, go out and stand on the courtyard stairs?" The buzzer rang again. "Please!" I pulled on my clothes, stepped out into the hallway, and found a door leading to a rickety inner staircase that had a kind of *Rear Window* view of several lit-up, empty-looking apartments. I heard Kate run past the door and down the main stairs towards the front gate. I lit a cigarette and stared straight up at the pale misty sky. Then I walked down to the courtyard, found a narrow passage out to the street, and went home.

The phone was ringing when I got in. It was Kate, of course, and we got into a fight. I hung up on her. But eventually we wound up at my place.

We argued then about a lot of things. Kate said, "It sounds like you just want a normal girlfriend," and I said, "You're so full of shit. I just want to know what the deal is. Do you want to be with me or not?" She said she was in love with me.

Kate would say things like "I think you're infinite." She would say, "You're like a church." She would bring me old records and picture books from the Purple Heart thrift store near our block or a bag of my favorite granola from the Rainbow Grocery. She would stand in the alley behind my place and shout, "Throw down the keys, Dino. I have the granola." She would tell me how much she loved me, and she would cry about things that had happened to her, and I would sing her to sleep with old Elvis Costello songs—she always wanted to hear the same ones—and then I would lie awake wondering what would happen to us.

Kate was always talking about New York and about famous writers she had met when she went to New York, and she would get letters from these guys in the mail and moan and groan about what slimeballs they were. She even asked me once if she thought she should open a particular envelope, and I said, "I think it's a bad idea; let me," and I grabbed it from her and held it out of her reach, and we laughed, and she wound up tearing the thing to pieces and throwing it in the trash. She carried a thin spiral note-book everywhere, a kind of diary, she said, and was always writing things down: she would just pop out with it when we were walk-ing down the street and scribble away. I didn't know half the things she mentioned—books and styles and whatever. And she would sometimes say things about Neil—that he didn't know much about Peru or something—that were about ten times more true for me. I would say so. She would say, "But you know other things," and I would say, "No, I don't, Kate. I really don't." She'd say she liked the lyrics to our songs.

On my twenty-fourth birthday, in mid-June, we walked up to the Haight for dinner and then saw a movie, *Picnic at Hanging Rock,* at the Red Vic. It was a foggy night: as we were heading back down the hill we couldn't even see the Bay. Beneath the fog, down in the Lower Haight, a single bus was climbing the hill toward us in perfect clarity. Kate said, "This city is so creepy at night. One night it's like *The Jetsons,* you can see a hundred miles of lights, and the next it's like this: it's like *The Wild, Wild West.* You know what I mean? They're like façades," she said, pointing to some Victorians we were passing, flat and square beneath the white sky. "It's like there's nothing up there. No space, no heaven. There's you, and me, and that's it."

I wanted it to be like that. I didn't want to think about anything else: not the band or her book, not our short-term leases, not anything.

For a while now, two songs from our record had been in heavy rotation on commercial stations in Silicon Valley and in the city, but sometimes, recently, when I heard them come on, I would turn off the sound. Kate would come out of the kitchen singing them, teasing me, and I would tell her to stop. She said she was proud of me; she said, "I think you're going to be great." But I was feeling superstitious as hell. A year ago, we were sending out our first tapes to college radio stations (cupped between stapled paper plates, which we autographed as a joke). It felt almost like bad luck that our songs were suddenly getting such airplay when nothing about the future—would the record get distributed? would we get a contract?—was certain.

I wanted to stay in bed with Kate. Nothing seemed more important to her, either, and we made love all the time. She would crawl on top of me, and every ounce of her body would fall into place, moving, and her whole neck and chest would get splotchy and red, and her nose would run, and her nails would cut into my hands—they would cut through my skin.

When her eyes were shut that tight, squeezing tears, and when I tried to imagine what she was seeing, it was always precisely that room, hers or mine, and the shape of our bodies, and it would make me almost sad.

One day in early August, Kate came over after work at the school and told me that she was going to her father's house in Sag Harbor for the month of September. She'd been talking about the idea for a while, but now she had a ticket.

She was going to have the book done by then and really wanted to take a break. I had told her, previously, that I didn't understand why we couldn't just rent a car and go to Carmel or something. But Kate was as broke as I was—soon she'd be waiting for her check from the publisher—and her father was paying for the trip.

When she returned in October, she was going to stay with me for a while, or we were going to get a place together.

She cried a little now when she talked about giving up her apartment. When it had come up in the past, Kate was the one who had acted like it was no big deal.

Sometimes when she got upset, I just didn't understand. The week before, for instance, she had gotten tears in her eyes when we were out for sushi in the Castro with Jack and his girlfriend, Stacey, who worked in a clothing store near there. Kate had suddenly said she didn't feel well, and I walked her outside. She told me she couldn't relax because she was thinking about her book, and then she started sobbing. "Do you want me to walk you home?" She said she didn't. She said, "I'm sorry. I'm just having a hard time." I couldn't help feeling that she simply didn't want to be there with us.

Now I said, "Is something else going on, Kate?"

"What's that supposed to mean?"

"You tell me, Kate. I really don't know." When she didn't say anything right away, I said, "Did you buy a round-trip ticket?"

"It's round-trip, it's round-trip. October 3rd." She looked down and shook her head. "That was a mean thing to say."

I apologized. After a while, we made love.

Later in the afternoon, she read me a chapter of the novel. The Murphy bed was still down, but now we were on the couch, mostly dressed. It was hot, the windows were open, and the shades were drawn over the gaps; they blew and bumped in the weak breeze.

When she finished, we talked about the book. She said, "I don't even care, at this point. I'm like, get it away from me, you know?"

"I know."

She laughed. "Dean's thinking, Mail it, mail it!" She moved closer to me on the couch. She pressed her forehead against mine and then scraped around to the side of my head and kissed me.

We were quiet for a couple of minutes, and I closed my eyes. Then Kate said, "The kids are so funny when I read to them." I lifted my head and looked at her. "The older ones—the four-year-olds—they'll point at the pictures and they'll go, 'I'd like to be that soldier,' or, you know, 'I'd like to be that rabbit.' The little ones don't get it, and they say, 'I want to be that *stone*.'"

We both laughed. My favorite kid at the school, Joshua, had been a heroin addict the first month of his life. Once, when I'd been there helping Kate, he'd stared at the mirror in the back hall and said, "The boy in the mirror looks like Joshua, but he's *not* Joshua." When I'd told Kate, she'd said, "He always says that!" She'd been busy getting one of the girl's shoes knotted up for the park. "And I always wonder, 'What's he know that I don't know?'" She'd made a funny, puzzled face. "But I kind of know what he means, don't you?"

We were still lying on the couch when Blue showed up.

Blue belonged to the gym across from my building, and he used to come by nearly every day after working out, and we'd have a beer and go over some songs or watch MTV. He came by less often now that Kate was around—once or twice a week.

He kept going in and out of the kitchen as I tried to talk to him. He wouldn't sit down. He lifted the shade from the kitchen window and looked out for a second then let it flop back down. I said, "Blue, man, trust me. The place is surrounded. Take a fucking seat."

We all laughed.

Blue looked bad. I knew that he was feeling the same sort of anxiety I was—probably worse. He was always hungover, and he looked washed out. His skin looked pasty. His hair seemed thin.

This was relative, of course, because Blue was a very good-looking guy. He had short dark hair, heavy-lidded blue eyes, and a thin, muscular body. He usually wore black Converse All-Stars and various T-shirts with the sleeves ripped off. Onstage, when he would switch from lead to rhythm on the guitar—when he came down hard on a chord after a pause—you felt like he could break the thing in two.

I sometimes thought Kate would have gone for Blue if he hadn't been so cold to her from the start. I knew she was attracted to him, in a way. She would say things like "Nice house, but nobody's home." For quite a while she had seemed afraid of him, but now they were more or less used to each other. When she came out with us after gigs, they would joke around like anybody else; she'd even gone with him to see X down at the Shoreline Amphitheater one night when I had to work. When we were alone she would still mock his affectations: the way he squeezed his forehead when he sang and so forth.

Absently, Blue picked up three oranges from the kitchen table and started juggling.

Kate said, "You're so good at that!"

Blue stopped immediately.

"No, keep going," she said.

"He's very good," I said. He could juggle five balls with ease.

"Have you talked to Michael?" Blue said. "The guy from Island is going to be there beforehand so we should try to be there by ten."

"He left a message."

"Where did you learn to juggle like that?" Kate asked.

"Santa Cruz."

He set the oranges back on the table.

"Well," she said, "if you guys ever don't make it big, you can always join the circus."

Blue said nothing.

Kate said, "You know what I mean, Blue. You know I'm joking."

"Whatever, Kate."

"Don't be an asshole, Blue," I said. "She's trying to be nice."

Our gig that night was at Monkey Sea, south of Market, somewhere we'd played half a dozen times, a place we liked. It was in a former meat locker on the second floor of an old warehouse, and there were numerous strings of monkey-face Christmas tree lights from Chinatown crisscrossing the ceiling and knotted around the beams. The bartenders brought booze up from the first floor in a hollow elevator shaft using a pulley system.

Blue and Jack and I had been living in the city for almost two years now and performing in it for longer than that. The whole scene was essentially familiar, and that familiarity was nice. You weren't jarred by whatever variety of weirdness you happened to come across: people fucking in the instant photo booth, or whatever. You were trying to grab the owner to give her your keys so the van wouldn't get towed; you were trying to remember people's names. It was like going to parties in someone's parents' basement when their parents were out of town.

Blue was drunk as hell. He was getting into rave-ups that went on about twice as long as the songs were supposed to be. Sometimes we would just jam endlessly in A: he'd keep building it up, drowning the dynamics. I'd start holding the notes, looking at Jack; we'd practically have to trick Blue into bringing it back to the head. But all in all, it was a good set. No real hitches.

Kate had stayed in to work. She'd asked if I would put her down on the list in case she caught a cab at the last minute. Sometimes I'd look up and see her there, bobbing around, holding a beer. She didn't make it tonight, and I was disappointed.

Blue, Jack, and I went to Uptown.

There were maybe a dozen people sitting on stools at the bar, mostly older guys, and some girls in the back room playing pool. Jack ordered shots of tequila and a round of beer.

I'd noticed Neil as soon as we came through the door. He was in the front room, off to the side, sitting with four or five others on a couple of old couches there, beneath a large, flat-looking painting of a black dog bleeding in the snow.

At the bar, Blue said, "Guess who."

"I saw him."

"Look again."

"What?"

"The brunette."

I had a moment's queasy rush, but it wasn't Kate. It was Kary Mead.

Kary Mead was a legend. Twelve years back, when she was about eighteen, she'd fronted a great San Francisco band, The Cadets—without a doubt one of the best punk bands in the country. They'd opened for The Clash at The Warfield in 1982 and, it is said, blew their cockney asses off the stage. By the late eighties, The Cadets had all sued each other and disappeared from the area, with the exception of Kary, who would still come out of the woodwork a couple times a year and put on a show with her new band. Every so often I'd see her out in public. Once, she was at the library, looking at microfilm, and I'd stood off to the side watching her. When I told the story later, Jack said she was probably looking up old reviews.

I said, "Let me just say what a surprise it is to have Neil and Kary Mead in the same line of vision."

"No shit," Blue said. He grabbed his beer and headed over.

In a few seconds, you could see Blue in his black leather jacket, standing in front of Neil. Neil leaned way back on the couch, looking surprised—even though I knew he'd seen us come in. As far as I knew, the two of them had remained on good terms.

Jack watched for a second and then turned around to face the bar and back room. He lit a cigarette. "Several babes," he said.

The bar itself had only one rail, but a big rectangle had been cut into the wall behind it so the people playing pool and pinball in back could order drinks more easily. The jukebox was playing some country/lounge tune, a kind of sweet faux-swing that was a little like Patsy Cline before she'd started making pop songs.

I looked at the girls again. They wore jeans and long shirts and a lot of loose, shiny bracelets, and they looked sexy and good in a frumpy way, but I said, "I'm not up for it, man. I'm tired." I turned back to Blue. "I want to see what this is about."

Jack glanced over at the couches. "Fuck Kary Mead," he said, but not angrily. He was in a good mood.

Blue stood drinking his beer, talking to Neil, who didn't seem to be saying much. None of the others were talking, either. It seemed pretty clear they were waiting for Blue to wander away.

Jack watched pool. When I turned to grab my beer, he said, "Where's Kate tonight?"

"She's working," I said. "Writing." I felt like a phony. "Who the fuck knows," I said.

It crossed my mind to call Kate now. But it was after one, and I was sure she wouldn't want to come meet us with Neil there. I considered calling her, anyway. The pay phone was visible by the bathrooms, and Neil would know I was calling Kate.

Jack said, "Let's shoot one game of pool."

I sipped my beer. "In a minute," I said.

I saw that Kary Mead was talking, and I got up and headed toward the couches. As I approached, I heard her say to Blue, "You're a true jackass."

Blue ignored her. He was saying something to Neil about the A&R person at Epic he'd talked to the other day.

He was too drunk to be subtle. At a club, near bar time, I'd seen him swoop down on some girl with braces and start dropping names and song titles like there was no tomorrow.

Kary Mead whispered something to a woman in her band, who laughed and turned away.

"Blue," I said. I almost apologized for him. He was drunker

than I thought. But it was also clear that these people were ass-
holes. They all knew who Blue was and were doing what they
could to make him feel like a zero.

"Blue, I want to hit the road soon."

"Why, man? I think you know everybody here. Josie and the
Pussies. Neil's Danish."

Neil's Danish was a bakery near his place.

"Blue."

"Fuck you."

I looked over at the bar for Jack and saw that he'd made his way
into the back room, where he was choosing a pool stick and talking to one of the women.

Turning back, I caught Neil's eye.

"What's up, Neil?" I said.

We both laughed.

"Not a lot."

"You play tonight?"

He nodded. "Kary was at Slim's. I sat in for Buna."

I didn't know who Buna was. "That's cool," I said.

Blue was gazing off toward the back room. Kary Mead was
looking down at her boots. It seemed to me so obvious that she
was jealous of Blue. That was all Blue wanted to see, and he
couldn't.

I said, "We'd love to stay and party with you folks all night." I
had my hand on Blue's shoulder, edging him toward the bar. He
shrugged it off. He didn't seem to know whose side I was on.

"You'd have a lot to talk about," Blue said. "You can talk about
Kate." He was looking at Neil.

"Blue, man," I said. "Shut the fuck up."

"All three of us can talk about her," he said.

At first this hardly registered. It was obvious that at this point
Blue would say whatever ugly thing he could think of.

Kary Mead looked up at him and said, "Blue . . . or whatever.
Just go. Everybody wants you to leave. You want to leave. So just
leave."

She got up and walked past us into the bathroom.

I looked at Blue, and I smiled, as if we shared some amused
perspective on all this, as if we were a band and this shit happens.
I clapped his shoulder again, and then I, too, walked away, into

the back room. Whatever his remark about Kate really meant, I wanted to look like I'd heard it before. I spent the next half hour or so talking to Jack and to the girls, and I said a few casual, random things to Blue whenever he hovered near Jack's chair between games of pinball.

On the ride home, with Jack behind the wheel chatting away and Blue in the backseat brooding, I started to get swamped by confused thoughts. It was easy to come up with half a dozen times when Blue and Kate could have gotten together, but the scenarios were vague enough that I wasn't terribly pained by them. I kept thinking of Kate's trip to Long Island. It seemed quite possible that Kate and I were through. I told myself I'd been expecting it. At the same time, I didn't really believe that it was over.

In any case, I was feeling something other than anger. I remember clearly how, when Jack turned onto my street and drove past the projects, my block looked the way that it had in the old days, before Kate moved in.

I'd left open a window in my apartment, but the cool night breeze still hadn't dislodged all the day's heat, and I sat on the carpet by the window smoking a lemon-flavored cigarette, all they'd had in the nickel cup that afternoon at the corner store. My ears were ringing.

Kate had left a message around one-thirty saying I should come over when I got in. "... Okay. Bye-bye, sweetheart." It was two-fifteen.

Now, for some reason, the image of her sleeping with Blue was vivid and excruciating. I really loved Kate. I imagined her leaving a message on Blue's answering machine. When I realized that's what I was thinking, I felt crazy.

I looked out over the building next door at the clear dark sky and the shimmering line of lights on the Bay Bridge, visible in the distance. For about three seconds I thought of calling my father, who lived in Las Vegas now, and who I hadn't seen since my older sister got married almost two years ago. He might—I thought—actually be glad that I called; he'd try to rouse himself and listen. But I imagined that he'd get impatient hearing the details about Kate and that we'd end up talking about him. He'd say something like "It doesn't sound good from here, guy. Now I'm not trying to tell you what to do... and it's awfully late here. As a matter of fact, I was out a little earlier with a friend of mine..."

When my cigarette burned out, I scraped it against the window ledge and flicked it down into the alley.

"I made soup," Kate said.

We were standing on the futon. I had already pulled off my jeans and socks. Her apartment was dark and smelled like lentils. I realized I was starving.

Kate disappeared into the kitchen, scurrying over the floor boards in the main room as though she were crossing a no-man's land, and came back with a coffee mug full of soup.

"Thanks," I said.

She was sleepy. She kissed me. "It's spilling, so..."

I swept the side of the mug with my finger and licked it, and then we sank down to the bed. Light came through the tiny closet window. I was still half-dressed. I sat against the wall with my legs crossed, and Kate lay down in front of me, the long way. She pulled a blanket over herself and my legs and then curled up close.

The soup was warm but not hot, so I was able to drink it. I leaned over to the edge of the bed and pushed the empty cup along the dusty floor until it hit the molding.

When I slipped down beside her, Kate rolled toward me and drew her top leg up lazily between mine. She reached her arm around me and was still. She was already half-asleep.

"Sing me a song," she murmured into the pillow.

"I'm really tired."

She gave me a feeble little shake. Then she slept.

I lay awake until four. When I finally did fall asleep, I dreamed about Kate. We were walking in the Mission, and I was upset with her—because it was dark out and she was going off alone to meet someone, one of the mothers from the school. I was heading to the Rainbow Grocery to get syrup and milk for pancakes. When I got to the store, it was closed, and the lights were off. Through the glass door I saw something move, and when I looked closely I realized the place was filled with black people—churchgoers. They were dressed up and dancing, but there was something sluggish about their movements, and there wasn't any music. It was a hot summer night, a Sunday, I remember, and this was a wedding.

I woke when Kate got up for work, and I asked if she minded me staying in bed for a while: it was rare that I didn't leave when she did. She said that that was fine, but I got the sense that she knew I was up to something.

"I guess you can just check the handle when you leave," she said. "You don't need my keys."

"No, I don't need your keys."

Ten minutes after she left, I walked over to her writing table and started looking around for her spiral notebook. There were papers all over the place, typed pages from the novel. The apartment didn't have a lot of hiding places, and after I looked through a stack of magazines next to her bookshelves, I began to think that she probably had it with her. As I gathered my clothes, it occurred to me to check beneath the futon, and there it was.

I sat on the edge of the bed, still undressed, and began to flip through it. My heart was pounding. The cool thing to do would have been to just go home. But it was too easy to imagine sitting there in my place, wishing I'd gone through with it.

At first, as I turned the pages, I didn't even read the words, but gradually I began to take it in. Mostly it was just passages for her book and random thoughts and notes about what she'd seen on the street: someone trying to sell *The World Almanac* for 1979 and an old pair of flippers—stuff like that. I saw my name here and there—short summaries of what we'd done together and talked about—and I kept moving through it. She mentioned meeting Neil for a beer and wrote down things that he'd said.

I looked carefully—I didn't want to miss anything, but I didn't really want to find anything, either. I looked for Blue's name. I was steadily flipping pages, hoping to quickly shut the book and be done with it.

There was a draft of a letter dated June 10th to one of the writers in New York. It was short and full of cross-outs, but in it she said she'd liked his book and was sending along some novel she thought he would enjoy. There was a formal tone to the thing: she didn't know the guy very well. She had given me the same novel, along with some earrings and a gift certificate for Tower Records, for my birthday. It occurred to me, as I continued going through the notebook, that she probably decided not to mail it to him, and had given me the book instead.

There was an entry on August 4th, three days ago; the rest of the pages were blank. I went back to the beginning—it started in May—and began skipping around in it.

Blue's name appeared twice. A month ago, after we'd all gone to a bar, she'd described the way he'd tapped her fingers with the box of cigarettes: "sexy gesture." And six days ago, after one of our shows, she'd written: "Blue thinks every woman in America should give him head."

I reread an entry about a fight we'd had, in June. "Horrible argument with Dean." She didn't go into much detail. She quoted me saying, "You're talking to yourself"—something I vaguely remembered—and then she described the way my place had looked, with the empty wineglasses and the candles.

I put the notebook back where I'd found it and pulled on my clothes. After tying my shoes, I dropped backward onto the bed and lay there in the sunlight, exhausted. After a minute or two, I sat up.

There was nothing much about Blue in the notebook, nothing surprising. And no confession of the sort I'd been imagining— that Kate was interested in someone else, or wanted to leave the city.

You wouldn't have paid more attention to my name than to any other. That didn't necessarily mean anything, I supposed. But I felt defeated, sort of hollow and dull. Her apartment seemed very empty just then, and its dozen or so objects appeared carefully set apart from one another: lamp, folding chair, bookshelves; my leather jacket, her little tin painted mermaid perched on the ledge of the window. I picked up my jacket from where it lay in the middle of the room and left, letting the door swing locked behind me.

At home, I ate two oranges and took a shower. When I got out, I noticed there was a message on the answering machine. It was from Blue. "Pick up if you're there, man." He sounded wiped out. He didn't usually call so early. "Well, listen. I've got some good news for us. I'll tell you about it. See you at noon."

We were supposed to go over a couple of new songs.

I immediately wondered if we'd gotten a contract. It could have been any number of things, I supposed, but it had to be fairly important, or Blue would have just said what it was. I called and got his answering machine. I couldn't reach Jack or Michael, either.

It wasn't even ten yet. I'd planned to go get some breakfast and then try to catch a ride to practice with Jack. Instead I grabbed my bass and headed straight to the studio, twelve blocks away, thinking maybe they'd gone over early for some reason.

They hadn't. No one was around. I set the case beside me on one of the couches and caught my breath.

The space was a big converted garage on Divisadero that smelled like must and beer and old cigarettes. We recorded in Marin, but day to day, for practice, this was it. We shared the place with two other bands and a singer named Wendel, a tall, pale guy in his early thirties who pretty much lived there. Behind a hung bedspread in the far corner, there was a mattress, and he would sometimes come in with his girlfriend and disappear back there while we played. They'd come out later going, "I liked that last one," or something like that, and then stroll outside. People were always pounding on the door, interrupting us, looking for Wendel, who was obviously selling junk. It was getting very old.

The place could be like a sweatbox after playing for an hour or two, but right now it was fine. I flipped through a wrinkled copy of *Playboy* for a minute—there were always about thirty of them sliding out from under the couches—and then tossed it back on the ground.

My hair was still wet from the shower, and I was in a sweat from hurrying over. Pretty pointless. But I really wanted to see Blue—and not only to find out what was up for the band. I wanted to talk about last night and get it over with. It seemed less likely that anything had actually happened between him and Kate. It didn't seem to matter as much anymore—there was no way Kate was going to end up with Blue—but I wanted to know. I thought I might be able to clear that one from my brain.

I lay down my bass behind some of the amps and left. I turned down Haight and headed back toward the Mission. It was already very hot. A girl in cutoffs was checking me out as she came up the sidewalk. She was twenty, twenty-one. She was smiling and I nodded, trying to think if I knew her. As she passed me, she said the name of our band and then said, "Right on."

It took me by surprise, and I mumbled, "Thanks."

It wasn't beneath me to flag someone like that down, but I was spacing out at the moment, and all it did was make me think of Kate and how sad the whole thing seemed. I'd been off in dreamland, telling Kate that we'd been signed.

Down by Steiner, there were a lot of people hanging out at tables outside the cafés, smoking cigarettes. There were motorcycles parked on the sidewalk, and someone was playing the Cowboy Junkies. I could easily imagine what it was going to be like walking by here on shiny, empty days like this while Kate was away. I could see myself in my apartment in the afternoon with all of her crap stacked in one corner, wondering if she was really going to come back. It was bullshit.

Kate was sitting on the hill near the top of Dolores Park. There were little kids running back and forth between her and the playground area twenty yards away. She waved when she saw me coming and then shielded her eyes from the sun with her hand. Beyond her, off in the far southern corner of the park, there were about twenty guys in Speedos lying on blankets, catching rays, and some of them had dogs running around over there, chasing each other.

As I reached the top, two of her kids came running up to her past me.

"What's up?" I said to her.

"Hey!" And then to the kids, "Look who's here. Ashley, David, say hi to Dino."

They knew me, but they were shy: they were four or five years old. They had something to show Kate and were waiting for her full attention.

"You're all sweaty," she said. "Wait a second, though. Little project going on here, right, Ashley?" I dropped down beside Kate and propped myself up on my elbows. Ashley had both of her fists tightly closed and was holding them out. You could see she had something in her right hand.

"What's the game?" I said to Ashley.

She was staring at her fists. She took a breath and said, "You have to guess—which hand."

"Ah-ha."

"We've only been playing for about an hour," Kate said.

It was totally obvious. Kate chose the empty hand. Ashley opened the other to display a large, bright green leaf that uncurled in her palm.

"Drats! Fooled again." Both kids were pretty pleased. "Good job! You know what?" Kate said. "I'm going to talk to Dean for a while now, so maybe we can play again later, okay?"

They ran off down the hill.

We kissed, and Kate moved the hair away from my forehead. "So what's going on? A little jog, apparently."

I told her I went over to the studio too early and decided to come see her. She said, "Are you okay?"

I said, "Kate, I wanted to talk to you."

We were side by side, facing the Bay. She looked at her watch and then looked down. She'd seemed nervous since I showed up. "That sounds grave." I didn't say anything until she looked at me. "But go ahead. What? It's about Long Island, right?"

"Well, yeah, that—"

"You could still come for a couple of weeks, you know. You should if you want to. It's really beautiful."

I was broke, we had gigs all month—and she knew that.

I said, "Well, you know I can't."

"My dad would lend me money until the check comes, and I already owe you some."

We'd had this conversation a month ago, and then it was dropped. It was only coming up now because I was scaring her. I could see how frightened she was, and I felt terrible. She was looking down again, and, as I watched, tears pooled into her eyes. When she finally raised them, she didn't look at me. She looked out over the water.

I started to think about the band again. It was Friday. We had a gig tonight across the Bay, in Berkeley. I thought about that girl who passed me on the street. A year ago, I would have been shocked. I could remember the first time that had happened and how it had seemed like one of the greatest days in my life.

Down below us was the Mission. Blocks away, you could see the top floor of the old post-adobe hotel on the corner of Valencia and 16th. It was an apartment house now with a Mexican market on its ground floor where we bought Hulk Hogan bars and flan that came on paper plates. A block or so from there, dwarfed by the distance, the big "17" hung over Mission Street.

For a second, I remembered clearly the moment Kate and I collided down there, and I felt a rush. There'd been nothing exactly deep about it. As soon as I saw that she wanted me, I was all over it: I didn't ask questions.

But just as quickly now, the sensation slipped away. I kept looking down there, concentrating, trying to pull that feeling out of all these others—like when there's a song you know, but you can't quite get it into your head. You go wait wait wait wait wait, because there it was, a second ago, and now it's about a million miles away.

I said, "Kate, let's get married."

She didn't answer. She was sitting with her knees up, looking at her hand brushing the grass by her shoe. Her mouth was set in a thin line. She looked halfway between angry and upset. I knew that look well, but I never knew quite what it meant.

"Do you want to marry me, Kate?"

Harry Ginsberg

from The Feast of Love

As a Jew, I am drawn in a suicidal manner toward the maddest of Christians. Kierkegaard, being one of the craziest and most lovable of the lot, and, therefore, dialectically, possibly the most sane of them all, is of compelling interest to me. All my life, I have tracked his ghost doggedly through the snow. Lonely, eccentric, and deranged, the man Kierkegaard (1813–1855) was drawn to philosophize about matters concerning which one cannot acquire *any* certainty whatsoever. Kierkegaard worried continuously about the mode in which one might think, or could think, about two unknowns: God and love. These were for the hapless Kierkegaard the most compelling topics. They bound him in tantalizing straps. Of the two vast subjects about which one can never be certain and should therefore perhaps keep silent, God and love, Kierkegaard, a bachelor, claimed especial expertise. Kierkegaard's homage to both was multifarious verbiage. He wrote intricately beautiful semi-nonsense and thus became a hero of the intellectual type.

I learned Danish in order to read Kierkegaard. His picture is on the wall in my study. I cannot write a word without his image up there, looking down at me.

As a member of the bourgeoisie, which is what I am, I live quietly in Ann Arbor, Michigan, a city of ghosts and mutterers. Everywhere you go in this town, you hear people muttering. Often this is brilliant muttering, *tenurable* muttering, but that is not my point. All these mini-vocalizations are the effect of the local university, the Amalgamated Education Corporation, as I call it, my employer. It is in the nature of universities to promote ideas that should not be put to use, whose glories must reside exclusively in the cranium. Therefore the muttering. There are exceptions, of course. The multimillionaire lawyers and doctors and engineers—how did they get into the university in the first placc?—live here among us in their, to quote Cole Porter, *stinking pink palazzos,* and motor about in their lustrous sleek cars massive with horsepower. The warped personalities, like myself, like my prey Kierkegaard, walk hunched over and unnoticed, or we wait at the bus stops, managing our intricate and tiny mental kingdoms as the rain falls on our unhatted heads. We wait for the millennium and for Elijah.

I live next door to Bradley W. Smith. I see him walking his dog, also called Bradley. What is this, that a man should name his dog after himself? The man runs a local coffee franchise, a modest achievement, in all truth. Megalomania can strike anywhere, I suppose is the point.

After he lost his second wife to another man, I decided to explain to him about Kierkegaard. In doing so, I first used the example of myself.

My wife is Esther, a tough bird, the love of my existence. She works as a biochemist for one of the local drug companies. It was Esther who years ago found out that the wonder medication Thalidomide deformed babies in the womb, gave them unnatural shapes, took away toes and fingers and entire arms. If Esther's mother hadn't joined the Party as a young woman (and who else but the Reds were trying to desegregate the public beaches in those days? who else had a *single* social idea worth implementing?), and hadn't dressed Esther in red diapers, and hadn't signed Esther up for the Party as a child, she would have been proclaimed, my Esther, from the rooftops. But somehow, in the shower of publicity, some measuring worm looked up her background, and, though Esther as a youngster was blameless, and not a Leninist but a reader of Trotsky, that was that.

We live, in all truth, a tranquil domestic life. We have a year or two to go before retirement. Mondays, Wednesdays, and Fridays, I cook dinner. My specialty is a beef burgundy, very tasty, you have to remember to cook it slowly, covered, of course, in the liquids so that the meat and the onions and the potatoes become tender. Tuesday and Thursdays are the nights when Esther cooks. We read, we talk, we play canasta and Scrabble. We feed the two goldfish, Julius and Ethel. *They must live.*

As is proper, the children—all grown—have left home. We have three. The oldest, our beautiful daughter, Sarah, is, like her mother, a biochemist. She is successful but, so far, unmarried. She would be a handful for any man. I mean this as praise and description. The middle one, Ephraim, is a mathematician and father to three wonderful little ones, our grandchildren. I have pictures here somewhere. Of the youngest, Aaron, who is crazy, I should not speak. And not because he blames me for the mess in his head. No: he deserves to be left alone with his commonplace lunacies—he calls them ideas—and given peace. He lives, it goes without saying, in Los Angeles.

After Kathryn, Bradley's first wife—a woman I never met, I should add—left him, Bradley became a manager of a local coffee shop and subsequently bought the house next door. He became our neighbor. He moved into the haunted house adjacent to ours, haunted not by ghosts but divorce. There was a divorce dybbuk living inside the woodwork. Young couples would purchase that property, they would take up occupancy, they would quarrel, the quarreling would escalate to shouting and table pounding, they would anathematize each other, and, presto, they would move out, not together, but separately. They would scatter. Then back it would go onto the real estate market. *Three couples* we saw this happen to.

I should explain. At first sight, each time they arrived, they were fine scrubbed American pragmatists you might see photographed in a glossy magazine. Blond, blue-eyed Rotarians, fresh owners of real estate, Hemingway readers, they would unload their cheerful sunny furniture from U-Haul vans. By the time they moved out, they would have acquired mottled gray skin and haggard Eastern European expressions. Even the children by that time would have the greenish appearance of owl-eyed Soviet refugees stumbling out of Aeroflot. Well, of course domesticity is not for every taste, but these young families emerged from that house bent and broken, like vegetables left forgotten in the crisper.

So, when Bradley arrived, alone except for his dog, we thought: The curse is over. The dybbuk will have to locate itself elsewhere. That was until Bradley met and married Diana. But I am getting ahead of myself.

* * *

This Bradley, an interesting man, invited Esther and me to dinner the second week he was installed in that house. A courageous gesture. He was not afraid of Jews. He served veal, which Esther will not eat. In the dining room, she picked at it delicately. She left small scraps of it distributed randomly around her plate. I said later, At least no ham, no pork, no shrimp mousse, no trayf. But Harry, she said, veal to me is like a frozen scream. I can't eat it. So don't eat it, I said. So I don't, she said. So?

The man, Bradley, had a certain hangdog diffuseness characteristic of the recently divorced. But he was trying against certain odds to be cheerful. He asked me about my work, he asked Esther about *her* work, and he listened pleasantly while we did our best to explain. These topics do not provide good conversation. He listened, though. He had large watchful eyes. I was reminded of an extremely handsome toad, a toad with class and style and good tailoring. He seemed to be living far down inside himself, perhaps in a secret passageway connected to his heart. Biochemistry does not scintillate at the dinner table, however, nor do neo-Kantian aesthetics. Only when I mentioned Kierkegaard did Bradley perk up. From behind a locked bedroom door, his dog simultaneously barked. I assumed that the dog had caught sight of the dybbuk or was interested in Kierkegaard.

Prompted by his interest, I said that Kierkegaard, the Danish philosopher, had been both unlucky and boorish in love. He had fallen in love with an attractive girl, Regine Olsen, and then he had concluded that they would be incompatible, that the love was mistaken, that he himself was complex and she was simple, and he contrived to break the engagement so as to give the appearance that it was the young lady's fault, not his.

He succeeded at least in breaking the engagement, in never marrying her. Cowardice familiar to many young men was probably involved here. Kierkegaard wished to believe that the fault lay with the nature of love itself, the *problem* of love, its fate in his life. From the personal he extrapolated to the general. A philosopher's trick. Regine married another man and moved away from Copenhagen to the West Indies, but Kierkegaard, the knight of faith, carried a burning torch, in the form of his philosophy, for her the rest of his days. This is madness of a complex lifelong variety. He spent his career writing philosophy that would, among other things, justify his actions toward Regine Olsen. He died of a warped spine.

Esther says that when I am seated at a dinner table, plates and food in front of me, I am transmogrified into a bore. Yak yak, she says. At the table she adjusted her watchband and raised her eyebrows to me. I felt her kicking me in the shins.

Still I pressed on.

Søren Kierkegaard maintained that everyone experiences love, everyone knows what it is intuitively, and yet it cannot be spoken of directly. Or distinctly. It falls into the category of the unknown, where plain speech is inadequate to the obscurity of the subject. Similarly, everyone experiences God, but the experience of God is so unlike the rest of our experiences that there, too, plain speech is defeated. According to Kierkegaard, nearly everyone intuits the subtlety of God, but almost no one knows how to speak of Him. This is where our troubles begin.

At this point I noticed Bradley's attention flagging somewhat. Esther kicked me again. She glanced toward Bradley, our new neighbor. Don't lecture the boy, she meant.

I raised my voice to keep his attention. Speaking about God is not, I said, pounding the dinner table lightly with my fist for emphasis, the same as talking about car dealerships or Phillips screwdrivers. The salt and pepper shakers clattered. The problem with love and God, the two of them, is how to say anything about them that doesn't annihilate them instantly with the wrong words, with untruth. In *The Philosophical Fragments,* Kierkegaard points out that the wrong words destroy love in a way that waiting for one's lover, delaying consummation, never can. In this sense, love and God are equivalents. We feel both, but because we cannot speak clearly about them, we end up—wordless, inarticulate—by denying their existence altogether, and, pfffffft, they die. (They can, however, come back. Because God is a god, when He is dead, He doesn't have to *stay* dead. He can come back if He chooses to. Nietzsche somehow failed to mention this.)

Both God and love are best described and addressed by means of poetry. Poetry, however, is also stone dead at the present time, like its first cousin, God. Love will very quickly follow, no? Hmm? Don't you agree? I asked. After God dies, must love, a smaller god, not follow?

Uh, I don't know. I'll have to think about it. Do you want some dessert, professor? Bradley, our new neighbor, asked. I got some ice cream here in the refrigerator. It's chocolate.

A very nice change of subject, Esther said, breathless with relief. Harry, she continued, I think you should save Kierkegaard for some other time. For perhaps another party. A party with more Ph.D.'s.

She gave me a loving but boldly impatient look, perfected from a lifetime of practice. Esther does not like it when I philosophize about love. She feels implicated.

Okay, I said, I'm sorry. I get going, and I can't help myself. I'm like a man trying to rid himself of an obsession. Actually, I *am* that man. I'm not *like* him at all.

Esther turned toward Bradley Smith. Harry, she said, is on the outs in his department. He does all the unfashionable philosophers, he's a baggage handler of Bigthink. What do you do, again, Mr. Smith? You explained, but I forgot.

Well, he said, I've just bought into a coffee shop in the mall, I have a partnership, and now I'm managing it.

This interested me because I've always wanted to open a restaurant.

Also, he continued, I'm an artist. I paint pictures. There was an appreciable pause in the conversation while Esther and I took this in. Would you like to see my paintings? he asked. They're all in the basement. Except for that one—he pointed—up there on the living room wall.

Esther appeared discountenanced but recovered herself quickly.

The artwork he had indicated had a great deal of open space in it. The painting itself covered much of the wall. However, three quarters of the canvas appeared to be vacant. It was like undeveloped commercial property. It hadn't even been compromised with white paint. It was just unfulfilled canvas. Perhaps the open space was a commentary on what *was* there. In the upper right-hand corner of the picture, though, was the appearance of a window, or what might have been a window if you were disposed to think of it representationally. Through this window you could discern, distantly, a patch of green—which I took to be a field—and in the center of this green, one could construe a figure. A figure of sorts. Unmistakably a woman.

Who's that? I asked.

The painting's called *Synergy #1*, Bradley said.

Okay, but *who's* that?

Just a person.

What sort of person? What were you thinking of?

Oh, it's just an abstract person.

Esther laughed. Bradley, she said, I never heard of an abstract person before. Except for the persons that my husband thinks of professionally. Example-persons, for example.

Well, this one is. Abstract, I mean.

It looks like a woman to me, Esther said. Viewed from a distance. As long as it's a woman, it's not abstract.

Well, maybe she's on the way to becoming abstract.

Oh, you mean, as if she's all women? *A symbol for women?* There she is, not a woman but all women, wrapped up in one woman, there in the distance?

Maybe.

Well, Esther said, I don't like *that.* No such thing as Woman. Just women, and *a* woman, such as me, for example, clomping around in my mud boots. But that's not to say that I don't like your painting. I do like it.

Thank you. I haven't sold it yet.

I like the window, Esther continued, and all those scrappy unpainted areas.

It's not quite unpainted, he informed us. It's underpainted. I splashed some coffee on the canvas to stain it. Blend-of-the-day coffee from the place where I work. It's a statement. You just can't see the stains from here.

Ah, I said, nodding. A statement about capitalism?

Esther glared at me.

You want to see my pictures in the basement? Bradley asked.

Sure, I said, why not?

Only thing is, he said, there're some yellow jackets nesting in the walls—or wasps—and you'll have to watch yourself when you get down there. Careful not to get stung.

We'll do that, I said.

About this basement and the paintings residing there, what can I say? I held Esther's hand as we descended the stairs. I feared that she might stumble. Wasps, likewise, were on my mind. I did not want to have her stung and would protect her if necessary. Bradley had located his paintings along the walls, as painters do, on the floor, leaning. Each painting leaned into another like derelicts reclining against other derelicts. He had installed a fervent showering bath of fluorescent light overhead. A quantity of light like that will give you a headache if you're inclined, as I am, toward pain. The basement smelled of turpentine and paint substances, the pleasant sinus-clearing elemental ingredients of art, backed by the more pessimistic odors of sub-surface cellar mold and mildew.

One by one he brought out his visions.

This, he said, is *Composition in Gray and Black.*

He held up, for our inspection, images of syphilis and gonorrhea.

And this, he said, is called *Free Weights.*

Very interesting, Esther said, scratching her nose with a pencil she had found somewhere, as she contemplated our neighbor's abstract dumbbells and barbells, seemingly hanging, like acorns, from badly imagined and executed surrealist trees, growing in a forest of fog and painterly confusion that no revision could hope to clarify.

And here, he said, lugging out a larger canvas from behind the others, is a different sort of picture. In my former style. He placed it before us.

Until that moment I had thought the boy, our neighbor, a dumb bunny. This painting was breath-snatching. What's this called? I asked him.

I call it *The Feast of Love,* Bradley said.

In contrast to his other paintings, which appeared to have been slopped over with mud and coffee grounds, this one, this feast of love, consisted of color. A sunlit table—on which had been set dishes and cups and glasses—appeared to be overflowing with light. The table and the feast had been placed in the foreground, and on all sides the background fell backward into a sort of visible darkness. The eye returned to the table. In the glasses was not wine but light, on the plates were dishes of the brightest hues, as if the appetite the guest brought to this feast was an appetite not for food but for the entire spectrum as lit by celestial arc lamps.

The food had no shape. It only had color, burning pastels, of the pale but intense variety. Spooky magic flowed from one end of the table to the other, all the suggestions of food having been abstracted into too-bright shapes, as if one had stepped out of a movie theater into a bright afternoon summer downtown where all the objects were so overcrowded with light that the eye couldn't process any of it. The painting was like a flashbulb, a blinding, cataract art. This food laid out before us was like that. Then I noticed that the front of the table seemed to be tipped toward the viewer, as if all this light, and all this food, and all this love, was about to slide into our laps. The feast of love was the feast of light, and it was about to become ours.

Esther sighed: Oh oh oh. It's beautiful. And then she said, Where are the people?

There aren't any, Bradley told her.

Why not?

Because, he said, no one's ever allowed to go there. You can see it, but you can't reach it.

Now it was my turn to scratch my balding head. Bradley, I barked at him, this is not like your other paintings, this is magnificent, why do you hide such things?

Because it's not true, he said.

What do you mean, it's not true? Of course it's true, if you can paint it.

No, he said, still looking fixedly at his creation. If you can't get there, then it's not true. He looked up at me and Esther, two old people holding hands in our neighbor's basement. I'm not a fool, he said. I don't spend my time painting foolish dreams and fantasies. Once was enough.

I could have argued with him but chose not to.

And with that, he picked up the painting and hid it behind the silly ugly dumbbells growing like acorns on psychotic trees.

What a strange young man, Esther said, tucked in next to me, several hours later, sleepy but sleepless in the dark. Her nightgown swished as she tossed and turned. He seems so nondescript and Midwestern, harmless, and then he produces from the back of his basement a picture that anyone would remember for the rest of their lives.

Oh, I said, you could say it's imitation Matisse or imitation-Hockney. Besides, I said, light as a subject for contemporary paintings is passé.

You *could* say that, Esther whispered, but you *wouldn't*, and if you *did*, you'd be *wrong*.

She gave me a little playful slap.

I only said that you could say that, not that you would.

You didn't actually say it.

No. Not actually.

Good, Esther said. I realized that she was agitated. I turned to her and rubbed her back and her neck, and she put her hands on my face. I could feel her smiling in the darkness. I could feel her wrinkles rising.

Harry, she said, it was a recognition for me, a moment of beauty. How strange that a wonderful painting should be created by such a seemingly mediocre man. Our neighbor, living in the Dybbuk House. How strange, how strange. Then she sighed. How strange, she said again.

Then the phone rang.

Don't answer it, Esther quickly said. You mustn't. Don't, dear, don't, don't, don't.

No, I must, I told her. I must.

I picked up the telephone receiver and said hello. From across the continent, on the West Coast, my son Aaron began speaking to me. In a voice tireless with rage, he cursed me and his mother who lay beside me. Once again I was invited to hear the story of how I had ruined his life, destroyed his soul, sacrificed him to the devils and angels of lost ambition. In numbing fashion he found words to batter my heart. Indictment: I had expected more of him than he could achieve. Indictment: I had had hopes for him that drove him, he said, insane. Indictment: I was who I was. Crazy, sick, and inspired with malice, he described his craziness and his sickness in detail, his terrible impulses to hurt others and to hurt himself, as if I had not heard this story many times before, several times, innumerable times. Razors, wire, gas. He called me, his father, a motherfucker. Then he broke down in tears and asked for money. *Demanded* money. From the nothingness and everlasting night of his life, he demanded cash. I, too, was weeping with sorrow and rage, holding the earpiece tightly to my head so that not a word would escape to be audible to Esther. Cupping my hand around the mouthpiece, I asked him if he had hurt anyone, if he had hurt himself, and he said no, but he was thinking about it, he planned every single minute in advance, he planned monstrous personal calamities, he needed help, he would ask for help, but first he had to have money *now*, this very minute, *my* money, superhuman quantities of it. Don't make me your sacrificial lamp, he said, then corrected himself, sacrificial lamb, don't you do that now, not again. I said, against my better judgement, that I would see what I could do, I would send him what I had. He seemed briefly calm. He breathed in and out. He pleasantly wished me goodnight, as if at the conclusion of an effective performance.

To have a son or daughter like this is to have a portion of the spirit shrivel and die, never to recover. You witness the lost soul of your child floating out into the ethers of eternity. Ethics is a dream, and tenderness a daytime phantasm, lost when night comes. Esther and I, eyes open, held each other until dawn broke. My darling wept in my arms, our hearts in ruin. We live in a large city, populated only by ourselves.

Kafka: *A false alarm on the night bell once answered—it cannot be made good, not ever.*

She and I

after Natalia Ginzburg

*"The following essay, 'He and I,' captures the seesaw of human
companionship and love with a patience and sensitivity to
interconnectedness that it is hard to imagine a male
essayist attempting, much less equaling."*
—Phillip Lopate

She is quintessentially French. I am, in the loosest sense of the
word, American. She always feels cold. I am always hot. In the
winter, even if it isn't chilly, she does nothing but complain about
how cold it is. Even in late spring, there are large, fertile fields of
goose bumps on her thin, beautiful arms, and I have known her,
even in the Middle East in late June, to wear a woolen sweater
around the house, to sleep in a lamb's wool camisole in August.

She speaks, since she doesn't speak much, only one language
well, though she seems to understand so much more than I do,
even in the languages she doesn't really speak. I, on the other
hand, can make myself understood in several languages, yet have
trouble focusing on the conversations of others.

She enjoys reading maps and navigating around in new places.
I hate it, and quickly grow impatient and ornery. After a single
afternoon in a foreign city, she will have mastered the public
transportation system, be able to find her way to the centrum
from the most desolate-seeming corners. I will get lost five meters
from my own hotel, or—worse yet—a new apartment. She hates
asking for directions, preferring to gaze patiently at an (to me)
indecipherable map for many moments. When we get lost, I am
quick to blame her. She blames no one, but busies herself looking
for secondhand shops and fruit and vegetable markets in whatever neighborhood we are lost in.

She loves old architecture, curved surfaces, rummaging among
the trinkets and memorabilia of other people's lives at flea markets, the scent of flowers and herbs. I am always impatient to get
where I'm going, missing virtually everything along the way. The

only two things I've ever been able to love completely and unconditionally are my own disfigured face in the mirror and sitting at my desk making a kind of music exclusively with words...though I love my son, and sometimes her, in a different way, as well.

She loves travel, unfamiliar places, a sense of the unexpected. I dream of living always in one place, burning my passport, etching an address in stone upon my doorpost, running for mayor in some town I will never again move from.

I love to eat in restaurants—bad restaurants, good restaurants, even mediocre ones. She always wants to eat at home: fresh vegetables and better food, she claims, at one-fifth the price. She hates the way I do the dishes and leave a mess after cooking. I like, on occasion, to do the dishes and cook, though I'm quite awful at the former, which I always do in too great a hurry, leaving all sorts of prints, smudges, and grease stains along the way.

She loves to watch a late movie—preferably a slow-moving, melancholic one of the French or Italian sort—and to have a glass of wine or two with dinner. I prefer rather superficial, fast-moving American films, fall asleep almost the second I enter the theater for anything later than the 7:30 showing, and can drink, at most, a glass of white zinfandel in late afternoon.

She has little patience for, or interest in, pleasantries among strangers, preferring to restrict her circle of acquaintances to those she is truly intimate with. I enjoy talking to the garbage collector, the mailman, making small talk with the meter reader and taxi driver. The greetings "How are you?" and "Have a nice day" do not cause me to rail against the superficiality of America and Americans.

She is shy; I am not. Occasionally, however, her shyness rubs off on me, or, alternatively—as in the case of landlords who are trying to take advantage of us or rabbis who are too adamantly in favor of circumcision—she loses her shyness and grows quite eloquent, even in English, her vocabulary suddenly expanding to include words like "barbaric" and "philistine."

She has no respect for established authority, and thinks nothing of running out on student loans, disconnecting the electric meter, or not paying taxes. I, on the other hand, though I have the face of an anarchist, am afraid of established authority and tend, against my own better instincts, to respect it. As soon as I spot a police car in the rearview mirror, I assume I have done something terribly wrong and begin to contemplate spending the rest of my life in jail. She, on the other hand, smiles shyly at the police officer, who quickly folds up his notebook and goes back to his car.

She likes goat's cheese, garlic, a good slice of pâté with a glass of red wine, tomatoes with fresh rosemary. I like sausages, raw meat, pizza, and gefilte fish with very sharp horseradish.

She claims that I am a Neanderthal when it comes to food, a barbaric American animal who will die young of high cholesterol, rancid oils, and pesticides. She is refined, has a sensitive palate and a nose so accurate it can tell the difference between day-old and two-day-old butter. When we lived in Cambridge, Massachusetts, she spent many days in search of the perfect, vine-ripened tomato and just the right kind of basil for making pesto. She can't stand, for example, pine nuts that are rancid. "Rancid," in fact, is one of the English words she uses most frequently.

At the cinema she hates to sit too close to the screen, and—if we're at home—refuses to watch movies on TV that are interrupted by commercials, claiming that it interferes with her "dream world." I like to sit near the front of the theater and tell jokes during the movie. I like almost any movie, as long as it is superficial enough not to disturb my worldview. She prefers dark, slow-moving, romantic tragedies, set to the music of Jacques Brel, which linger in her imagination for many days after, causing her to question, or reexamine, almost everything in her world. She remembers the names of films and actors, and prefers actresses who embody a kind of low-key sensuality and dark reserve. I adore those who are brazenly sexual and whore-like in their demeanor. If, for example, as in Roman Polanski's *Bitter Moon*, there are two women, one of whom is subtly beautiful, sensual, and slightly tragic, the other who is vulgar, brazen, hedonistic, and rather shallow, it is always certain that she will prefer the first. I always prefer the second.

On those rare occasions when we've seen a film we both liked, she will, the next day—even the next month—remember every small detail of it: the weather in a particular scene, the shape of an awning, the way a blouse or a cloth napkin lay against the protagonist's arm or lap. I, on the other hand, will remember nothing, not even the plot, as if some premature and obliterating dementia had overtaken me during the night. Somewhat sheep-faced, I will ask her to remind me what the movie was about, who was in it... on occasion, even, what its name was, all of which she will generously do, never even pausing to comment upon my infirmity.

Though I am rather smart about books and literature, it is the rare film in which I am even able to follow the plot line, much less unravel the mystery, so that, after we leave the theater (assuming I haven't fallen asleep), I will usually need her to explain to me exactly what happened, who was related to whom, and why, at the end, a photograph of one character's daughter mysteriously showed up on the wall of a seemingly unrelated character's living room. When she does, I am inevitably embarrassed about my simple-mindedness and lack of insight, a shortcoming she seems either oblivious to or willing to overlook.

I either love or hate people, and find myself utterly incapable of having any interest in those I am indifferent to. She, though often equally indifferent to the same people, always seeks to find something interesting and unique about them, a pursuit I have neither the time nor patience for. Something in even the most uninspiring of persons arouses, if not her conversation, then at least her curiosity, and—once she has been engaged with someone in any way—she retains a certain ongoing loyalty to them I can neither relate to or comprehend. Though far less extroverted than I am, she will carry on a correspondence with any number of people, in all sorts of countries, and keeps a list in her address book of all the birthdays of everyone she has ever known and liked.

I consider every crisis a catastrophe, and will begin to fidget nervously and despondently whenever I am confronted with a late train, a rescheduled flight, or an incompetent waitperson. She considers each of these events a hidden opportunity, a portent from the gods, yet another manifestation of the world's independence and revivifying fickleness.

Though I have somehow been appointed the "breadwinner" of our family, I am extremely lazy. My favorite activity, as Freud said of poets, is daydreaming, my buttocks wedged firmly in a chair. She is never idle, raising domesticity to an art form, a Buddhistic perfection in every ironed crease.

Being a devotee of Bishop Berkeley's formulation to the effect that, if you can't see it, it isn't there, I prefer neatness to cleanliness. My idea of housecleaning is to sweep the large dustballs under the bed, stuff plastic and paper bags sloppily into a kitchen cabinet, cover the bed hurriedly with a creased down comforter, cram my underwear (freely mingling the soiled and the clean) into a dresser drawer. She is almost maniacally clean, sniffing each of my shirts and socks daily to make sure they don't need to be washed, vacuuming in corners, changing the pillowcases and sheets with the regularity of tides.

I like to buy cheap things, particularly clothes, frequently wearing them once or twice until they fray in the washer or loose their shape, and then cart them from place to place without ever wearing them again. One of the things she seems to enjoy most is to go through my clothes closets, reminding me of all the cheap items I bought and never wore, or which I have worn once, washed, and which are now "totally out of shape." She buys clothes almost never, but always things of good quality, preferring to wear the same few things (always immaculately clean) time and time again.

I fancy myself a great dancer and a sex object. She thinks of herself as physically awkward and more sensual than sexy.

I can type like a madman and, albeit reluctantly, use a computer. She considers a keyboard a postmodern artifact.

I like to drive. She likes to navigate. On those few occasions on which she drives our car, I nag her relentlessly about shifting at the wrong speeds, or squeezing too hard on the brakes. When she navigates and we begin to lose our way, I immediately become so ornery and hostile that, on at least one occasion in Budapest, she threatened to get out of the car and go home on her own. In countries known for their dangerous drivers, she insists I do *all* the driving, an affirmation of my manhood I accept reluctantly, though I don't object to being in control.

I am the kind of person who can do many things at once, most of them rather middlingly. She does only one thing at a time, but always with a sense of perfection.

I like to cook without recipes, freely mixing Marsala wine, mustard, artichoke hearts, candied ginger, maple syrup, and plums, hoping something capable of being digested will emerge. She always uses a recipe—except for things she has made before—but everything she makes is successful and delicious.

I would have been a rock star, or a concert pianist—or perhaps, even, the proprietor of an illicit sex club—had I felt freer to follow my lyrical and immoral heart's calling. She would have been a sister in a Carmelite monastery, or a gardener.

She is an enthusiastic and natural mother. I am a reluctant, though not unsuccessful, father.

She could have been many things, all of them having something to do with taking care of others or using her hands: a nurse, a dentist, a carpenter, a potter, a refinisher of furniture, a restorer of antiquarian books. I, though I like to imagine otherwise, could probably have done only the one thing I am doing now: putting words to paper.

I like to live part of my life in the *if but only* mode of wishful thinking and fantastical alternatives. She accepts the life that life has given her as her one possible destiny, without complaining.

She doesn't like to think of money—in fact, her refusal to think about it has, on occasion, gotten us into trouble. I, while I don't like to think of it either, am usually left with the unpoetic task of having to worry about it. Since I have been with her, in fact, hardly a day has passed without my thinking of it . . . almost constantly. She, on the other hand, worries about many other unpoetic tasks in our lives which have nothing at all to do with money.

I can imitate people from many countries, and with many different accents. She is too much herself to imitate anyone.

I like to have some kind of music playing whenever I am not reading or working. She usually prefers silence, or only to have music on when she is actually *listening* to it.

I will continue to eat even when I am no longer hungry, just for the pleasure of it. She eats only as much as satisfies her hunger on any occasion. I abhor all forms of table manners, eating with my fingers, chewing with my mouth open, taking food freely from others' plates, licking my fingers at the table, stuffing my mouth with large quantities, burping and passing gas. She never eats before being seated at the table, waits for everyone else to do likewise, chews only small morsels at a time, and eats so slowly, and with such deliberate pleasure, that I have usually finished what is on my plate well before she is actually seated. Only twice in our eight years together have I observed her passing gas. Burping, never.

As soon as I make a decision, I immediately, and relentlessly, tilt towards wanting the other alternative. She immediately accepts, and begins to implement, any decision she has made. She often says that I am a neurotic and "special" kind of person, that she feels that, living with me, this kind of behavior is the "statue quo." Occasionally, when I am in one of my periods of manic reconsideration, she smiles slightly in her slightly smiling French way, as if to say, "*Oy vey*, what a case I am married to."

I like to eat on the street—frequently, and mostly greasy and unhealthy foods—which accounts for the fact that most of my clothes have grease and/or coffee stains on them, souvenirs of my animalistic habits she claims American washing machines are incapable of eradicating. Most of all, I like to devour greasy Hungarian sausages at stand-up counters in Budapest. She likes to eat only "*à table*," quietly, savoring every morsel of, say, pâté with, preferably, a glass of red wine. Among the tastes in life I can truly not abide are *pasteque*, fennel, and every form of anise, all of which she has rather an affection for.

I am often angry at others, friends, foes, and family alike, and like to hold, and nurse, these angers for as long as is humanly possible, until I can almost feel them eating at my liver, like an earthquake with numerous, sustained aftershocks. She is incapable of sustained anger or hostility and would, I believe (perhaps already has), forgive me the most egregious deeds and betrayals, an attitude I have no desire to test to its limits. Even in her case, I like to remind her as often as possible of the ways she has disappointed and betrayed me. She, on the other hand, rarely mentions my betrayals and weaknesses.

I never cry, even when I am truly unhappy, yet I have a tendency to grow teary-eyed whenever an athlete experiences some major triumph, or after the last out of the World Series, when the players all rush to the mound and hug each other. She cries easily, even at sentimental movies whose pandering to sentimental feelings she despises.

I will take any kind of pill or medicine anyone recommends in order to relieve pain and discomfort. She prefers "natural" remedies. Although I am not terribly Jewish by religious conviction, I wanted to have our son circumcised when he was born. She felt it to be a pagan ritual tantamount to permanent disfigurement, and began assembling propaganda from various anti-circumcision organizations around the country which depicted vast armadas of mutilated children with heavily bandaged penises. She won... she usually wins.

I think she is beautiful, but too thin, and am constantly after her to try and gain weight. She thinks she is less beautiful than I do, but comments frequently about her "beautiful arms." When she was younger, in California, she wore her hair very short and looked like a kind of postmodern French punktress on her way to the wrong discotheque. Now, I think, she is much more beautiful and womanly, and, like I am, a bit older.

When we met in Ecuador, she had rather gray hair and was wearing purple nylon pants and a yellow sweatshirt. She seemed, at first, more interested in reading her mail than in talking to me, a fact which I soon realized was due more to her shyness—and her passion for her mail—than to lack of interest in me. On the two-hour bus ride between Quito and Otavalo, across the equator, I slowly began to realize that she was quite beautiful, in an undemonstrative sort of way, and that night, as a way of getting myself into her room and closer to her bed in the hotel where she, her female traveling companion, and I were staying, I planned to borrow her toothpaste. But she wasn't, I discovered, as shy as she seemed, and it turned out I didn't need to do that. The next morning I remember her companion bringing two glasses of fresh-squeezed orange juice to the room, along with coffee, and then our walking, hand in hand, above the town of Otavalo, where we finally sat in a small restaurant and her friend, Annick, took our picture. I looked very happy in the photo, though not too handsome. She looked happy, too, and quite lovely.

We stayed in several very lovely, and inexpensive, small Ecuadorian hotels during those days, and I remember, not even a week after not having to borrow her toothpaste, looking down at her one night (or was it afternoon?) and saying, "I think I love you." "I think I love you, too, Gringo," she replied. She used to call me "Gringo" in those days.

I remember talking to her an awful lot back then, and thinking to myself how attentively, and compassionately, she always listened. I myself am *not* such a good listener, except on occasion, so that—along with the sweet way she always said "uh-huh, uh-huh..." and "yes...yes" when I was telling her a story—it made a real impression on me. Back then, I don't remember her being nearly as cold, or quite as thin...but, then again, we were in love and in Ecuador.

Sometimes, now, when I realize we have been together for more than eight years and have a seven-year-old son, I think that this is one of the major miracles of my life...and I'm sure she does also. I was so romantic then, that night in Otavalo, and so was she when, hardly a week later, she got on a plane from Quito to the United States and followed me to Boston. I remember her calling me, as we had planned, but suddenly having a sense that the call wasn't quite long-distance. When she told me she was standing at a pay telephone across the street at Porter Square, I ran down the stairs, not even bothering to button my shirt or pull up my zipper, and took her into my arms and carried her halfway up to my fourth-floor, rent-controlled apartment.

I was stronger in those days, and healthier, and so, maybe, was she. We were not so young, but very much in love, and there was a scent of laundry, somehow, wafting through my windows as we made love, on a mattress located on my study floor, for the first time in the United States of America.

Now, as I write this, I am sitting in Israel, and we will soon be in Paris, then in Provence, and then back in the United States of America, the only country whose language I have truly mastered. I no longer live in that rent-controlled apartment, and that mattress, I am quite sure, is no longer on the floor. She is still beautiful, though—perhaps even more so—with her knowing eyes and beautiful smile and lovely French voice, and she is still, as a friend of mine once described her, *"une chouette"*—an owl. Which is a wiser, more deliberate animal than a fly.

A Profile by Don Lee

L orrie Moore hasn't had a full night's sleep in three and a half years. It's not what you think, however. She has not, like one of her characters, fallen prey to love woes or obsessive-compulsive panic. If anything, Lorrie Moore is far tougher than most people would suspect. It's simply that she has a feisty three-and-a-half-year-old son. "This particular parenting experience has been like a large nuclear bomb on the small village of my life," she says.

The author of two novels and two short story collections, with a third, *Birds of America,* due out this fall, Moore has lived in Madison, Wisconsin, for the past fourteen years. Since 1984, she has been teaching at the University of Wisconsin, where she is now a professor of English. By all appearances, she has had a remarkably stable writing career. "I've rarely felt any pressure to publish," she concedes. "I really feel like I'm writing what I want, at a pace that is the natural one." Indeed, her biography reads like a model of serendipity, a guide to "How to Become a Writer"— the title of one of Moore's earlier stories, which begins: "First, try to do something, anything else." The irony of that line speaks volumes of her literary and personal temperament. While success has come quickly and easily to her, she has worked hard for it. Like most writers, she runs through dozens of drafts before getting a story or a book right, going back and forth from longhand to the computer, revising and polishing. And while Moore's fiction is renowned for its wit and humor, filled with repartee, pithy one-liners, and wisecracks, she considers the essence of her work to be sad.

Nicknamed "Lorrie" by her parents, she was born Marie Lorena Moore in 1957 in Glens Falls, New York, a small town in the Adirondacks. Her father was an insurance executive, her mother a former nurse turned housewife. Moore, the second of four children, remembers her parents as rather strict Protestants, politically minded, and culturally alert. A quiet, skinny kid, Moore fretted, quite literally, about her insubstantiality. "I felt completely shy, and

Joyce Ravid

so completely thin that I was afraid to walk over grates. I thought I would fall through them. Both my younger brother and I were so painfully skinny, it still haunts us. Here we are, sort of big, middle-aged adults, and we still think we're these thin children who are going to fall down the slightest crevice and disappear."

Academically precocious, she skipped ahead in school, earned a Regents scholarship, and attended St. Lawrence University. There, as an English major, she was the editor of the literary journal and won, at nineteen, *Seventeen* magazine's fiction contest. It was her first publication, and it unearthed some surprising facts about her parents. Her father revealed that he had had literary aspirations of his own. He'd been in a writing class with fellow students Evan S. Connell and Vincent Canby at Dartmouth; he brought down some stories from the attic that he'd once sent to *The New Yorker*. Her mother, too, had wanted to be a journalist. Yet her parents' revelations did not necessarily strengthen Moore's resolve to become a writer.

Her expectations for herself were modest. Entering St. Lawrence, she hadn't been exactly bursting with ambition. "I think I probably went to college to fall in love," she laughs. "I had the same boyfriend from the second week of college until I was twenty-four.

I don't recommend it. But I have to tell you what it allowed—it allowed me to study, and write, and have a very serious student life, whereas other people were still busy shopping around for boyfriends and girlfriends." After graduating, she moved to Manhattan and worked as a paralegal for two years, then in 1980 enrolled in Cornell's M.F.A. program, where she was in a class of five—two fiction writers and three poets—who were thrown together with second-year students to make up a single workshop.

As she became more devoted to her writing, she found that music, her first love, was now a distraction. Like her father, she played the piano, and even had had a professional gig as a freshman, at a reception for Eugene McCarthy. (She'd been playing in a dormitory lounge, the dean of women students heard her, and she asked Moore to provide background tinkle for the reception the day after the next. She was paid fifteen dollars.) But at Cornell, she decided she had to give up music. "It was eating into similar energies," she says. "The typewriter and the piano were actually similar ideas, for my mind and for my hands. I was completely unaccomplished musically. Nonetheless, I was having ecstatic experiences in the practice room at Cornell and wasn't getting any writing done. So I had to choose." Slowly, the sacrifice began to redound, as her stories were accepted at magazines— one by *Ms.*, for which they paid her but never ran, others by *Fiction International*, John Gardner's *Mss.*, and *StoryQuarterly*. The publications were encouraging, but she was still not convinced they would lead anywhere. "I remember thinking, rather naïvely, that I would give myself until I was thirty, and if I hadn't published a book by then, I would probably have to find something else to focus on, that I obviously just was completely deluded and I didn't know what I was doing."

In 1983, when she was twenty-six, Knopf bought her collection, *Self-Help*, comprised almost entirely of stories from her master's thesis. One of Moore's teachers at Cornell, Alison Lurie, had mentioned that her agent, Melanie Jackson, was looking for clients. Neither Moore nor her classmates really knew what an agent was. "I sent her the collection, and she sent it to Knopf, and they took it. Now, I realize, that doesn't happen ordinarily," Moore says. *Self-Help*, which was published in 1985, produced a flurry of attention, reviewers comparing her to everyone from Grace Paley to Woody

Allen. Six of the nine stories are written in the second-person mock-imperative, ironically imitating self-help books for contemporary women, particularly in regard to romance. One story begins, "Understand that your cat is a whore and can't help you." Another, called "How to Be an Other Woman," starts, "Meet in expensive beige raincoats, on a pea-soupy night," then continues, "After four movies, three concerts, and two-and-a-half museums, you sleep with him. It seems the right number of cultural events."

By this time, Moore had been hired at the University of Wisconsin, but Madison often proved too lonely for her, and, whenever she could, she returned to Manhattan. "It was all very difficult," she says. "I lived in Little Italy for the summer, then found an apartment in Hell's Kitchen. I kept moving back to New York to worse neighborhoods and paying more rent." Not incidentally, the predicaments of East Coast sophisticates landlocked in the Midwest became a motif in Moore's next two books. *Anagrams,* her first novel, published in 1986, features Benna Carpenter and Gerard Maines, occasional lovers who live in Fitchville, U.S.A. The novel is structurally anagrammatic, the characters' relationships and occupations changing from chapter to chapter; Benna also has a daughter and a best friend who are, the book reveals, imaginary. "It got many bad reviews," Moore says. "I actually had to stop reading them. I just couldn't take it anymore."

Her next collection in 1990, *Like Life,* received raves, the eight stories showing a growing narrative authority, accompanied by her distinctive wit and mordant observations about love in the modern age. In "You're Ugly, Too," Zoë Hendricks is languishing in Illinois, teaching college history. It's not that different from her last job in Minnesota, where her blond students assumed, because she is a brunette, that she is from Spain. She escapes to New York to visit her sister, who pairs her with a man at a party. Zoë braces herself for the initial conversation: "She had to learn not to be afraid of a man, the way, in your childhood, you learned not to be afraid of an earthworm or a bug. Often, when she spoke to men at parties, she rushed things in her mind. As the man politely blathered on, she would fall in love, marry, then find herself in a bitter custody battle with him for the kids and hoping for a reconciliation, so that despite all his betrayals she might no longer despise him, and in the few minutes remaining, learn, perhaps, what his last name was, and what he did for a living, though probably there was already too much history between them."

"You're Ugly, Too" was the first of many of her stories to be published in *The New Yorker* (and then to be reprinted, with regularity, in annuals such as *The O. Henry Awards* and *The Best American Short Stories*), but, in 1989, it was a controversial piece for the magazine. "All through the editing process, they said, 'Oooh, we're breaking so many rules with this.'" Robert Gottlieb had taken over as the editor, but the turgidity of his predecessor, William Shawn, still gripped the institution. "I could not say 'yellow light,' I had to say 'amber light,'" Moore remembers. "And that was the least of the vulgarities I'd committed."

In her next book, the short novel *Who Will Run the Frog Hospital?*, which came out in 1994, Moore took a different tack and focused on adolescence. Lauded as her richest work, the novel has Berie Carr, a thirty-seven-year-old photography curator, in a childless, failing marriage. During the three weeks that she is in Paris with her husband, who is attending a medical research conference, Berie replays the summer of 1972, when she was fifteen. She worked as a cashier at an Adirondacks amusement park called Storyland, where her beautiful best friend, Silsby Chaussée, was costumed as Cinderella.

Moore took the title for the book from a Nancy Mladenoff painting, which depicts two girls worriedly standing over a pair of bandaged frogs—injured from too many kisses. The novel evokes the fairy-tale purity of Berie and Sils's love for each other, as well as their hopes for the future, beyond this fallow period when they have "no narrative": "it was liquid, like a song...It was just a space with some people in it." Yet, heartbreakingly, the novel is just as much about the end of possibility, the realization that the narrative—all that waiting—has arced prematurely into disillusionment: "By then my parents had moved from Horsehearts to the east coast of Florida with my grandmother, who, when I visited, stared at me with the staggering, arrogant stare of the dying, the wise vapidity of the already gone; she refused to occupy the features of her face. The living didn't interest her; she grew bored when anyone spoke. In her yawn I could see the black-and-white dice of her filled teeth, the quiet snap of her spit, all gathered in a painting of departure. It is unacceptable, all the stunned and anxious missing a person is asked to endure in life. It is not to be endured, not really."

Birds of America, Moore's new book—her fifth from Knopf with the same editor, Victoria Wilson—is her longest yet. "Almost three hundred pages," she marvels. "Unbelievable. You could keep a small door open with this." Of late, Moore has become more interested in the novelistic terrains of place and time and memory. She also notes the inclusion of children in her most recent work. She realized after the fact that nearly all twelve of the stories in *Birds of America* have a jeopardized child in them—most of them written well before she herself became a mother.

Moore is taking the next year off from teaching to work on a new novel. "It's on my own nickel, so we'll see if we end up in a shelter," she says. "Having a child, you can start to feel money pressure, and if you get a bad review, you might think, How's my kid going to go to college?" The new novel will be a marked departure for her. "It's actually about hate. It's hard to get in the same room with it. It may not be a book that is possible for me to write."

Lorrie Moore claims her literary ambitions have become more prosaic than ever. "I used to stay up all night and write and read, and I was quite obsessive. But now it's a much more modest endeavor. When your life gets crazy and complicated, your hopes turn into 'I hope I get enough sleep so that I can get some writing done this year.'"

BOOKSHELF

THE COAST OF GOOD INTENTIONS *Stories by Michael Byers. Mariner Books/Houghton Mifflin. $12.00 paper. Reviewed by Fred Leebron.*

In nearly every story in *The Coast of Good Intentions,* a debut collection by Michael Byers, there is the beguiling and disconcerting sense that all the *real* action is happening offstage, that offstage people are cheating on their dead wives or watching their children die, while onstage the characters preside with a kind of measured restraint and intelligence. Set in the Pacific Northwest, these nine careful tales evoke a realism that is complex and ambiguous.

"Settled on the Cranberry Coast" is a frankly sweet but never saccharine story about a retired schoolteacher, his old high school crush, and her granddaughter slowly weaving a life together in a dusky moment of their lives. "I was drunk but not drunk enough to say what I wanted," Eddie explains, as he yet again shies from the chasm of boundless intimacy, "that we don't live our lives so much as come to them, as different people and things collect mysteriously around us. I felt as though I were coming to Rosie and Hannah, easing my way toward them." While such fatalism may seem easy, the writing does all the hard work: the mist "hung up in the trees like laundry," the granddaughter "was sweaty and smelled like sun and dirt and meat."

The stories are novelistic in how generously they dwell in the shades of doubt and decision endured by the central characters, and how deeply they explore with a compellingly languid pace the breadth of details that make up their resilient lives. In "Shipmates Down Under," two geneticists watch helplessly while their six-year-old daughter struggles with an undefinable life-threatening disease, only to discover that she will survive while their marriage most probably will not. "I think I'm fairly nice," Harriet insists to Alvin. "Well," he says. "Sometimes." The argument rages, abates, finishes but does not finish, devolves to sleep. "And, to my surprise," Alvin admits, "she huddled against me, her breathing deep and even, directly into my ear, as if she were imparting secrets without words, without secrecy."

Many of the characters in *The Coast of Good Intentions* are, like the spurned professor and the spurned secretary of "Blue River, Blue Sun," destined to live lives whose shining moments are best described as "solidarity forever." Joseph is fifty-six, and his wife has just left him; Paula is thirty, and her husband has left her. "Move on. That's right. Move on. It's time," Paula urges the professor. When they finally do, "her expression was full of happy desperation, her eyebrows high on her forehead, her little breasts wiggling as she leaped toward him."

The forceful quiet of these stories and the deft slide of their endings, as if they could keep going but simply decide to stop, are evidence of a serious and sophisticated vision. All of these characters—and the very talented Michael Byers—have something more ethereal in mind.

Fred Leebron is author of the novel Out West *and co-editor of* Postmodern American Fiction: A Norton Anthology. *He teaches at Gettysburg College.*

DEFINITION OF THE SOUL *Poems by John Skoyles. Carnegie Mellon Univ. Press, $24.95 cloth, $11.95 paper. Reviewed by H. L. Hix.*

The best poems in John Skoyles's *Definition of the Soul* find solace in small scale. Their particular skill—announcing the Looming whose umbrage prompts them, but answering with barely lumen enough to light the singer's face and his next step—represents one of the best possibilities of the lyric.

The title poem, which opens the book, employs precisely this pattern. Its large problematic, defining the soul, has overwhelmed many minds, from Plato and Aristotle to the present. The title's ambiguity affords Skoyles two options: tender a finished definition or navigate the act of defining. He chooses the latter. Rather than attempt to transcend the problematic (a vain striving for survey at which abandon hope all ye who enter), Skoyles walks carefully through its shadow, cupping his hand in front of the candle he carries. "The attempt to separate my soul from yours," speciation without prefatory genus, the shift in scale that lets the poem work, "is like wringing out a handkerchief/ wet from something spilled." That spill sets the tone, by its suggestion that trouble has generated the affinity of the two souls. The poem continues with anecdotal indications of the relation between its *I* and its *you*, and ends with a metaphor that hints at a future for the souls no less troubled than their past: "The attempt to separate my soul from yours / is like the creaking of a lamppost / against a sapling in the wind. / Soon someone will come / and hack through the more fragile one."

The epigraph that prefaces one of its poems summarizes the whole second section: *"Halfway through life, one begins looking back."* The prototypical poem in the section, "Without Warning," replicates the same approach—large-scale problem, small-scale solution—that reappears throughout all three sections of the book. To the overwhelming burden and oppressive threat posed by midlife crisis, Skoyles answers with a tiny, apparently trivial incident he turns into a toehold. "A yellow leaf / rushing the asphalt / makes you swerve off the road, / tires grinding the grassy sleeve." With a pre-modernist ease and self-assurance modeled on predecessors like Oliver Wendell Holmes and grounded in our flickering recollection that poetry may still be able to delight *and* teach, Skoyles finds the lesson he needs: "instead of stopping / you plow along, / finding that getting off like this, / through the grit and straw, / has a great sweetness."

As with the soul, so with providence itself. In "Little God," prime exemplar of the explicit religious preoccupations in the book's final section, Skoyles still explores definition, this time more by perambulation than penetration. Through an estimable act of negative theology, we learn all we need to know about Skoyles's "little god" by its very absence from Skoyles's observations and its failure to fulfill his yearnings. He tells his little god to observe with him the "thin drunkards" who "wrap their chests / in a vest of old headlines," and "the fire escape's / homemade cross / marking the death / of our super / who jumped to end / his unspeakable ache." He longs for "the cushioning touch / of a supreme hand / the way the chapel ceiling / shows it," but his little god will send no Lazarus to "press a bead of water to [his] lips."

If the book's first poem represents one promise of the lyric, its last lists one of lyric's ultimate ambitions: "to pronounce / the words of this world / in the language of the next." The project with which Skoyles begins—a "Definition of the Soul"—may be de-finite, insusceptible to culmination, but undertaking it does render him the figure with which he ends, a "Patron of the Impossible."

H. L. Hix's most recent books are Understanding W. S. Merwin *(South Carolina, 1997),* Perfect Hell *(Gibbs Smith, 1996), and* Spirits Hovering Over the Ashes: Legacies of Postmodern Theory *(SUNY, 1995). He teaches at Kansas City Art Institute.*

WHERE SHE WENT *Stories by Kate Walbert. Sarabande Books, $19.95 cloth. Reviewed by Don Lee.*

Kate Walbert's first collection, *Where She Went,* gives us haunting portraits of two women—a mother and her daughter—both trapped by itinerancy. While Marion Clark, a bride of the fifties, finds nothing but ennui in her many moves across the country, she encourages her daughter, Rebecca, to wander abroad for adventure. Yet, despite their best efforts and hopes, Rebecca arrives at an emotional emptiness remarkably parallel to her mother's.

Where She Went is divided into two halves, the first devoted to Marion, then Rebecca, going roughly in chronological order. The fourteen pieces that make up the book are more vignettes than stories, largely elliptical and fragmentary in style. Individually, they are not quite complete, but they accumulate in power, Walbert's prose always lyrical, images and phrases recurring to great effect—for instance, in the description of dusk as *"l'heure bleue,"* or the blue hour, "that time of early evening when the world seems trapped in melancholy, and all its regrets for all its mislaid plans for the day are spelled in the fading clouds."

At twenty, Marion takes the train from Indiana to New York with twelve dollars in her pocket. She gets a job as a secretary at an insurance firm, and, within a year, she meets Robert Clark, an efficiency expert, "a man of routine, precision, a company man." They marry as virtual strangers—he proposes after three dates— and, to a large degree, they remain strangers over the next thirty-six years, as Marion dutifully packs up the house to follow her husband from one job assignment to another, from the suburbs of Rochester to Norfolk to Baltimore. It is a stultifying existence, but Marion, like most women of her generation, rarely voices dissent, even after falling into deep depression with the loss of her second baby—a sister for Rebecca—to a heart defect. Although

Marion privately and repeatedly pledges to leave Robert, she never does. Some of the book's vignettes are structured as first-person monologues addressed to her daughter, and, in one of them, Marion explains: "We had all abided by some silent code. We spoke of our children and our husbands and our husbands' jobs. We played bridge. We got drunk on Friday and Saturday nights at dinner parties."

On the other hand, Rebecca, when she is twenty, has access to freedoms that would have been unimaginable for her mother. She travels with her college boyfriend to Jamaica, where she dallies into a pointless affair with a resort owner, telling him, "My mother wants me to do everything she never did." After graduating, Rebecca journeys to Italy and sends postcards to her mother, who wants vicarious reports on "our world tour," but then she returns to Manhattan and settles into a numbing life of boredom and loneliness. She works as a typist at a newspaper, then edits children's primers, and lives in a studio apartment in a squalid neighborhood. She reads Neruda, jogs, dates, goes to a synagogue and then a church, looking for "an order, a system." She saves for another trip to Europe, but, once there, feels disappointed, adrift; she makes up reports of lovers and escapades for her mother.

A few years later, she marries a sculptor from California, but, on their honeymoon in Istanbul, she halfheartedly asks for an annulment: "She has done something terribly wrong, she knows. Something she should repent. But she isn't sure where to go, whom to pray to, what to say. She hears voices rising in no epiphany, only confusion, repeating Marion's wishes." Rebecca, like her mother, is unable to articulate the root of her unhappiness. Travel and marriage have only accentuated the sadness of mislaid, unrealized lives—hers, Marion's, her sister's: "in our family she survives, constant in her absence, as if she took with her certain letters from our family alphabet. There are words we can no longer pronounce, gaps within them, whistles, holes that leave us breathless, beached."

THE WAY OUT *Poems by Lisa Sewell. Alice James Books, $9.95 paper. Reviewed by David Daniel.*

Lisa Sewell's first collection of poems, *The Way Out*, explores territory that's not fit for the timid; whether she's writing about the body's generation or its decay, or of love, or sex, or of abortions, she does so with a precise, lidless eye. One welcomes her careful charting of the fleshy world and all of its difficulties when so many poets, upon surveying this type of terrain, seem eager to escape into shadowy metaphysics or soft-focused romance. In "Two Lessons in the Sacred," a poem that, among other things, discusses various funereal rites, Sewell writes of the people of Benares: "The poorer families must tend to their own pyres, / keeping watch until the skull explodes." Such attention to the physics of our bodies—and this is just one instance of many—may or may not make for good poetry, but it certainly shocks and challenges the reader, responses which are made interestingly complex because Sewell's images are often quite gracefully rendered. "Two Lessons" ends with these lovely lines: "There is nothing to take away from that place / except the burning that stays in your clothes / and the long memory of the journey." The poet's subtle transference of "long" from its predictable home next to "journey" to its brilliant new one alongside "memory" gives the poem and its ordinary sentiments a memorable body.

While Sewell's acuity and tenacity, to this point, are the most distinctive aspects of her poems, her voice and its philosophical foundation are less consistent. Her voice, at its best an appealing mixture of rhetorical elegance and mundane anecdote, sometimes wavers in and out of awkwardness, though it steadies as the book progresses, and culminates in a fine poem, "Human Nature," that begins, "When someone presses his mouth to mine, I don't hesitate, / I open my lips." Such wit, such pluck, is endearing, and it is also indicative of the book's greatest merits: the poet embraces her own vulnerability with enough charm and confidence that the poems, at least, no longer seem vulnerable. The voice at these moments becomes buoyant and rangy, and, consequently, the matter of the poem more fully flowers. Too often, though, the poems seem philosophically underdeveloped, sprinkled, for instance, with allusions—to Dante, to classical and Judeo-Christian mythology, to Nietzsche—that appear more to support the poems than to enrich them; the allusions' complexities and ironies, and hence the poems', are at times left rather frustratingly unexplored. It's as if Sewell is at a crossroads: one road leads to the irresolvable ironies of our greatest ironists; the other tries to eliminate that complexity and create a world without irony, or one in which, when irony is discovered, the discoverer feels triumphant over it rather than awed by it. It is to Sewell's credit that she's flirting with the great path, the one that will do justice to her unusually penetrating eye. This is a first book that's worth reading.

*Books Recommended by
Our Advisory Editors*

Madeline DeFrees recommends *Adam Chooses,* poems by Michael Spence: "These spare, understated poems have the elegant design and the formal ease we've come to expect of Michael Spence's work. The stance is reminiscent of James Wright's *Green Wall* poems in their escape from 'that vacant Paradise' to the celebration of the here and now." (Rose Alley)

George Garrett recommends *The Buddha in Malibu,* stories by William Harrison: "A collection of seventeen short stories set in Hollywood, Africa, and the future." (Missouri)

David Gullette recommends *Bite Every Sorrow,* poems by Barbara Ras: "Barbara Ras has written a dazzling first book of poems—C. K. Williams's choice for this year's Walt Whitman Award. She favors long, opulent, clever lines, as when she falls for a man in Central America: 'I loved the gesture for wait, two hands pumping the air waist high / as if depressing invisible brakes, and the avocado man singing / *a-gua-ca-te* all the way down the street.... Once he said, You watch for snakes while I sleep, / and laid his head on my belly and slept, / while cinders the size of bougainvillea petals arrived / from a burning across the valley.' These poems, and this poet, catch us unawares." (LSU)

Jane Hirshfield recommends *Except by Nature,* poems by Sandra Alcosser: "Sandra Alcosser's second collection is filled with pleasures: descriptions that make the reader shiver with delight, vivid moments of the human heart refracted, and passionate inquiry." (Graywolf)

Don Lee recommends *Watermark,* poetry and prose edited by Barbara Tran, Monique T. D. Truong, and Luu Truong Khoi: "A fascinating and surprising collection by a new generation of Vietnamese American writers, delving into identity and displacement with energy and grace." (Temple)

Robert Pinsky recommends *The Odes of Horace,* poems translated by David Ferry: "David Ferry's versions of Horace have an immense formal appeal: they sound ravishing when you read them aloud, and that appeal to the senses is one of the ways that this book rescues us entirely from the stereotype of Horace as a kind of silvery, genteel man who valued calmness. This is a passionate, various book of poetry, one of the great renewable resources for poetry, made available with unprecedented success by Ferry's freely invented English equivalents to the Latin lines and stanzas." (Farrar, Straus & Giroux)

Gary Soto recommends *Babylon in a Jar,* poems by Andrew Hudgins: "Hudgins can't get over his Southern childhood, which he drags as lovely narrative poems into his adulthood in Cincinnati. Perhaps the South does have manners, as Flannery O'Connor once said, but Hudgins's characters, mostly men, have such inconsistent manners: one moment they are brutes with their pale beer, and, in the next, tenderhearts sitting among begonias and impatiens. Where are we going to find a better book of poems this year?" (Houghton Mifflin)

New Books by
Our Advisory Editors

Ann Beattie, *Park City: New and Se-lected Stories:* Nearly five hundred pages long, this generous and sparkling collection of thirty-six stories is as much a cultural chronicle as it is a showcase of Beattie's enormous talents. She goes from the seventies to the present (eight of the stories are brand-new), incisively charting the relational and familial issues of the day. (Knopf)

Andre Dubus, *Meditations from a Mov-able Chair,* essays: This new collection of twenty-five essays is a radiant follow-up to *Broken Vessels.* Confined to a wheelchair since a 1986 accident, Dubus reflects on writing, Catholicism, divorce, family, and everyday life in a handicapped-inaccessible world. Resonant, thoughtful, passionate, and superbly written. (Knopf)

George Garrett, *Days of Our Lives Lie in Fragments: New and Old Poems, 1957–1997:* Garrett has long been admired for his fiction, but for the past forty years, he has amassed a large body of poetry as well. From bawdy satires to quiet lyrics, Garrett's poems splendidly show his affection for the world through unique sensibilities. (LSU)

DeWitt Henry and **James Alan Mc-Pherson,** *Fathering Daughters: Reflec-tions by Men,* essays: This remarkable, moving collection offers nineteen essays on a subject about which very little has been published: the relationship between father and daughter. Henry and McPherson have broken new ground, soliciting stirring, often heartbreaking essays from the likes of Rick Bass, Phillip Lopate, William Peterson, and Adam Schwartz that probe more than the issues of parenting and gender, but also adoption, race, and manhood. A must-read for every father and daughter. (Beacon)

Howard Norman, *The Museum Guard,* a novel: Norman's third novel is an exquisite tale set in Halifax just before World War II. DeFoe Russett, orphaned at age eight, lives in a hotel and works as a museum guard with his uncle. DeFoe begins a tormenting affair with Imogen Linny, the caretaker of a small Jewish cemetery, who becomes obsessed with a Dutch painting called *Jewess on a Street in Amsterdam.* Norman once again delivers odd, charming characters to us with haunting prose. Excerpt on p. 108. (Farrar, Straus & Giroux)

POSTSCRIPTS

Miscellaneous Notes · Fall 1998

COHEN AWARDS Each year, we honor the best short story and poem published in *Ploughshares* with the Cohen Awards, which are wholly sponsored by our longtime patrons Denise and Mel Cohen. Finalists are nominated by staff editors, and the winners—each of whom receives a cash prize of $600—are selected by our advisory editors. The 1998 Cohen Awards for work published in *Ploughshares* in 1997, Volume 23, go to Maxine Swann and Mark Doty:

MAXINE SWANN *for her story "Flower Children" in Fall 1997, edited by Mary Gordon.*

Born in 1969, Maxine Swann grew up on a farm in southern Pennsylvania. She attended state public schools until the age of twelve, then an all-girls' private school in the nearest city, Baltimore, and, finally, for two years, Phillips Academy (Andover), from which she graduated in 1987. After a year spent in Alaska, London, and, briefly, France, she entered Columbia College in 1988 and studied, most notably, with Mary Gordon.

In 1991, Swann went to Paris on an exchange program, but then ended up staying, not completing her degree in comparative literature at Columbia until 1994. During these years in Paris, she worked sporadically as a translator and English teacher and, most significantly, began writing screenplays with Argentine film director Juan Pablo Domenech. In 1994, they received both a writing and a development grant from the European Script Fund for their first feature screenplay, *Limbo*. Also in 1994, Swann entered the graduate program in French literature at a branch of the Sorbonne, Université de Paris VII, from which she received her master's degree in 1997 for a thesis on Proust's style. Since November 1997, she has been in Punjab, Pakistan, staying with her friends Lauren Ingram and Tamur Mueenuddin, who have launched a project to provide reproductive health care to Pakistani women in rural areas. In Pakistan, Swann has been teaching English and sports at a village girls' school, continuing her collaboration with Juan Pablo Domenech, and writing her first novel. She plans to return to France this fall and then eventually move back to the U.S. "Flower Children" was her first publication. Besides the Cohen Award, the story has won a rare "triple crown" for literary prizes, selected for this season's *The Best American Short Stories, The O. Henry Awards,* and *The Pushcart Prize.*

About "Flower Children," Swann writes: "All stories, I think, are in the end a very dense mixture of memory and imagination, with the doses varying each time. 'Flower Children,' I see now, was a story I'd been trying to write since I'd begun writing. It is, in a sense, a condensation of nearly all the stories, pages, and even poems that I wrote in grade school, high school, and then college. In her writing class at Columbia, Mary Gordon, taking my efforts seriously, pressed me further towards it, also introducing me to the Austrian writer Ingeborg Bachmann, whose work eventually led me to find the form in which to say what I wanted to say. The story itself I wrote a year or so later while in Paris. Its germ I discovered one afternoon when I was home on vacation in my mother's house. I remember feeling desperate that I would never write. I sat down at the table and, almost out of pure stubbornness, it seems to me now, came up with a refrain:

> *The children don't understand how the tree frogs sing...*
> *They don't understand why their father was here and now is gone...*
> *Although they kill things themselves, they don't understand why*
> *anything dies or where the dead go or where they were waiting*
> *before they were born...*

"That found, the rest of the story came somewhat easily. In her essay 'My Vocation,' Natalia Ginzburg describes the first time she wrote a 'serious piece': 'It came from me like a miracle in a single night, and when afterwards I went to bed I was tired, bewildered, worn out.... I was seventeen and I had failed in Latin, Greek and mathematics. I had cried a lot when I found out. But now that I had written the story I felt a little less ashamed.... I had written my story on squared paper and I had felt happy as never before in my life; I felt that I had a wealth of thoughts and words within me.' When I finished 'Flower Children'—and the last part I wrote in a rush one night late—I felt much the same way. I knew that the story was true in the sense that it was the first thing I'd written that was whole and right. I felt, I remember, a delicious sensation of lightness, went promptly to bed, and slept very hard."

MARK DOTY *for his poem "Mercy on Broadway" in Spring 1997, edited by Yusef Komunyakaa.*

Ted Rosenberg

Mark Doty was born in Maryville, Tennessee, in 1953. His father was a civilian member of the Army Corps of Engineers, a job that necessitated move after move for the family. When Doty was seven, they left Tennessee for Tucson, Arizona, where his father worked on the Nike Zeus missile project, and from there, they were transferred to a series of towns in Florida and California. In the mid-sixties, Doty returned to Tucson, where the poet Brenda Hillman was his classmate in a high school creative writing class. He soon dropped out, however, and quietly enrolled in the University of Arizona, in part because he'd met a professor, the poet Richard Shelton, who was supportive of his fledgling work. It took some time before university administrators gleaned that Doty did not have a high school diploma, but they were surprisingly accommodating, only asking him to take an extra literature class. He studied with Richard Shelton until he got married and, once again, dropped out. "This was 1971," Doty says, "and dropping out was simply what one did." Eventually, he earned a bachelor's degree in literature from Drake University in Des Moines, Iowa, and then, from 1978 to 1980, was a graduate student at Goddard College in Vermont, in the old M.F.A. program founded by Ellen Bryant Voigt. His teachers there were Jane Shore, Barbara Greenberg, and Thomas Lux. "It was a life-changing experience," he says. "I read a great deal of poetry I'd never encountered before, work that opened out new realms of possibility. Before long, I had an M.F.A. and a divorce certificate, and a new life began."

Doty is the author of a memoir, *Heaven's Coast,* and five books of poetry, including *Sweet Machine* (HarperFlamingo, 1998) and *My Alexandria* (Illinois, 1993), a National Poetry Series winner, selected by Philip Levine, which subsequently won the National Book Critics Circle Award, Britain's T. S. Eliot Prize, and *The Los*

Angeles Times Book Prize, and which was a finalist for the National Book Award. A recipient of fellowships from the Guggenheim Foundation and the NEA, Doty lives in Provincetown, Massachusetts, and Houston, Texas, where he teaches in the graduate writing program at the University of Houston.

About "Mercy on Broadway," Doty writes: "Most of my poems begin in an experience of recognition, but I often don't know what it is I am recognizing. This poem's no exception. My partner, Paul, and I had been together just two months when we went to New York for a weekend; Robert Jones, my friend and my editor at HarperCollins, had loaned us his apartment near the corner of Eighth and Broadway, close to NYU. The building where Robert lived then had concrete balconies which faced onto Broadway, and since we were about three or four stories up, the noise of that particularly raucous intersection blared up and bounced off the concrete walls, so that the city seemed one huge seamless wall of noise—New York mixed by Phil Spector! Out for a walk, we encountered the bowl of turtles the poem describes on the sidewalk in front of a tiny Chinese gift shop. They seemed startlingly green and alive, and weirdly out of place in the hustle and collision of that block, where there are countless street vendors, kids hanging out in front of McDonald's and the sneaker shops, a whole micro-universe, both social and commercial.

"When I went to write in my notebook a few days later, it was the memory of those turtles which emerged, seemed to insist on my attention. When I have that sort of feeling, I usually begin in description, to see where the process of saying what I've seen will lead, to see what clues my descriptive language will contain as to what I'm really writing about. The turtles proved to be inseparable from the noisy, unbroken life of the street. Probably that perception—of unbroken life—led the poem in the direction it eventually took, over many drafts, through a process half improvisational 'singing' and half meditation. It's such an exhilarating part of writing, that discovery of what the poem wants or needs to be. And in this case there was a particular pleasure in celebrating the street song, the ephemeral stuff of style, the flashing human stream of this moment.

"It's often in this exploratory process that I discover my poems are conversations with other poems, too. In this case, it's 'Crossing Brooklyn Ferry,' of course; I hope that the line 'Broadway's no one, and Broadway lasts' stands in that stream which pours out from Whitman's poem, the testament of one who saw the city as a great matrix of bodies, of the temporary self taking its place in the permanent stream. Hart Crane furthers Whitman's tradition, and Frank O'Hara—poets for whom the city is a zone of permission, where we're shoulder to shoulder in the human enterprise, our aspirations made visible. Just a few nights ago I stood on Fulton's Landing in Brooklyn, where the ferry used to depart for Manhattan, and listened to Galway Kinnell read Whitman's extraordinary poem, which seems so alive and strange still; it's as if it comes to us from the future, not the past. It was twilight, and the lights on the bridge had just come on, and suddenly poetry did that old, still-startling thing: it made me shiver."

ANNUAL PRIZES Our congratulations to the following writers, whose work has been selected for reprint in these anthologies:

Bliss Broyard's "Mr. Sweetly Indecent," Maxine Swann's "Flower Children," and Meg Wolitzer's "Tea at the House," all from the Fall 1997 issue edited by Mary Gordon, will be included in *The Best American Short Stories 1998*, with Garrison Keillor as the guest editor and Katrina Kenison as the series editor.

Marilyn Hacker's "Again, The River," from the Spring 1997 issue edited by Yusef Komunyakaa, and Donald Hall's "Letter with No Address" and Alan Shapiro's "The Goat," both from the Winter 1996–97 issue edited by Robert Boswell & Ellen Bryant Voigt, will appear in *The Best American Poetry 1998*, with John Hollander as the guest editor and David Lehman as the series editor.

Maxine Swann's "Flower Children" has been chosen for *Prize Stories 1998: The O. Henry Awards* by editor Larry Dark.

Three stories and three poems have been selected for publisher Bill Henderson's *The Pushcart Prize XXIII: Best of the Small Presses*: Patricia Hampl's "The Bill Collector's Vacation," Maxine Swann's "Flower Children," and Meg Wolitzer's "Tea at the House," all three stories from the Fall 1997 issue edited by Mary Gordon; and Toi Derricotte's "Invisible Dreams," Martín Espada's "Thanksgiving," and Barbara Tran's "from *Rosary*," all three poems from the Spring 1997 issue edited by Yusef Komunyakaa.

CONTRIBUTORS' NOTES

Fall 1998

ALICE ADAMS was born in Virginia, grew up in Chapel Hill, North Carolina, and graduated from Radcliffe. She has since lived mostly in San Francisco. She is the author of ten novels, most recently *Medicine Men* (Knopf, 1997). A short story collection, *The Last Lovely City,* is due out in February 1999. She is at work on a new novel, *After the War.*

CHARLES BAXTER is the author of six books of fiction, most recently *Believers* (Pantheon). He is also the author of a book of essays on fiction, *Burning Down the House* (Graywolf). He teaches at the University of Michigan and lives in Ann Arbor. "Harry Ginsberg" is a chapter from a current novel-in-progress, *The Feast of Love.*

MICHAEL BLUMENTHAL is a poet, novelist, and essayist whose most recent book of poems is *The Wages of Goodness* (1992). The story included in this issue is from his just-completed novel, *Weinstock in Exile.* His new book of poems, *Dusty Angel,* will be published by BOA Editions in 1999. A collection of his essays from Central Europe, *When History Enters the House,* was published by Pleasure Boat Studios last March. He lives in Austin, Texas.

ROBERT BOSWELL is the author of *American Owned Love, Living to Be 100, Mystery Ride, The Geography of Desire, Dancing in the Movies,* and *Crooked Hearts.* He teaches at New Mexico State University and in Warren Wilson College's M.F.A. Program for Writers. He lives with his wife, the writer Antonya Nelson, in Las Cruces, New Mexico, and Telluride, Colorado.

MAX GARLAND's first book of poems, *The Postal Confessions,* won the Juniper Prize in 1994. Recent poems and stories have appeared in *New England Review, The Gettysburg Review,* and *The Best American Short Stories.* He is the recipient of an NEA fellowship for poetry and a James Michener Fiction Fellowship.

WAYNE HARRISON grew up in Connecticut and received his M.F.A. from the University of Iowa Writers' Workshop earlier this year. His stories have appeared in *B&A New Fiction* and *The Coe Review.*

PAM HOUSTON's first collection of short stories, *Cowboys Are My Weakness,* won the 1993 Western States Book Award and has been translated into nine languages. She edited an anthology for Ecco Press entitled *Women on Hunting* and wrote the text for a photography book called *Men Before Ten A.M.* Her second book of fiction, *Waltzing the Cat,* will be published by W.W. Norton this fall. She is currently at work on a book of essays.

GISH JEN is the author of two novels, *Typical American* and *Mona in the Promised Land*. Her short story "Birthmates," which originally appeared in *Ploughshares*, has been chosen for *Best American Short Stories of the Century* and will be included in a collection to be published next year.

PAUL LESLIE lives in San Francisco. He is at work on a collection of short stories.

VICKI LINDNER is a fiction writer and essayist whose stories have appeared in *Fiction, Chick-Lit: Postfeminist Fiction, Witness, The Little Magazine, The Kenyon Review, New York Woman, Ploughshares,* and other magazines and anthologies. The recipient of an NEA fellowship—as well as two grants from New York State—for her short fiction, she teaches at the University of Wyoming.

NANCY MLADENOFF is a painter currently residing in Chicago, Illinois, and Madison, Wisconsin. Her work has been widely exhibited throughout the United States, including the International Print Fair and the ABC No Rio Gallery in New York, the Chicago Cultural Center, the Milwaukee Art Museum, and the Tucson Museum of Art. She is represented by the Carol Hammer Gallery in Chicago and the Dean Jensen Gallery in Milwaukee. Her paintings were featured in the August 1997 issue of *New American Paintings.*

HOWARD NORMAN's excerpt in this issue is from his new novel, *The Museum Guard*, which has just been published by Farrar, Straus & Giroux.

BRADLEY J. OWENS has published stories and essays in *The Threepenny Review, The Christian Science Monitor,* and elsewhere. He has been a Jones Lecturer in Creative Writing at Stanford University, where he received his M.A. in English. He was, most recently, the Carl Djerassi Fiction Fellow at the Institute for Creative Writing at the University of Wisconsin, Madison.

SHEILA M. SCHWARTZ is the author of *Imagine a Great White Light*, which won the Pushcart Editors' Book Award in 1990. She recently completed a novel, *Lies Will Take You Somewhere*... She teaches fiction writing at Cleveland State University.

MONA SIMPSON is the author of the novels *Anywhere But Here, The Lost Father,* and *A Regular Guy.*

DEBRA SPARK is the author of the novel *Coconuts for the Saint* (Faber & Faber, 1995; Avon, 1996). She teaches at Colby College.

MEG WOLITZER's story "Tea at the House," which appeared in last fall's fiction issue of *Ploughshares*, was chosen for *The Best American Short Stories* and *The Pushcart Prize.* Her new novel, *Surrender, Dorothy*, will be published by Scribner next spring. She lives in New York City.

SUBSCRIBERS Please feel free to contact us by letter or e-mail with comments, address changes (the post office will not forward journals), or any problems with your subscription. Our e-mail address is: pshares@emerson.edu. Also, please note that on occasion we exchange mailing lists with other literary magazines and organizations. If you would like your name excluded from these exchanges, simply send us an e-mail message or a letter stating so.

∼

HOW IT WORKS *Ploughshares* is published three times a year: mixed issues of poetry and fiction in the Spring and Winter and a fiction issue in the Fall, with each guest-edited by a different writer of prominence, usually one whose early work was published in the journal. Guest editors are invited to solicit up to half of their issues, with the other half comprised of unsolicited manuscripts screened for them by staff editors. This guest-editor policy is designed to introduce readers to different literary circles and tastes, and to offer a fuller representation of the range and diversity of contemporary letters than would be possible with a single editorship. Yet, at the same time, we expect every issue to reflect our overall standards of literary excellence. We liken *Ploughshares* to a theater company: each issue might have a different guest editor and different writers— just as a play will have a different director, playwright, and cast—but subscribers can count on a governing aesthetic, a consistency in literary values and quality, that is uniquely our own.

∼

SUBMISSION POLICIES We welcome unsolicited manuscripts from August 1 to March 31 (postmark dates). All submissions sent from April to July are returned unread. In the past, guest editors often announced specific themes for issues, but we have revised our editorial policies and no longer restrict submissions to thematic topics. Submit your work at any time during our reading period; if a manuscript is not timely for one issue, it will be considered for another. We do not recommend trying to target specific guest editors. Our backlog is unpredictable, and staff editors ultimately have the responsibility of determining for which editor a work is most appropriate. Send one prose piece and/or one to three poems at a time (mail genres separately). Poems should be individually typed either single- or double-spaced on one side of the page. Prose should be typed double-spaced on one side and be no longer than twenty-five pages. Although we look primarily for short stories, we occasionally publish personal essays/memoirs. Novel excerpts are acceptable if self-contained. Unsolicited book reviews and criticism are not considered. Please do not send multiple submissions of the same genre, and do not send another manuscript until you hear about the first. Additional submissions will be returned unread. No more than a total of two submissions per reading period, please. Mail your manuscript in a page-size manila envelope, your full name and address written on the outside, to the "Fiction Editor," "Poetry Editor," or "Nonfiction Editor." Unsolicited work sent directly to a guest editor's home or office will be ignored and discarded; guest editors are formally instructed not to read such work. All manuscripts and correspondence regarding submissions should be accompanied by a self-addressed, stamped envelope (S.A.S.E.) for a response. Expect three to five months for a decision. Do not query us until five months have passed, and if you do, please write to us, including an S.A.S.E. and indicating the postmark date of submission, instead of calling. Simultaneous submissions are amenable as long as they are indicated as such and we are notified immediately upon acceptance elsewhere. We cannot accommodate revisions, changes of return address, or forgotten S.A.S.E.'s after the fact. We do not reprint previously published work. Translations are welcome if permission has been granted. We cannot be responsible for delay, loss, or damage. Payment is upon publication: $25/printed page, $50 minimum per title, $250 maximum per author, with two copies of the issue and a one-year subscription.

FATHERING DAUGHTERS
REFLECTIONS BY MEN

EDITED BY DEWITT HENRY AND JAMES ALAN MCPHERSON

"**Powerful, savvy, inimitable**—there's no collection that can match *Fathering Daughters*. . . . **Heartbreaking, courageous**—above all, loving."
—Howard Norman, author of *The Bird Artist*

"**An intelligent, insightful, multi-voiced mosaic** depicting a man's experience as father to a daughter."
—*Boston* magazine

RICK BASS	MARK PENDERGRAST
ALAN CHEUSE	WILLIAM PETERSEN
NICHOLAS DELBANCO	SCOTT RUSSELL SANDERS
GERALD EARLY	ADAM SCHWARTZ
DEWITT HENRY	SAMUEL SHEM
HOWARD JUNKER	GEORGE H. SMITH
ROGER KAMENETZ	GARY SOTO
PHILLIP LOPATE	M. G. STEPHENS
JAMES ALAN MCPHERSON	FRED VIEBAHN

AVAILABLE IN BOOKSTORES • HARDCOVER $24.00

 BEACON PRESS, BOSTON   w w w . b e a c o n . o r g

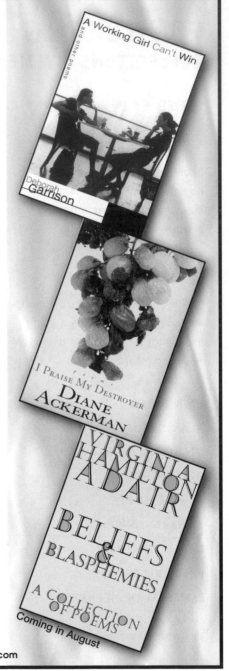

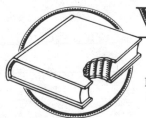

M.F.A. in
Creative Writing

M.A. in
Writing & Publishing

Located in historic Boston, right on "The Common," Emerson College offers an exciting community for writers and aspiring publishers. Home to the nationally renowned journal *Ploughshares,* Emerson's graduate program nurtures new voices and provides diverse opportunities for study in an environment of discovery and growth. Class sizes are small, with enrollments limited to twelve students in workshops.

Graduate Admission
100 Beacon Street
Boston, MA 02116
Tel: (617) 824-8610
Fax: (617) 824-8614
gradapp@emerson.edu
www.emerson.edu/gradapp

EMERSON
COLLEGE

Current Faculty in the Department of Writing, Literature & Publishing:

John Skoyles, Chair
Jonathan Aaron
Douglas Clayton
William Donoghue
Robin Riley Fast
Eileen Farrell
Flora Gonzalez
Lisa Jahn-Clough
DeWitt Henry
Christopher Keane
Maria Koundoura
Bill Knott
Margot Livesey
Ralph Lombreglia
Gail Mazur
Tracy McCabe
Pamela Painter
Donald Perret
Michael Stephens
Christopher Tilghman

Adjunct Faculty include:

David Barber, Sam Cornish, Andre Dubus III, Marcie Hershman, William Holinger, Kai Maristed, George Packer, Martha Rhodes, Elizabeth Searle, Jessica Treadway

Concentrations in:

Fiction, Poetry, Non-Fiction, Screenwriting, Children's Literature, & Publishing

BENNINGTON WRITING SEMINARS

MFA in Writing and Literature
Two-Year Low-Residency Program

A. BLAKE GARDNER

FICTION
NONFICTION
POETRY

Jane Kenyon Poetry Scholarships available
For more information contact:
Writing Seminars
Box PL
Bennington College
Bennington, VT 05201
802-440-4452, Fax 802-447-4269

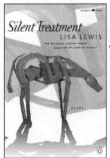

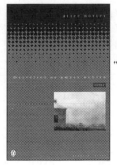

Ploughshares

a literary adventure

Known for its compelling fiction and poetry, *Ploughshares* is widely regarded as one of America's most influential literary journals. Each issue is guest-edited by a different writer for a fresh, provocative slant—exploring personal visions, aesthetics, and literary circles—and contributors include both well-known and emerging writers. In fact, *Ploughshares* has become a premier proving ground for new talent, showcasing the early works of Sue Miller, Mona Simpson, Robert Pinsky, and countless others. Past guest editors include Richard Ford, Derek Walcott, Tobias Wolff, Carolyn Forché, and Rosellen Brown. This unique editorial format has made *Ploughshares*, in effect, into a dynamic anthology series—one that has established a tradition of quality and prescience. *Ploughshares* is published in quality trade paperback in April, August, and December: usually a fiction issue in the Fall and mixed issues of poetry and fiction in the Spring and Winter. Inside each issue, you'll find not only great new stories and poems, but also a profile on the guest editor, book reviews, and miscellaneous notes about *Ploughshares*, its writers, and the literary world. Subscribe today.

Sample *Ploughshares* on the Web: http://www.emerson.edu/ploughshares

---